MW01134313

The Forest & Pale Green Dot

Justin Groot

This book is a work of fiction. Any references to historical
events, real people, real brands, or real places are used
fictitiously. Other names, characters, brands, places, and events
are products of the author's imagination, and any resemblance
to actual events or brands or places or persons, living or dead, is
entirely coincidental.

///

Copyright © 2017 Justin Groot
Cover by Madison Porter (@Positron_Dream) and Tiffany Le
All rights reserved.
ISBN-13: 978-1978358003

For everybody who's ever told me "Slow down,"
"Trust your feet," "Use your braaaiiiin..."

In my defense, it's harder than it sounds.

SPECIAL THANKS TO

Doug Bramlett
James "Dicer214"
Christian Best

When was the first time you saw the forest?

I was nine. A dense fog had descended on New England, where my family was spending an impromptu vacation, but we persevered, loaded up the car and drove out early to beat the crowds. Headlights slipped through the murk like phosphorescent eyes. My father hunched over the wheel, muttering more than usual. My mother had been gone for sixteen months. In the back seat, I held my little brother's hand.

We parked near the coast and climbed the trail to a lighthouse on the cliffs.

Television had not prepared me for the view. Fog boiled away into treetops without end. Green canopy unfolded all the way to the horizon. A bird cried out and was answered. Wind snickered through the leaves. In the distance, at the very limit of my vision, something huge began to move.

1

Date: Tue, 29 Mar 2017 15:11:45 -0800 (PST)
From: L. Alvarez
Subject: Re: More preposterous claims
emanating from your department
To: T. Porter

Since giving the Senator another geology lesson
strikes this public servant as an egregious
misuse of time and tax dollars, she would kindly
direct the Senator to an informative video,
available on various streaming services,
wherein Neil deGrasse Tyson traipses across a
tremendous calendar, pontificating at tedious
length on what humanity's twelve thousand years
amount to, on a geologic scale, which (spoiler)
is nothing. Should the Senator continue, after
watching this video, to feel the need to harass
this public servant with his laughable belief
that things on Earth have always been precisely
as they exist today – let alone to continue
addressing her as "young lady" – he is kindly
invited to fuck a lawn mower.

After nine months, Sergeant Rivers decided it was time for our first expedition. He split us into trios. I expected him to group me with Zip and Lindsey Li, since the three of us spent most of our time together, but instead I wound up with Sam Vazquez Jr. and Hollywood.

I didn't mind Junior. Hollywood was another matter.

"Put me in Li's group," I said.

Sergeant Rivers was seven feet tall, and he moved with the slow precision of someone who'd spent a lifetime accidentally smashing objects in his vicinity.

"Excuse me?" he said.

"Look, Tetris," said Hollywood, "we know you'll miss your little girlfriend out there, but if you really can't go four days without a blow job, I'm sure Junior will fill in."

I took a step. Zip grabbed my shoulder, but it wasn't me Hollywood needed to worry about. Li's current expression typically preceded somebody's nose being broken by about fifteen seconds.

"Next recruit to dispute an order packs their bags," roared Rivers. "I've got nipple hairs that mean more to me than you do."

He directed a cycloptic glare at each of us, the mess of interlocking scar tissue in his empty left eye socket crumpling horribly.

"As for you," he said, turning to Hollywood, "keep your god damn mouth shut."

I was pissed all day. So was Li.

"I don't know what you've been telling people, Tetris," she said, right before we turned in for the night, "but we're just friends. I'd never date you in a million years."

Hollywood, three bunks over, let out a hoot.

So then I couldn't even fall asleep. Not that I was into Li. I was just trying to figure out what was so wrong with me, that she'd say something like that.

When I woke up, it felt like someone had crammed cotton balls into the space behind my eyes. The hour-long ride to the coast passed in a hazy blur. Each time I slipped into sleep, my head tipped forward, waking me up again.

At the Coast Guard checkpoint, a bleary-eyed guardsman lifted himself out of his chair and came to check our credentials. A helicopter puttered overhead, following a row of concrete towers that receded down the coast like the pylons of some long-crumbled bridge. Rivers expelled us at the forest's edge and drove away without a word.

It was cool enough that I didn't want to stand still, so I shuffled my feet on the dewy grass. The sun sat fat and low behind us, sending rays of light that pelted into the forest and scattered. Trees like cathedral columns stretched into dim infinity. Their bases were obscured by plants that clawed over one another, battling for whatever scraps of sunlight made it through. Tapestries of moss hung from low branches and rugged contours of bark.

A distant creature made a sound like water drops in a deep bucket. Others crooned and squealed and sang. We waited for a while, but nothing showed itself. Only the canopy moved, shifting veils of brilliant green.

Hollywood rocked on his heels, drawing air through

flared nostrils. His blond hair was just short of the insubordinate length at which Rivers would order it all shaved off.

"Finally," he said, and headed down the slope.

Rangers only brought one assault rifle on expeditions, typically a SCAR-17, since it was more important to pack light than to be heavily armed. Naturally, Hollywood had demanded to carry our rifle. He led the way through the forest with springy, cheerful steps. Junior and I grimaced behind him. At least this wouldn't take very long. Two days in and two days back: a fraction the length of a normal expedition.

My personal mission was to grit my teeth and avoid getting in a fight. Maybe, if this went well, Rivers would put me in a different group next time. The whole thing was probably an attempt to teach me a lesson about working with people I didn't like, which, frankly, was a lesson Rivers could stuff right between his sickeningly well-defined glutes.

For a long while it was silent and still. A few hours passed. We kept our eyes on the ground, avoiding colorful plants and scum-rimmed puddles, as we worked our way between the enormous trees. Right when I'd begun to wonder if the entire day would pass uneventfully, branches just out of sight began to snap, and we took cover in a bank of ferns. Something went crunching by, obscured by a tangle of vines and foliage. Red-brown bulk and rippling muscle showed through the gaps. Whatever it was, it was big, especially for this close to shore. Blood thumped in my ears. The gear I'd grown used to carrying in training—backpack, sidearm, grapple gun, body cameras—suddenly felt unwieldy and conspicuous. I held my breath and glanced at the others.

Hollywood was smiling. I wanted to elbow him in his bright white teeth.

When we could no longer hear the creature's passage through the reeds, we continued on our way. By noon we were further into the forest than I'd ever been. Green-gold motes of pollen or dust drifted in the air, glittering when they crossed columns of sunlight. The trees here made the ones by the coast look like saplings. We'd passed the edge of the continental shelf, where the earth sloped sharply downward and the forest rose to take its place. Everywhere around us, there were cave-ins, green ravines leading into darkness. Five hundred feet down, you'd find the loamy remains of trees that predated the pyramids.

My head began to throb. A thumb-sized horsefly landed on my arm and popped like a grape when I swatted it.

Ninety-eight percent of the sun's light is blocked by the canopy. Because there's hardly any light to work with, shadows are hard to spot. If I hadn't happened to glance up at the right moment, I wouldn't have noticed the carpet snake gliding down on its broad, wing-like rib cage until it was far too late.

"Incoming," I shouted, drawing my pistol. The creature's twenty-foot wingspan billowed at the edges. I opened fire. Each hit created an sputtering fountain of black blood. The crescent mouth gaped stupidly. Fangs shone white and sharp inside.

As the carpet snake crumpled and fell, its tender underbelly ruptured, I slammed a new magazine into the pistol. Hollywood and Junior were already arming their grapple guns. Gunshots drew attention. We'd have to lie low for a while.

"Nice eye," said Junior when we were safe on a branch high above.

I didn't trust my shivering lips to respond.

When the forest seemed to have forgotten we were there, we rappelled down and went to look at the creature's body. It was gone. Something had dragged it into a nearby ravine, leaving a trail of squashed vegetation the width of a snow plow.

"How much you think that thing weighed?" asked Junior.

"Five hundred pounds, easy," said Hollywood. He blew a bright pink bubble.

I squinted at him. "You brought gum out here?"

The bubble, baseball-sized, popped. "Got a problem?"

I shrugged, remembering my mission.

We took it slow. Thickets of curled pink flowers lined our path. The flowers gave off an odor of rotting flesh, drawing clouds of curious flies.

In some places the trees grew so thick together that they became a maze with towering bark-lined walls. Most of the time, there was a moist, earthy aroma, like the smell in the woods back home after it rained. But then there were spots that smelled even worse than the pink flowers. When you came across one of those, you hustled through. You hoped the odor originated from a rotting carcass, because the living things that smelled like that were uniformly horrifying.

We'd just exited one of those awful-smelling areas when we called it a day. Darkness would be falling soon, and we wanted to be up in the branches before then, tucked away in our camouflaged sleeping bags.

I only managed two hours of sleep that first night. Nothing had prepared me for the barrage of sounds. I held my breath after every rustle and screech. My eyes strained to pierce the sludge at the aperture of the sleeping bag, but as hard as I pushed against it, the darkness pushed back harder.

Surely the monsters could hear me breathing from the forest floor. When the jaws closed around my skull, would I have time to feel the pain, or would my death come quicker than my nerves could sense it? I braced myself and hoped for the latter.

In the morning, purple bags lurked below Junior's bloodshot eyes. I must have had those too. My muscles and tendons were gritty with sleep deprivation, and my head pounded. Thinking about the length of the day ahead made me physically ill.

Hollywood looked like he'd scored ten hours on a fluffy king bed. He chattered all through breakfast. As we lowered ourselves to the forest floor, I actually heard him whistling—whistling!—until something out of sight unleashed a mucousy roar. That shut him up.

A few hours of walking later, I ducked behind a tree to relieve myself and came face-to-face with an enormous brown insect, its mouth yawning in a toothless grin. I leapt back, but the bug didn't move. After a moment I realized the eye sockets were empty. It was a gigantic version of the exoskeletons that dotted the trees in my back yard every fall.

I must have yelled, because Junior poked his head around the corner.

"Well, that's horrifying," he said.

I prodded the husk with a finger. It was thicker than I'd thought, and tough, like fiberglass.

"In Baltimore we get a big cicada swarm every seventeen years," said Junior. "Last one was in 2013. Sky turned black. You'd step on them everywhere. The smell was awful."

Hollywood came to have a look.

"Neat," he said. He leveled the SCAR at the exoskeleton and fired off a burst.

The gunfire was impossibly loud. Junior's nostrils doubled in size. He picked Hollywood up by his pack straps. "Are you insane?"

Junior was almost as big as Rivers. Definitely not a guy you wanted to fuck with. Two months ago, when Scott Brown decided he'd had enough and tried to stab Hollywood with a knife from the kitchen, it had been Junior who stepped in and hurled the would-be-assassin through a wall.

Hollywood slithered out of the pack and danced away. "Was curious if these were bulletproof," he said, sticking a finger through one of the neat round holes. "Looks like they're not."

"I'm going to murder you," hissed Junior. He threw the pack at Hollywood, nearly knocking him down. I searched the canopy for movement. The forest crashed and rumbled, awakened from its slumber.

"Relax. We'll hit the branches and wait it out."

"Not an option," I said, stomach flattening, as a tarantula the size of a bus broke through the leaves and skittered down a trunk toward us.

We ran. Hollywood, out front, hefted the SCAR in both hands and leapt a fallen branch. Junior and I could barely keep up. We tore through a dense patch of vegetation and across a porous section of forest floor, weaving between pits with hungry black gullets.

Up ahead, a flesh wasp hovered, swollen stinger twitching in the air. Hollywood led us left. The flesh wasp buzzed after us. The giant insect's sting carried an overpowering paralytic venom, but the awful part was that it also injected a larva. After stinging you, the wasp would continue on its way, but your misery would only have begun: in the days that followed, the larva would devour you from the inside, assuming something didn't find you lying there first.

Soon our path was blocked again, this time by a fleet of blimp-sized jellyfish. Filled with hydrogen gas, the jellyfish wobbled gently off of tree trunks and each other as they floated through the forest. Curtains of silvery tentacles draped beneath them, dredging for warm-blooded prey.

The jellyfish blocked every direction except the one we'd come from, and they were drifting steadily toward us.

I spun and found the tarantula clambering into view. Its legs were the diameter of telephone poles. The flesh wasp was nowhere to be seen.

"Junior," I said, "you've got incendiary rounds, right?"

"Yeah," said Junior.

"In your pistol?"

"Yeah."

"Give it to me."

He handed it over. The tarantula observed, frozen except for its fidgeting mouthparts, as the wall of tentacles rustled closer.

"When I fire," I said, "run straight at the spider."

Junior opened his mouth, but I held up a hand.

"Hollywood," I said, "Hit it in the eyes."

He popped a piece of bubble gum into his mouth. "Mh-hmm."

The jellyfish were a few yards away, looming like purple storm clouds. I took aim with Junior's pistol.

"Three two *ONE*," I said, and fired.

The foremost jellyfish erupted into flames. It sagged out of the sky, a sudden sun in the perpetual dusk.

Hollywood ran toward the tarantula. The SCAR's roar cut through the din. Bullets pinged worthlessly off hairy armor. For a moment I saw flames reflected in the huge black eyes. Then the tarantula wheeled and fled.

Behind us, a second jellyfish went up, a dull pop followed by a crackling boom. Then a third, and a fourth. We bolted back the way we'd come. The blaze wouldn't spread far—forest trees were notoriously fire-retardant—but the amount of hydrogen we'd set alight would turn the rest of the vegetation into a whirling inferno.

A safe distance away, we grapple-gunned onto a branch. Fingers of smoke curled after us.

Jittery with adrenaline, I turned on Hollywood.

"You are actually the stupidest person alive," I said.

Hollywood blew a bubble. "Chill."

"You almost got us killed," said Junior, rapping the body camera on Hollywood's chest with gigantic knuckles.

"We were never in any real danger," said Hollywood.

"You're such a fucking idiot," I said.

"Suck a dick."

"Fuck you."

I wanted to rip his throat out. I wanted it so bad for a second that my vision went red and I actually reached toward him, forgetting that we were sixty feet above the forest floor—

Junior smacked my hand down.

"That's enough," he said.

I decided to retie my boots.

"We've still got a few hours until dark," said Junior. "Then two days to get home."

Hollywood blew a bubble, popped it, and slurped it

back in.

"If you do something like that again, I'll kill you," said Junior, grabbing Hollywood's chin and forcing him to make eye contact.

"Real scary," said Hollywood.

I slept much better that second night, and awoke refreshed, emboldened by the adventures of the previous day. This was why I'd left home with everything I owned in a ragged red duffel bag. The miserable months of training had served their purpose. I'd been a loser with no future; now I was a master of nature, a commando, a badass without peer. Yesterday I'd faced the worst the forest could throw at me and survived. Nothing could kill me now.

My feet had barely touched the ground when I heard the screams. Distant but unmistakable: a human female screaming, in agony or fear.

Junior and I froze, but Hollywood didn't waste a second. He clipped the grapple gun to his belt, cradled the SCAR like a football, and crashed off through the undergrowth.

Half a second later, Junior followed. My heart jumped up and down, terror clumping in my throat, but I didn't have a choice. I scrambled after them.

2

If rangers tend to be a little odd, it's because
they have a job no truly sane person would want.
A ranger's career is extremely lucrative, of
course, since the television programs they film
pull better ratings than anything except the
Super Bowl, but their average lifespan clocks
in at a meager four years. Not a lot of time to
enjoy the fruits of one's labor. If there's a
more dangerous career, we haven't found it yet.

- *Roy LaMonte: Against All Odds,* Theodore
Hunker, Salvador Press 2018

The first time I saw Lindsey Li, at six a.m. on the first
day of training, she was blocking the entrance to the
sleeping quarters, doing pull-ups on the doorframe. She
didn't let me through until she'd finished the set.

"You're early," she said when she dropped to the floor.
I'd never seen such potent disinterest on someone's face.
Later, when I learned the number of other recruits, and

the number who would wash out before the final cut, I understood why.

I found my cot and sat down. All five pounds of my worldly possessions had been surrendered at registration, and I felt the missing weight like an amputated limb. I fluffed the flimsy pillow and examined the RangerCorp logo on the sheets. The shoes I'd been issued were too tight.

"Where are you from?" I asked. Li ignored me and went back to pull-ups. I watched the complex movement of muscles in her tank-topped back. Her exhalations were curt and precise. I reclined on my cot and studied the ceiling.

By eight a.m. the room was packed, awash in nervous chatter and the squee of rusty bedsprings. Sergeant Rivers' arrival shut everybody up. He took us outside and set us running. By the end of that first hellish day, he'd ejected thirty recruits. The month of conditioning that followed winnowed us down from two hundred and fifty to seventy-five. I barely survived, but nothing Rivers did could faze Li. Running, climbing, weightlifting, lugging sacks of grain up steep hills . . . she crushed it all.

She'd been training since she was six years old. She was world-class fast, strong, and quick-thinking. I was world-class at nothing. Same with Zip, except when he was on a climbing wall. The two of us outlasted countless stronger, faster, and quicker-thinking recruits because we were simply more stubborn. More desperate. Li continued to ignore us and everyone else until the number of recruits had dwindled to thirty. At that point it was twenty-eight indefatigable freaks of nature, Zip, and me. Then Li started sitting with us in the mess hall.

Up until then she'd invariably sat in the corner by herself. To say that we were unsure how to respond when she plopped down next to Zip would be a stupefying understatement. For a while we kind of just watched her chew. Conversation at the surrounding tables ceased.

"Trade you for your broccoli," she said, offering an apple. Zip wordlessly obliged.

Except for economical movements of her fork, she was motionless. Zip and I exchanged a worried glance and went back to eating.

"I've seen you two up on the roof after curfew," she said after a while.

I blanched. "You're not going to tell anybody, are you?"

"Can I join?"

There was one other thing to mention about Li: it was absolutely impossible to imagine her screaming. She was the type to go teeth-gritting and defiant to the grisliest grave. So even though she was the only woman among the recruits, soon to be the only woman among the active rangers, and therefore the only woman who could conceivably be out here, two days from the coast, where distinctly feminine screams were echoing through the trees—I couldn't quite bring myself to believe that they were coming from her.

3

Date: Wed, 5 April 2017 18:12:04 -0800 (PST)
From: D. Weaver
Subject: subdermals
To: D. Cooper

You've got to talk to Rivers. He gets like this every year. You and I both know there's no room for transparency when it comes to the subdermals. 'Vaccine implants' line has flown for years. It's simple and the recruits accept it without question. Can't change unless we want another PR catastrophe.

    Running through the forest is like driving an SUV the wrong way down an interstate: it's possible, technically, but you'd really prefer to avoid getting yourself into that situation to begin with. Every step you take, you have a sneaking suspicion that you missed some deadly clue, that your weight will fall on a mess of leaves concealing a trapdoor spider's lair or a sinkhole hundreds of feet deep. There's no time to check your path, so you pray to God and plant your feet on whatever looks most solid.

I was acutely aware of the danger, and I knew Junior was too, but that didn't stop us from following Hollywood. The screams were getting fewer and further between, but they were still coming.

I burst through a thick patch of razorgrass, covering my face to protect it from lacerations, and stumbled into Junior's back. My momentum carried me past him, and I just had time to realize we were beside an enormous chasm when I tumbled over the edge—

Junior yanked me back with a single huge hand. I'd drawn my pistol as I ran; it slipped out of my grasp and vanished into darkness.

I stood panting beside Junior and Hollywood as we listened for another scream.

"Look," said Junior. On the other side of the chasm stood a tall gray obelisk. It was detailed with a network of fine lines. Against the biological backdrop, its sharp edges were almost profane.

"That's not supposed to be there," said Junior.

Was it throbbing, or was that my imagination? I closed my eyes, rubbed them, and looked again.

"Gimme the floodlight," said Hollywood, peering into the chasm.

Junior rooted mechanically in his pack. Hollywood snatched the floodlight from his hands.

"We should get over there," said Junior. "I've never seen anything like that in the videos, the books, nowhere." He raised a hand above his eyes, squinting. "Are those words?"

Hollywood panned the floodlight over the abyss. The circle of light traveled down the far slope, traversing a network of vines, musty wood, and fungi. It struck me as surreal, almost dreamlike, that he didn't seem to care about the obelisk. I was still shivering from my near-fall. What was he looking for?

Junior yelped. I glanced up just in time to see a shape vanish into the trees.

"There was a person," said Junior, scrambling along the edge. "Tetris, did you see him?"

"Who?"

"I'm going to look," said Junior. "Somebody was over there. I swear to God."

I couldn't detect any movement. For a long, heavy moment, everything was dreadfully still. The only sound was the blood thunking in my temples. Then Hollywood sucked in his breath, the bushes near Junior rustled, and things began to happen very quickly.

Thirty feet below, the floodlight revealed a grinning reptilian face. Clusters of black eyeballs gleamed like river stones. The creature opened its massive jaw, revealing row after row of recurved teeth, and an odor of death wafted up. Out of the gaping mouth came a piercing shriek, the woman's scream we'd heard before, except that this time the noise continued endlessly, increasing in intensity as the creature scrabbled with wicked claws up the wall.

Hollywood dropped the floodlight. It fell toward the monster, the beam of light ricocheting wildly. I turned to shout at Junior, who stared wide-eyed back at us. He could hear the shriek, but hadn't yet glimpsed its source.

"Junior!"

An enormous scorpion, heavy with dull black armor, exploded out of the trees behind him. The stinger snapped, whiplike, and skewered Junior through the torso. The point popped out the front of his chest. As it lifted him off the ground, his feet kicking and his big hands slapping at the segmented tail, Hollywood yanked my arm.

"Run," he said, and led the way.

We barreled back through the razorgrass, stumbled across a tree branch bridging a ravine, and broke into a sprint on the shaking ground beyond.

Behind us, the shriek became a throaty roar, as the reptilian creature sensed the possibility of our escape. I heard a new sound, a heavy whump-whump like mattresses falling to the floor, and snuck a glance back. The creature had taken flight on a set of rippling, scaly wings. It loomed behind and above us, close enough that I could feel its hot breath against my neck.

We weaved between obstacles, Hollywood a few feet ahead of me. No chance of grapple-gunning to safety if the thing could fly. We'd have to lose it in the maze of undergrowth.

We'd just rounded an enormous tree trunk when Hollywood stepped on a moss-and-silk trapdoor and plummeted out of sight. I grabbed the straps of my pack and leapt in after him.

The tunnel was steep and slick, lubricated by webs. There would be a spider in here with us, even now rushing toward this section of its burrow.

I'd dropped my pistol into the chasm. Hollywood might have a chance to produce one of his weapons, but the fall through the trap door would have taken him by surprise, and anyway the spider would get to him in moments.

As my slide accelerated, I saw Hollywood up ahead on a flat spot in the tunnel, headlamp flicked on, hand reaching for the pistol at his side. Beneath him: the spider, hairy legs blurred as it charged from the web-wrapped depths.

One of the spider's front legs pinned Hollywood's gun arm to the floor. The beast leaned in, pedipalps parting to reveal a pair of bulbous fangs—

I fired my grapple gun. The silver spearhead flashed across the cavern, trailing an impossibly thin strand of carbon nanofilament, and shattered the section of carapace beneath the spider's left eye cluster, hardly losing any momentum as it burst out the other side and embedded itself in the wall. Thick green-black goo exploded from the point of impact, showering Hollywood. Countless limbs spasmed in death. With a grunt of exertion, Hollywood planted a foot against the abdomen and shoved, sending the body shuddering back down the tunnel.

"Thanks," he said, wiping the stinking blood out of his eyes.

As I craned my neck to listen out the opening of the burrow, the cries of the winged creature grew fainter. I recalled its scales, a queasy mixture of blue, black and green.

"What was that thing?" I asked.

"That," said Hollywood, "was a fucking dragon."

4

"It's not healthy for our kids to watch this stuff."

"It's just nature."

"I'm sure your viewers agree that it's not just nature."

"Just animals, at the end of the day. And, yes, a few particularly ornery plants."

"Prairie dogs are nature. Lion cubs are nature. This is different."

"They put a parental advisory ahead of every episode. Isn't it your responsibility, as a mother, to keep your children from watching them?"

"You have to draw the line somewhere, Bill. And I'm telling you, these ranger programs are corrupting our youth. My son watched an episode at his friend's house and peed the bed every night for weeks."

"…"

"I don't see what's so funny about that, Bill."

I sat beside Hollywood in a windowless room. Across the table, Sergeant Rivers doodled on a yellow pad. Stars, tornadoes, a skull and crossbones or two. A man in a suit stood behind him, fiddling with his tie.

"Why are we here?" demanded Hollywood. "You've got the bodycam footage."

"Nobody thinks you did anything wrong," said the man behind Rivers in a voice as smooth as Vaseline.

Rivers shifted on his tiny chair. "Agent Cooper just needs you to walk him through it one more time."

There was definitely something going on with Rivers. Frustration? Maybe a sparkle of wry amusement? He'd started drawing a castle. Was working on the parapets.

"We heard screams," I said.

"What kind of screams?" asked Cooper. "It wasn't clear from the bodycam audio."

I shifted. "It sounded like a woman screaming."

Cooper tilted his head like a puzzled dog. "Douglas, what do you think?"

"Nobody calls me that," said Hollywood.

"Did you think the screams sounded human?"

"Yeah, I did," said Hollywood.

"So you chased after them."

Cooper approached the table with lazy steps, hands buried in his pockets. Even sitting down, Rivers was taller.

"Well, excuse me for thinking somebody needed help," said Hollywood.

"Two days into the Pacific Forest? Who could it possibly have been?"

"We thought it might be Li," I said.

"Your fellow recruit, Lindsey Li?"

"Yeah."

The hands emerged from Cooper's pockets and planted themselves on the table.

"You knew her expedition would depart much further down the coast."

"That didn't occur to us at the time, sir."

Cooper's smile reminded me of the dragon's. "Tell me about the clearing. What you found."

"Big pit," said Hollywood.

"Nothing odd?"

Hollywood shrugged.

"Junior saw something," said Cooper.

"There was an obelisk," I said.

"Now we're getting somewhere."

"On the other side of the pit. Junior was going to look."

"Douglas, did you also see the obelisk?"

"Could have been a rock," said Hollywood.

Agent Cooper pulled out a chair beside Rivers and sat, unbuttoning his jacket. Settling back, he steepled his fingers and peered down his slender nose.

"Tell me more about the obelisk," he said after a while.

The image in my head was fuzzy. All I could conjure was the blank look on Junior's face when the scorpion impaled him. As if he expected to wake up from the nightmare at any moment.

"I think there were words on it," I said.

Cooper threw his head back and laughed, startling

Rivers, whose pen snapped. Hollywood nearly knocked me out of my chair trying to dodge the spray of ink.

"Fuck," said Hollywood.

"Watch the language," barked Rivers, holding half a pen in each monstrous paw.

Cooper hadn't taken his eyes off me. "Are you a conspiracy theorist?"

"No, sir."

"Hieroglyphic script on mysterious monuments... sounds like the kind of ridiculous fantasy those people trot out to justify their hypotheses about an ancient civilization hidden beneath the trees."

"I'm not familiar, sir."

"I think I agree with Douglas. It was probably just a rock."

"If you say so, sir."

Cooper leaned close. I examined the doughy folds of his face, his beady little pupils.

"Can I trust you not to spread this 'obelisk' story? The nutjobs have enough to work with already. The last thing we need is any more misinformation."

Hollywood snorted. "Is that what this is about?"

"Of course not," said Cooper. "This is about the young man, Junior, and the unfortunate circumstances surrounding his death. Can you talk me through the events from your perspective?"

It was a long, silent drive back to training camp. Riding with Rivers was always an ordeal, since his single eye and generally forceful disposition tended to send him careening into lanes already occupied by unsuspecting motorists. He never checked his blind spots, just wrenched the wheel and trusted everyone else to get out of the way.

That night I couldn't fall asleep, so I tiptoed outside. It was chilly. Clouds of insects swarmed the lights that lined the path to the grapple gun course. I went to the corner of the barracks and climbed the gutter.

Li was already up there, sitting on the edge of the roof.

"Hi," I said. She didn't respond. I sat beside her. She squinted at something in the darkness across the training field.

"Hollywood said you thought you heard me screaming," she said.

"Maybe."

She shook her head. "Why?"

"It sounded like a girl."

"Fuck off."

"What?"

She winged a shard of brick at a light post below. The bulb shattered.

"If I'd been there, Junior wouldn't have died," she said.

I pinched the loose skin on my kneecaps and twisted, hard.

"My dad told me that some things mimic human noises. Screams, shouts, laughter," she said.

"Never came up in class."

"Pretty rare, I think. But I would have known."

"I didn't want to go. Hollywood went, we followed."

"You could have stopped him."

"Maybe."

We sat in silence. I went over the scene in my head: Hollywood breaking into a sprint, the slow seconds before he slipped out of sight. Could I have convinced him to come back?

"How do you think they learn those noises?"

"Hmm?" I said.

"The human noises. How do they learn those screams? You think rangers teach them, when they die?"

"Could be."

"Doesn't explain the laughter, though."

I shivered. "Cold out here."

"It doesn't add up, Tetris. That everything in the forest is just a dumb animal. I don't buy it."

I considered telling her about the obelisk. About the person Junior thought he saw. After the talk with Agent Cooper, though, I kept my mouth shut. She wouldn't believe me anyway.

"Our first couple of weeks," she said, "Junior was the only one who treated me like a normal person."

It was too dark to see her face.

"What about me?"

"Oh, come on."

We watched moths spar with the remaining lamps.

"I want to get some sleep," she said. "No way Rivers will give us a break tomorrow just because Junior's gone."

When she reached the edge of the roof, she paused. Scratched the back of her head and cleared her throat.

"Don't beat yourself up, Tetris," she said. "It wasn't your fault."

After a long and awkward moment, she climbed down the gutter. I stayed up there for a long time, looking at the stars.

"Sorry, Junior," I said, but my voice sounded flat and cold.

5

Air Force fighter jets brought down a 1,200-ton tentacled creature on Monday after it penetrated the Coast Guard perimeter west of Los Angeles. 50 were killed and at least 300 injured in the rampage, the worst since 2004. In Washington, questions have once again been raised as to the efficacy of current Coast Guard countermeasures.

"Bigger guns would certainly go a long way," Coast Guard chief Donald McCarthy told the Post.

A few years later, Zip and I drove down to Portland to meet Li's family. We took Zip's pride and joy, a decades-old, beat-up red Corvette. The roof was cracked, so it leaked when it rained, which in Seattle was a fairly significant issue, and the seat belts didn't work—they just hung across your chest like lasagna noodles—but Zip's love for the car was boundless and all-forgiving.

"I don't understand your refusal to buy a new car," I said, gripping the edge of my seat as the scarlet death trap rattled over a pothole. "What else are you doing with those paychecks?"

"Saving," said Zip. "I'm not—"

"—a big spender, yeah."

I fingered my two thousand-dollar watch. In two years as a ranger I'd acquired a spacious apartment and an orange muscle car, taken trips to Europe and Asia, and outfitted myself with a wardrobe that was, if not fashionable, then at least expensive. Meanwhile my bank account hovered around empty, and my credit card bills were multiplying.

Zip patted the dashboard. "I'm going to drive this thing until the wheels fall off, and then I'm going to buy new wheels."

I'd taken a rough fall at the bouldering gym the day before, and my ankle was killing me. Climbing with Zip was humbling. Not as bad as when we'd first started, when I'd lacked the technique to tackle anything higher than a V3, but still pretty bad. Zip annihilated routes with holds the depth of credit cards, moving like a praying mantis, relentless and self-assured. Even after all the practice, I still found myself trembling through routes a person with half my strength and a bit more technique could have managed with ease.

You could tell Zip was good by the way veteran climbers watched him. Respect and jealousy battled it out on their leathery faces. Sometimes people clapped.

The Li family lived in a brick mansion up on a hill. Li's silver convertible was in the driveway. When we rang the doorbell I considered running. What if they laid out a bunch of little forks and spoons, and I didn't know which to use for what?

Zip was as calm as ever, though his right hand curled and uncurled, squeezing an imaginary tennis ball. His family had been just as dysfunctional as mine. Neither of us would ever have invited our friends over.

I fidgeted with my tie. Today was the first time I'd seen Zip in a button-up. It was a size too small. I hadn't noticed until it was far too late.

The door opened.

We were not devoured.

It was pretty awkward, though. I went for the handshake while Mr. Li offered a hug; I switched mid-flight to go for the hug and ate a massive shoulder as he tried to match a shake no longer being offered... Zip barged through the door after me, discovered that there wasn't enough room in the foyer for all five of us, and tried to step back outside just as Mrs. Li offered her own hug. Zip whipped back around to return the hug, which she'd already abandoned, then tried to pretend that he hadn't seen it, fake-stumbling to explain all the jerky movements, except that he ended up actual-stumbling and knocked an expensive-looking urn off its table. Li caught it, of course.

"So," said Mr. Li, beaming at his daughter over the dinner table, "You've been on how many expeditions together, now, the three of you? Nine?"

"Thought it was ten," said Zip.

I lifted mashed potatoes to my mouth. Noticing Mr. Li looking my way, I nodded, hastening to swallow.

"We're shooting for the record," I said.

"Which one?"

"Most expeditions by the same trio," said Li. "Record is twenty-six."

"Sixteen more expeditions?" exclaimed Mrs. Li.

"Jeez, Mom, have a little faith."

Mrs. Li sawed her steak vigorously. I gathered there was something of an ideological divide in the Li household when it came to Li's career choice.

"You don't have to worry, Mrs. Li," said Zip, puffing out his chest as his shirt buttons held on for dear life. "She's in strong, capable, dare I say *dashing* hands."

"Ha," barked Li. "When that velociraptor went for your esophagus, who, exactly, evaporated its face?"

"What about when you were about to step on that boomslug?" said Zip. "Who was it, again, who said 'Li, please take care not to step on that boomslug, lest you perish in an immolation of your own creation?'"

"I wasn't about to step on anything," said Li. "I was well aware of the slug, and as I recall, your oafish shout in that instance caused quite the—"

"Li thinks she's our daddy."

"You're damn right I'm your daddy."

"Boomslug?" said Mrs. Li weakly.

Zip crunched into a Brussels sprout. "Explosive invertebrate, bright orange, very bad to step on, but luckily pretty hard to miss, unless you're—"

"—which is why I didn't miss it, dumbass, I—"

"I saved Li from a crab once," I said.

"Zip would have fallen in those beetleflowers if I hadn't—"

"Anyway I'm like eighty-five percent sure I had the velociraptor situation under control."

"That is such a load of—"

Mr. Li cleared his throat. Silence materialized.

"As long as we're trading stories," he said, "has she told you the one about the lions?"

"Dad."

"It's a great story."

"It really isn't."

"Go on," said Zip.

Li glowered at him. Zip stuck out his tongue.

"It happened on a trip to the zoo," said Mr. Li, "when Lindsey was seven years old."

Mrs. Li laid a hand on his arm. "This still gives me nightmares."

"We stopped to consult a map, and when we looked up, she was gone."

"Poof."

"We searched the area—no luck. It was summer, and the crowds were positively teeming. Eventually we decided to find an information booth, a security guard, somebody who could help. Except there were no employees in sight. One finally went tearing by, holding his hat to his head. I grabbed his arm. What was going on?"

"Some kid had gotten into the lion enclosure," said Mrs. Li.

Zip whooped.

"We found her cuddling with a lioness," said Mr. Li. "They hadn't laid a paw on her."

"It was all over the news," said Mrs. Li.

"She was famous."

"Twelve million views."

"An appearance on a late-night television program."

Mrs. Li wiped her lips. "I still think that's why she became a ranger."

"Not true," said Li.

"The things you put me through," said Mrs. Li, turning to me. "What about your parents? Don't they worry?"

The last time I'd heard from my dad was the day I left home, when he'd unleashed one last eyeball-bulging rant. Did that count? I looked to Zip for help.

"My parents are too busy working to worry," he said.

Mrs. Li narrowed her eyes, and Zip looked sheepish for perhaps the first time ever, but then Mr. Li boomed a laugh.

"Understandable," he said, putting a hand on his wife's shoulder. "Lucy's a neurosurgeon, so God knows she works hard. Me, on the other hand..."

"You have your gardening," said Mrs. Li.

Now Mr. Li joined Zip in looking sheepish.

"Have to keep busy somehow," he said.

This was a man who had battled the forest for nearly a decade. Thirty years older than Zip or me, he maintained comparable muscle mass. It was simply impossible to imagine his hands cupping a plant bulb or trimming a rose bush. Tearing weeds out of the ground, though: that I could imagine him doing. Mercilessly.

"This expedition record," said Mrs. Li, "who holds it currently?

"Roy LaMonte and the Briggs brothers," said Li.

"I knew Roy," said Mr. Li. "Fantastic poker player. Terrific mustache. Shame the way things turned out."

"Still better than what happened to the Briggs brothers," said Li. She stabbed with relish at her Brussels sprouts. "Mom, how come you never made these when I was growing up?"

"Your father does all the cooking these days, dear," said Mrs. Li. "Mind if I ask what happened to the Briggs brothers?"

Mr. Li clicked his tongue. "Not appropriate dinner conversation, I'm afraid. Suffice it to say that the forest got them."

"Pass the salt, please," said Li.

"The steak's more than salty enough as it is," said Mrs. Li. "You'll give yourself a heart attack."

Li's incisors gleamed. "Least of my worries, Ma."

Mrs. Li passed the salt.

"Poor Roy," mused Mr. Li. "After that trip—amazing that he made it out, by the way—he was raving mad. Wouldn't stop talking about the things he'd supposedly seen."

"What'd he think he saw?" I asked.

"Fantasies. Towers, pyramids, you get the idea. People, too."

My fork, laden with another mound of potatoes, froze just short of my mouth.

Mr. Li raised a silver-flecked eyebrow. "Is something wrong?"

The look Li gave me said: Tell me later.

"No," I said, and cleared my throat.

That night, Zip and I flipped a coin to see who got the guest bed. I lost and headed to the living room to set up on the couch.

I was digging for my toothbrush when Li came down the stairs. She looked amazing. I couldn't quite figure out why—the pajamas weren't revealing or form-fitting, so maybe it was the shapelessness itself that made it hot, somehow—but for a couple moments I forgot not only what she'd come down to talk about, but also the English language and my own name besides.

"What was that?" she asked.

"Uhm?"

"You know what I'm talking about."

I gave up on the toothbrush and sat back on the couch. "It's probably nothing."

Li perched, cross-legged, on an armchair across from

me. "Tell me, Tetris."

I took off my watch and stared at it. The ticks reverberated in my fingertips.

"Before Junior died," I said, "I thought I saw something. Something like what your dad described, across the chasm."

Shadows cast Li's features into stark angles and planes.

"An obelisk," I said. "Script all over it. Junior saw it too. That's why he left us behind."

"And you thought Roy LaMonte—"

"Junior said he saw a person."

"Like, a human person?"

"That's all he said. I didn't see anything. Well, I saw something, but I couldn't tell what it was."

I strained to picture the scene, the shape vanishing into the forest. Might as well have tried to remember my mother's face.

Li stared out the window. I looked too. There was nothing to see. I imagined Junior stepping into view, pressing his face against the glass. In my imagination, his eyes were shiny and black, even the parts that should have been white. When he opened his mouth, blood dribbled over his parched bottom lip.

My eyes watered. I peeled my gaze away from the window.

"You sure you saw something man-made?" said Li.

"I don't know," I said.

"I wonder," said Li, unfolding her legs.

"What?"

"Nothing."

She stretched, hands linked above her head. At the apex of the stretch, her shirt lifted up just far enough to reveal a strip of midriff. I averted my eyes.

"Enjoy the couch," she said.

"Beats a tree branch."

I watched her climb the stairs.

When she was gone, I went to the bathroom and brushed my teeth. Then I returned to the living room and turned off the lights. The whole time, I studiously avoided glancing out any of the windows.

Immediately after falling asleep, I began to dream. I stood by the chasm in the forest where Junior had died. No matter how I stared into the darkness, though, I couldn't make out the obelisk on the other side.

The chasm seemed much deeper and darker than before. I knew that if I stood beside it too much longer, it would drag me in, but my feet stayed rooted to the ground.

At first, the forest was silent, but after a while I began to hear a rustling.

When I turned around, Junior was there, held aloft by the scorpion that had killed him. The stinger poked out through his chest, but his legs were still, not kicking the way I remembered. The scorpion blinked its many eyes, and I got the feeling it wanted to say something, if only its mouthparts were capable of articulating more than a complicated hiss.

"TETRIS," said Junior, in a voice far too deep, as blood dribbled down his chin.

Reluctantly, I brought my gaze up to his face. His eyes were as black and shiny as the scorpion's.

"I'm sorry, Junior," I said.

"Under your skin," said Junior in that awful, grating voice. His mouth was full of worms. "Your skin, Tetris. You have to know—"

I jolted awake before I could hear any more. Sweat slicked my body from neck to ankles, and my heart thumped violently against my ribs.

6

We've figured out physics. We've put humans in orbit, on the moon, and in a few years we'll be sending them to Mars. We've mapped the globe, split the atom, cured cancer, and perfected plumbing. But there's still one question we haven't answered. One place right here on Earth that remains a total mystery, because we've only scratched its surface: the World Forest. That's what rangers are for.

- RangerCorp promotional brochure

On the ninth day of our eleventh expedition, with a lemony aroma in the air, we came across a creeper vine.

"Check it out," said Li, slinging the SCAR-17 across her back.

I crouched beside her. The vine was thick and sinewy, an inert green snake. It trailed into a crevice a few feet away.

Li gave it a poke with a stick. The vine tugged the stick from her hand and hissed out of sight.

A year or two earlier, this would have filled me with dread. Now I just grinned, imagining the plant's frustration when it discovered that its tendril had been fooled. No tasty morsel this time.

This expedition, we'd set out much further down the coast, near San Diego. The previous team assigned to this region had gone missing, presumed dead. Apart from a slight temperature increase, it was more or less the same forest.

"I was thinking about what you said, Tetris," said Zip.

"Hmm?"

"About me not spending my money."

"Oh."

"There's one thing I'd blow it on."

"Girls."

"Well, I mean, other than that."

"Climbing gear."

"Got plenty of that already."

"As far as I know, those are the only expensive things you like. So."

"Tacos."

"Tacos. Are not expensive."

"I mean the best tacos. In the world."

"Even good tacos are not expensive."

"Somewhere out there, there is a man who has spent his entire life making tacos."

"Or woman," said Li.

"And this man—"

"Or woman."

"—who I presume lives on a Mexican mountaintop somewhere, far from distractions, and makes tacos day in and day out, feeding them to the wildlife, because the customer is a hassle, see, the tacos themselves are the point—"

I had a bug bite the diameter of a quarter on my neck, but I refused to scratch it.

"Impoverished taco hermit is about the worst job I can think of," I said.

"You clearly haven't worked in a funeral home," said Zip.

"Please, God, no, I take it back."

"When I was fifteen, I started helping my dad with the embalming."

"Here we go."

"You don't want to know what we had to do to those bodies," said Zip.

"No more than the first time."

"First you suck out all the blood and replace it with embalming fluid. Fasten the eyes and mouth shut. All the leak-prone orifices have to be plugged. If a person's been decapitated or something, you have to piece them back together."

"No doubt. No doubt."

"A lot of the time when we pump the embalming fluid in, the deceased gets an erection. If it's a dude. We have to, like, tape it to his leg."

This was new information. The image rose at once: a mourning family crowded around an open casket, everyone studiously ignoring the tent in the pants of the silver-haired occupant.

"The worst I saw was a guy who got run over by a forklift."

"Totally 'forked' up, huh?"

"Tore his legs off. Dragged his top half across ten yards of gravel."

"Real talk: how does that even happen?"

"Dunno. Runaway forklift."

"Those can't possibly go more than ten, fifteen miles an hour."

"My dad was an artist. Sewed the two halves together, repaired the skin, and rebuilt the skull with putty. You would have thought he died of a heart attack."

I thought of my brother, small and bald and cold in the casket.

"People say the forest's so dangerous," said Zip, "but out on land you can get torn to shreds by a forklift. You can slip off a grapple gun course. You can trip getting off the bus and break your neck."

"Wow, you might be on to something," I said. "Wait— which is the place with snakes the size of subway trains, again?"

"Dead is dead," said Zip. "It doesn't matter whether it was a drunk driver or a subway snake that killed you."

We edged around a ravine as a distant creature skreeled and sang.

"What you really have to watch out for," said Li, "is an inebriated subway snake."

Zip had just opened his mouth to respond when a clatter of chitinous legs rose from below. We drew our grapple guns and rocketed away.

A flood of giant spiders burst through the floor, scrabbling over each other and onto the trunk of our tree. Up they climbed, zeroing in like bloodhounds drawn to a scent.

"There," said Li, pointing at a tree some distance away. We fired our grapple guns and swung across. The rush of air made my eyes water. Spiders flooded after us. Tens of thousands of them. I'd never seen anything like it. The producers would eat this footage up if we survived long enough to bring it home.

By the time we'd landed and rearmed our grapple guns, the spiders were halfway up this tree too.

"We've gotta go higher," said Zip.

Only sunlight could drive these things away. It was worth the risk of brushing the canopy. Our grapple guns fired, one after the other, and we zipped to a thick branch far above. The spiders kept coming.

"If y'all have any bright ideas, I'm listening," said Li.

At this altitude, the tree's sway was noticeable. Another jump and we'd be in the canopy proper, where the grapple guns were useless.

"They'll stop climbing," said Zip.

The spiders continued climbing.

"You'd think the light would have turned them away by

now," said Li.

There was something large and scaly hidden in the leaves twenty or thirty feet above us. Four orange eyes blinked in counter-clockwise order, then vanished.

The spiders knocked each other off as they flowed up the trunk, hundreds flailing through empty air at any given time, crunching into the horde like leggy cannonballs.

"Another tree," I said. "They'll have to climb the whole thing again."

We swung to another tree. Sure enough, the flood of spiders began scaling this one too. From this height, their shapes were indistinguishable. They were an amorphous black mass, geologic in scale.

The ones on our previous tree continued to climb. It was clear that they intended to skitter across and sandwich us from above.

"We can hardly be worth the effort they're exerting," I said.

"Speak for yourself," said Zip.

"They'll give up," said Li, pointing out another tree.

But spiders were already scaling that one, along with every other tree in the vicinity. The net had begun to close.

An ominous rumble joined the maelstrom. As our tree shuddered, the spider-covered ground puckered and swelled. Out burst the twirling maw of a creature so immense it could have swallowed the Washington Monument. All mouth and neck, with no eyes I could see, the worm didn't eat the spiders so much as drink them, sucking them down its bright pink throat.

Our tree teetered, its root network upended.

"Go," shouted Li, and we fired our grapple guns, swinging free just as the tree went thundering down. The impact sent others tumbling like gigantic, groaning dominoes. Denizens of the canopy shrieked and roared, searching for a stable place to take hold. A dragonfly zipped by in a panic, and enormous mosquitoes cruised aimlessly overhead.

We prepared our grapple guns again. The spiders had become the prey. Away they scuttled, retreating into to the tangled depths as the pink creature slurped them down like water droplets off a leaf.

A few jumps later, when we paused to catch our breath, I began to shudder. I clamped my mouth shut, but my chest shook harder and harder, until finally it all came spilling out, a deluge of painful, hiccuping laughter. Zip and Li must have felt it too, because they grinned like toddlers meeting a cat for the first time.

"Those stupid fucking spiders," I choked, wiping my eyes on my sleeve. "Did you see—did you see?"

Li spat. The three of us watched the glob of spittle tumble, shrink, and vanish.

"Fuck," she said, savoring the word, drawing it out like a death row inmate taking her last drag of a cigarette. "I love you guys."

Zip snickered.

"Yeah, okay, I take that back," she said.

Warmth pulsated in my veins. This was why I was here.

Zip unwrapped a protein bar and took a bite.

"I've got a story," he said with his mouth full.

"Always bragging about your conquests," said Li.

"Not that kind of story," said Zip.

I grabbed a protein bar of my own.

"Sunday afternoon," said Zip, "I roll out of bed, put on my flip-flops, and head to the gas station for a bite to eat."

"You're the only person making three hundred grand a year who's ever used 'gas station' and 'bite to eat' in the same sentence," said Li.

"I grab the usual—hot dog, sour gummy worms, onion rings, 76-oz blue slushie—and I've got all this shit cradled in my arms as I go flip-flopping up to the register."

Zip took a big gulp from his canteen.

"So I'm standing there with my arms full, trying to figure out how to retrieve my wallet from my pajama pants, and the cashier is glaring at me, because no matter how many days in a row he sees me, I am still a buff black man, and therefore probably a criminal. Same old everyday shit."

"Downright quotidian," said Li.

"Until a skinhead walks in and pulls a gun. Shirtless, full-body tattoo, swastikas aplenty, red eyes, the classic package. Standard citizen, at this point, would be unnerved. But I'm three feet from this thug as he waves the pistol, bellowing about the Reichstag or whatever, and all I can do is stare at his twiggy little legs. Up top he's got biceps, shoulders, et cetera. Except he's never heard of squats, never caught wind of dead lifts, and he looks like you could knock him over with a squirt gun.

"Well, I must have chuckled, because this fine Southern gentleman invades my personal space, leans over me, and positively shrieks the N-word.

"'*Gib mir dein wallet*,' he screams, and jams the pistol in my sternum, which knocks the slushie out of my arms. This makes me very upset. It is his first major error.

"I tell him no problem, one wallet coming right up. I lean down and place the hot dog, onion rings, and gummy worms beside the spreading slushie mountain. Then I straighten, produce my wallet, and hand it to him. The whole time, we're staring right in each other's eyes, it's like the climax of a fucking rom-com.

"He's got my wallet now, and this is where he makes his second mistake, because he pulls that Glock back and flips the wallet with his other hand to see what's in there. Soon as he breaks eye contact I leap to the side and grab his arm—the gun goes off, BLAM! Shatters the glass in the beer section—and I snap his wrist. Gun falls into the slushie puddle, I kick it away, and as this dude's starting to scream I shove his legs out from under him and slam his face on the linoleum. And I swear to you, friends—I swear that this man's bald head bounced."

"Every word of that story is imaginary," said Li.

"I have the police report to prove it," said Zip. "Remind me to show you when we get back."

"What happened next?" I asked.

"Thug was out cold in a puddle of blue-raspberry blood. Cashier issued another slushie free of charge, so I

53

sipped on that until the police arrived."

"You crack his skull open?" I asked, hungry for details. What had the impact sounded like? Had his body spasmed around, or gone straight limp?

Zip shrugged. "I didn't hang around long. Had a date that afternoon."

"Oh, of course," said Li.

"Point is," said Zip, "I think this job changes us. Even with that gun against my chest, I wasn't scared."

"I bet that asshole's skull cracked wide open," I said, satisfied by the thought. "I bet he's fucking dead."

"Huh," said Zip, and took another drink from his canteen.

7

On the eleventh morning of our expedition, we came to the edge of a canyon.

It was a gash so broad and deep that the canopy could scarcely bandage it. Branches strained to nuzzle across the gap. Sunlight snuck through, harsher than a camera flash, and painted jittery shadows against the chasm's walls.

The light pierced a mile into the depths, a descent criss-crossed by fat, grasping roots. Nothing moved.

We set out along the edge. Half an hour later, we found a fallen tree that bridged the gap. The ravine curved away forever. I probed a sore tooth with my tongue. The bridge-tree must have fallen recently, because blue sky poured through a canopy-wound overhead.

Blue was a rarity in the forest, existing only to denote poison. For instance: blue frogs the size of meat lockers.

They would leave you alone, but if you ever had the misfortune to touch one, the toxins coating their skin would squirm through your pores and liquefy your organs.

We crossed, quickly but carefully, along the very center of the trunk. Safe among the trees on the other side, I exhaled.

"Felt like an ant on the sidewalk out there," I said.

Zip adjusted the straps of his pack. "Twelve-year-old me must have murdered twelve billion of those."

"How unique," said Li.

"I don't think you grasp how seriously I took my quest of entomologiful eradication."

"Entomological."

"'Fuck ants,' essentially," said Zip. He tried to turn a shudder into a shrug. "I hate ants."

That night, a storm rolled over the forest. As we settled into our sleeping bags, a soothing drone of raindrops masked the normal nighttime sounds. Distant thunder grumbled. Rainwater slithered through the leaves and fell in intermittent three-hundred-foot pillars.

The way our tree swayed back and forth, you could tell that the storm was stirring up fierce winds above the canopy, but by the time it reached us, the gale was toothless. A gentle swirl of fresh, wet air was all that remained, and we drank it in with relish.

Kept awake by the sound of rain, I stared out the top of my sleeping bag and remembered Boy Scouts. On a camping trip at Badger Falls, when I was thirteen, it had rained every night for a week. On that trip, I'd been the only kid without a dad. At night I pressed the wall of the tent and watched the droplets accumulate. Hoping to taste pure rainwater, I licked up some moisture I collected this way, but it tasted like my palm—the acrylic sting of bug spray mixed with salty sweat.

In the forest, rangers collected water via condensation nets. Tonight, with the rainfall providing extra moisture, those nets would fill our canteens in minutes. That was pure rainwater, or close enough, but by the time you took a drink, it tasted like the canteen.

Asleep at last, I stood on the forest floor, in the dark, alone. The storm had passed, and all was still, until a thousand spiders crawled up from below. They encircled me, crowding against each other so that their hairy legs scrabbled and interlocked. Fangs gleamed between innumerable pedipalps, but the fear I felt seemed disconnected from the spiders somehow.

Out of the darkness swayed Junior, held aloft by the scorpion's stinger.

"Tetris," he said with a carnivorous smile. His teeth were much too long.

I peered into his black eyes.

"You haven't been listening to me," said Junior, his voice resonating in my bones.

The spiders chittered and rubbed their mandibles together. They coated the tree trunks, clinging to the bark with hooked feet, a swarm ten thousand strong, every eye fixed on me.

"It's under your skin, Tetris."

I could feel it, the skin of my neck crawling, something wriggling to escape. I fought the urge to tear myself open. My palms stung, and I discovered that my fists were clenched, the fingernails digging deep ruts. Any moment now, the nails would burst out the backs of my hands...

"Can't you leave me alone?" I begged.

The forest was silent. Junior considered my words. The spiders shifted their focus to him, waiting for the response.

"No," said Junior at last, and the horde of spiders writhed, screaming.

The scorpion clacked its claws, and silence fell again, although the spiders continued to spasm. Their mouthparts flagellated madly.

"Trust your eyes, Tetris," said Junior, oblivious to the roiling chaos. "Trust nothing else."

The floor gave way, and I fell into bottomless darkness, unspeakable shapes contorting and shrieking all around me.

In the morning I had purple crescents underneath my eyes.

"What kept you up?" asked Li.

Zip, packing his sleeping bag, thought the question was meant for him.

"I slept like a koala," he said. "Love it when it rains."

"Not you. Tetris looks like a gorilla punched him in each eye."

"I punched him back," I said.

"I'm sure you did."

"You think there's a way they could make these breakfast bars taste better, but they don't bother, because it's cheaper this way?" asked Zip, unwrapping one as he spoke.

"Is that mulch or plastic?" I asked, grabbing one out of my own pack.

"Mulch," said Zip.

"Trade you," I suggested. Plastic, which was supposed to taste like key lime pie, left a slick, acrid residue on the roof of your mouth. The blueberry bars might taste like mulch, but at least they went down properly.

Zip shrugged and tossed it over. When I tossed mine, I must have put some crazy spin on it, because it bounced off Zip's hand and tumbled out of the tree.

"God damn it, Tetris," said Zip, peering after it. "I'm never gonna find that thing."

We finished packing and rappelled down. As Li checked the magazine in the SCAR, Zip rooted through the brush for his breakfast.

I scanned the undergrowth, half-expecting to see dream-Junior's smirking face. My jaw throbbed. I placed fingers against the base of my ear and felt the joint pop. Must have been gritting my teeth again. Wearing my molars down to nubs.

Zip's yelp shattered the silence. Something that sounded like a bird, but was almost certainly not a bird, squawked three times in response.

"Are you nuts?" hissed Li.

"Look at this," said Zip.

"Keep it down," said Li, but she went to look. I stayed where I was.

Newly-fallen leaves covered the ground. They'd shrivel and lose their color within a few hours, but for now they draped like veiny doormats all around. Not for the first time, I marveled at their size. Skeletons of tough cellulose kept the green skin rigid, like bones in a bat wing.

Actually, it was kites they reminded me of. I wondered if you could get a forest leaf to fly, at least in the brief period before it began to decay. Not that I'd ever—

"Tetris, you've gotta see this," said Li.

"What's that look like to you?" asked Zip.

A prickling chill started at my scalp and broadened as it went. Past the tangled matrix of branches and leaves was a gray tablet etched with complicated symbols.

"Is that what you told me about?" asked Li, hunched over my shoulder.

"You guys keeping secrets from me?" said Zip, letting the bush wobble back into place.

"I think it is," I said, scratching my neck.

Li stowed the rifle and wrenched away chunks of vegetation. Zip and I bent to help. Much of the tablet lay underground, so we dug with our fingers. Soon the soil was everywhere: caked under our nails, smeared on our cheeks, gritting between our teeth.

I couldn't believe it. Right there, a few inches away, was a tangible contradiction of everything we'd been taught about the world. Perhaps it was a sci-fi movie prop that had dropped out of a plane? The symbols resembled no language I'd ever seen. They were all sharp corners and fine details. Hieroglyphs? No two were alike. The symbols were large, several inches across, and their contours were complicated by fractal appendages.

When I'd seen the obelisk, it had been too far away to judge its composition. With my hands against the gray tablet, I was even more confused. The material was too uniform, too featureless, to be stone. Yet it was cool and smooth as a granite countertop.

Not metal. Not plastic. But not stone, either, at least no stone I'd ever seen.

"You guys have got to tell me what this is," said Zip.

"I've got no fucking clue," said Li. "Tetris told me he saw something covered in symbols. That's the extent of my expertise, here."

I sat back on my heels. "This is a lot smaller, but yeah, it looks similar."

"There's no way," said Zip, scanning the treeline.

The cuts in my palms sang.

"I'm freaking out, guys," said Zip.

"Cool it," said Li. "We'll take pictures and bail. Once we're out, somebody will tell us what we're looking at."

I remembered Agent Cooper leaning over the table, breathing his acrid mouthwash breath.

"They know," I said.

"What?"

"I think they know," I said. "Those fuckers. I think they know."

"Stay with me, Tetris," said Zip.

"When Junior died, the FBI questioned me and Hollywood," I said. "I thought they wanted to know what happened with Junior, but the government guy, the agent, he didn't care about that. What he cared about was the obelisk."

"Obelisk, right." Zip glanced at Li. "Obelisk?"

"It's why Junior died," I said, suddenly exhausted. "He was going to look. They must have seen it in our footage, flagged it down."

Zip nodded several times. "Yes yes yes. Okay. Yes. Alright. Just so you know, though, you sound like an absolute wacko."

"That's what the agent said!"

"Mhhmm."

"Remember the story Li's dad told? Roy LaMonte saw obelisks, structures, people—"

"LaMonte was a nutjob," said Zip. "That guy could find evidence of ancient civilizations in a Burger Hut parking lot."

Li's fingertips tapped the SCAR's stock.

"Oh, come on," said Zip, "you can't possibly believe this."

"The Briggs brothers died on that trip," she said.

"Wouldn't he have shown the pictures? Taken a video?"

"It all goes through the government first," I said. "It's a condition of the subsidies. They could have censored it."

We stared at the tablet. Was that a slight glow,

hovering around the edges, or was it my imagination?

"You realize that the FBI will see our footage, too," said Zip. "The body cameras. Everything we're saying right now is recorded. If you're right, and they're trying to cover something up, we are totally fucked. As soon as we turn this in, they'll lock us away, or worse."

"So we don't turn it in," said Li. "We take the footage straight to the news networks."

I considered that. It wasn't like they were waiting for us when we came out of the forest. Our return wasn't a scheduled event. Typically, we headed as close to east as we could manage, and wherever we wound up on the coastline, we radioed for pick-up. We could slide under the radar and hitchhike to the nearest town. At any public library, we could hop on computers, make copies of the evidence, and send it everywhere, like an email chain letter. Backups upon backups.

"I'm with you," I said.

Zip ran a finger along an indented symbol. His shoulders shrank. For a moment he resembled a middle-schooler, disappointed in his report card, imagining the look on his father's face when he brought it home.

"I wish we'd never found this," he said.

"Me too," I said, startled to discover that it was a lie.

8

We couldn't pull ourselves away.

"What if there's a whole city up ahead?" said Li.

I wiped my palms on my pants to sop up the sweat, but the fabric only drew further moisture from my pores.

"This is making my nuts shrivel up," said Zip. "I've got a couple of raisins down there."

I kept expecting the tablet to vanish the second I dragged my eyes away.

"We should turn around," said Li, but she didn't move. The toe of her boot drew circles in the dirt.

"Yes, heading for shore is definitively correct," said Zip, who also didn't move.

Strains of a violent argument reached our ears. Deep bellows, like an elephant defending its water hole, followed by a rapid-fire series of avian shrieks.

"Fuck it," I said, checking the mag in my pistol. "Let's go."

Onward we went, miners drawn into unplumbed depths by visions of sparkling jewels. We didn't find a city. For five hours, we didn't find anything at all, except endless, identical trees. Tangled vines and towers of steaming excrement began to seem familiar, as if we were walking in circles, although I'd been checking my compass every five minutes. Our voices grew taut and thin. Zip spat strands of phlegm into the undergrowth, and I wondered if his mouth had the same sulfurous taste that mine did.

Eventually we stopped for lunch.

"I wonder if Sergeant Rivers knew about this," said Li around a mouthful of protein bar.

I thought back to the interrogation, the look on Rivers' face.

"No clue," I said.

Zip balled up a wrapper and hurled it into a ravine.

Li scratched her nose with the back of her arm. "You guys hear how he lost his eye?"

"I suppose you're going to tell us," said Zip.

"One of his teammates got nabbed by a creeper vine."

I leaned against a tree trunk and counted blades of razorgrass. Heavy perfume wafted from some flowerbank out of sight. I'd already heard the story, but I didn't mind listening to Li's voice.

"Per company policy, Rivers and his remaining partner were supposed to turn around. Instead they rappelled down the hole."

"Dun dun dunnn," said Zip.

"There was a cavern underneath. No bottom in sight. The plant was perched on a fallen tree with vines coming off it like puppet strings. Rivers got down there and pulled the missing guy out, but it had already started to digest him."

Zip probed his ear with a pinky finger. "And then he got acid in his eye. The end."

"Even less cool than that. On the way up, something huge grabbed his partner, who was carrying the unconscious guy. Rivers kept going, but the grapple line came whipping down and pow—no more eye."

"There's a moral in there somewhere," said Zip, scrunching his face in mock concentration.

After lunch we went back to walking. Just when I'd begun to think that there was nothing out here, we found a tall gray pillar in a clearing no different from the thousands of others we'd crossed.

It was the biggest structure so far. Featureless and smooth, it was bare of hieroglyphs except for a convoluted labyrinth etched at its peak. On the far side of the clearing, a trio of enormous ants wriggled in the tangled threads of a seventeen-story spider web.

Li crept closer to the gray structure, and I followed, keeping an eye on the wobbling web.

"I don't like this," said Zip.

I laid both palms against the obelisk. It was cool and damp as a stone plucked from a riverbed, with the same smell of earthy nothingness.

"Guys, come on," said Zip, as a pair of bloated red spiders crept out of the canopy. Their titanic abdomens throbbed like human hearts.

"Gimme a lift, Tetris," said Li, peering at the markings. I bent, allowing her to clamber onto my shoulders.

The spiders ambled down the web. Their lazy movements suggested that they'd already feasted today, and the ants were a happy surprise, like a slice of cake discovered in the fridge. The larger spider grasped an ant and administered a bite. At first the gyrations only intensified, but after a moment they faded to twitching, and then the ant was still.

The spider spooled greasy thread from its rear and transformed the ant into a tightly-wrapped cocoon. Its companion wove a similar casket for the second.

As I let Li down off my shoulders, the third ant bucked and clacked its pincers. Sheer will or an act of God allowed it to tear itself free, and it tumbled fifteen feet to the ground.

Time slowed.

The ant lumbered in our direction, two legs still bound with silk. The spiders plopped down after it.

Zip dove left. Li and I flung ourselves right. The ant brushed between us and plummeted through the floor, dragging a good portion of the clearing with it. The first spider flew after it. Like bystanders during a bank robbery, we tried to make ourselves as small as possible.

The second spider paused at the edge of the new-formed pit. Its abdomen swelled and contracted. While it considered a descent, it noticed Li and me crouched beside the obelisk.

Li let loose with the SCAR, stitching a path of bullets from its eye-cluttered face down the length of its abdomen. On the other side of the pit, Zip unloaded his handgun.

For a moment the spider wavered, four of its legs pulling it towards Li, the others reaching for Zip. It settled on us, but we were already seeking cover in a thicket. Meanwhile, Zip emptied another magazine, and the spider wheeled to face the hail of bullets.

Zip scrambled up a tree trunk. At full speed, the spider could have plucked him off the bark like a grape, but another barrage from the SCAR and my own pistol kept it off balance.

The climb was nothing for Zip. I'd seen him scale a glass office building just to impress a girl. By the time the spider reached the base of the tree, he was well out of reach.

Then he fucked up. He could have kept climbing and grapple-gunned to safety, but instead he stepped onto a branch directly above the spider and fired six shots into its chitinous head.

The spider rammed into the tree, sending shivers up the trunk, and Zip's branch gave way with a groan, dropping onto the spider's upward-gaping maw—

A pincer boomeranged across the clearing, trailing goopy black bile. Zip threw himself free and rolled to a stop at the edge of the pit. Again Li's SCAR roared.

The spider staggered, orange goo gushing from a dozen spouts. As it floundered away, a leg lashed out, catching Zip full in the chest—

For a moment he floated in midair, eyes as wide and disbelieving as Junior's had been. Then he was gone, hurled unceremoniously into the abyss, and blood pumped thick and heavy through the red corridors of my skull.

9

Zip's parents hated each other, but, for religious reasons, they refused to get a divorce. They also refused to use birth control. It wasn't a great combination. Zip was their fifth child, and by that point they'd quit even trying to come up with names, which is how he wound up Zachary Taylor Chase.

"The most fucked up thing in my childhood was the way we went through pets," Zip told me once at Thai Restaurant, our favorite Thai restaurant. Palm-sized silver fish swam fin-to-fin in an endless slow arc around an aquarium beside us.

"My dad spent most of his time at work," said Zip. "There, or the bar, or his girlfriend's place. Avoided our house like it was radioactive."

I'd skipped breakfast that morning, and my stomach was beginning to turn on itself.

"He sounds like a piece of shit," I said.

"That's what he was afraid we'd think," said Zip, "so he kept bringing home puppies. For the optics."

I sipped my water.

"My mom hated that," said Zip. "She was already raising six kids by herself, and she didn't like animals to begin with. Plus these dogs were a representation of my dad. Three of them ran away, two got hit by cars, and another one died in our backyard because she refused to take him to the vet."

"He could at least have gotten you fish, or something."

"Oh, he did. We had fish for a while. Keeping them alive is impossible, though."

"Can't be that hard."

"Don't feed a fish for a couple of days and it'll die. But if you feed it too much, that'll kill it too."

"Like the pandas at the zoo. The ones they can't convince to mate. Isn't evolution supposed to weed that out?"

"I don't think fish even want to be alive," said Zip. "If the water's too cold, too hot, too blue, too wet—any excuse they find, they'll pounce on it and die, and then when you find them floating at the top of the tank they give you that look, like it's your fault—"

He puffed his cheeks, widened his eyes, and furrowed his eyebrows.

"That's good," I said. "That's a reproachful fish, right there."

Zip bought a pug puppy when his first paycheck came through. His apartment didn't even have furniture. He was sleeping on a pile of blankets. Getting a dog was priority number one.

He named the puppy Chomper. Chomper was a big fan of me, so much so that he lost control of his bladder every time I visited. At first Zip found this hilarious, but by the sixth or seventh time he was exasperated.

"Can we stop coming to my place?" he said, grabbing paper towels off the fridge.

"Your TV's bigger," I said. Chomper was running figure eights through my legs, so I leaned down to scratch him behind the ears.

"You're a good boy," I said. His little pink tongue drooped happily out of his mouth.

"Don't say that," said Zip, mopping. "Don't tell him that."

Even Li liked Chomper, and she hated dogs.

Whenever Zip went on an expedition, he left Chomper with his sister. The worst part of watching him vanish into the pit was knowing that he'd never retrieve his dog.

The darkness yawned.

"We're going after him," I said.

"No shit," said Li.

A few months earlier I'd run into Sergeant Rivers at a bar near RangerCorp headquarters. After a few drinks I asked if he thought he'd made the right decision by trying to save his partner. He tightened his lips and rubbed the rim of his empty eye socket.

"The smart thing to do," he said, "is not always the right thing to do."

Side by side, Li and I rappelled into the abyss.

10

The pit was cool and dark and bottomless. There was no trace of the ant or the spider. Perhaps the ant still fled, somewhere far below, the spider trailing frothing ribbons of drool a few feet behind.

The firepower we'd unloaded on the surface had not gone unnoticed. Furious cries barraged us as we sank through the soupy gloom. Our headlamps painted rolling ovals across the forest's tangled brown skeleton.

How long would we look before giving up? The thought provoked a whiplash of guilt. What kind of friend was I? But if he'd fallen far enough, there wouldn't be any point in finding him. It didn't make sense for us to die too, did it?

If only we'd listened to him and left. If only the branch had held. If only the spider's leg hadn't happened to find him. Was the barrier between life and death really that thin?

Li whistled. She'd found Zip's body on a ledge protruding from one of the earthy walls. I willed him to turn and look up at us, give a toothy grin, but his body remained still.

Something hairy was clambering up from the depths. Through the decaying infrastructure, I glimpsed matted fur and long gray fingers with multiple joints. Fingers thicker than telephone poles snaked around branches and outcroppings as the beast hauled itself upward.

"Go," said Li, planting both feet against me and exploding away. I swung toward Zip, flicking the grapple gun to allow more line to flow. I left enough slack to land on the ledge with room to spare, but the edge gave way beneath my feet, sending dirt and half-eaten wood spiraling down while I scrabbled for purchase.

Zip remained inert as I reached his side. Dozens of hand-sized insects leapt off his body, fleeing my headlamp. There was no time to check his pulse. I hooked his belt to my line and hefted him over my shoulder.

The ascending beast unleashed a guttural roar. It was an ape with dull black eyes and a mouth that sucked in a roomful of air with each breath. Tree trunks gave way before it like rotten toothpicks.

I tripped a button on the grapple gun and began to rise. A spider crawled out from under Zip's shirt and onto my neck, leaping away before I could bring my hand around to swat it. The sensation of legs prickling my skin remained.

The SCAR crashed and spat. Li, twenty feet above and ascending rapidly, sprayed at flies burrowing out of the opposite wall. The flies were translucent, like rice paper, with bright red eyes and convoluted organs. One leapt into space and clasped itself around Li's legs. The proboscis prepared to plunge into her stomach—

Calmly, almost casually, Li jammed the barrel of the SCAR against the insect's head and fired. The fly exploded, drenching her in fluid, and the jittering limbs released her. I watched the segmented body tumble past. The ape snagged it out of the air and tossed it down its gullet.

Grunts and roars merged with buzzing flies and the throaty voice of the SCAR to form a clobbering wall of sound. I fired into the maelstrom as the surface neared. The insects seemed reluctant to pounce, but greedy enough that they didn't want to leave us alone, even as more of them crumpled under the flood of hot lead. When Li vanished over the edge, the swarm followed. My line whizzed me up and over. Li helped me to my feet. We unhooked ourselves from the grapple guns—no time to unwind the hooks—and blitzed across the clearing toward the spider web. Zip bounced, heavy and limp, on my shoulder.

Knocked out of the air by one of its fellows, a fly thwacked against me. I struck out and felt delicate exoskeleton crunch. My fist came away soaking wet.

The ape fought through the aperture in the floor, bellowing.

We slid under the web and ran hard. With no grapple guns to carry us into the branches, we had to find another kind of cover. Flies whapped like baseballs against the web, tangling themselves in the thick silk. I glanced back and saw what looked like hundreds of the fat insects trapped, roiling, and then the ape bulled full-speed into them, tearing a path with its ferocious hands.

The ape's incisors gleamed when it roared. It wrenched the web away from its face to fix hideous eyes upon us. The web, lumpy with flies, trailed after it like a demented wedding dress.

A third spider, larger than the previous two, fell out of the trees and blocked our way. We cut left, but the spider wasn't interested in us. Furious at the destruction of its web, it leapt toward the ape, wrapping around the beast's hulking arm and plunging fangs into the thick, muscular shoulder.

The ape spun. I tackled Li as the cape of fly-filled spider web whipped just overhead. As we rose, the ape yanked the spider off its arm and spiked it into the ground. Then, looming tall, it spread its hands apart—

The merciless palms closed with a thunderclap on the spider's swollen abdomen, which popped like a kickball in a trash compactor. Orange-red juices spurted everywhere, spattering our necks with foul-smelling drops. The ape set to work tearing the legs off, stuffing them into its mouth as the spider screamed and writhed. A descending gray fist crushed the head and stilled the twitching pincers.

Li and I reached the place where our hooks were secured and hastened to free them. Moments later we were soaring up to safety and the sweet smell of clean canopy air.

We swung from tree to tree, dodging creatures that dive-bombed the opposite direction, until finally we reached a place where the forest was quiet, and the canopy still, and we laid Zip down to find that breath still came, measured and slow and strong, through his corrugated lips.

11

Zip's left leg was broken. It was purple and lumpy and when he woke the first thing he did was sit up and try to touch it. That's when we realized he had a broken rib, too, because as fast as he'd sat up, he flapped back down again.

"Oh, fuck," he said. "My ribs —"

We unzipped his jacket and pulled up his shirt. His chest was a patchwork of bruises.

"My leg," he said. "Oh, fuck, guys, I'm dead. I'm so fucking dead."

"You're going to be fine," said Li.

"We're twelve days in," said Zip. "You can't get me out."

"Yes we can."

"Listen to yourself."

"You can walk."

"My leg's splinters. I can't fucking walk."

"We'll make crutches."

Zip's face was drawn tight over his cheekbones. It made me uncomfortable to look at him. I scanned the canopy and tried not to think about what a broken leg meant in the forest. Sometimes even a sprained ankle was enough.

"I'm not letting you die," said Li.

"Tetris," said Zip, "you gotta take care of Chomper, okay? Can you promise me that?"

I dug at the grime under my fingernails. I had dirt and dried insect blood everywhere—the corners of my eyes, the creases in my palms, the sweaty crevices in my joints—but it was thickest under my nails.

"I don't care if I have to carry you over my shoulder the whole way," I said. "We're taking you home."

Zip let his head fall back.

"You're welcome, by the way," said Li. "We fought King Kong for you, stud."

Zip moaned. We gave him ibuprofen capsules.

"You need a splint," said Li.

"I need a lot of things," said Zip.

Li and I gathered sticks. We wrapped the leg with bandages, then strapped on the splint.

"Fixed," I said, and Zip almost smiled.

Night came quickly. I dreamed I was back at my brother's viewing, the casket open, but instead of Todd it was Zip lying stone-faced inside. A second Zip stood beside me, examining the corpse with an undertaker's eye.

"Top-notch embalming," said the living Zip. "Looks like I'm just asleep."

In the morning Zip's eyes seemed to have receded back into his skull, and his teeth were clenched together, but he'd regained a bit of his normal cheer.

"If we make it out of here, I'm getting a bright pink cast," he said.

"That'll suit you, I think."

"Women love an injured man. This may turn out to be a net positive."

He leaned on me as we trudged along. I had to hunch so he could put his arm around my neck. Soon my spine was on fire.

"I'm just glad it was me and not you," said Zip. "There's no way I could carry your fat ass."

"Runt like you? Of course not."

Not since my earliest expeditions had I felt so vulnerable on the forest floor. If something jumped out at us, I'd have to swing Zip across my shoulders and make a run for it, which in most cases would be an exercise in futility. The pressure on Li was tremendous, too, because she had to keep watch all by herself. But this was Li we were talking about. All day long, she threaded us around ravines, trap doors and sink holes, lithe and sure-footed, a panther with two stumbling cubs in tow.

We pushed hard, but it was like wading through pudding, and after three days we'd only made two days of progress.

"This is going to take forever," observed Zip as we settled in for the third evening. "We're going to run out of food."

"So we skip dinners," said Li. "Starting tonight. The food will last."

We slept with our stomachs pinching. In the morning, the breakfast bars and gel packets hardly seemed a meal. I wished for a stack of pancakes and a sheaf of bacon strips. And fast food hash browns, the kind I ate on road trips as a kid. All of it steaming on a shining platter in front of me.

On the fourth day we crossed paths with a herd of pill bugs. We hauled ass into a tree and watched them pass.

Forest pill bugs had the bulk and personality of terrestrial cattle. They grazed on whatever they passed, and wouldn't hurt you unless you went to spectacular lengths to piss them off. When confronted by a predator, they curled into armored balls and scattered like a handful of flung marbles.

Zip leaned against the trunk with his eyes closed. His face was linen-white and drawn.

I nudged him. "You doing okay?"

Zip remained silent.

"Looks like it's time for more ibuprofen," said Li.

"Morphine, please," said Zip.

"Not yet," said Li.

Zip looked like he was settling in for a nap. Li scooted closer to me.

"It's going to get worse," she whispered in my ear. "Every step he takes, the broken edges are grinding on each other."

She made her hands into fists and rubbed the knuckles against each other.

Her face was grimy and smeared. It was also painfully

beautiful. I wanted to cradle her head and put my thumbs on her cheeks and wipe away the dirt. I wanted to kiss her on her tight-pressed lips. She was right there! Zip was half-asleep. I could do it. Lean in and kiss her. I wanted...

I whipped my head away. No. What the fuck was that?

Zip was dying. This was not the time to entertain adolescent fantasies. Li had made it abundantly clear that she wasn't interested in me. I had to crush that feeling, throw it down a mineshaft and bury it with concrete.

Li waved a hand in front of my face. "Hello?"

Below, the pillbugs stripped the forest floor clean, mouthparts milling industriously.

A few nights later I dreamed myself back to my dad's house in Indianapolis. I was sipping a glass of lemonade on the porch. Hollywood was there too. He sprawled on a lawn chair with a hat pulled low over his eyes. Only his jaw moved, grinding away at a lump of bubble gum.

The sky hung low and red and empty. No clouds, no sun, just the dull, uniform color of congealing blood.

"You should listen to him, you know," said Hollywood, chewing his gum.

I peered at the red sky. "Who?"

Then a scorpion began to clamber over the white picket fence, and I wrenched myself awake.

My sleeping bag was sticky with sweat. I tried to chase the nightmare away with memories of home: bright summer days at the court by the public pool, heat radiating pleasantly off the blacktop, the rubber-and-leather smell of the basketball transferring to my palms.

Shockingly clean sneakers with soft, fat laces.

Clean shoes sounded amazing. Socks, too. We'd reached the stage of the expedition when rotating between three pairs no longer kept them remotely fresh. Grime had infiltrated every crevice of my body, causing a perpetual, slow-burning itch. I would have traded half my expedition payout for a shower.

Sleep, when it returned, was torn jagged by rapid-fire dreams in which I ran or climbed or flew, fleeing something I was afraid to turn and glimpse.

The next morning was dim and gloomy. Nobody felt like talking. We downed our food bars and continued the trek, obsessively checking our compasses to make sure we were heading as close to due east as possible.

Zip pulled further and further into himself. I dragged him along, and his legs moved, but his mind was miles away. He never asked for painkillers, so we kept an eye on his jaw, and when he clenched it harder than usual we knew it was time to administer another dose.

Around lunch we came across the body of a subway snake. It was rare to see one on the surface. This one must have thrashed furiously when it died, because a wide swath around its corpse was scraped clear of vegetation. Its ridged body curved and rolled out of sight like a levee tracing the edge of a tortuous river. The tip of the tail might have been half a mile away.

The snake's mouth gaped, a cave bristling with serrated teeth, the heavy jaw dislocated. Jettisoned from the mouth, in a puddle of snake vomit, was the half-digested corpse of a giant blue frog. Even for an animal as large as the snake, the toxin coating the frog's skin would have proved lethal in minutes.

The three of us stood, transfixed, imagining the snake in motion. Thousands of tons of scales and muscle, rippling in tune. It must have downed a mountain of meat every day. How else could it keep its ravenous bulk satisfied?

"What a shame," said Li.

Out of nothingness this gigantic creature had grown, a universe of trillions and trillions of cells, over decades, maybe even centuries, and the whole system had collapsed one day because it took a bite out of the wrong frog. Now scavengers would clean it down to the bone. A shining white skeleton would be all that remained, and then the forest would swallow that too.

The snake's skin swelled and we stumbled back, fearing that breath had returned to its mighty lungs. Instead a centipede burst through the thick hide, sniffing the air with its antennae. Out of the gap poured an odor so foul that my breakfast began to rise up my throat.

"Wonderful," I said, and spat.

As we turned to leave, skin wriggled all down the side of the snake. The scavengers were already hard at work.

Late one afternoon, as the forest began to dim, we heard a woman scream.

"Don't go chasing after that, now," said Li.

I smiled. "I believe that's the first joke anybody's told in a week."

"Face it, guys," said Zip, quiet and gravelly. "I'm the funny one. Without me you're boring."

"Well, yeah," said Li. "Why do you think we're trying so hard to save you?"

That night it rained and rained. In the morning Zip moaned and refused to move. We checked his splint and saw that the wrappings were soaked through with blood. As we unwrapped his leg, a sickening smell assaulted us. A spear of bone had punctured the skin of his calf. The whole area was lurid, yellow and red, and humming with infection.

We slathered the wound with antiseptics and bandaged it carefully. While Li put together a stretcher, I managed to get Zip to swallow some antibiotics, along with a few gulps of water.

Off we went, Zip strapped to the stretcher between us, four or five days from shore. If we were lucky, we could make it there in three.

12

At first, the jostling of the stretcher was enough to keep Zip awake. He was even alert enough to spot a flesh wasp and croak at us to get down. But the next day he hardly opened his eyes, and the day after that, we couldn't wake him up. His forehead was aflame.

"Trees look like they're thinning out to you?" I asked, lifting the stretcher over a fallen branch.

"Yeah," said Li, "yeah, we're almost there. Today, I think."

"Today," I repeated. I could feel the forest laughing at us.

By the evening we were close. The trees grew smaller, the canopy hanging lower and less dense overhead. There were even a few gaps in the leaves, puzzle pieces of darkening sky. Soon it would be night.

Without discussing it, Li and I came to the same conclusion. We weren't stopping. We flicked our headlamps on and increased our pace as much as we dared.

"Time to radio for pickup?"

"We can't," said Li. "They can't know we're back."

"Zip's going to die," I said.

"I'll call 911 on my cell," said Li. "As soon as I've got service."

I grimaced but didn't argue. If we were truly uncovering some insidious government conspiracy, falling into their hands would put all three of our lives in danger. But waiting for cell coverage instead of using the radio would push back our call until we were only a few minutes from shore.

So, the new plan: call 911. Sneak back to civilization in the ambulance, set Zip up in a hospital, then bolt for the nearest internet-equipped PC to post our footage. Hollywood lived in San Diego. Maybe he'd help. Although something told me he wouldn't be interested in involving himself.

Our ranger careers were finished. We were breaking six contract clauses and a handful of federal laws. The lawyers would say we were putting Zip's life in danger, stealing expedition footage and releasing it outside the company's channels for personal gain. At best, Li and I were headed for jail. At worst, the government would find a way to make us disappear.

Walking through the forest at night made the hair on my arms stand up. Darkness pressed in on the cone of light from my headlamp. I tried not to think about the predators that could be stalking us, lurking just out of sight. The list was long. But we had to be close to the shore.

After a while, Li paused. We put down the stretcher and she rooted through her pack for her phone.

"One bar," she whispered triumphantly, flashing the screen my way. She dialed 911.

"Hi, we need an ambulance along the shoreline south of San Diego," said Li, keeping her voice low and flicking her beam around the clearing. "We're coming out of the forest with a critically injured person."

The darkness rustled and trilled as Li listened to the voice on the other end.

"No, I don't have a more precise location," she said. "Get rolling and I'll call when we're out."

Something trumpeted. The ground shook. Li shut the phone, yanked up her end of the stretcher, and ran. I struggled to keep track of the ground beneath my feet, scarcely avoiding tripping over the branches and vines that zipped into view.

We ran for a long time, until red daggers filled my lungs. At last the trumpeting grew distant, as whatever had chased us gave up or found more promising prey. We kept running: the trees ended up ahead. The incandescent eyes of a Coast Guard tower glimmered through the leaves.

As we stood, blinking and gasping, under the floodlights, an ambulance came barreling down the slope, trailed by several unmarked black vans.

Li ripped off her headlamp and ran a hand through her close-cropped hair.

"They already know," she said.

In a moment we were encircled. Out of the ambulance sprang paramedics, who rushed to Zip and transferred him onto a stretcher of their own. Out of the vans came a dozen men in bulky black body armor. They trained their rifles on us as the paramedics wheeled Zip away.

"Drop your weapons," shouted one of the soldiers, and we obliged, tossing them into a pile: the SCAR, the pistols, and the grapple guns. Li slung her pack to the ground, and I followed suit, rolling my aching shoulders.

"Easy," I said.

"Hands on your head," screamed the soldier.

Too tired to protest, I lifted my grimy hands and rested them atop my head. Li crossed her arms across her chest and glared. Looking at her, I dropped my arms back to my sides.

"I said hands on your heads!"

"That's enough," said Agent Cooper, stepping out of the rightmost van. "They're cooperating. Stand down."

His smile was uncomfortably wide, and I expected a slim tongue to come flickering through the teeth.

"Welcome back," said Cooper. "We'll take care of Mr. Chase. But you two are coming with me."

13

Cooper sat across from us in the back of the van with the smile still plastered across his face. After a while he donned a pair of sunglasses. Li curled and uncurled her fingers, sometimes cracking the knuckles. I reclined with hands on my knees. Why hadn't they handcuffed us? Didn't they know what we were?

I eyed the soldier next to me. His head was a boulder perched atop mountainous shoulders. There was a comparatively tiny pistol in a holster at his side. I could grab the gun before he could react, put an incapacitating round in his knee cap, turn, and drop the other guard. Li would pick up on the plan as soon as I moved. She'd lunge across the aisle, knock Cooper out, and move on to the soldiers who flanked him—but then what? And what if something went wrong? What if we had to kill someone?

That's what Cooper was counting on. We weren't murderers.

Still, the lack of respect irked me. I'd like to see these thugs survive three days in the forest, weighed down by bulky body armor and assault rifles. The vests might stop bullets, but foot-long teeth would slice through them like lasers through tissue paper.

In the 80s the US Army tried sending a full battalion of soldiers into the forest. These were the best of the best: steely killing machines, bristling with the most fearsome weaponry available. For the first time, it was thought, military technology would give mankind a fighting chance against the denizens of the forest. This was the experiment. High-caliber automatic weapons, armor-piercing rounds, shoulder-mounted rocket launchers, flamethrowers that spewed their searing payload a hundred yards—how could anything composed of mere flesh and bone withstand such an assault?

Dutifully, in a nod to the experts who counseled vigorously against any excursion of this size, the battalion was accompanied by five ranger guides.

At first, the expedition met little resistance. Flesh wasps and other airborne creatures were terminated on sight, reduced to bloody globs by shoulder-mounted missiles. Spider burrows were identified and cleared with grenades. Raising everyone's spirits, a marauding subway snake was brought low by blistering fire from machine guns and rocket launchers. Minimal casualties were sustained.

By the fourth night, the battalion had fallen into a routine. After making camp, the soldiers would set up a perimeter of floodlights, leaving a full quarter of their number on watch at any given time. Around this bubble of light, the forest roiled and screamed, but anything that ventured inside was driven back by a flood of lead.

The soldiers began to feel safe. They grew confident, no longer fearing the titanic creatures that gnashed their teeth in the darkness.

But the forest had not given up. Insistently, it probed the contours of the bubble the men had constructed. It knew that they were most vulnerable at night. Men had to sleep. The forest did not.

Deep in the fourth night, as the lookouts' eyelids grew heavy, the forest struck.

An oval of floor beneath the sleeping soldiers crumbled away, revealing a leviathan all serrated teeth and yawning gullet. Half a company was lost at once, sucked into the whizzing rows of teeth. As the creature flopped its hideous mass higher, foul cyclone breath washing over the bubble, a second assault was launched. A thousand spiders, screeching in unison, rushed down the trees and fell upon the scattered soldiers.

The noise must have been terrific. Suddenly it was every man for himself, and all military discipline was forgotten. Muzzle flash lit the clearing in lieu of the overturned floodlights, and flamethrowers wielded in panicked disarray set vegetation and piled carcasses alight.

As the defensive perimeter crumbled, new predators came stampeding in from all sides, elbowing their way into the bloodshed.

To their credit, some of the soldiers weathered the storm, collapsing inward into a core so dense and tight and well-armed that it could not be breached. If the fearsome creatures had worked together, these remaining humans would have been swiftly devoured, but once the battle was underway the forest turned on itself. The humans crept away, and when morning came the light revealed that thirty had survived. Among them: three of the five rangers.

Licking their wounds, the survivors headed for shore. Without a battalion's full firepower to deter them, guerilla predators nipped at the party from all sides—a trapdoor spider snatching one man and vanishing into its tunnels, a blood bat descending silently and soaring back to the canopy with human prey in its talons—and the nights were fraught with terror.

Of the nine hundred men who entered the forest, only two survived.

The van rolled to a bumpy stop.

"Get out," said Cooper.

We stepped into an empty parking lot beside a long, squat building. Towering floodlights bombarded us with artificial light. The brightness hurt my eyes. The building only seemed to have one floor, but its footprint was enormous, the corners far away in the distance. There were no windows.

Taking his time, Cooper stepped out the back of the van and sank his hands into his pockets.

"Come on," he said, and motioned with his chin.

"No," said Li. She planted her muddy boots on the asphalt. "We're not going anywhere until we get some answers."

Cooper was inscrutable behind his sunglasses. "You'll get your answers. Inside."

"Fuck you."

He sighed and brushed dust from his suit jacket.

"I'm not the bad guy," he said. "Which, I realize, is what the bad guy would say. But I'm saying it nonetheless."

They ended up having to handcuff us after all.

14

In a gray, windowless room, with uncovered light bulbs beating down, Li and I waited for Agent Cooper to return.

"I hope he brings cheeseburgers," said Li.

Our handcuffs were linked to the table through steel loops.

"They questioned me and Hollywood in a room like this," I said.

Li didn't reply.

I'd last seen Hollywood in a San Diego dive bar. I arrived just as the biggest dude in the place smashed a barstool over his blond head. As the whole establishment descended into bedlam, I dragged Hollywood out the door and a respectable distance down the street. In return I received a drunken wallop in the eye.

"This is why nobody likes you," I said as I staggered away.

He wrapped himself around a telephone pole like it was the only stationary object on Earth.

"Hey, Tetris, you know what?" he said as his head lolled to the side.

"What?"

"Go fuck yourself."

Agent Cooper came through the door with an enormous paper bag cradled in his arms.

"Not quite cheeseburgers," he said. "There's a great Indian place around the corner. Gimme a sec, I'll grab some plates."

He placed the bag on the table and left. Li stretched against the handcuffs and managed to tug the food over. Rooting through, she laid each dish on the table. Despite myself, I was pleased. Indian food was my second-favorite cuisine. It dawned on me that Cooper probably knew that.

"They have us under surveillance all the time, you think?" I asked.

"Motherfucker even knew our orders," said Li. "Chicken korma, vegetable pakoras, lamb biriyani. No mango lassi, though. Good thing Zip's not here. He'd throw a fit."

We munched on the pakoras while we waited. They were the crispy kind: my favorite.

The door was ajar. I considered the odds of a successful escape. Even if we got out of the handcuffs, we'd passed countless security checkpoints on the way down. Still, it seemed sloppy to leave that door open. A play to make us feel at ease?

"Sorry about that," said Cooper when he returned. "Break room was out of plates. Had to run up a floor."

He unlocked our handcuffs and stacked them, then leaned back and watched us tear into the food.

"Not polite to stare at somebody when they're eating," said Li with her mouth full. "Your mother never teach you manners?"

Cooper smiled. "She certainly tried."

"Where'd you take Zip?" I asked, wiping my mouth.

"Hospital in San Diego," said Cooper. "He should be alright."

The food was delicious. I had to force myself to slow down. Gorging yourself after an expedition was a great way to land a crippling stomachache.

"I'm sure you have more questions than that," said Cooper.

Li wiped her fingers one at a time.

"I'll try to fill in some blanks," said Cooper. "First: those body cameras don't just record."

"Yeah, no, that's pretty obvious, now," said Li.

"Signal can only reach us when you're fifty miles from shore, but that still gives us plenty of time to screen the footage before you arrive."

"You knew about the monolith," I said. "You knew about the tablet, about what LaMonte saw, everything."

Cooper nodded. "Yuuup."

"Why cover it up?"

He leaned across the table. "Time for some game theory."

Li snorted.

"Let's say we knew there was something in there," said Cooper. "Something big and scary. An entity we didn't fully understand. What would we do?"

"Warn everyone," said Li. "And then kill it."

"Come on. Would we want to advertise its presence to the world? Would we want to get everybody riled up before we fully understood what it was, and what it wanted, and what it was capable of?"

He seemed to be waiting for a response, and I enjoyed refusing to give him one.

"No, we would not," said Cooper. "We would not want that. It would cause panic. More importantly, from a strategic perspective, it would tell the thing in the forest—the entity, the civilization, whatever it was—it would tell it that we knew it was there."

"People have a right to know," said Li.

Cooper laughed uproariously.

"Oh, that's a good one," he said, wiping the corner of his eye. "That's one of my favorites."

"So the whole ranger program is fake?" I asked.

Cooper slowly regained his composure. "Well, rangers would probably have developed anyway. But yes, we use it as a sort of camouflage. You're not just filming television. You're also gathering intelligence."

"So what's in there?" asked Li. "What are we dealing with?"

"When you're finished eating," said Cooper, "I'll take you to someone who can tell you everything we know."

We followed Cooper into an elevator and he hit the lowest button. The elevator hummed as it plummeted. Cooper's suit was immaculate, well-pressed, pin-striped, and perfectly tailored to his slight frame. Beside him, Li was coated in grime, mud caked on her boots up to the ankles. Her face was dark with dirt. Both of us left clods of dried mud and brown smears everywhere we went.

"No guards this time?" asked Li. "Guess you figured out they wouldn't be much help."

"I wouldn't be so sure about that," said Cooper, straightening his tie.

"You don't give rangers enough credit," I said. "Just because those guys are bigger doesn't mean they're more dangerous."

Cooper examined me, eyes half-lidded.

"You're more cocky than I remembered," he said. "I thought Rivers was supposed to beat that out of you."

"Just honest," I said.

"The big gentleman beside you in the van? He was a POW for a week or two in Afghanistan," said Cooper. "When they tried to interrogate him, he snapped the restraints."

"Strong dude," I said. "I get it."

"They shot him four times, point blank. Two in the shoulder, two in the gut. He killed eight of them with his bare hands."

Li shifted her weight to the other foot.

"After that he had a weapon. Escape from the camp was easy. But he had to cross the desert, walk a hundred miles, with no food and only the water he could carry."

The elevator jolted to a stop. With an airy ding, the doors parted.

"I'm not saying you don't have a hard job," said Cooper.

"Just that you're not the only ones."

He took us through a maze of corridors, finally stopping before a pair of double doors.

"Try to behave," he said, and pushed them open.

On the other side was an enormous pit of a room with descending tiers connected by waffled steel steps. Complex machinery chimed and blinked. In the center, at a table with a hologram projected above it, stood a woman in a white lab coat with hair past her shoulders.

"Hey, Coop," she said. "Who are they?"

She spoke quietly, but somehow her voice still reached us. Cooper trotted down the steps.

"Rangers," he said.

"I can see that," said the woman. "They're going to get dirt everywhere."

She wasn't wrong. You could trace our progress by the debris we left behind.

"Sorry about that, ma'am," I said.

"This is Doctor Alvarez," said Cooper. "She's the best we've got."

"Try not to touch anything," said Dr. Alvarez.

Li walked around the table, examining the hologram, which depicted a slowly-twirling molecule. Dr. Alvarez wore a thin glove with blue spots on the fingers. When she motioned with the gloved hand, the hologram shrank and vanished.

"You're too young to be a doctor," said Li.

"Apparently not. What are you here for?"

"The forest," said Cooper. "Tell them everything."

"Everything?"

Cooper spread his arms and beamed. "Everything."

Dr. Alvarez tapped a few keystrokes and a green globe materialized overhead.

"The Earth," said Dr. Alvarez. "Familiar enough. Continents. The World Forest. Past certain latitudes, the polar wastes."

As she spoke, she twisted the gloved hand, and the globe rotated accordingly.

"Can either of you tell me how life on Earth originated?"

I looked at Li. Science hadn't been my best subject. To be fair, I hadn't really paid attention in any of my subjects.

"Single-celled organisms in lakes," said Li.

"Close, but wrong," said Dr. Alvarez.

Li furrowed her brow. "Wait a minute."

"That's what they teach you in school," said Dr. Alvarez, "but I assure you: it's wrong."

A few more keystrokes and the Earth was replaced by a blue globe with a single gigantic continent in the middle.

"This is the Earth," said Dr. Alvarez, "one billion years ago."

I watched the globe as it spun. "What's all the blue?"

"Water," said Dr. Alvarez.

My head thumped. The blue orb slowly turned.

"Where's the forest?"

"Exactly," said Dr. Alvarez.

Li tugged her earlobe. "You're telling me the whole planet used to be one huge lake?"

"They're called oceans," said Dr. Alvarez, "from the Greek 'okeanos,' meaning 'great river.' It's there, in the oceans, that life on Earth began."

I was suddenly very tired. I looked for a place to sit down, but everything was covered in blinking buttons and dials.

"How do you know?" asked Li.

"Geological records," said Dr. Alvarez. "Until about sixty-five million years ago, seventy percent of the Earth's surface was covered by water. After that? No more oceans. Instead, forest."

She tapped a few more keystrokes. "The World Forest is not natural. It's not supposed to be there."

The globe morphed once again. Now I recognized the outlines of the modern continents, but instead of the forest and white-brown polar wastes, these continents were surrounded by dazzling blue.

"That's what the world is supposed to look like," said Dr. Alvarez, with just the slightest hint of sadness.

I couldn't comprehend that much water. Couldn't even picture it. Whole continents of water. You could swim for years and never make it across.

"Something, or someone, put the forest there," said Dr. Alvarez. "And it's our job to figure out why."

15

After a while my eyelids started getting heavy and I could no longer keep track of what Dr. Alvarez was saying. My mind would wander away mid-sentence, and when it returned she'd be firing off incomprehensible multisyllabic words.

Dr. Alvarez caught me yawning. "You going to let these kids sleep?"

Cooper jumped.

"Oh, yeah," he said. "C'mon, I'll show you to your room."

"You're not letting us go?" asked Li.

"It's not like that," said Cooper. "We've got something to discuss tomorrow. We could put you up in a hotel, but there are perfectly comfortable accommodations within the facility."

Perfectly comfortable accommodations turned out to be a cold concrete room with two cots and a yellowing bathroom.

"This is going to earn you a one-star review on TripGuide," said Li.

"Very funny," said Cooper. "There's a call button on the wall if you need anything. I'll send fresh clothes down. Soap and toiletries are in the bathroom."

"Dibs on the first shower," said Li. I winced. The floor would be a muddy mess by the time I got my turn.

"Do you give this tour to all the rangers?" I asked.

Cooper paused in the doorway. "You think this happens to everybody?"

"Finding spooky shit? Happened to me twice already."

"Not to inflate your already cumbersome ego by implying that you're special, but this is a once-in-a-decade occurrence. The vast majority of rangers go their entire career without finding anything."

I tried to read his face, but as usual it was illegible behind bland corporate geniality.

"Get the clothes," said Li. "If you need me, I'll be checking the shower for cameras."

After Cooper left, I followed her into the bathroom, where she was scouring the ceiling.

"Find anything?"

"Nope," she said. "Probably bugs in the vents, though."

"Do you believe him?"

"About what?"

"That nobody ever finds anything in the forest?"

"Sure. Maybe."

She balanced on the rim of the tub, examining the rings holding up the shower curtain.

"Isn't it weird, then? That I found it twice?"

She laughed. "What do you want me to say? You're the chosen one?"

"It just creeps me out, is all."

Li hopped down and put a hand on my shoulder.

"Look," she said, "we have no reason to think they're being honest. They're putting on an act, all this buddy-buddy shit, trying to make us feel like part of their fucked-up team. I'm not buying it."

After a few seconds withering in her raptor gaze, I nodded.

"That's what I'm worried about right now," said Li. "That and Zip. Fuck the tablet. I don't care anymore. I just want to know that we're getting out of here, and that Zip's alive."

While she showered I had another crisis of willpower, imagining her stripped bare, the hot water steaming off her skin. I thought about going to the door, asking—did she mind if I joined her?

Stupid.

When she finally emerged, wrapped in a towel, her legs clean and wet and exposed, something must have shown in my expression.

"What?" she said.

I planted my eyes on her face. "Umm."

"Oh. I get it."

"Nothing," I said. "Sorry. No. I mean, no. Not that."

"Am I going to be safe sleeping in the same room as you?"

"I have no idea what you're talking about."

She laughed. "Your turn, bud. Believe I used up all the hot water."

She hadn't, of course. It was like a hotel: you could stay in there for hours and the heat would never fade. I closed my eyes and let my skin turn red. The first shower after an expedition, I always cranked the heat up until it hurt, because the dirt and toxins of the forest had worked their way deep into my pores. I had to roast myself, all the grime and dead skin peeling away, and emerge like a molting lizard with a fresh new exterior.

Li was already asleep when I finished. Her eyes were closed, her mouth ajar. For a minute or two I stood there looking at her. Then I shook myself and finished toweling off.

I was unconscious within seconds of slipping under the covers.

In the middle of the night I heard a noise and woke up. Li wasn't in her bed. Her empty sheets were pulled aside, tangled. Light trickled around the edges of the bathroom door. The fan whined insistently.

"You alright in there?" I called.

Nothing. I waited a few seconds. Still no response. She probably couldn't hear me over the fan.

Back in my apartment, I sometimes spent nights staring at the dark rectangle of my bedroom doorway, imagining what'd I'd do if someone—something?—glided into view. Something tall. Something even darker than the black rectangle out of which it emerged, except for a glistening mouth. The fear made no sense. But maybe that was the problem: to make a rational judgment about the safety of your surroundings, you needed sensory data, which darkness denied.

When I listened closely, I thought I heard a tapping sound. I held my breath and inclined my head, trying to locate the source. It was probably a pipe, or something to do with the air conditioning. I had noises like this back in my apartment complex. I closed my eyes and tried to sleep.

Tap. Tap tap. Tap tap tap.

The bathroom door slammed open, and I sat up to look. It was Junior, eyes a coruscant black, with blood positively gushing from his mouth. The blood came between his teeth in a torrent, spreading across the floor in sticky waves, and I knew that it would fill the room and drown me.

"Tetris," said Junior through the rush of blood. "Do you understand now? Do you understand, Tetris?"

"Understand what?" I shouted, standing as the sticky red tide rose, lapping at the edges of my cot. "Understand what?"

"Tetris!"

I looked down and saw that the blood had vanished. The room was dark, the bathroom still. Li sat in bed, rubbing her eye with a fist.

"What the fuck, dude?"

"Sorry," I said, lying back down. "Just a nightmare."

I curled up under the sheets, heart jackhammering

away.

"I've never heard you talk in your sleep," said Li.

"Hmm," I mumbled.

"That better not become a habit," she said. "You can't shout like that in the forest."

"Guess I'll be duct taping my mouth," I said.

"Guess so," said Li, and rolled to face the wall.

16

In the morning Cooper took us to the cafeteria for breakfast, then back to Dr. Alvarez's lab for what I presumed to be round two of Forestology 101. This time, though, he got straight to the point.

"We've got a mission for you," said Cooper.

"Course you do," said Li.

"Out in the middle of the Pacific, there are a number of volcanoes, most of them inactive, that protrude above forest level," said Cooper. "Since the sixties, we've maintained a base on one particular chain. The name of the chain is Hawaii."

"Hawaii?" I said, rolling the word over my tongue.

"Proto-Polynesian for 'Place of the Gods,'" explained Dr. Alvarez.

"Course it is," said Li.

"The reason we set up a research station there," said Cooper, "is that there's a major electromagnetic distortion a few miles off shore."

"We've been conducting experiments as discreetly as possible," said Dr. Alvarez, "but there's only so much we can learn without sending people in."

"So you want us to go," I said.

"Correct," said Cooper.

Dr. Alvarez pulled up the hologram of the alternate-Earth again. Its sapphire oceans rotated before us.

"You two simplified things tremendously when you stumbled across those artifacts. Obtaining clearance for this was going to be a nightmare. You're the obvious choice for the mission."

"What do you mean, 'you two?'" demanded Li. "What about Zip?"

Cooper grimaced. "That's where the bad news comes in."

My stomach flattened. Zip was dead, I could feel it.

"Zip's not going on any more expeditions," said Cooper, and I turned away, screwing my eyes closed.

"Motherfucker," said Li. "You let him die?"

"What?" said Cooper. "No, he's not dead. He's in the hospital and looks to be making a full recovery. But they had to take his leg off."

I remembered the foul odor that had spewed out of Zip's wound, the way the punctured skin oozed with blood and yellow pus. No more rock climbing for him, then. Although, knowing Zip, he'd figure out a way to do it with three limbs. But our trio wouldn't be setting any expedition records together, that was for sure.

"Fuck," said Li.

"Sorry," said Cooper. "But we only needed two of you anyway. The third slot goes to a scientist."

My eyelids peeled wide.

"No way," I said. "That's a suicide mission. We're not dragging dead weight out there."

"They won't be dead weight," said Cooper.

"Like hell they won't," said Li.

"The person we're sending has been training for months," said Cooper. "They might not be on the same level, but they'll know how to look out for themselves."

"Why?" I asked. "Why can't you send rangers and look at the footage afterward, like you always do?"

"We don't know what's out there," said Cooper, "and we don't know if it'll still be there when we look a second time. We might only have one shot."

"It's a suicide mission," said Li. "You want us to plunge into God knows what kind of clusterfuck, and you want us to do it with somebody we don't trust, somebody we can't possibly trust."

"Look," said Cooper, "at least give this person a chance. Let them show you what they can do. If they can't win you over, if you still want out, we can't force you to go."

"We can walk away?" asked Li. "You'll let us walk away?"

Her teeth were bared, the canines sharp.

"Of course," said Cooper. "It's a free country. Although if you agree to participate, you'll be compensated more than fairly."

Li's eyes flicked back and forth across his face. She

turned to me and twisted her mouth in a way that said *fuck it*.

"Alright," she said.

"So who's the third guy?" I said. "When do we get to meet him?"

Dr. Alvarez stirred. I'd almost forgotten about her.

"It's me," she said.

Li laughed. She leaned against the stairs, head tilted back as far as it could go, and shook with hooting laughter.

"Oh my God," she said when she'd recovered somewhat. Her cheeks were pink. "Well, I can tell you one thing, and that's that you're going to have to cut off all that beautiful hair."

"I know," said Dr. Alvarez stiffly. "I have been putting it off as long as possible."

"Oh boy," said Li. "Oh boy."

"You should take some time to think about it," said Cooper.

"No shit," said Li. "Get me out."

She headed up the stairs. I gave Dr. Alvarez a smirk and followed. After a moment Cooper came along and held the door for us.

In the hallway Li rounded on him.

"Doc better be real fucking impressive," she said.

"We'll bring you back in a couple of weeks," said Cooper, "and you can put her through whichever kinesthetic rigmarole you desire."

"I want to see Zip," I said.

"I've got a car waiting," said Cooper.

Just like that, it was over. We were free. Li and I sat in the back seat and looked out our opposite windows.

"You folks mind if I play some music?" asked our driver after a few minutes of silence.

"Whatcha got?" asked Li.

"Taj Mahal," said the driver. "Taj Mahal and the Phantom Blues Band."

"Sounds great."

So we listened to Taj Mahal and watched the highway markers whip by. It was a bright day, the sun high in the sky, no clouds in sight.

"I don't know what to say," sang Taj Mahal, "I must have had a real bad day."

During the last year of Todd's life, I'd spent countless days at the hospital, as the doctors administered chemotherapy or radiation or whatever five-percent-chance treatment they were trying that month. Nowhere was more impersonal and lifeless than a hospital. People bustled everywhere, but you were invisible to them, your misery inconsequential. Your whole life might be falling apart, but that wouldn't stop them from telling jokes and laughing as they strolled past.

We asked the lady at the information desk for Zachary Chase and she gave us his room number. Three burly men in poorly-fitted suits lounged on spindly chairs outside. They eyed us lazily as we entered.

Zip was asleep. The muscles of his face had finally relaxed, allowing his mouth to hang open. He snored quietly. His eyes, closed, were inset and dark.

"You better let him sleep," said the nurse. "It's going to be a few days before he's up to entertaining visitors."

We sat beside his bed. The EKG machine beeped.

"I'm glad he's okay," I said, because it was the only thing to say.

"Me too," said Li, looking at the place where his leg should have been propping up the blankets.

Outside in the sun, our driver leaned against the car, smoking a cigarette.

"Back already?"

"He's asleep," I said.

The driver dropped the cigarette and rubbed it out with his heel. His smile revealed a wide gap between his front teeth. It didn't look bad—just made him seem friendly.

"I can take you back to your cars, if you want," he said.

"That'd be great," said Li.

"Agent Cooper booked rooms downtown."

"Nice of him," I said.

"Mh hmm," said the driver, and opened the door.

At the hotel I dropped my bags beside the minifridge and plopped on the bed with my laptop. After finagling the complimentary internet to life, I pulled up a high-resolution satellite image of the planet.

It was the same old picture. The forest was everywhere you looked, outlining the continents, a dark, implacable green. Over the top swirled thick white clouds. On land: lighter green, yellow, brown... jungles and deserts and plains. Then the caps of the globe: brown smeared into white. Frigid wasteland. I zoomed in on the northernmost edge of the Pacific Forest. The transition was abrupt, rough-edged. The treeline fizzled out, and northward from there it was muddy and cold.

I zoomed back out and looked at the whole globe again. It was ugly.

This green-brown sphere with naked poles was diseased, syphilitic, balding. I closed one eye and recalled the world Dr. Alvarez had shown me, boundless clean water glittering blue. That was the planet I wanted. What had happened to get me stuck with this one instead?

That night, a rare thunderstorm rolled over San Diego. The windows shuddered, rain pelting against them in waves. I didn't feel like sleeping, so I watched a James Bond marathon. Around midnight I got a text from Li.

You still up?

My heart rate tripled. Did that mean what I thought it meant? This late at night, was there any other reason to send that text?

"Yeah, wanna come down the hall?" I typed, then backspaced it out.

After trying it a few different ways—"Yeah, want to hang out?" "Yeah, what's going on?"—I settled on the simplest possible reply:

Yeah

As I waited for her next message, James Bond drove a sports car out the side of a supervillain's ice fortress. Translucent shards sprayed in all directions. The car floated languorously in midair. The camera cut to a close-up of Bond's face, his cheeks smooth, no stubble, the corners of his lips hooked upward in a mischievous smile. Then the car touched down and time returned to normal.

Right when I thought I'd waited too long to reply, my phone buzzed again.

I can't sleep.

A few seconds later:

Can I come over?

I stared at the text bubble with those words in it.

Sure, room 205.

I dropped my phone and surveyed the room. Earlier, when I'd rooted through my duffel, I'd strewn clothes all over the place. Now I stuffed them back inside. My sneakers were scattered beside the door; I straightened them out.

I looked at my reflection in the bathroom mirror and couldn't help but laugh. What was I worried about? I flexed, practiced a broad grin. What did I think was going to happen? Something in my head had come unplugged. I was a teenager on his first date, trying to decide whether to put an arm around the girl during the opening credits of the movie.

When she knocked I counted to five before opening the door.

Her eyes were bright and sharp, not the least bit drowsy.

"Hey," she said, and I stood aside so she could come in.

"Raining pretty hard out there," I said, hands in my pockets.

"Sure is," she said.

For a while we watched drops come splattering out of the darkness against the wide window.

"What are you up to?" she asked, as if she couldn't tell.

"I'm watching a James Bond marathon," I said.

"Neat," she said, and sat down on the bed. After a moment I joined her.

On the screen, James Bond leaned against the bar at a classy party, exchanging sultry glances with a woman in a low-cut red dress.

"They're gonna bang," said Li.

"A bold prediction," I said.

Sure enough, James Bond followed the woman to her personal rooms. She draped herself against the doorframe and craned her neck back.

"Do you think you're enough of a man for me, Mr. Bond?" asked the woman in her huskiest voice.

"Oh, I always rise to the occasion," said James Bond.

"Thousands of years from now, archaeologists are going to discover movies like this and make all sorts of conclusions about our society," said Li.

"And they'll mostly be right," I said.

"Not everybody's a violent, sex-crazed solipsist."

"What's wrong with sex?"

She looked at me. "Nothing. I'm just saying, it's all some people think about."

"That's evolution's fault, though."

She shook her head. We watched the rest of the movie in silence. When the credits rolled, she yawned and stretched, reaching above her head.

"I actually get so bored watching TV," she said.

"Me too," I said. "I get bored most of the time, actually. Not sure what I find fun these days."

"Everything outside the forest is so beige."

I grinned. "Actually, I can think of one thing that's fun."

"Stop."

"What?"

"I hear enough of that from Zip."

"I mean, I don't kiss and tell the way he does, but my appreciation for the fairer sex is probably comparable."

"I don't doubt it."

I couldn't tell if she was giving off positive signals or not. My hands were sweaty, and my mouth was dry, but I decided to press on anyway.

"C'mon," I said, "you can't tell me you don't get the same urges."

"No comment," said Li.

"We rangers," I said, "we're good-looking guys, right? In great shape. Strong chins."

She laughed.

"Not my type," she said.

I stuck an arm out, tugged back my shirt sleeve, and flexed.

"What's not to like?"

Li looked at my bicep, then back at my face, and doubled over laughing. She shook, practically crying, and after a while she put a hand on my knee. The laughing made my heart plummet, but the hand on my knee took the sting away.

"Tetris," she said, "you're like a brother to me. I could never, ever think about you that way. I'm just not attracted to you. Sorry."

I kept my stupid grin up, although I could feel the edges drooping.

"What?" I said. "No, I mean—that's not what I was saying—I would never suggest that—"

"I'm not an idiot," she said, leaning into my shoulder. "It's sweet, actually. I'm very flattered."

I picked up the remote and flicked through the channels.

"Sorry," she said, "I just want to be up front, you know? Avoid any confusion."

"Sure," I said, punching the channel-change button. "It's fine."

"I care about you, man," she said. "We've got a good, solid friendship. Isn't that enough?"

"Of course," I said. Everything she'd said was reasonable. Why did I feel so bitter?

I put the remote down and we watched a few minutes of some Spanish-language soap opera, her cheek still leaned against my shoulder. My mind did barrel rolls five miles above. After a while, she clicked her tongue and patted my chest, then slid off the bed.

"Alright," she said. "I'm going to sleep."

"Goodnight," I said, getting up to walk her out.

"Sleep well," she said.

"You too," I said, and closed the door behind her.

Alone in the room, I paced to the window, hands behind my head. Stupid. She was bored, couldn't sleep, had wanted to come hang out. That was it. That was all it was. Why'd I have to make it into a disaster?

I tried to sleep, but between my fear of another Junior dream and my mind's determination to replay fourfold every millisecond of the evening with Li, I rolled from side to side for hours. Even the dull patter of rain couldn't lull me into unconsciousness.

Cooper met us in the hotel lobby for breakfast.

"Take a week or two off," he said, sliding an envelope across the table. "Tickets for your flight back to Seattle."

"Thanks," I said, battling a yawn.

"When Zip's doing better, we'll send him home. Maybe you can meet him at the airport."

I rubbed my exhausted eyes and made an affirmative noise.

Cooper stirred his coffee. "About the way we picked you up—"

"Don't sweat it," I said, although I could tell it was Li that Cooper was worried about. She hadn't said much, and it wasn't because she was busy eating. She'd barely touched her stack of pancakes. She had a cold glare fixed on Cooper.

"Sorry about any confusion," he said. "We really are on the same team. Just had to exercise caution, you know?"

"Understandable," I said, wanting to get out of there as soon as possible.

Cooper must have felt it too, because he took one last

gulp of coffee and pushed his chair back.

"We'll be in touch," he said, and mimed a quick salute before shrugging into his suit jacket and striding away.

"I can't stand that guy," said Li.

"I noticed," I said, "and I think he did too."

"Good."

I munched on a strawberry. My appetite was still in overdrive, and it felt amazing to sink my teeth into something firm and juicy. As I ate, I eyed Li, trying to be discreet. She hadn't said a word about the previous night, and if she didn't bring it up I had no intention of ever touching on it again.

I needed a girlfriend. That's what I needed.

We went to visit Zip before our flight, but he was asleep again, snores whistling through his nose.

"You just missed him," said the nurse. "He woke up this morning and had a snack. Poor thing's been through a lot. Going to sleep like a koala for a while."

At the airport I defeated Li in a best-of-five rock-paper-scissors match to secure myself the window seat on the plane. My strategy was to pick "rock" every time and let her overthink her own move.

"I can't believe I let you win three times with rock," she said, glowering.

I shrugged. "Some people just aren't cut out for the high-octane world of competitive rock-paper-scissors."

When I got on the plane and worked my way back to row twenty-three, there was already somebody in my seat. I scrounged in my pocket for my boarding pass. 23D. That was mine, alright. I gave its occupant another look.

It was Junior. His black eyes pulsed. The hole in his chest dribbled pus and maggots as he leaned toward me, extending a hand. When he opened his mouth, his teeth were sharpened to fine points.

My head ballooned. Dizzy, I stumbled back. Nausea came at me in wriggling waves, and I closed my eyes, focusing on keeping my breakfast down. For a moment all I could hear was a tinny ringing.

When my hearing returned, I looked again.

Junior was gone. The other passengers were staring at me. I had practically fallen into the lap of a suited man across the aisle. Muttering an apology, I hoisted myself off of him.

"What's going on?" asked Li.

Despite my wobbly legs, I managed to cram my duffel into the overhead bin.

"Nothing," I said, lowering myself into the seat. "I'm fine."

I closed my eyes, trying to slow my heart with deep, calm breaths.

You're losing your mind, said the voice in the back of my head.

I stomped it down and reached for the magazine in the seat-back pocket.

17

Our eyes concealed behind sunglasses, Li and I watched Dr. Alvarez scurry through an obstacle course. She vaulted a series of fences and climbed a net with ease. On the balance beam that followed, she looked shaky for a moment, but recovered and finished it out quickly. The next few obstacles gave her no trouble at all. To complete the course, she had to ascend a rope and ring a bell. It took her a while, but not as long as I would have expected.

"All in all," said Cooper, "an unquestionably impressive display."

Li had her arms crossed and a foot tapping furiously. She checked the stopwatch.

"Sixty-five seconds," she said, and tossed it to Cooper, who nearly dropped it. "My turn."

Dr. Alvarez came over, slick with sweat and trying not

to pant. As Li set up, the doctor cleared her throat. I became aware that she was staring at me.

"How did I do?"

In shorts and a tank top, with her hair cut short, she no longer looked like a scientist. Her chin curved up to pointy cheekbones and eyes as sharp as a diamond-tipped drill.

"Fine," I said. "Stumbled on the beam. Took too long at the end. Otherwise, fine."

"I see," said Dr. Alvarez.

Cooper indicated to Li that he was ready, and she streaked into the course. Over the fences she flew, up and over the net, along the balance beam at a sprint. The rest of the course passed in a blur. Scaling the rope took mere moments.

"Thirty-eight seconds," said Cooper when Li jogged over.

"So," said Li, "turns out sixty-five is awful."

"He said it was fine," said Dr. Alvarez, pointing at me.

Li rolled her eyes. "He's being nice because he thinks you're cute."

I made a strangled noise.

"I was being nice because I'm a nice guy," I said.

"Run it again," said Li.

Dr. Alvarez gave her a sour look. "I don't have my breath back."

"Exactly," said Li.

This time Dr. Alvarez finished in seventy-nine seconds.

"That's what I thought," said Li. "No endurance."

"This is unfair," said Dr. Alvarez, face the color of a

raspberry.

Li's glare was equal parts rage and pity. She planted a finger in Cooper's chest. "I want out. She's out of shape and her attitude's all wrong."

Cooper tried and failed to brush the hand away. "You carried a cripple through the forest for a week and a half. How is this harder than that?"

"It's not," said Li, "but that doesn't mean I want to do it."

Cooper turned to me. "What about you?"

I fiddled with my car keys. "If Li's out, I'm out."

"I thought you might say that," said Cooper. "Which is why we're prepared to offer you each ten million dollars for this expedition."

My jaw fell open.

"What?" I squawked.

"Forget it," said Li. "You can't bribe someone into suicide."

"What she means is, can we get back to you tomorrow?" I said, grabbing Li's arm.

"I thought we were going to swing by the grapple gun course," said Cooper.

"I'm sure she's a regular old expert," I said, pulling Li away. "Gotta go! Talk to you soon."

"Well, okay," said Cooper. Dr. Alvarez smoldered beside him.

In the car, Li slammed her door shut. I dropped the keys in a cup holder.

"Are you out of your mind?" she said.

"Ten million dollars, Li. Christ! Do you understand how much money that is?"

"Won't do us any good if we're dead."

"We won't die," I said. "In fact, it's safer this way, because we can retire afterward. Survive one trip and we're set for life. Otherwise we're risking our lives on expedition after expedition."

"What happened to being an explorer?" she asked. "I thought you weren't in this for the money."

I considered this and backtracked.

"It's not just about the money," I said.

"What, then?"

"You heard Cooper. This is some top-secret world-altering shit. They've got a whole electromagnetic whatchamacallit out there, just begging to be probed."

She shook her head, but I could tell that I was getting through.

"What was it you told me back in training? That the forest had to be more than what it seemed? Now we've finally got a chance to figure out the truth, and you want to chicken out?"

"I don't want to think about this right now," said Li.

"I could use a drink too."

"Not what I meant. It's four in the afternoon."

"So?"

Li sighed. "Fine."

Hamilton's Tavern had just opened an hour ago. It was deserted. At one end of the bar, a pair of businessmen dug into sloppy burgers, leaning over their plates to keep the juices from dribbling onto their clothes. At the other end of the bar sat Hollywood.

"You've got to be kidding me," said Li.

Hollywood turned at the sound of her voice.

"Ha," he barked.

"Haven't seen your ugly mug in a while," said Li, taking a seat beside him. I sat on her opposite side.

"I've been staying off the radar," said Hollywood, rubbing the bridge of his crooked nose. His drink was mostly gone.

"Any expeditions recently?"

"Nah," said Hollywood.

The bartender came by. He was a round man with eyebrows like fuzzy caterpillars.

"What can I bring you folks?"

"Recommendations?"

After enduring a long-winded spiel on the merits of various local craft breweries, I ordered something called a Speedway Stout. Li asked for a cider.

As we waited for the drinks, Li filled Hollywood in on our latest expedition. She left out the tablet and the structure in the clearing. The rest of the story was delivered in meticulous, gory detail, down to the precise velocity with which orange goo exited the abdomen of a spider upon forced implosion via gigantic ape fists.

"Anyway," said Li when she'd finished, after we sat in silence for a minute or two, "How have you been?"

"Truth is," said Hollywood, scratching his chin, "I've been kind of fucked up."

"What?"

Hollywood's eyes flicked over Li's face, then mine, as he dug at the dirt under his fingernails.

"Forget it," he said, and finished his drink.

The skin of my arms pebbled up.

"You can't say something like that and then say it's nothing," said Li.

"I'm fine," said Hollywood.

"Bad dreams?" I suggested.

Hollywood tilted his head. His fingers ceased their fidgeting.

"No dreams," said Hollywood pleasantly. "Have you been having dreams, Tetris?"

It spilled out before I could stop it. "Dreams about Junior. Except his eyes are black and he's got a hole in his chest."

"Sucks," said Hollywood, with a sarcastic whistle. "PTSD, maybe?"

I grimaced. If I was actually going crazy, the last thing I wanted was for Hollywood to know.

"Is that what happened the other night?" asked Li, scrunching her eyebrows. "When you jumped out of bed screaming?"

Hollywood chuckled. "Some things never change."

"Fuck off," said Li.

"When's the wedding? Dibs on best man."

"You can be a bridesmaid," I offered.

"If I ever get married, I'm not inviting either of you," said Li.

"Ouch," said Hollywood.

When Li turned away, Hollywood's eyes flitted across her body. Suddenly I was furious. What right did he have to ogle her in public?

He caught me staring and grinned. His canines were yellow.

"Hollywood," said Li.

"What?"

"How much would they have to pay you to take a random civilian on an expedition?"

"A little extra, I guess. Ten thousand bucks?"

"It wouldn't worry you that you couldn't trust her?"

"You think I trust rangers?"

I made a mental note that this was the most stereotypically "Hollywood" thing I had ever heard.

"Look," said Hollywood, leaning on the bar, "every time we go out there, it's with the understanding that nobody, however experienced, is immune to the occasional fuck-up. Zip fucked up, didn't he? And he was an acceptably competent little munchkin."

"The chances would be so much higher."

"That doesn't matter if you respond to fuck-ups intelligently."

"You mean you'd let them die," I said.

"Hell yeah," said Hollywood. "I admire what you did for Zip, but you have to admit it was stupid."

"We knew we could save him," said Li.

"I counted six or seven places where you should have been dead," said Hollywood.

"But we're alive."

"Point is, you got lucky," said Hollywood.

I replayed the scene in the forest, replacing Zip with Dr. Alvarez. Would we have descended into the pit for her?

"I can't believe you'd take someone along only to abandon them," said Li. "That's disgusting."

"Come on," said Hollywood. "Long before we left, I'd tell them: look. If you fuck up, I'm not risking my life to save you. You'll just fucking die."

Which must have resonated with Li, because in the morning she greeted Dr. Alvarez and Cooper with open arms.

"Doc," said Li, "you can come along."

Dr. Alvarez smiled. "Thanks for giving me a chance."

"I'm not finished. You can come along, but you have to understand one thing: I'm not risking my life to save you."

"Reasonable."

"If you fuck up, I'm leaving you to die. Understood?"

The smile wavered a bit. "Understood."

"I mean, we're not going to actively try to get you killed or anything," I offered.

"Don't let him take the edge off of it," said Li. "I don't give you good odds. This is fifty-fifty, at best."

"Okay," said Dr. Alvarez.

"Are you okay with that? Are you okay with a fifty percent chance that this mission kills you? Is it that important to you?"

Dr. Alvarez looked at Cooper. He shrugged.

"Yes," said Dr. Alvarez.

Li squinted at the clouds sailing across the sky. Dopplered strains of a passing car's music overlaid the sound of distant crows interfacing.

"Alright," she said. "When do we start your training?"

"Whoa," said Cooper. "What do you mean, 'start?'"

"She needs two months, at least," said Li. "Put her in with Rivers' next batch."

"She's already had months of perfectly intensive training," said Cooper.

I got up in his face. "Sell her short on this and it'll be your fault when she dies."

"I'll do the training," said Dr. Alvarez.

Then she smiled at me, and something inside me melted, and I realized maybe I did think she was cute after all.

18

My answering machine was blinking when I arrived in my apartment. I hit play and untied my shoes.

"Hey, it's your dad."

I almost slammed the delete button, but stopped with my finger hovering above it.

"Just wanted to check in and see how things were going. Call me back if you want. Miss you."

Then a few seconds of silence before the click that signified his hanging up. I put my shoes back on and went to visit Zip.

When I rang the bell he came over on his crutches and yanked the door open.

"Welcome, welcome," he shouted, beaming.

Chomper the pug ran tight ovals around us, emitting breathless little barks. I rubbed him behind the ears.

"Would you look at that," I said. "He didn't even pee himself."

"Don't jinx it," said Zip. "Hurry up. I'm watching a

documentary about Magellan."

I followed him to the living room. There was a hint of impatience, but otherwise he seemed to have the hang of the crutches.

"Who's Magellan?"

"You really didn't learn a thing in school, huh?"

"Dead Italian people were never a top priority."

"Ferdinand Magellan was one of the greatest explorers in history," said Zip. "Dude flew an airship around the world back in the 1500s."

"Oh. That guy."

"And he was Portuguese, not Italian."

"Of course. What'd they give him?"

"Hmm?"

"For finishing that trip? Did they make him a knight? Did the Portuguese have knights?"

"Oh, Magellan himself didn't make it."

"I thought you said—"

"No, his crew finished the journey without him. Somewhere off the coast of Southeast Asia, Ferdy got cocky and floated too close to the canopy. Pterodactyl snatched him right off the deck."

"No shit."

Chomper had his tongue out. He mostly sat on the couch next to Zip, but every once in a while he hopped down and ran over to me for a pat on the head.

We watched the documentary for a while, but I could tell that Zip was no longer interested. He kept reaching for his phone to check the time.

"Okay," I said, "you've obviously got questions."

He flicked the TV off and tossed the remote aside. "One moment you're dragging me through the forest. Then I wake up in a hospital bed."

"They didn't tell you anything?"

"I mean," said Zip, "this sleazeball came to visit a couple times. Dressed like Frank Sinatra but without the handsome."

"What'd he say?"

"*You're not in trouble. Your friends are fine.*' Bullshit like that."

"Anything else?"

"Said if I kept my mouth shut about the tablet they'd set me up with a fat pension."

"Must have been Cooper," I said. "Smiled like a snake?"

"Yeah."

"Me and Li have seen a lot of him."

I could tell he felt left out, so I filled the silence with the first thing that popped into my head.

"The forest's not supposed to be there," I said. "It's supposed to be water."

"What?"

"Like, instead of forest—everything that's forest, is supposed to be water."

"That's two thirds of the globe."

"I know," I said. "They showed us what it would look like."

"Are you allowed to be telling me this?"

"Fuck them," I said, electrified. "I'm telling you. I don't

care what they think."

His shoulders relaxed. "What do you mean, 'supposed to be?'"

"Millions of years ago, we went from having water to having forests. And they think it has something to do with the tablets."

Zip rapped his knuckles against his leg. "Why did they tell you that? Why not just tell you to shut up, the way they did with me?"

I watched his face carefully. "They want us to go on an expedition."

He snorted. "Right."

"Me and Li and a scientist. We're supposed to investigate a magnetic disturbance. Or something. I'm not totally clear on that part."

Zip rubbed his eyes and rested his face on his palms. All I could see was the taut line of his mouth.

"You alright?"

He took a moment to respond. "I'm so pissed, man. That should be me out there, but I fucked up, and I'm going to have to live with that the rest of my life."

"At least you're alive," I said.

"I kinda wish I'd died," said Zip. He scratched Chomper behind the ears. "I don't mean that."

"You better not," I said, trying to think of what Li would say.

Get over yourself, fuckface. I went through hell to save you. Where's my thank-you card?

"What am I going to do, Tetris? I mean, what am I

going to do with my life?"

"What does anybody do? Find a job. Find a girl. Chill out and enjoy yourself."

"Right," said Zip, but he didn't sound convinced.

"Look," I said, "we're hitting Thai Restaurant for dinner. Want us to pick you up?"

I was pleased to see him brighten at the thought.

"Thank God," he said. "I mean, my sister's great. She's been going light years out of her way to take care of me. But... let's just say she's not going to be winning a cooking show any time soon."

When Li and I picked him up, he'd put on a nice shirt and rolled up his empty pant leg, fastening it with safety pins. At the restaurant he even managed to grin when the waitress, who'd seen us often enough to notice the missing leg, asked what happened. After regaling her with the tale—in this version, the culprit was a Tyrannosaurus Rex, and the story did not end well for the reptile in question—Zip even managed to requisition her phone number, scribbled upon a napkin, which he carefully folded and placed in his pocket.

And for once, instead of making a snarky comment, Li gave Zip a congratulatory smack on the back, and then we were all laughing, and for the first time in a long while I knew that everything was going to be okay.

19

The dreams were getting worse. They came in low and hot over the trees and through my bedroom window at night. In the mornings a shadow of myself was sweated into the sheets, leaving a faint, salty silhouette even when the fabric dried. I started switching them out twice a week.

One day at the grocery store, hand-length centipedes writhed among the oranges. I had to step around a pool of blood beside a yellow "Wet Floor" sign in Aisle Six. I ignored the hallucinations and went to check out. At first the cashier seemed normal enough, but when she turned to grab my receipt, her cheek had a ragged hole. Clean white teeth showed through like rows of gum pellets.

I never called my dad back, but I didn't delete his voicemail, either.

The night before the flight to Hawaii, I sat in bed watching shapes glide across the walls. Sometimes I could tell that they were shadows, chased by headlights passing on the street. Other times they were driven by no light source I could detect. If I stared straight at them, the shapes froze, pretending to be natural. It was only out of the corner of my eye that I could catch them moving.

According to policy, rangers were supposed to report for psychological evaluation at the first sign of mental instability. I had a feeling I was way past that point, but there was no way I was turning myself in. Not now, one expedition away from ten million dollars. I could buy an awful lot of top-notch psychiatric care with ten million dollars. I wanted the money so bad that I'd started to come up with worst-case scenarios, to prepare for the potential disappointment. Maybe Cooper would turn out to be a lying sack of shit. Maybe Congress would cut funding for whatever agency Cooper belonged to. Maybe nuclear war would break out. But mostly I constructed lists of all the things I'd buy when the check came through. A midnight-silver electric sports car. A lifelong subscription to every magazine in America. Even when I totaled up everything I could imagine, it didn't come close to denting ten million dollars.

I wanted to tell Li. I wanted to come clean and tell her about the time I saw Junior on the plane, about the centipedes and the cashier's cheek-hole and the insomnia and the night sweats and everything. But as hard as it had been to convince her to come along, I couldn't give her any excuse to back out.

And yet...

I had a sneaking suspicion that I was putting her life in danger. That I was going to get all three of us killed. Because the psychological instability rules existed for a reason, and the reason was that crazy people tended to last approximately as long as a strawberry Popsicle in the forest.

But this was ten million dollars we were talking about. So when I lugged my duffel onto the plane and plopped into the seat beside Li, and she asked what was wrong with my eyes, I told her not to worry about it.

Soon we were soaring over the Pacific and I was slumped against the window catching up on sleep.

Hours later I woke to find Li deep in the thickest book I'd ever seen.

"What's that?" I asked.

She licked a finger and turned the page. "What were you doing instead of sleeping last night?"

"Watching Seinfeld reruns. That a crime?"

Li slowly shook her head. "It's *Infinite Jest*."

"What?"

"The book, dumbass."

I looked at it. It was twice as thick as the Bible.

"What's it about?"

"Tennis."

"That whole thing's about tennis?"

"There's other stuff, too."

"I didn't know you liked to read."

"Nothing else to do."

I smacked my lips and swallowed, trying to clear the sour crust of saliva from the roof of my mouth.

"How long was I out?"

Li checked her watch. "Five hours."

I sidled past her to stretch my legs in the aisle. We were the only passengers except for a few people I didn't recognize up in the front. The empty seats creeped me out. I was used to planes that buzzed with tangled conversation and the rustling of magazines. Except for the thrum of the engines, this plane was silent.

I noticed Sergeant Rivers a few rows behind us. His single eye was focused downward, perhaps at a book of his own.

"Hey," I said, "I didn't know Rivers was coming."

Li tapped her bookmark against the page and raised an eyebrow.

"Rivers," I said, and went to point. Then I saw that his face was sloughing off, sliding into his lap, the eye-holes and mouth elongating like putty as the skin pulled loose from his red-slicked skull, and I had to grab a seat and close my eyes to stop the flood of nausea.

When it passed, I straightened and tried to pretend that nothing had happened. Li gave me a positively eviscerating glare.

"Alright," she said, "I've had enough. What is wrong with you today?"

"Stupid joke," I grunted. I was having a hard time concentrating over the ringing in my right ear. I fought the urge to stick a finger in there and silence it.

"You were making a joke? And then you keeled over, I assume because of how awful your joke was?"

I tried to smile and managed at least to bare my teeth.

"Airsick," I offered. I forced myself to glance back at

the place where I'd seen Rivers. The seat was as empty as the rest of the plane.

I wondered what I'd see next. A headless Zip hang-gliding across the sky? Hollywood swinging like Tarzan through the forest?

"I don't understand why you're lying," said Li.

"I tried to make a joke and got airsick right at the punchline. Arrest me."

"Fine. Don't tell me. Jeez."

I felt guilty, but the guilt was nothing compared to the relief of escaping detection. Wiping sweat from my forehead—why was I sweating? The cabin was freezing—I went to the back of the plane to relieve myself. I stayed in the bathroom a long time, staring into the vibrating mirror.

When we stepped onto the sprawling black runway in Hawaii, Dr. Alvarez and Cooper were waiting for us.

"Welcome to paradise," said Cooper.

Tropical trees, draped with vines and moss, encircled the airstrip. In the distance, guard towers rose above the jungle. Beyond that reared the spine of a green-black mountain, curving away to the south.

It was hot on the tarmac. I shouldered the duffel, waiting for them to lead the way, but Cooper stayed put.

"How was the flight?" he asked.

"It was fine," said Li.

"Yes," I said briskly. "It was fine."

Dr. Alvarez squeezed her lips in a way that said I don't believe you, but I am not about to pry. Cooper seemed oblivious.

"Great! Come on, I'll give you '*El Grande Tourino*,' as they say!"

He took us to a dull gray Jeep, babbling all the while. As we drove, Dr. Alvarez delivered another unprompted lecture.

"It's likely that islands like these would have been tourist hotspots in a world with oceans," she said. "The edges would be covered in sand. Like a lake shore, but much finer and softer material, eroded by the water and deposited on the coast over millions of years."

I watched the foliage zip by. Every once in a while there was a burst of color as a tropical bird, startled by our passage, took flight.

"What would it look like?" I asked. "All that water?"

"There would be waves," said Dr. Alvarez. "You've probably seen waves on lakes. But ocean waves would be different. Much more powerful. When they hit the shore, the tallest ones would crest, curling up and tumbling down."

I'd imagined a flat plain of water, still and placid and boundless. The way Dr. Alvarez described it, oceans sounded as violent and chaotic as the forest.

The military base was encircled by a seventy-foot buffer of bare dirt. The trees were gone, but no one had bothered to clear the stumps, which dotted the no-man's-land like pimples. As we pulled through a gate into the complex, we passed scaffolding that bridged a gaping hole in the wall. A crane worked to clear debris.

"What happened there?" asked Li.

"Oh, we had a little incident," said Cooper. "Nothing to worry about."

"Whatever it was took a big chunk out of your base," said Li. Piles of rubble indicated places where buildings close to the wall had been flattened.

"Nothing duct tape and elbow grease can't fix."

I tried to guess at the size of the creature in question. "Subway snake?"

"Bingo," said Cooper. "Have no fear. The beast was brought low by good old-fashioned American grit and ingenuity."

"Sure," said Li, eying the high-caliber weaponry mounted on the parapet.

"I'll admit: the forest doesn't want us here," said Cooper. "It keeps sending eviction notices, but we are some persistent squatters indeed."

His voice oozed confidence, but his Adam's apple bobbed when he glanced at the wall. I had a feeling he couldn't wait to head back to the mainland. His fear soothed my nerves. I might be losing my mind, but at least I wasn't a coward.

"How far is the shore?" I asked.

"Five miles," said Dr. Alvarez.

Li wiped sweat off the tip of her nose. "You've got subway snakes coming five miles up the coast to screw with you?"

Cooper tried to fix his tie. The hot, soggy air had rendered the fabric hopelessly flaccid. I would have bet serious money that his suit jacket concealed sweat stains the size of Rhode Island.

"Guess we do," he said. "Maybe you can help us figure out why."

20

Li and I didn't talk much that night, even when Cooper took us to the room where we'd be staying and finally left us alone. She could tell that I was keeping something from her, and she didn't like it. I couldn't blame her. I'd own up to everything the instant the expedition was over.

In the room we'd been assigned, the bedspreads were generous, patterned inexplicably with palm trees and setting orange suns. The floor was scuffed. The light switches were canted. Three vaguely impressionist landscape paintings were bolted onto the walls. The overall effect was of a bad hotel pretending to be a mediocre hotel. I fell asleep immediately.

Soon I dreamed I woke up in the room with Li. Everything seemed normal—she was in her bed, fast asleep, and so far blood wasn't seeping out of cracks in the walls or anything—but I could tell it was a dream. I felt no fear, just dull expectation. Maybe I was getting used to the nightmares. The terror was gone, replaced by cool acceptance of whatever fucked-up vision I was about to face.

Something pulled me to the window. I surveyed the dark arteries of the base. In the distance, searchlights from guard towers played back and forth, scanning the stump-ridden no-man's-land. The beams of light spat fleeting yellow polygons across the ramparts.

The realness of these dreams continued to amaze me. When I pinched my arm and twisted, I felt the sting. I closed my eyes and listened. The only sound was Li's breathing, taking in air and then, after a long silence, letting it out softly. She breathed like she was rationing oxygen, holding onto each lungful until it became pure carbon dioxide.

Gradually, I became aware of another sound, a soft plopping like clumps of peat falling out of a wheelbarrow.
Plop. Plop.

It came from outside the window. Reluctantly, I opened my eyes and looked.

In the center of the street, clumps popped up and away from a growing mound. I fixed my eyes on the bulge, ready to witness the birth of whatever lay beneath.

Slowly, patiently, a black dome emerged. Long antennae frisked the air. Satisfied with the taste, the dome revealed itself to be the head of an enormous centipede. Out into the open it wriggled, hairy with a million terrible legs, freeing itself from the ragged wound in the earth.

More centipedes followed the first, side-winding out of the hole and dispersing in all directions. So far, this was one of the tamer dreams. There was something cathartic about watching them emerge. Something about the way they shed their cloaks of dirt.

"Tetris?" said Li.

I smiled. "This is the part where I look and you've got eight eyes, or your arms have been torn off, right?"

"What?"

I turned to look. Dream-Li was sitting up in bed, rubbing the corners of her eyes. Her body parts appeared to be intact.

"What's going on, Tetris?"

"This is a dream," I said, and snickered.

"This is not a dream, Tetris," said Li.

"Ha! Arguing with a dream," I said. "Guess I really am losing my mind."

"You dumb—what the fuck is *Tetris get out of the way!*"

Something thunked against the window. I spun to see a centipede pressed against the glass. It reared back, a hundred legs writhing in the air, then slammed against the window again.

The glass spiderwebbed. I fell out of the chair, kicking my legs like propellers, suddenly very, very afraid.

"Okay," I said, "not a dream."

"Not a dream not a dream not a dream," agreed Li. "Where's my gun?"

They hadn't given us weapons yet. I scrambled to the corner and tugged on my jeans. Li dressed in equally frenzied fashion while the centipede explored the cracks in the glass with its complicated mouthparts.

"Guns," said Li. "We need guns. Big ones."

The centipede rammed its head through the glass and came slithering in.

We flung the door shut behind us and ran down the hall, pounding on the walls.

"Wake up," I shouted. "Wake up! Wake up!"

A distant alarm began to wail. The centipede exploded through the closed door and slammed against the opposite wall before steadying itself and hurtling after us.

"Down the stairs," said Li.

"You want to go down there?"

"You want to get trapped on the roof?"

We took the stairs three at a time. Outside, chaos reigned. Floodlights reflected off the carapaces that glided everywhere. A Jeep careened past, dragging a centipede that fought to wriggle aboard. The centipede scream-hissed as a barrage of point-blank shots tore its face to bits. When the bullets reached its brain, the unwanted passenger let go all at once, spasming in the street. Freed of the weight, the Jeep veered left. The driver had scarcely regained control when he ran right over another centipede and the whole vehicle vaulted into the air. Dimly, I noted the arc of the fluids that splooshed out of the creature where the tires had made contact, the orange and green mural those fluids left on the wall of the building adjacent.

Then the Jeep face-planted into a wall, and whatever munitions it had been carrying went up with a roar. For a moment a sun bloomed, the floodlights dim in comparison, and then Li was tugging me in the opposite direction as bits of Jeep and God-knows-what-else rained down around us.

We came across the desecrated body of a soldier—it was his top half; a smeared trail of blood led into an alley, where his lower half was presumably being devoured—and Li snagged the rifle out of his stiff fingers. She checked the magazine as we ran.

"Mag's full," she called.

Gunfire. I looked up just in time to see a centipede lunge at a soldier standing on the roof. It tackled him into space, his weapon spraying into the sky, and somersaulted over us. The centipede hit the pavement upside down with a crunch. As the creature writhed, Li stepped up, jammed the barrel against its chin, and pulled the trigger.

Miraculously, the soldier seemed to have survived. I vaulted the centipede's death throes and skidded to his side.

"Where's Cooper?" I asked, helping him to his feet.

"Who?" he choked, blood dribbling out of his mouth. His legs hung limp.

"Can you stand? Hello?"

The soldier's eyes rolled back.

"His back's broken, Tetris," said Li. "Leave him."

I wiped blood off his face. The soldier was my age or younger, his cheeks smooth, with a shadow of stubble along his chin. I swung him across my shoulders.

"Oh, God, Tetris," said Li. "You can't move someone whose back is broken."

"We can't leave him here," I said. "Go."

She went, and I followed. We ran, and in the distance somebody's flamethrower lit up the night, a blossoming orange flower, and we kept on running.

21

We found Dr. Alvarez in the turret of an armored vehicle near the center of the base. She grinned bright enough to light up the courtyard when she saw us.

"Evening," she said. Around us, burly soldiers manned improvised barricades. They hardly seemed to notice our presence, so intently did they peer into the gelatinous darkness.

"Where's Cooper?" asked Li.

"Down below," said Dr. Alvarez, clapping a gloved hand on the armored roof.

"I knew we'd find him cowering," said Li.

"Not cowering," shouted Cooper, his voice bouncing, muffled and irate, out of the depths of the vehicle. "Someone has to stay back and dispense strategic guidance to our boots on the ground."

"Positively Patton-esque of you," said Dr. Alvarez, giving me a wink I couldn't help but feel was a bit flirtatious. I shifted the unconscious soldier to a better position across my shoulders.

"We need a medic," I said.

Dr. Alvarez pointed to a nearby tent.

"Incoming," shouted someone.

Dr. Alvarez took hold of the machine gun and hammered away. Her whole body jittered with the recoil.

"Jesus," muttered Li, tugging my arm. "She's not what I expected, I'll give her that."

The doctor's lips pulled back from her teeth in a gleeful predatory sneer. As we headed toward the medical tent, I thought I heard her laughing, although it was hard to tell over the fusillade.

"I think I like her," I said, looking for a place to lay the injured soldier down.

"I know," said Li.

"Not like that."

As a medic rushed over, Li gave me a look that said: *Yes, like that.*

"Okay, maybe," I admitted, trying to lower my human cargo as gingerly as possible onto the gurney.

"If it gets you to stop pining after me, I guess I can't complain."

The way she said it pissed me off. What kind of friend would taunt you about something like that?

"Was he bit?" snapped the medic.

"I don't know," I said. "Maybe? One of them tackled him off a rooftop."

The medic had wide, round eyes, like a baby's, and his

helmet was a couple sizes too large. The effect was more Pee Wee Herman than grizzled battlefield doctor. He bent over the injured soldier, checking his pulse.

If it gets you to stop pining after me. Christ. She probably derived some sick satisfaction out of rubbing it in. As if the initial rejection didn't hurt enough.

"He's dead," said the medic, waving an orderly over.

I stared at him. All the shit about my crush on Li sure seemed insignificant now. There was an intolerable silent ringing inside my chest. "What?"

"Get out of the way, buddy. He's gone."

The orderly wheeled the stretcher away. I thought about how close I'd been to the centipede in our room, the horrible face pressed against the window. Not the closest I'd been to death. Still—very close. That glass couldn't have been more than a quarter-inch thick.

As a kid I'd been fascinated by multi-legged creatures. Fat spiders perched atop webs in every corner of my garage. The biggest ones lived up in the crevices where the garage door slid into the ceiling. Those only came out at night. Sometimes I'd go out with a flashlight to have a look. They were big enough that I could see them looking back at me. The shiny eyes never blinked, no matter how long we stared at each other.

Sometimes I made it my mission to exterminate them. Sprayed them off their webs with insecticide, watched them crumple up and ricochet off the concrete. Spiders shrank four or fivefold when they died. Shriveled up like they were trying to hide. They never made a sound. Or maybe they made the same sounds that forest spiders did, and their voices were too quiet to hear.

No matter how many I killed, the spiders always came back.

Once, when I was twelve, my dad put his foot in an old sneaker and a brown recluse bit him on the ankle. I was there in the basement when it happened. He swore and slapped at the spider, over and over, pulverizing it with the heel of his hand.

When the brown recluse had been reduced to a leggy smear half on his ankle and half on his palm, my dad took the sneakers upstairs and put them in a garbage bag, then tied it off and dumped it in the trash bin outside. Didn't say a word the whole time. A few hours later, a vivid red bulls-eye mark had formed on his ankle; he went to the urgent care clinic down the street. I stayed home and scoured the basement with a flashlight and my trusty can of insecticide, knocking over promising hidey-holes.

Someone in the med tent screamed and screamed. I couldn't think of anything to say to Li, so I walked away.

The night had assumed a ringing silence. In the distance, a few tongues of flame still tickled the sky. The worst of the assault seemed to have passed.

Cooper must have felt it too, because he'd ventured into the open. He stood beside Dr. Alvarez, scraping at grease spots on his plaid pajama sleeves.

"Nice PJs," said Li.

"Yes, well," said Cooper, his frown intensifying, "I didn't have time to don the proper accoutrements."

"Accoutrements," whooped Dr. Alvarez, her cheeks flushed.

"You alright there, Doc?" asked Li.

Dr. Alvarez clapped a hand on Li's shoulder. "I have never felt better in twenty-eight years."

"We'll see how you're doing once the adrenaline wears off," I said.

The next morning, Dr. Alvarez could barely keep her nose out of her oatmeal.

"Sorry for all the trouble last night," said Cooper as he peeled a banana. His suit was a notch or two more disheveled than usual.

"We still heading into the forest today?" asked Li, an eyebrow arched in Dr. Alvarez's direction.

"Perhaps not," said Cooper. "We'll take the afternoon off and get you a good night's sleep."

"How do you know the same thing won't happen again tonight?" I asked.

"If something like that happened every night, there wouldn't be a base here," said Cooper.

My sausage patty had grown several tiny human eyes. I pushed my tray away.

"Not hungry?" asked Li.

"Lost my appetite," I said. The ringing had returned. Please, I thought, not now.

I rubbed my eyes, and when I opened them again, the sausage patty was its normal eyeless self. Even the ringing had receded somewhat. Which felt like a good sign. Maybe I could control it? I made a mental note to confront the next vision head-on, to try and will it out of existence.

"You were a bundle of laughs last night, Doc," said Li.

"Humpf," said Dr. Alvarez, yawning into the back of her hand.

"Can tell a lot about somebody by the way they act when their life's in danger," said Li, smirking at Cooper.

Cooper cleared his throat and squinted across the room, pushing omelette around his plate.

That afternoon, the three of us—Li, Dr. Alvarez, and me—sat on the roof in lawn chairs and watched the breeze rustle the jungle. Nobody said much. Li read her gigantic book, which she'd salvaged from our room, licking a finger each time she turned a page. I closed my eyes behind dark glasses and savored the warmth of the sun. Soon we'd be back in perpetual dusk.

"What's the worst thing out there?"

I ignored the question, partly because the heat had lulled me to the brink of sleep, and partly because I wasn't entirely sure the words had come from Dr. Alvarez and not my own tormented subconscious. Li closed her book, the reams of pages meeting with a thunk.

"You learned all about the forest," said Li. "Don't you have your own opinion? Flesh wasps? Lots of people pick the flesh wasps."

"Well, I didn't learn everything," said Dr. Alvarez. "Anyway it's different in the classroom. You've been out there. What are you most scared of?"

I wondered if they thought I was asleep.

"None of the monsters keep me up at night," said Li,

"because when you think about it there's nothing evil in them. Just a bunch of animals trying to survive."

"So—nothing scares you?"

"That's not what I said."

"Sounded like it to me."

"I mean, sure, some deaths seem more unpleasant than others, and I want to avoid them. Like getting drained out by a mosquito. Doesn't sound fun. All the fluid in your body sucked out just like that—*bloop*. But as long as I use my brain, it's never going to happen. I'm smarter than the forest. I'm smarter than the mosquitoes and wasps and lizards and snakes. So the only thing that scares me is the chance I might fuck up."

A breeze passed over, carrying a sweet, leafy smell. When I listened closely I could hear Dr. Alvarez breathing in the chair beside me. I wondered what it would be like to kiss her. Somehow I imagined her lips as softer than the average set of lips. My own lips were chapped, scraped raw. I had an awful habit of biting them, tearing away at loose skin, especially when I was stressed, which these days was most of the time.

Maybe after this expedition I could retire to a villa somewhere with Dr. Alvarez and snog her fluffy soft lips day in and day out. No stress. We could grill steaks in the back yard and toss tennis balls to a cadre of adorable huskies. The word "snog" was just perfect for what I wanted to do to Dr. Alvarez's lips.

"Actually, there's one thing that does scare me," said Li.

"Hmm?"

"That fucking tablet," said Li. "Because whatever made that tablet—it isn't dumb. It might even be smarter than me. It's smart, and for all we know it's evil too. And that's the scariest fucking thing I can imagine."

22

As we delved into the forest, it became increasingly obvious that Dr. Alvarez operated as a sort of parachute slowing the expedition's forward momentum. She insisted on stopping every fifteen yards to pluck samples of vegetation or animal dung with a pair of steel pincers that hung at her hip.

"Honestly, Doc," said Li on the second day, "I understand that you came out here to perpetrate some serious science, and as far as I'm concerned, more power to you. But if we keep on at our current ratio of science to walking, we're never going to get anywhere."

"Yes, of course," said Dr. Alvarez, prodding with the tip of her pincers at a bulging yellow plant bulb. "It's all so fascinating, you know?"

"I'd be careful with that," I said, pointing at the bulb. "You're not going to like the smell that comes out if you pop it."

Dr. Alvarez gave me a wide-eyed look of impending guilt, steel pincers frozen mid-prod.

"Oh, no," I said. "Don't even think about it."

"But you can't just say something like that and expect me to leave it alone," said Dr. Alvarez. "Now I have to pop it. You know that. It's basic human nature."

"Oh, Christ," said Li, "at least let us get to the other side of the clearing first."

Something big rustled through a thick stand of razorgrass.

"Up!" hissed Li, and the three of us readied our grapple guns.

I aimed and fired in one fluid motion. Hook secured, I zipped upward, a few milliseconds behind Li. Then Dr. Alvarez's bolt, fired a bit late and well off the mark, careened against the trunk and rebounded into emptiness. As it flew, trailing its impossibly thin cord, the missed hook generated a horrible silence.

"She missed," I said, hanging upside-down with my feet braced against the branch. Before Li could respond, I dove into space, cord whizzing out of my grapple gun as I fell toward the doctor, who stood, dumbstruck, facing the quick-rippling wall of razorgrass—

Out into the open stampeded a towering avian creature, dubbed the "Megadodo" by rangers, a blunt-beaked, dim-eyed, fat-bodied bird with splayed pebbly talons and tufts of down jutting every which way. Confronted by Dr. Alvarez, with another human plummeting from the sky and a third not far behind, the Megadodo squawked and fled, stubby wings flapping.

"Oh my God," said Dr. Alvarez, a palm pressed against

her cheek.

"I thought you knew your way around a grapple gun?" said Li, dropping to the ground with the thoughtless grace of a gymnast.

"I do, I just—"

"You should be dead. Actually I'm mad that you aren't dead. Because that is the saddest, most mind-blowingly imbecilic first-week-rookie fuck-up I have ever seen."

"I'm sorry, Li, I just—"

"I can't believe it! I knew this was going to happen. Tetris, did I not say that this was going to happen?"

I retracted my grapple gun's line. Thank God it had been a Megadodo and not a snake or a scorpion. Watching another decent person get impaled by a stinger seemed like exactly the kind of thing that would push me over the edge into prescription-strength insanity.

"Ninety-nine-point-nine percent of things that produce that kind of noise in razorgrass are class-one badass motherfucking forest things you *do not want to fuck with*," said Li, very conspicuously *not* shouting. "You are the luckiest person I have ever met, Doc, you know that? You miss your fucking grapple and don't even run, just stand there like a cow in a slaughterhouse, slack-jawed, mooing, and the thing that comes out of the bushes is a motherfucking MEGADODO?"

Dr. Alvarez, to her credit, met Li's gaze.

"I'm sorry," she said, "but I do know how to use the grapple gun. It must have been nerves. I haven't missed a shot like that in months."

"We're turning around," said Li. "I thought I could watch you die, Doc. I really did. But when you missed that grapple, a thirty-wheeler hit me full in the chest."

"We can still do it," said Dr. Alvarez. "I'll be careful, okay? I won't rush it next time."

I squatted in a footprint left by the Megadodo. When I lifted my head, a fourth person had appeared in the clearing. It was Junior, legs crossed as he leaned against a trunk. He grinned at me over Li and Dr. Alvarez. The scorpion was nowhere to be seen, although the hole in Junior's chest remained, crawling with flies.

I'd almost forgotten how tall he was. I stared him right in his featureless eyes, willing him to disappear.

He kept smiling.

"You're not real," I muttered. "You're a hallucination. Go."

Junior's smile broadened. A red worm poked out of his ear.

I closed my eyes and counted to five. When I opened them, instead of vanishing, Junior strolled toward me, pulling the worm out of his ear hand over hand. It just kept coming. He passed between Dr. Alvarez and Li and dropped three feet of worm, coiled and wriggling, at my feet.

"Not real?" he said, smile morphing to a sneer. "Why don't you listen? Why don't you listen why don't you listen WHY DON'T YOU LISTEN LISTEN LISTEN—"

"Go!" I shouted, as his words reverberated in my skull, leaving divots and keening pain. With a sarcastic leer,

Junior vanished.

I felt the ground where he'd stood, temples pounding. Li and Dr. Alvarez stared at me.

"Excuse me?" said Li.

"Go on. With the mission, I mean," I said, dusting my hands on my pants. "Doc fucked up. It was a wake-up call, sure. But she'll be more careful from now on."

Dr. Alvarez beamed at me in a way that would normally have left my entire body tingling. At the moment all I could muster was an upward contortion of my lips.

She didn't ask to stop even once the rest of the afternoon, and most of the next morning, although I caught her staring wistfully at just about every discarded arthropod exoskeleton, cluster of flowers, and pyramid of excrement we passed.

The next few days passed quickly. Though the forest screeched and trilled, its inhabitants left us alone. Part of this was due to Li's grim, silent concentration as she led the way, SCAR at the ready. At the slightest rustle of undergrowth, she would raise a hand to stop us, and we'd stand listening, holding our breath, until Li decided it was safe to proceed.

At night, I was tortured by nightmares. I lost track of the ways I saw Dr. Alvarez, Zip and Li murdered in these dreams: disemboweled, swallowed whole, set aflame by fire ants. Mercifully, I never cried out or attempted to wriggle out of my sleeping bag. I merely woke, again and again, repeating words of reassurance to myself as sweat pooled in the inlets of the bag's acrylic interior.

On the fifth day we came across an antlion pit and paused to drink out of our canteens.

"Stay away from that," said Li, pointing at the pit. It was longer than it was wide, a dirt-sloped trench, the bottom out of sight unless you approached the edge.

"What's in there?" asked Dr. Alvarez.

"Mobile home-sized bug with totally wacko pincers," I said, miming with the thumb and index finger of my left hand.

"Ah," said Dr. Alvarez, "Myrmeleon Maximus. Colloquially, an antlion."

"Yeah," I said. "That."

"I wish I could get a look," she said.

"No you don't," I said.

The forest moves at several speeds. At the low end, there's the imperceptible rate at which the trees grow, elbowing one another out of the way as they scramble for sunlight. Then the speed with which creeper vines extend, measurable on a daily if not hourly basis. The gradual creep that a tarantula employs as it pads on hairy legs toward unsuspecting prey.

But because the forest is an inherently violent place, these periods of slow, careful movement are always followed by explosive bursts of speed. The tree, after many years, creaks and tumbles to a crashing demise. The creeper vine, triggered by contact, snaps reflexively inward, undoing weeks of careful growth in a ravenous instant. The tarantula strikes so fast and suddenly that it appears to teleport.

Li saw the iguana first. It crept over a fallen branch, spines standing up along its back, red eyes narrowed. In its mouth, which hung open a few degrees, triangular teeth bristled.

Dr. Alvarez and I only noticed the iguana when Li opened fire. It bulled past us, tail slicing the air and knocking Dr. Alvarez off her feet. The iguana closed the distance before Li could react. A swing of its heavy head— it didn't dare open its mouth under the hail of bullets— sent her flying with a rib-cracking thump. The SCAR skittered to a stop near the antlion pit.

Li hit a tree trunk and tumbled down. Across the clearing, I pulled my pistol's trigger as fast as I could, flinging rounds into the creature's scaly head. It turned to face me and I pivoted right, sliding into a patch of tangled weeds. Then the iguana was on me, tearing at the vegetation as I tried to wriggle deeper, the hot greedy breath washing over me—

There came a familiar gunpowder roar and a whistle of bullets through the reeds. I cowered, making myself as small as possible, and the iguana's breath vanished. It lumbered across the clearing toward Dr. Alvarez, who lowered the SCAR she'd picked up and ran. My heart dropped as she approached the antlion pit, the existence of which she must have forgotten in the heat of the moment. She was about to die in spectacularly gruesome fashion, and I couldn't pull my eyes away—

My breath sucked through my teeth as Dr. Alvarez took a running leap and vaulted the antlion pit, simply soared across the gap, scrabbling a bit on the far edge but making it up and out nonetheless, a nearly unbelievable act of athleticism and nerve, and then, as the iguana pursued, the antlion's titanic pincers erupted like a sick insectoid jack-in-the-box, closing around the iguana's midsection and dragging it into the pit.

As I struggled out of the weeds and Li rushed to Dr. Alvarez's side, a swarm of pillbugs came bouncing and rolling like gray-plated cannonballs out of the undergrowth. They bolted across the clearing, around and over the iguana as it spasmed and snapped its jaws and bled in tall wet spurts, and I had to dive out of the way to avoid being flattened. But before I even picked myself up, I realized things were about to get even worse, because pillbugs never moved like that unless something was chasing them, and sure enough after the pillbugs came a bowel-looseningly gigantic praying mantis, four stories tall, serrated forearms folded up near its thorax, the thorax itself like an electric-green rocket booster.

The mantis was less interested in us than the battered iguana, which had begun to emit guttural shrieks, one of its front legs dangling by a translucent strand of connective tissue as the remorseless antlion's pincers closed and opened and closed again. The mantis latched onto the iguana with razor-blade arms, and a tugging match ensued. Li and Dr. Alvarez took advantage of the distraction to grapple-gun away.

I watched the mantis and antlion fight over the iguana. With a terrific slippery tearing sound, the mantis ripped the top half of the iguana clean off, guts and blood fountaining while the head's eyes bulged, the shrieks cut short. The iguana's intact forearm continued to windmill, slapping hopelessly against the mantis, which dragged the head-and-upper-torso a few feet away and began to tear off thick strips of flesh.

Frozen by the gore, I took longer than I should have to notice a second praying mantis, this one stalking carefully toward me, feelers quivering above its head. I grapple-gunned at once, but the mantis followed, wings flaring as it scampered up the trunk. I undid the grapple as fast as I could to prepare for another jump. When I fired I knew it was too late, the mantis was too close, and I took a chance and leapt into the air, praying that my hook would latch in time. Dropping like a stone, I watched the hook close around a branch across the clearing, and slammed the button to cut the slack, transforming my downward momentum into a wild swing forward. At the lowest point in my swing, I hurtled past the iguana-devouring mantis, which lifted its head, quivering meat dangling out of its dainty mouth.

I retracted the line and rose, swinging back toward the mantises but ascending rapidly. As I passed overhead the ground erupted and a creature of truly titanic size, summoned by the chaos, emerged. It was shaped like a Komodo dragon but covered in matted black hair, and it had two ravenous, toothy mouths, stacked on top of each other, as if God had designed the thing with one mouth and slapped a second one underneath just for the hell of it. The antlion sucked its half of the iguana into the depths. The mantis with the other half ripped off one last scaly bite and fled, leaving a heap of bloody leftovers, which the hairy monster snarfed down at once. As its lower mouth chewed, the head whipped around, tracking the mantis as it retreated up a tree—my tree, as it happened. With a multivocal cry, the double-mouthed beast set off in pursuit.

I stood on a branch I'd thought was safe, once again aiming the grapple gun and preparing for an emergency leap, when the mantis skittered past me, trailing a shower of iguana bits. Before I could fire, the hairy creature was on me. The grapple gun flew from my hand and I tumbled down the length of the creature, managing to grab hold of the thick tangled hair just short of its rear haunch. Stunned, I clung to the creature's side, wrapping my arms in hair to keep from falling off because I could think of no alternative.

The creature smelled like wet dog times a million. My pack bounced crazily, threatening to tear me off and send me tumbling through open space. I squinted past tons of raging animal muscle and saw the canopy approaching fast, the mantis a few meters ahead. Then leaves and branches whipped by and I had to hide my face. Either the creature hadn't noticed me holding on or it didn't care, and either way I didn't see a whole lot of options besides sticking it out and hoping we wound up on the ground long enough for me to dismount.

With a crash and a sudden shift of momentum that

nearly flung me skyward, we crested the top of the tree. I was blinded by the sun, hot and huge against a motionless sky. In the distance, the mantis buzzed away, wings a blur as it soared above the wind-rustled canopy. The creature I rode unleashed a roar from both mouths. It clung, teetering, to the top of the tree. I heard an odd clicking sound and turned to see a flat tick bigger than me making its way through the matted landscape of fur. The tick's eyes were dull and expressionless, but its slavering mouthparts betrayed its carnivorous intentions.

I pulled out my pistol and shot the approaching tick four times in the head.

With a roar, the hairy beast reared on its perch and contorted itself to try and get a look at me. I lost my grip on the pistol. Somehow, impossibly, the tick crept closer, ruined face hanging loose. I climbed laterally away, toward the underside of the creature, but then an enormous hawk came screaming out of the sky and sank its talons into the hairy flesh mere inches from my face—

Each of its talons buried deep as a railroad spike, the hawk flapped its wings, gouging at the beast's eyes with a wicked beak. As the beast writhed and tumbled, both mouths snapping, I lost my hold. Jettisoned away from the melee, I fell through thick leaves and bounced to a bone-jarring halt against a wall of sharp twigs. Covered in gashes, including one on my neck that I prayed had missed my carotid, I woozily surveyed the place I'd landed.

It was a bird's nest, complete with eggshell fragments

and a disarray of discarded feathers.

Suddenly I understood why the hawk had picked a fight with such a gigantic foe. From the other side of the nest came three fledgling hawks, whose roundness and curious mannerisms would normally have provoked a smile and an "awww" from me, except that in this case they were large enough to regard me as an afternoon snack.

"No," I said, as the three fledglings hopped closer. "No, guys, trust me, don't even think about it."

With my grapple gun and pistol both gone, I settled for drawing one of my climbing picks, leaving my left arm free as I circled the nest.

"Don't do it," I warned the foremost fledgling.

"SKREE!"

As I climbed the lip of the nest, brandishing my climbing pick, a fledgling worked up the nerve to charge. Sensing a way out, I sidestepped and lunged onto its back as it passed. We tumbled out of the nest, ripping through leaves and branches, and then into open air, my arms wrapped around the fledgling's neck. Down we plummeted, the rushing air intensifying into a roar. The forest floor loomed.

"Come on," I screamed. "Fly!"

Screeching, the fledgling flapped its wings, and our descent slowed. No matter how it tried, the bird couldn't gain altitude with me on board, but it managed at least to flatten our trajectory, so that when we hit the ground we rolled instead of splattering.

Still, the speed at which we made impact was bone-splintering. Through the undergrowth I flew, glancing off rocks and roots, until I came to rest against a massive tree trunk.

The last thing I saw before blacking out was Li descending like an angel on her grapple gun's line, looking like she'd just witnessed a miracle and couldn't help but wonder if it wasn't all one big and elaborate trick.

23

"You're hurt," said Li.

"I'm fine," I said. "Scrapes and bruises. A few minutes to catch my breath and I'm ready to go."

Li bit through her protein bar and chewed viciously.

"We're almost there," said Dr. Alvarez, dangling her legs off the branch.

"Doc's right," I said, forcing a used car salesman's grin across my face. Everything hurt. My right shoulder throbbed in a way that implied it had popped out of its socket at some point before being jammed back in.

I was swabbing antiseptic on the gash in my neck when a sliver of something twitched in the wound. I probed with my fingers and gingerly pulled the splinter out.

It was the vaccine implant they'd injected back in training, a one-inch shard of silver material. I frowned. They'd said this would dissolve in weeks. What was it doing in my neck years later?

Under your skin, Tetris.

I hurled the splinter away.

"How many days, Doc?" asked Li.

"Two," said Dr. Alvarez. "Three at most."

Li tore off another chunk of protein bar. "You know what I just realized?"

I opted not to venture a guess. My mind ran laps around the vaccine implant. More lies. What else were they lying about?

As Li stared me down, I pulled my eyebrows up in an attempt to intensify what I hoped was a good-natured smile.

"Do you know the fact that is suddenly crystallizing for me," said Li, "as I sit here on a branch in the middle of the Pacific Forest, having this Eureka-style epiphanic moment of slow-dawning realization?"

"Would you care to inform me?"

"As I sit here, in the most dangerous place on Earth, between two woefully inadequate companions—stop, let me finish—between two *woefully* inadequate companions, one of whom has absolutely no business being here, and the other—upon whose body I struggle to find a single bruise-or-gash-free square inch of skin—who, as a result of recent events, is in possession of neither a grapple gun nor a firearm—what I begin to realize, Tetris, as you wave your hands and bulge your eyeballs in this most blatant fake outrage—what I realize is that all of this, the whole fucking Category 5 shitstorm we've landed ourselves in, is all one hundred percent your fault."

"No," I said, trying very hard to un-bulge my eyeballs.

"It's greed," said Li. "Ever since Cooper said the words 'ten million dollars,' your brain has been firmly switched off."

"No."

"Listen to yourself," she hissed, leaning close. "Just for one minute, snap out of this self-destructive spiral and consider what you're suggesting."

"I am listening to myself," I said, bandaging my neck. "Hello, me, what's that? You think we should keep going? Roger that, me, you're coming in loud and clear."

"Tetris."

Despite the guilty pleasure I derived from the proximity of Li's face, I found myself unable to meet her eyes. Instead I worked on swabbing a gash on my forearm. It stung. Everything stung.

"This isn't you, man," said Li, almost whispering. "I know you. You're smart. You're careful. You're risk-averse. I know you, Tetris, better than anybody knows you, and I know that you are not yourself right now."

"Then who am I?" I asked, watching red spiders wriggle out of holes in my arm and mill around on the surface. I scratched at them, but my fingers slid right through.

Li leaned back. She seemed deflated, no longer trying to meet my eyes.

"I don't know," she said. "But you're not you."

I closed my eyes and thought about telling her.

"Okay," I said, "the truth is, I've been having

nightmares."

Li took another bite of her protein bar. Dr. Alvarez, who had spent the past few minutes scooting closer, peered around Li's shoulder.

"I know that," said Li. "You've mentioned that five or six times now."

"They're getting worse," I said. "Like, every night. I'm stressing out. That's why I'm not myself."

Li chewed and scanned me. There. I'd told the truth. She wouldn't be able to find any trace of a lie on my face.

"But that doesn't mean we shouldn't go on," I said, trying to capitalize on the foothold of honesty I'd found. "They're just dreams, Li. We're so close. I can share Dr. Alvarez's grapple. And you know the pistol wouldn't have dented hardly anything anyway."

"We'll be careful," added Dr. Alvarez. "We can move slow. Take four days instead of two."

Li chewed and chewed.

"My God," she said at last, crumpling the empty wrapper and flinging it into space. "I can't believe I'm actually considering this."

At which point I knew the battle had been won.

The rest of the afternoon passed in a torturous muddle. It took significant willpower not to stagger. The tendons in my neck stood out like ski lift cables. Despite Dr. Alvarez's suggestion that we take it slow, Li strode ahead, muttering under her breath. When we turned in for the night, I hit my sleeping bag thinking I was far too exhausted even to dream. Instead I tossed and turned, head rattling with the same old blood-drenched nightmares.

In the morning I was too nauseous to eat, aching hunger or no. As we pushed forward, the floor sloped down, and the needles of Dr. Alvarez's various instruments wobbled. I stumbled along in the back, beset by faces in tree trunks that sneered or laughed, revealing mouths packed with canine teeth. The ringing in my ears was joined by a constant percussive throbbing. Once, I thought I saw Todd, bald from the chemo, standing on the other side of a clearing. When he vanished, a wave of sadness crashed over me.

That afternoon, a fog descended, beginning as a few wisps of gray and swiftly coalescing to a thick sheath that obscured my view of the tree-faces. At first I thought the fog was my imagination, but then Li stopped us for a quiet discussion and I realized the others saw it too.

"What the fuck is this, Doc?" asked Li. "I've never seen fog this thick."

"I don't know," whispered Dr. Alvarez. The fog reflected our voices back at us.

I tugged my pack straps tighter, probing absentmindedly at my thigh for the grip of a pistol that wasn't there.

"Well, we can't grapple out of it," said Li, peering upward for branches and finding nothing but fog.

"We might be close," said Dr. Alvarez. "The fog might be a product of the anomaly."

I watched Li breathe. Her face was illegible.

"Okay," she said. "What do we do?"

I cleared my throat. The sound echoed grotesquely.

"We go forward," I said.

The drumming had worked itself beyond my inner ear. There was no way I could hear anything sneaking up on us. As thick as the fog was, we wouldn't see a subway snake until we'd walked smack into its scaly flank.

Close together, practically touching, we edged forward. Dr. Alvarez juggled her instruments, whispering navigational suggestions in Li's ear. I focused on filling my lungs with wet-smelling air. Moisture beaded on my skin.

Finally we came to the end of the fog. Beyond lay a circular clearing with a giant hole in the middle. Fog, extending upward to the canopy, swirled around the perimeter as if butting against tall glass walls.

The drumming in my skull had ceased. Aside from the walled-off fog, everything was back to normal.

"Is this it?" asked Li quietly.

Dr. Alvarez didn't answer. Retrieving a high-powered flashlight from her pack, she padded toward the lip of the pit.

After a moment, Li and I followed. My legs were heavy. They took my full concentration to move, as in a dream. Our boots crunched explosively on the leaves.

Dr. Alvarez pointed her flashlight into the abyss. The cone of light caught dust particles floating in the air, but revealed no bottom. The darkness at the center of the pit remained unbroken.

She pointed the beam at the opposite wall and gradually tilted downward. The circle of light grew wider and wider as it descended, revealing a root-and-vine-riddled cross-section of the forest's innards. As it fell, the illuminated area grew more dim, until finally it vanished. No bottom.

Li produced her flare gun and aimed into the center of the pit. Before she fired, she looked at each of us, asking permission with her eyes.

We nodded. The air in the clearing froze, anticipatory and thick.

The flare gun coughed. I thought I saw the cylindrical wall of fog ripple in response. The hot-sputtering flare arced down, painting unnerving patterns of crimson and shadow.

Down the flare flew, a dwindling red star. It never hit bottom, just shrank and shrank, until finally it vanished altogether.

"No way," said Li, speaking for all of us. A slimy anxiety in my stomach forced me away from the edge.

"How deep?" I asked.

Dr. Alvarez scratched her head.

"Must be at least a couple of miles," she said, staring down.

I imagined falling in, plummeting for miles in unadulterated darkness. Would you pray for the pit to be bottomless, as you tumbled through the empty air? Or would a bottomless pit be even worse?

Near the top of the fog walls, tree trunks began to emerge.

"The fog's fading," I said.

Spurred on by my words, it flowed away in all directions, subsuming into the forest floor. The three of us stood, unable to breathe, staring at what its departure had revealed.

Clinging to the trees that encircled the clearing, with clusters of round black eyes bulging above grinning, toothy jaws, were at least a dozen specimens of a creature I hadn't seen since the day Junior died.

The long bodies of the dragons glistened with blue-black scales. Half-extended wings jutted as their spear-shaped skulls sniffed down at us.

They covered every angle of retreat except one. A single, obvious escape route, between two wide-spaced trees.

All sound had ceased. The dragons smiled, waiting.

Dr. Alvarez ran for the gap. Li and I followed. Behind us, a human laugh built in pitch and intensity over the heavy whump-whump of wings.

We crashed out of the clearing, Li quickly taking the lead. I hung close behind Dr. Alvarez as we vaulted a log and hit the ground at a sprint, our backpacks jumping and jostling. Here the floor was a ragged mess of branches and pitfalls. Li never glanced back. My heart pounded in my ears as I followed, bruises and tender joints forgotten.

With our pursuers close enough that we could feel the rush of air from their wings, Li took a hard left, Dr. Alvarez and I scrambling after her. We slid through a patch of razorgrass, then under a mossy overhang and into the open, where a dragon wheeled to cut us off. It shook the ground when it landed, flaunting its full wingspan. Li fired the SCAR as she ran, zig-zagging into a corridor between two fallen trees.

Down the narrow passageway we flew, dragons lighting on the trunks as we passed, jamming their snapping jaws into the gap. It was hard to tell their roars from the roars of the forest as it awakened. I could hardly hear my own frantic breathing.

Near the end of the passageway, the ground began to swell. As we leapt clear and stumbled to our feet beyond the fallen trees, a subway snake burst out of the bulge, shaking off huge clods of dirt, which thudded like mortar shells around us. Li headed toward a thick patch of undergrowth, Dr. Alvarez close behind. A dragon plummeted from the sky to our left and scrambled along the ground on all fours, mouth widening in preparation for a strike.

The subway snake hurled its Brontosaurian bulk across the clearing and clamped huge jaws around the dragon's unguarded torso. The crunch of so much raw meat colliding at such incredible speed released a shock wave that nearly knocked us off our feet. One wing trapped, the dragon flailed and shrieked, scrabbling at the snake's gigantic head.

We thrashed through the undergrowth. Probably the majority of the dragons were now occupied, but Li seemed to think it was a good idea to put more distance between us and them before risking a grapple. My ankles emitted white shrapnel-bursts of pain as I fought across the weed-strewn ground.

Beyond the thick vegetation, we found ourselves before a chasm bridged by a fallen tree. Li wasted no time scurrying across, arms extended for balance. Dr. Alvarez and I followed.

Midway across, my foot plunged into a soft pit of decayed wood, and I tripped. Picking myself up, I felt a whoosh of air and snapped around to glimpse the descending shape of a dragon. With a sickening crack, the dragon landed on the bridge behind me. Li's SCAR roared, but the sound was lost in the splintering of the dead tree's core. At first the bridge sagged mildly, and I thought for a moment it would hold, but then the dragon stepped clumsily about, shrieking as it tried to maintain its balance, and the whole bug-eaten tree crunched downward beneath its feet—

Wishing like hell for the grapple gun I didn't have, I caught a glimpse of Li and Dr. Alvarez staring down from the edge of the chasm, above me now as I scrambled up the crazily-leaning trunk, and then the dragon took off, kicking the two tree-halves downward, my stomach leaping against my throat, and I fell, unbelieving, into bottomless darkness.

24

Up on the wall of the Hawaiian fortress, leaning on the parapet a few dozen meters from the gate, stood Lindsey Li. She wore sunglasses and stared across the stump-scarred no-man's-land into the jungle. Every once in a while she worked up enough spittle to fire a glob over the edge.

The soldiers on watch had learned to leave her alone. Trying to engage her in conversation provoked an emotionless stare that screamed "not-to-be-fucked-with." Privately she was the subject of much discussion, standing up there as she did in the same spot every day. Her companions—the weaselly agency guy and the academic chick who'd known her way around a machine gun—had returned to the mainland a few days back. But this one, the first female ranger any of them had ever seen, had stayed behind.

Li wasn't sure why she'd stayed. She knew Tetris was dead. She and Dr. Alvarez had circled back after the chaos died down and taken a look in the chasm where he'd fallen. Hadn't found anything except spiders, which had chased them right out of there. She felt no doubt whatsoever. So why did she keep coming out here?

Guilt, probably. She felt guilty. Because if she'd asserted herself, really refused to take "no" for an answer, they would have turned around, and Tetris wouldn't have died. All that shit she gave him for being greedy, and in the end it turned out she was just as greedy as he was.

Not for the money. It was the mystery that called to her, the desire to understand. So she'd held her tongue and let Tetris goad them on, and what had they found?

A hole in the ground.

That was it. That was what Tetris had died for: an abnormally deep ravine.

She spat and watched the globe of spittle wobble and spread until it was too small to see.

******

I regained consciousness in total darkness. Waking

took several minutes, and at first I didn't realize what was happening, only that the darkness was changing somehow, gliding over itself on well-oiled rails. I had a sense that something lurked behind a thick black curtain in front of me.

It was quiet. Dead, dull, deep-buried silence. I thought I heard a trickling, some faraway subterranean stream.

Was I dead?

I lay on a bed of soft material. Moss, maybe. It was cool against my neck. I found that I could work my fingers into it, through tightly knit, fine-leafed vegetable matter that sprang back into place when my fingers retreated.

The moss held water like a sponge. As I felt around, dew transferred in fine drops to my skin. I lifted some of the moisture to my mouth, expecting the clear taste of a quick-running mountain stream, but tasted only my grimy fingers.

Slowly, as the murk of sleep faded away, I discovered that the lower half of my body had vanished. I felt at my legs. They were still attached. I couldn't feel them, though, even when I prodded and pinched the skin through my pants. I slid my hands along my thighs, the flesh dead and silent beneath my fingertips. Then, right above my hips, I felt sensation return.

Touching my lower back provoked a spike of white pain so intense that I nearly bit through my tongue trying to keep from crying out. My hand came away drenched with blood. I wrenched myself up on my elbows and tugged my heavy legs into a sitting position. Groping in the dark, gasping from the pain, I found a mossy slope—a root, maybe. I dragged myself closer.

Leaning against the slope, I closed my eyes and tried to distract myself by taking an inventory of what I'd lost.

My pack: gone. Grapple gun and pistol: both gone. Gone, too, were my legs, and with them any hope of survival.

Li and Dr. Alvarez were gone. I'd never see them again. Neither would I see Zip, or my dad, with whom I would never have a chance to make amends. I'd never get a chance to track my mother down.

The whole hopeful narrative of the life I'd planned began to shudder and crumble before me. Why?

I began to cry.

I stifled the sound at first, but the sobs bubbled up out of my chest with too much force. Then I realized I didn't care if some monster found me, I was dead no matter what, and I stopped holding back.

I hoped Li and Dr. Alvarez had continued running instead of trying to save me. They probably hadn't. Which meant I had killed three people instead of one. And it had been me who killed us. How many warnings had I ignored? How many chances had I thrown away? I'd imagined myself to be invincible. That seemed obvious, now. The ultimate arrogance. Other rangers died; I could accept this fact. But not me. I was different. I was smarter, quicker, guarded by luck.

But the forest knew better. The forest had laughed at my arrogance and snapped my spine like a Popsicle stick.

I shouted something beyond comprehension. My voice plowed into the mossy walls and died. I sucked in air and screamed, no words, just a furious animal cry, trailing off only when my lungs deflated completely. Again I screamed, and again, and then out of the darkness came an enormous grasping claw, wrapping itself around my head, and a voice beside my ear breathed a single word:

TETRIS.

I flailed, trying to wrench myself free, but the grip on my skull was far too firm, and at once I was bound on all sides, crushed inward, unable to shout, hardly able even to breathe, and it was only my eyes that could move, rolling in their sockets as I strained to see something, anything, of the creature that now possessed me.

TETRIS, said the voice, in my other ear this time.

"What are you?" I gasped, and suddenly it became excruciatingly bright. I had to screw my eyes shut to keep from being blinded, and when I peeled them open, I was in a room with shining white walls. I sat, immobilized by invisible restraints, atop a wicker chair, across the table from a flickering image of Junior.

"Junior?" I said, the horror of the earliest dreams returning in full force.

NOT JUNIOR, whisperscreamed the voice, as Junior inclined his head, eyes flickering from normal to shiny and back again. His mouth remained clamped shut.

"You're it," I said. "You're what lives in the forest."

The image flickered, bathing Junior head to toe in blood.

NOT LIVE. INCORRECT NOT LIVE. AM. AM AM AM AM AM.

Now the voice came from inside me, somehow, resonating in my bones.

"I don't understand," I said.

SHOW, THEN, said the voice, and an image slammed across my view.

I saw the Earth, the ocean-Earth with all its glittering blue. It floated like a jewel in boundless starry space. I sat atop a huge, round, cavernous rock, and watched the Earth grow before me. Deep in the asteroid, I saw/felt a seed, a kernel, a core, a not-quite embryo. And as the asteroid plunged into the atmosphere, I saw that the continents were foreign, somehow, clumped together, and I understood that this was not some alternate reality, this was Earth, the real Earth, my Earth, before the forest, sixty-five million years ago.

And then the asteroid flung hunks of plasma as the ravenous atmosphere tore at its skin, and inside I felt the seed/kernel/embryo stir, not grasp what was happening, precisely, but feel in some deep instinctual place that it was time, that life was near, and then the asteroid hit the planet and was obliterated, and I was obliterated, and the Earth was obliterated, great banks of dust rising above the shaking ground and filling the prehistorically starry sky.

Time jumped, and I shrank to the size of a virus, deep in the ocean beside the towering embryo from the asteroid's core, and I watched as molecules began to pull apart around me, as atoms, even, bared their neutrons and protons, stimulated somehow by the embryo, electrons zipping around in panic. I felt a sensation of zooming, time quickening, and my field of view changed. The embryo grew, adding to itself exponentially, tearing apart matter in a bubbling frenzy and glomping freshly-minted molecules onto extensions of itself, on every edge, every fractally-divergent extremity sucking in water as the organism grew and grew and grew and grew, and then, as time quickened further, millenia flashing past, the oceans dwindled and the forest spread, and I finally began to understand.

"You *are* the forest," I said, and the image vanished. I sat across the table from Junior, who smiled, revealing teeth that changed as frequently as his eyes, first clean and white, then bloodied, then sharp and multi-peaked like a piranha's.

AM FOREST. AM AM AM.

"The nightmares," I said, "the hallucinations—you sent those?"

YES.

I gritted my chipped and aching teeth. "Why? Why torture me?"

NOT INTENDED. NOT NIGHTMARES NO JUST MESSAGES. MESSAGES FILTERED POLLUTED TWISTED BY TINY PRIMITIVE HUMAN MIND, HUMAN BRAIN WITH PRIMITIVE PSYCHIC RECEPTORS VERY FAR, FAR FAR FAR VERY FAR AWAY.

I looked at Junior, focused on him. Found that, with a

bit of concentration, I could stabilize his appearance.

"You were trying to communicate," I said.

YES.

"But I never got anything out of those dreams. That's all I thought they were. Dreams."

HAD TO BRING—HAD TO BRING A HUMAN. HAD TO BRING YOU.

"That's what the obelisk was? What the tablet was? What Roy LaMonte saw? All to bring someone here?"

YES. YES YES YES.

"Could have just sent a letter," I said. "Seems like that ought to be within the capabilities of a giant sentient forest."

Without warning, I found myself staring at another image of the globe, this time the familiar Earth with forests instead of oceans.

SIXTY-FIVE MILLION YEARS OF LIFE.

I watched sixty-five million years whip by in thirty seconds, the continents gliding and morphing into their familiar shapes.

THEN—HUMANS.

And I watched as humans appeared, spread across the whole planet, built factories and extinguished ecosystems and, finally, began to probe in earnest at the borders of the forest. I felt the forest's curiosity, its confusion... and, beneath it all, an unmistakable tinge of fear.

SIXTY-FIVE MILLION YEARS OF FOREST. TEN THOUSAND YEARS OF THIS.

Images whipped by: primitive humans perfecting fire.

The first airships floating over the canopy. Wars on the continents, hundreds of thousands of deaths in the trenches, blood and gunpowder and screams both verbal and psychic, and then the biggest, brightest scream of them all, a flash of light over Hiroshima, and then, before the first shock had faded, again at Nagasaki—

Here the image froze. The view rotated, swiveling around the blooming mushroom cloud with its impossibly bright point of origin, and through the image it was somehow relayed to me how the forest had felt at that moment, watching the cloud rise, seeing, finally, after sixty-five million years, the birth of a terrestrial force that had the capacity to cause it harm.

DO YOU SEE? asked the forest.

"I see," I said.

The forest brooded.

NEED TO KNOW, it said, IF HUMANS CAN BE TRUSTED.

I snorted. "And that's why you brought me? To probe in my brain, figure out whether you could trust me? What happens if you decide you can't?"

A flurry of images, a million swollen bulbs, lurking in the canopy all around the globe, filled to near-bursting with what I understood wordlessly to be an incredibly potent neurotoxin.

"You're going to kill us," I said. "You're going to flood the air and kill us all."

NO, said the forest. DO NOT WANT TO.

The image vanished, the white room vanished, and I

found myself back in darkness, still encapsulated by what I now recognized as a form-fitting cage of throbbing plant matter.

BUT, said the forest, MIGHT HAVE TO.

"Why?"

BECAUSE OF THIRTY THOUSAND NUCLEAR WARHEADS POINTED AT MY NEUROLOGICAL CENTERS.

For some reason this struck me as hilarious. Perhaps I'd lost enough blood to drive me to delirium, but either way I couldn't stop my chest from shaking. I tried to put my finger on what I found so funny, and eventually it occurred to me:

"Cooper said we couldn't let you know that we knew you existed," I said. "And now you're saying that you yourself are afraid to let them know that you already know that they know that you exist?"

Silence.

CORRECT.

"Why can't we just tell each other outright? Why this skulking in shadows?"

IF EACH ACTOR HAS THE POWER TO DESTROY THE OTHER, WITH NO CHANCE OF REPRISAL, AND BOTH ACTORS UNDERSTAND THIS FACT, A PREEMPTIVE STRIKE IS THE MOST STRATEGICALLY SOUND DECISION.

I scrunched my eyebrows together. The volume of the voice had decreased significantly, while the messages themselves had grown more complex. As if the forest was calibrating to my mind.

"I don't understand," I said. "In that case, why haven't you already killed us off?"

The silence stretched on so long that I began to think it had forgotten about me.

BECAUSE, said the forest, its tone somehow reluctant, I MAY NEED YOUR HELP.

It showed me another image of the modern-day Earth. Then the view swiveled, away from the planet and out into empty, star-speckled space.

SOMETHING IS COMING, said the forest. SOMETHING FROM FAR AWAY. COMING FAST. SEVEN REVOLUTIONS, PERHAPS, BEFORE IT ARRIVES.

The stars vanished.

"What is it?" I asked.

DO NOT KNOW. BUT FEEL IT COMING, AND FEEL... MALICE. HUNGER TEETH MERCILESS APPETITE DARK RAVENING HUNGER.

I shivered, although the air down here was warm, almost too warm. My skin pearled with sweat.

"And you want our help with it, whatever it is."

IN SEVEN REVOLUTIONS, CAN ONLY DO SO MUCH. NEED DECADES CENTURIES MILLENIA TO PREPARE. BUT WITH HUMANS, IN SEVEN REVOLUTIONS—WITH MY HELP—

Silence, again, as the forest either absorbed itself in thought or waited for my response.

"I have so many questions," I said.

ASK.

"If you wanted us to get here so bad, why not clear the monsters out of our way?"

The forest, amused: LIKE ASKING A HUMAN TO KEEP WHITE BLOOD CELLS FROM ATTACKING BACTERIA.

"Why did you stop at the coasts? Why not grow over the entire planet?"

LIKE ASKING A FIT HUMAN WHY DID HE NOT GROW TO BE FOUR HUNDRED POUNDS WHEN HE HAD ACCESS TO THE REQUISITE NUTRIENTS.

I chewed at loose skin on my lips. The pain in my back had only grown worse.

"Well," I said, feeling gloomy again, "I don't think I can help you explain things to the rest of the humans. My back's broken. I'm bleeding to death."

For a long time, I sat in my cage, listening to the burble of the faraway stream, waiting for a reply.

The forest had abandoned me. Either it had already learned everything it wanted to know, or it had no use for a human without functioning legs. Both options were equally depressing.

God, I didn't want to die. I pressed a hand against the wound on my lower back and felt the lifeblood seeping out. This was how I was going to go, huh? Meek and silent, buried deep underground, accepting my fate without a fight?

"Hey," I shouted, my voice hoarse. "Hey, is that it? You leaving me to die?"

Still the silence dragged on. I strained against the bonds, then gave up, counting heartbeats in my aching temples.

Something stirred in the darkness.

IT MAY BE POSSIBLE TO FIX YOU, said the forest at last. BUT THERE WILL BE A COST.

A thrill of hope shivered up my spine. I licked my ruptured lips.

"If it saves my life, I'll pay any price," I said.

There was definitely a stream in the distance, trickling endlessly onward.

LIKEWISE, said the forest, as tendrils plunged into my lower back, my spine, and the back of my skull, unthinkable white-hot pain slamming me unconscious.

*****

Once, in first or second grade, Li had just about burned her house down trying to bake a cake. She still had nightmares about the egg-draped, icing-smeared kitchen, flames billowing out of the oven. Had stuck around to try and put it out and barely made it out in time. When the firefighters arrived, she was trying to get the neighbor's garden hose to reach the crackling inferno. Years later, she retained a deep aversion to cooking.

"I can't believe my eyes," her mom had said when she made it back from work and saw the wreckage.

That stupid cliché had been bouncing around Li's head ever since. But she never really understood what it meant, until one morning on the ramparts of the Hawaiian base, when someone who looked an awful lot like Tetris came strolling out of the jungle, arms swinging empty-handed at his sides.

And if she closed her eyes at first, and rubbed her sunglasses on her shirt, and had to take a second look to be sure, she could have been forgiven, because, sunglasses or no, her eyes reported that Tetris's swinging arms, and the skin of his faintly smiling face, were tinged the unmistakable light-green tone of upper-canopy leaves.

Book Two

Pale Green Dot

1

"There has to be something you can give me."

"No."

"Some tidbit. Some morsel."

"Which part of 'no' is giving you trouble?"

"Jack, I've got a green humanoid allegedly ambling out of the Hawaiian jungle. Hundreds of eyewitnesses. Seasoned soldiers, here, alleging this. I've got paragons of reconnoitering reliability informing me that this person was seven feet tall and a screaming electric green. The color of nuclear waste in cartoons, Jack. One gentleman insisted under polygraph that there were vines sprouting from the green person's footprints."

"Ridiculous."

"If green men really are strolling out of the forest, isn't that something the head of the Coast Guard ought to know about?"

"I have nothing to share at this time."

"Do I look like a reporter?"

"Don."

"Then why are you bullshitting me? I'm just trying to do my job."

"Then do your job."

"Jack."

"And stop fucking with mine."

"Here I was thinking the CIA director's role was to acquire and share intelligence."

"Can we get the check? Miss?"

"Surely, Jack, this is within your job description, what I'm requisitioning here."

"Hello? Miss? Okay, thanks. Thanks, yes, you'll be right over. Right."

"Surely you can point me in a promising direction, at the barest minimum."

"Service at these places is not what it used to be."

"Surely."

"Pleasure as always, Don."

*****

They were insects wriggling beneath a magnifying glass. Insects in tailored suits and silk ties. It was all Toni Davis could do not to smile.

"I don't know, ma'am," said Jack Dano, Director of Intelligence of the CIA.

"What do you know?"

"Something turned him green," said Dano. "Whatever it is, he can talk to it. Telepathically. And he no longer sleeps."

Toni leaned back in her excellent chair. Buffed leather, soft where it was supposed to be soft and firm where it was supposed to be firm. The man beside Dano had clearly been wearing his suit for several days straight. His eyes were bloodshot and wild.

"What did you say your name was?" she asked.

"Dale Cooper, Madam Secretary," said the disheveled man. "I oversee the ranger program."

"You're the one who sent him out there."

"Yes, ma'am."

"Well," said Toni, tossing the report onto her teetering to-do pile, "I suppose you've got him in a cell somewhere?"

The men adopted a stony expression she'd seen a million times before.

"You better not be torturing him," she said.

"Of course not," said Dano.

She squinted. "What, then?"

Dano's mustache gave a nervous spasm.

"Madam Secretary," said Cooper, "we have, presently, less-than-full knowledge of his precise geographic whereabouts, is the thing."

"We lost him," said Dano, and exhaled hard through

his nose.

Toni tapped her pen a few times. She retrieved the report from the pile and flipped it open.

"In that case," she said, eyes running down the page, "I suggest you get out there and find him."

*****

Just when he thought the sore spot on his lip was going to heal over, Cooper always managed to bite it again. His bottom teeth angled outward because he'd never worn his retainer as a teenager. For decades he'd just lived with it. He could hardly go back to the orthodontist now.

But the lip thing kept happening. It was worse when he was stressed, because then he forgot to chew carefully, and it only took a few overzealous bites to draw his lip into the line of fire. Then the injured tissue swelled up, making it even harder to avoid biting it again.

When Cooper bit his lip at lunch with Jack Dano, immediately after the trainwreck meeting with the Secretary of State, it was the fourth time in a week. His eyes watered. He stuck a grimy finger in his mouth to gauge the damage. It astounded him that he wasn't bleeding.

"You look awful," said Dano, pausing with a fat wad of spaghetti wrapped around his fork.

"Mrrfghul," said Cooper, probing the tender spot with his tongue.

"When was the last time you slept?"

Cooper pushed his plate away. "On the plane."

Dano tried to figure out how to fit the ball of pasta into his mouth. The problem was the bits of spaghetti dangling off, which positioned themselves inconveniently no matter how he turned his fork.

"Get some rest," said Dano.

Cooper rubbed a stain on his tie. "It's my fault."

"Irregardless."

"I should have told them about the subdermals. Full disclosure, to build trust. Whatever happened to him out there, he found out anyway. The girl's was on the floor in a puddle of blood. Did I tell you that? She cut it out herself."

"Thought you installed them next to the carotid?"

Cooper took a sip of coffee and swallowed hastily as it seared his lip. "Apparently she deemed it worth the risk."

"Not stationing an agent outside the room was pushing your luck," said Dano, wiping sauce from his trim white beard.

"I didn't want them to feel like prisoners."

"Mission accomplished."

"I figured we could always track the subdermals if they ran."

"We'll find them. This is America. They've got nowhere to go."

*****

Vincent Chen watched the Arizona horizon skate past.

Everything was a featureless light-blasted brown. The sky shone white-blue. There were no clouds.

"What agency did you say you were with?" asked the Navajo County sheriff. His fingers around the wheel were gnarled brown roots.

"Not important," said Vincent.

"It's got to do with aliens, don't it."

Vincent shifted, trying to find a position that alleviated his aching shoulder. "No."

"Man reports an alien stole his truck, and you roll up the next day?"

"We've got a warrant on a serial killer who's known to paint himself green."

The sheriff scratched his nose. "How about that."

A sixteen-wheeler whipped by in the opposite lane, a hammer-blow of air and sound. The car shuddered.

"No aliens," said Vincent firmly.

After a while the sheriff slowed the car and turned onto a dirt road. Vincent gripped the edge of his seat. Every rattle jarred his shoulder. Three years and it still hadn't healed, physical therapy be damned.

When they rolled to a stop in front of a ranch house, Vincent shoved the door and stepped out. He quelled an urge to stretch as the owner came out to greet them.

"Howdy, Sheriff," said the rancher, hands resting on suspenders that struggled to contain his enormous belly.

"Vincent Chen," said Vincent.

"Scott Brown," said the man. He shook Vincent's hand, turned, and spat. "About time one of you types made it out here."

"Tell me what happened," said Vincent. He didn't know why the man was faking a Southern accent, and he didn't care.

"Around one o'clock something kicked over the rain bucket. Made a hell of a clatter. Figgered it was an animal."

Vincent spotted something red and moved to investigate. A blood-soaked rabbit lay with legs splayed, a chunk torn out of its middle.

"Yes sir," said the rancher, lumbering over, "that there's where he was. When I turned on the floodlights, he was chowing down. Blood everywhere. Big tiger-type fangs." He demonstrated with his fingers. "Skin green as a grasshopper."

Vincent pulled a pair of latex gloves from his bag.

"Sheriff, you know I ain't the type to leave my shotgun far from hand. And the day I let some alien trespass on my property is the day I vote for Sharia law. Plus I wanted to catch him, you know, just to have some proof."

Scott pointed to a spray of droplets that darkened the ground beyond.

"You hit him," said the sheriff.

"Clipped him in the shoulder," said Scott. "But the bugger made it to my truck."

The sun careened off the sand. Vincent lifted the rabbit's body into a plastic bag.

"Ain't the first time I seen one of them, neither. They're all over these parts. Was blue lights in the sky last summer. And I found a bone out in the boonies what don't belong to nothing terrestrial. I can bring it out, if'n you like. Imagine it'd interest a man of your profession."

"Did he have a companion?" asked Vincent.

"Yes sir. Drove the truck. Definitely another alien." Scott spat again, eagerly. "Want to see that bone?"

"He don't want to see your god damn bone," said the sheriff.

"All due respect, sheriff, I feel it might have some-"

Vincent forked blood-spattered dirt into a second evidence bag and straightened, knees creaking.

"That'll be all," he said.

Scott followed him to the car. "You got one of them mind-erase guns? Pull the trigger and I lose my memory?"

Vincent turned.

"That's what my real gun is for," he said.

As the sheriff drove back down the bumpy road, Vincent lifted the evidence bag and examined the rabbit. He imagined biting into a living animal, the fur and skin giving way, little bones crunching and splintering as hot blood thump-thumped out.

He put the rabbit away and went back to watching the horizon.

*****

Sixteen Hours Earlier

Tetris spotted a sliver of furry movement as he rounded the corner and dove in pursuit. He put a foot down in a bucket and tumbled, but the noise was nothing compared to the locomotive in his head. Kicking free, he muscled up and out of tickling grass as the rabbit cut hard right. Long feet splashed sand into the moonlight. It was dark, but he felt the heat and zeroed in, fingers closing around the thrumming neck. *Snap.* Before his brain caught up, his teeth had plunged into the wonderful hot flesh.

He took three bites before he realized what he'd done.

"Oh God," he mumbled, mouth packed with twitching rabbit.

He swallowed anyway.

Harsh lights snapped on. A window squeaked upward, un-muffling a dog's furious barks, and then the blue-black sky cracked open and something kicked hard against his shoulder, spinning him into the sand. The rabbit slipped through his fingers.

Li shouted from the truck. He staggered up, brain rebooting, concrete feet picking up speed. Blood simmered on his tongue. Another shot sliced the night in half, but this one was well off the mark. He hauled himself into the passenger seat just as Li gunned the engine and pulled away. The door fought back when he tried to close it.

"Your mouth," said Li, punching the light in the ceiling.

He wiped rabbit blood with the back of his good hand. They hit a bump at forty miles an hour and his head smacked the roof.

"I'll pull off the road when we get some space," said Li.

He'd already torn his shirt down the middle, revealing green-tinted torso. Getting the arm out of its sleeve wasn't going to happen. He focused on dragging the seatbelt across his body.

Stop moving.

He ignored the voice and scrabbled the buckle against its silver sheath.

You've got an artery open. I can't close it if you're flailing around.

"Pull over," said Tetris.

"We're not even at the highway," said Li.

"I said pull over."

She hit the brakes. "I don't like that tone."

He pressed himself against the seat as a wad of tentacles wriggled and flexed inside his shoulder. Hands tugged at his sleeve. Li slipped a knife beneath the fabric and neatly opened it. The skin beneath was riddled with holes.

"Buckshot," she said.

We can push that out later. Just bandage it for now.

"Got to stop the bleeding," said Li. "Must have hit your brachial artery."

She flopped half into the back seat and rifled through her pack.

"You're going to owe me five new shirts," she said, grinning, as she pressed cool cloth against his wound.

"Are you enjoying this?"

"Hold," she said, pushing his good hand against the fabric. "I need to see what's wrong with your mouth."

She had her hands on his jaw before he could protest.

"My mouth is fine," he said, jerking away.

The grin vanished. "Your mouth is bleeding."

"It's not my blood."

Oh boy.

"It's not his blood, he says."

"I was eating a rabbit. On accident."

"Why'd you keep telling me you weren't hungry?"

"I *wasn't* hungry."

You're photosynthesizing, said the forest. *But your body needs more than glucose.*

"You've got to be kidding me," said Tetris.

"What?"

"Some kind of craving," he said. "Photosynthesis. Missing nutrients."

Li brushed his hand away and leaned on the wrappings. Blood was streaked across her face like war paint.

"So on top of everything else," she said, "it turned you into a vampire."

Tetris closed his eyes. The forest roamed the confines of his mind like a barely-suppressed memory.

Soon they were back on the highway, blasting toward a gradually-brightening blade of Arizona sky.

2

A cop pulled them over just past the Illinois border. It was four a.m., and Tetris had been driving in silence for hours. Li slept in the passenger seat. Now she sank down, stretching, a predator taking inventory of every sinewy limb. The lights painted her face elaborate patterns of red and blue.

"Fan-fucking-tastic," she said, and slithered out the door, closing it just before the officer came around the corner.

Tetris rolled down his window. "Evening, sir."

The officer directed a flashlight into the cab. Tetris averted his eyes.

"Your taillight's out," said the officer. His hand rested on the smooth grip of a pistol.

"Sorry about that," said Tetris.

"I'll need to see your license and registration."

"They're at home."

Beneath the flashlight beam, Tetris watched the hand on the gun.

"Your face is green," observed the policeman.

"I have a condition."

"You do, huh?"

"Mexican florobotulism. It's quite contagious."

"I'm going to need you to step out of the vehicle."

Tetris stayed where he was. His shoulder throbbed.

"Officer," he said, "I promise to get my taillight fixed at the very earliest opportunity."

"Get out of the vehicle." Fingers slipped around the pistol grip. "Now."

Tetris unbuckled his seat belt. "This is a very bad idea."

The pistol came out of its holster.

"I can't let you arrest me," said Tetris. His heart stomped around in his chest.

"Exit the vehicle and place your hands on your head," said the officer, stepping back as the pistol came up.

Tetris unlatched the door.

Li melted out of the darkness, grabbed a fistful of hair, and smashed the man's face into the upper edge of the open window. Tetris threw himself sideways as the gun discharged. The bullet ripped past his ear. As the cop's cranium rebounded, blood and spittle pinged Tetris's face.

The officer made an animal noise when Li twisted his pistol wrist. The gun dropped. He was significantly larger than her, and when he spun around he knocked her back a few feet, but then Tetris rammed the door hard against his spine.

Li finished him off with a strike to the gut. She had him handcuffed before Tetris was even out of the truck.

*****

Tetris watched the sun rise over flat soybean countryside and a diminishing ribbon of gold-lined highway. With another set of eyes, he watched a tarantula the size of a mobile home make its way through the forest. Pollen shimmered in the air. The spider, moving in nervous bursts, crossed a patch of undisturbed soil.

Pincers erupted from the center of the clearing, followed by a hypertrophied column of iridescent yellow muscle. A worm, hundreds of segments long, each segment edged with tunneling spikes.

The worm snapped its jaws around the spider's abdomen. Despite the flailing limbs, both worm and meal vanished in a single swift retraction: *shwoop*. The ground puffed a few times, breathing. Spurts of glittering dust rose and fell. Then the clearing was still.

*****

They stopped at a rest station so Li could get some food out of a vending machine. Tetris slouched in the passenger seat, peering out the shattered window. A child

219

walked by, trailing his mother by a couple of steps.

"Mommy," he said, "that man is green."

"That's nice," said the mother, tugging him along.

They ditched the pickup in a riverbed outside Maple, Illinois. The sign at the edge of town said "Population: 157." The first vehicle they came across was an ancient red SUV. It was unlocked. The keys were in the cup holder.

"Small towns," said Li, drumming on the steering wheel as they drove away.

Tetris didn't reply. He was watching the low-slung houses roll by, counting satellite dishes and dogs chained to trees, while he picked buckshot out of his shoulder with a pair of tweezers.

3

The Washington Post's receptionist glared balefully over thick-rimmed glasses.

"I fail to see how painting yourself green constitutes news," he said.

Li laid her palms on the counter. "It's not paint."

"It looks like paint."

"Well, it's not."

Tetris went to peruse the magazines in the waiting area.

Tell him about the photosynthesis, said the forest. *Tell him you healed a shotgun wound in three days.*

"He'll love that," muttered Tetris.

Constrict his throat until the lack of oxygen renders him unconscious?

In the corner, the security guard's stiff posture did little to hide his keen interest in the argument unfolding at the front desk.

"Maybe let us handle this one," said Tetris.

The guard first?

"Trying to get me shot again?"

"What was that?" The receptionist had the phone against his ear and a finger hovering over the dial pad.

"Look," said Tetris, waving a dog-eared men's fashion magazine, "I'm a ranger. I'm bright green. I've got a big story about the thing that turned me green. The least you can do is put me in front of a reporter."

The receptionist flattened his lips. After a moment he returned the phone to its cradle and reached for a bottle of antacid tablets.

"Or," said Li sweetly, "I suppose we could always take our story to the Times."

Five minutes later they were sitting in senior reporter Janice Stacy's office as she tapped a pen against bright pink lips.

"Let me get this straight," said Stacy. "The whole forest is one giant, large, very big alien. From outer space."

"Correct."

"And the government knows."

"Correct."

"And every American ranger has a secret implant in their neck. For, like, mind control, presumably."

"Tracking," said Tetris, "and a kill switch."

"A kill switch."

"To keep us from falling into enemy hands."

"Any other scoops while we're at it? UFOs? Lizard

people?"

Tetris didn't reply.

Stacy scratched at an unsightly residue on the arm of her chair. A few wisps of hair had escaped her bun and were undulating in the air conditioning.

"Where did you obtain this information?"

"The forest told me," said Tetris.

"A giant alien made of trees, from another galaxy, that speaks English."

"I can tell you the exact temperature in any coastal city, anywhere in the world. Right now."

Stacy chewed the end of her pen and watched Li pace the floor-to-ceiling window that served as one of the office's walls. People kept poking their heads out of their cubicles to gawk.

"Mumbai," said Stacy, and turned to her computer.

Tetris tilted his head. "Eighty-six point four degrees Fahrenheit."

The mouse click-clicked. "Osaka."

"Seventy-eight degrees Fahrenheit and raining. It's been raining for the past forty-seven minutes. Year-to-date rainfall is one thousand, two hundred and thirty-three millimeters." He scratched his shoulder absentmindedly. "There are, at this precise moment, one hundred and ninety-three international flights over the world's forests. I can show you the exact position of each one and supply arrival times."

Stacy set the pen on the desk.

"Let me get my editor," she said.

The story ran on the front page. Li and Tetris, who'd spent the night on air mattresses in Stacy's office, emerged the next morning to a horde of reporters, TV vans, and curious passersby. It took an hour to walk the six blocks to the south lawn of the White House, shoving cameras out of their faces the whole way.

Tetris planned on saying a few words to the press when they arrived, but he didn't get a chance. A cadre of suit-clad agents dragged them into the back of an unmarked van.

"You shitheads can't touch us," said Li, relieving a burly hand of its grip around her wrist. The hand's owner yelped.

"You're not under arrest," he said, cradling his fingers and scooting away. "The Secretary of State wants to see you."

Li took an apple out of her pocket and buffed it on her sleeve.

"In that case," she said, biting in with a crunch, "proceed."

The van inched through the mob. Fists rang against the anodized walls.

*****

Toni Davis wasn't sure what color she'd expected him to be. A slight, sickly-green tint, perhaps. But no, he was green with a capital "G," head to toe. Practically Granny Smith-colored.

"Madam Secretary," said Tetris, "you're staring."

"I understand you to be something like an ambassador."

"Sure."

"Well, Mr. Ambassador—"

"Call me Tetris, please, ma'am."

"In America, as in any country, Tetris, we have laws. And while certain action films may have given you ideas to the contrary, we expect ambassadors to abide by those laws. Diplomatic immunity only goes so far."

Tetris looked at Li, who shrugged.

"I'm not sure I understand," he said.

"In the past seventy-two hours, you've publicized highly sensitive state secrets, assaulted a police officer, and stolen three separate motor vehicles."

"Borrowed," said Li.

"Congress is crying treason. Congress wants your little green head."

"Look," said Tetris, "you fuckers put a pod of neurotoxin in my neck. I don't need a lecture on right and wrong. That's wrong."

The subdermals pissed Davis off too. If she'd found out in advance, discontinuing them would have been at the top of her list. Even leaving aside the ethical implications, the program had been guaranteed to set off a scandal whenever the press unearthed it, and the last thing this administration needed was another scandal.

She went with the explanation Cooper had offered. "It's no different from the cyanide pills we used to issue U2 pilots."

"Except those pilots knew in advance," said Li. "They had a choice."

Davis pretended to make a note on her pad.

"I don't think you can blame us for running," said Tetris. "They'd be dissecting me as we speak."

"Of course not," said Davis. "We can't even waterboard you anymore."

"Have you met Cooper?" demanded Li.

"Anyway," said Tetris, "a little transparency never hurt anyone."

"What an unfathomably stupid thing to say," said Davis.

Tetris opened his mouth and closed it again.

"You just told every country with a coastline that a giant alien monster lives next door," said Davis.

"They had to find out sooner or later," said Tetris, "because there's something even bigger on the way."

Davis tugged at an earlobe. There was a painting on the far wall that she looked at when she was thinking. Golden fields rippling in a stiff wind, the mountains in the background jagged and tipped with snow.

"Well?" said Tetris.

Davis clicked her pen and leaned over the desk. "Are you going to explain what that means, Tetris, or are you going to sit there like a vegetable all afternoon?"

*****

Vincent Chen was in the Kansas City airport, bumping elbows with a clump of other travelers beneath a small, square television, when he got the call.

"Yes?" he said.

"They're in DC," said Cooper.

"So it seems."

"I assume you're en route?"

"Wheels up in forty-five."

"Roger that."

As Vincent hung up, the station replayed a portion of the footage they'd been broadcasting all morning. The camera zoomed in on a green face, emotionless eyes above a rigid jaw. That, Vincent knew, was not a human being. It was a husk manipulated by a remorseless alien foe. A fat, tendriled parasite wriggled in that hollowed-out skull. Vincent remembered the rabbit with its ragged bite marks. The mouth on the green thing's face looked normal enough, but it was full of teeth designed to tear into living flesh.

"No word yet as to where the so-called Green Ranger was taken, or whether he was telling the truth in his interview with the Washington Post," said the newswoman.

The man next to Vincent turned to a companion. "What's his dick look like, you think?"

The companion considered.

"Definitely some wacko shit," she said. "The image that's coming to mind—and don't judge me, here—is a cucumber with teeth."

"Or is his pelvis straight-up smooth, like an action figure?"

Vincent fought his way out of the crowd and headed for the security line.

4

"Say the words 'tissue sample' one more time," said Li, advancing on a blue-jawed doctor, "and I'll shove those forceps so far up your rear that they'll have to invent a whole new procedure to extract them."

Days of Senate hearings, boardroom briefings, press conferences, and hush-voiced agency interviews. Everyone everywhere asking the same six questions over and over. Nonstop medical appointments, doctors poking and prodding and drawing dizzying amounts of blood. Tetris tugged absentmindedly at the gauze taped over the latest needlehole and wished, above all else, for silence.

"Do I look like—no, *you* listen—tell your boss to come down and talk to me *mano e mano,* capiche? We've seen six doctors today. No more."

There'd been bright points, of course. Dr. Alvarez

blasting around a boardroom table for a rib-flexing hug. The perpetually chastened look on Cooper's face, especially apparent in the presence of Secretary of State Toni Davis.

"-out of my face before I tear it to shreds. That could be Mozart's fucking signature, dude, what will it take for you to understand I don't give a shit?"

"There's no cause for alarm, miss. It's a routine—"

"I'm counting backwards from three, little man, and when I reach one—"

Davis didn't seem like a politician, and of course she wasn't; during the second round of Apollo missions, she'd become both the first African-American and the first woman ever to set foot on the Moon. Tetris had never read her autobiography, *Fuck Your Opinions I'm Doing It Anyway*, but he'd seen display cases full of hardcover copies, her many immaculate smiles gleaming like snowbanks.

At this point it seemed to Tetris that he'd met every member of the United States government except for the President himself, the latter having been called away to attend an international summit in Paris. The summit concerned climate change, but had taken an abrupt turn when Tetris made his existence known. Now the various heads of state were clamoring for more information on the forest, demanding their own ambassadors, and filling the air with fiery rhetoric re: the violation of their coastal borders by the monsters that sometimes spilled out of the verdant depths.

It was a life of continuous noise, without even sleep to interrupt it. When he closed his eyes, he saw the canopy, billowing green.

*****

Ben Jonas was in a store buying clothes for his wife's birthday, which was tomorrow. With everything going on at the White House, he hadn't had time to find a gift online. So here he was, at the mall, his least favorite place, an hour before closing time. Desperate for something, anything, to purchase.

An alarmingly attractive attendant swooped down. "Doing alright?"

"What size would you say the person in this photograph is?" he blurted, shoving his phablet in her well-rouged face.

"Err," she said.

"Aim high and I'm calling her fat," he said grimly. "Aim low and she'll feel like a cow."

"The eternal struggle," agreed the attendant, curls bouncing.

Ben watched her adjust a bra strap. There was something unsettling about her proportions. Alien, almost. He was disgusted. He definitely did not have a boner. How did they get away with wearing such revealing clothing? He was a married man. Old enough to be her father. Okay, he definitely had a boner, it was such a fucked up time to have a boner, what was wrong with him? Everything in his life had been one huge catastrophe since junior prom, when Jace Plaudit pantsed him while he was dancing with Cindy Ducksworth, and the whole school saw his yellowing whitey-tighties with the hole in the rear, and of course he'd had a boner then too—

"Maybe a 12?" suggested the attendant, biting her bountiful lip.

"I'll be taking my business elsewhere, thank you very much," snapped Ben, and trundled out.

*****

You know, said the forest, *if it's more ambassadors they want, we can make more.*

*****

"Come on, man, I brought you out here to have a good time."

"I am having a good time."

"You flinch after every hit."

"It's an awful noise."

"It's an amazing noise. Throaty. You can tell a home run by the sound, you know. It's like a gunshot."

Vincent's shoulder twinged. He drove his thumb deep into the soft tissue and rubbed.

"Ah, shit, my bad," said his brother. "Poor choice of words."

The fans beside Vincent were shirtless and screaming.

Little beads of redolent sweat kept flying off them. They stood and cavorted, shouting, at all times, except between innings, when they sat to gulp beer out of enormous plastic cups.

"You've got to move on eventually," said his brother.

"I have moved on."

A hit, that horrible crack, and the fans went berserk. The all-important white speck vanished in the humming lights and reappeared, plummeting. An outfielder caught it neatly.

"Come on!" shouted Vincent's shirtless neighbor, taking a swing at the air. The other one scowled with his hands behind his buzzcut head.

"It wasn't your fault," said Vincent's brother.

"It wasn't my fault, it wasn't my fault, do you have any idea how many times I've heard you say that?"

"It wasn't, though."

"Look, whose fault it was doesn't change anything. It's meaningless. You think it matters whose fault it was?"

"Don't take it out on me, I'm your last brother, you're—"

"—just wanted to hang out, relax, and not use my fucking brain for five fucking—"

"Hey," shouted the red-faced fan, "can you take your little Communist Party somewhere else?"

"What was that?" said Vincent.

"Vince," warned his brother.

"You heard me, Comrade Ching Chong, I can't hear the damn—"

Another bat crack like a femur snap and Vincent was out of his seat, rising fast, buoyant with electric energy that infused his fists and lifted, at least for a moment, the gray veil over his viscera.

*****

"Go away, Lucia."

Dr. Alvarez slid a finger across the china cabinet. Tsked at the coat of fuzzy dust that accumulated.

"You need a housekeeper, Dave."

"I can't afford a housekeeper," said Dave. He slapped the arm of his wheelchair.

She picked up a photo and wiped it clean. Her own seven-year-old eyes stared back at her. "I could—"

"I don't want your handouts," he said.

"Dave."

"She's long gone, Lucia. Why are you here?"

"I need to check in every once in a while. For my peace of mind."

"No you don't."

She surveyed the graveyard of plastic-wrapped furniture.

"This isn't a way to live," she said.

He turned up the volume. Conservative talking heads traded barbs about national security and the insidious Green Ranger. Dr. Alvarez climbed the stairs, careful not to touch the banister. All the pictures were still on the wall, though some of them were slanted.

Her old room was bare. Even the bed was gone. Where her Marie Curie poster had once hung, the wall was a marginally lighter brown. The floorboards were submerged in gray dust.

Dave was waiting at the bottom of the stairs. A string of spittle connected his chin to his chest. He didn't seem to notice.

"It's your fault, you know," he said.

"What?"

"It's your fault she's dead."

Dr. Alvarez looked at him.

"There was enough for us to live on," he said. "From the settlement. Until you. That's why she went back to work."

The television warbled.

"You think I don't think about that?" she said, harsher than she'd intended.

Dave spat into the dust and wheeled himself away.

*****

Cooper fiddled with an emerald cuff link. Took it out, examined it, put it back.

"Self-defense," said Vincent.

"Bruised trachea, three snapped fingers—"

"He popped me a good one in the eye."

"I can see that. Meanwhile he walked or rather had to be *carted* away, after being hurled down several levels of bleacher, with—"

"He slipped. With great enthusiasm."

"All the scrutiny our department is getting, it seems like a spectacularly bad time for a senior agent to be throwing fists at a ball game."

"They won't be pressing charges."

"I should hope not."

"But. Off the record?"

"My lips are sealed."

"Shithead had it coming."

"That I do not doubt."

*****

"How are you doing, Li?"

Li dunked fries in a paper cup filled with ketchup. "I'm alright, Doc. You?"

"You've been pushing yourself hard."

"I'm going to go ahead and blame your boss for that."

"Cooper means well."

"Neurotoxin pods do not equate, in my mind—"

"Those were an error."

"You're not apologizing, though."

Dr. Alvarez shifted on the red plastic. "I've told you I didn't know about them."

"Sure."

"It was an error. One that I am inclined to believe Cooper regrets."

Their Secret Service agents were posted outside. Stringy clouds whisked across a sky tinged orange by fast-food glass.

"Can't help but notice numerous glances in the direction of the restroom," said Dr. Alvarez.

"He's been in there a long time."

"He's a telepath who spits out buckshot like grape seeds. I'm certain he's fine."

"Again, I'm going to have to blame y'all for the paranoia."

"Everybody always assumes you two are together, don't they?"

The last of Li's soda gurgled through her straw. She sloshed the ice around. "You don't?"

"No."

"We're failing the Bechdel test right now, you know."

"I suppose we'll have to have further conversations, then."

"Do grapes even *have* seeds?"

"Originally, sure. We engineered it out of them."

"If the seeds are gone, how do they grow new grapes?"

Dr. Alvarez opened her mouth, frowned, and closed it.

"Ha! Stumped," said Li.

"I've made a mental note to look into that."

"At last, a factoid the Doctor does not know."

"You would be surprised just how much falls into that bucket."

*****

"What's their plan?"

"He's scheduled to speak to NATO in Paris on the twenty-first. Two days after that, he leads an expedition into the forest. Brings rangers from five or six countries."

"To turn them into plants."

"To turn them into—whatever he is."

"So it's spreading."

"It's six guys. I share your concerns, but it's hardly a pandemic."

"That's the thing about pandemics, Vince: they always start small."

*****

When John Henry, Chief Legal Adviser of the United States Department of State, arrived at his spotless spartan square of an apartment, there was a big evil spider smack in the middle of his marble countertop. Next to the peaches. The peaches he'd been salivating over his entire commute. Fresh, organic, local-ish peaches. So the insecticide spray was out of the question.

He and the spider regarded each other. John Henry made a long and high-pitched sound of distress. His skin was crawling in twelve directions, seeking any avenue off his skeleton. He hated all bugs, but spiders were the worst.

The spider tested the air with a long, waving leg. A brown recluse, perhaps? Known to be aggressive. The vicious serial killer of the arthropod world. Slowly, with great poise, John Henry removed his shoe.

*****

In State Department headquarters, Sasha Montessori and Toni Davis watched the late-night news and dug into freshly delivered pizza.

"How's morale, Sasha?"

"Mmph."

"I wish we could get everyone to see things our way."

"Our?"

"I trust him."

"Can't hurt to be cautious."

"Stationing bombers over the forest goes beyond cautious. Tripling the Coast Guard's budget is blatant opportunism."

"Wouldn't be a real crisis if everyone wasn't trying to turn it to their own advantage."

"JFK have to deal with this shit?"

"You're hardly JFK in this scenario."

Davis caught a strand of half-melted cheese and lifted it to her mouth. "Sometimes, in this administration—"

Sasha grimaced and bit into another slice.

"This is an amazing opportunity," said Davis. "Why are we ruining it with subterfuge and bickering?"

"Because we're human, boss."

"Thank God *it's* not."

5

They were three hours into the flight, thirty thousand feet above the Atlantic Forest, when one of the engines switched from a steady thrum to a keening shriek of metal on metal. It happened with a bang and a shuddering lurch to the left. Smoke whipped past Tetris's window. The plane screamed downward, a steep, spiraling plummet, and he knew in his berserkly-beating heart, as his body rose and strained against the seatbelt, that everything was over. Unique connection to the forest or no, he was going to die.

Five minutes later, he was still very much alive. The noise had not abated. There were fewer screams now, most of the screamers having opted for sobbing into their laps, but the plane's alarms continued to blare, on the off chance that anyone had yet to grasp the gravity of their situation. Furious currents howled against the fuselage, battering it left and right and up and down, but the groaning wings remained attached.

Li had adopted his grim silence, but first she'd been sure to express, matter-of-factly and at great length, her conviction that the plane would come apart when it impacted the canopy. It would, she predicted, fling twisted metal and human debris in all directions.

The wind shrieked vindictively past his window. Everything shook.

I can't tell where you're going to land, said the forest.

Tetris bit his lip and tasted copper.

Get the pilot going in a straight line.

He sucked in a breath and unclicked his seatbelt.

Li yanked his arm.

"I'll be right back," he screamed, tapping the side of his head.

*****

Vincent's reality was a shattering field of glass. Memory-panes flew innumerably by and burst into shards. At some point in the preceding minutes, there had been a very loud noise. The plane had lunged left. Now Cooper was bent in half, praying, and Vincent was crunching the odds of survival. Today would have been his mother's fifty-seventh birthday. Fire and smoke swirled dragonlike past the window.

The green ranger staggered downhill, brushing Vincent on the way by. There was only one reason that someone in this situation would rush in that direction: to reach the cockpit and finish the job.

Vincent caught Tetris at the door, hit him low in the back, and felt the green skull clock the edge of the doorway with a sweet, satisfying *thwock*. The plane tilted even further, and together they slid, Vincent wrapped around the formidable waist, holding on for everything in the universe. Tetris bucked and spun, planting his feet against Vincent's chest, then pushed off as they tobogganed past the lavatories. Vincent grasped at the jackhammering feet. A boot caught him in the teeth.

"Get off!"

Vincent ignored the blood flowing into his eye. A boot hit his face a second time. It seemed harder to dodge these blows when he couldn't hear. It was very likely that his nose was broken.

Fine. He'd wanted to take the saboteur alive, but a couple more blows like that and his consciousness would ebb. He unholstered his pistol and brought it up—

Tetris bucked out of the way, but Vincent still would have adjusted his aim and hit the shot if Cooper hadn't come flying and tackled him. The pistol discharged through the wall, leaving a whistling eraser-tip of vivid blue sky.

The three of them tumbled, all flailing legs and arms, into the C-32's onboard conference room.

Vincent searched for the pistol. It was past Tetris's head, caught on the edge of a chair. Tetris kicked free and reached it first. He ejected the magazine and racked the slide, then flung the empty gun away. Shouted something inaudible.

Vincent struggled, but Cooper was wrapped around him like an octopus. The engines devoured his voice.

"Let him go, Vince," shouted Cooper in his ear.

Vincent kept fighting, but Tetris was already gone.

*****

The plane was crashing. It was going down. There were unspeakable noises coming through the window, and what Ben Jonas wanted to know was where was his oxygen mask? The plane was going down and he couldn't breathe. An oxygen mask was supposed to come out of the ceiling, yellow with an elastic cord, he was supposed to affix his own mask before assisting his neighbor—

The yellow mask would come down and he would put it on and everything would be okay, he would breathe slowly and surely, maybe close his eyes and take a little nap. *Oxygen will be flowing, though the bag may not inflate.* Ben punched the ceiling. Slammed it with both hands. Where was the mask? What had he done?

He sobbed, and the plane fell out of the sky like a dropped sausage, and a green man went down the aisle smelling like a thunderstorm, barging into the cockpit and shutting the door behind him.

The plane came whistling out of the cavernous cloud-swirled sky. Sunlight glinting off the wings would have caught the carnivorous attention of countless canopy denizens, had they not been otherwise occupied.

The thing that had the monsters snapping at one another as they fled was a substance rather like thick green gelatin, which oozed by the megaliter out of the tops of the trees. It formed rolling bubbles and waves above the canopy, blooming upward and dripping through the interlocking branches to splat in heaps on the forest floor.

As the plane approached the rubbery green goop, it extended its landing gear. A pillar of smoke straggled behind it. After a long moment of consideration, the landing gear retracted.

The underside of the plane made contact, skipping lightly across the surface, then gliding, kicking up towering ripples. As it skidded, the plane sank and slowed, until finally it was halfway submerged. It inched forward. It stopped.

Gradually the green substance dissolved and drained away. As it vanished, the plane settled lower, sliding backward, tail inclined toward the ground.

The last part to be swallowed was the cockpit. Then the plane was gone, and the treetops sprang back to their normal positions. A breeze ruffled the canopy as if nothing had happened at all.

*****

Tetris, who'd taken a seat in the forward compartment, unstrapped himself and hurtled into the cockpit. The pilots were busy at their consoles.

"You have to get away from the windows," he said.

Outside, ancient branches twirled into the patchwork sky.

"We're radioing for help," said the co-pilot, glancing at Tetris over a formidably bushy mustache.

"If anything moves," said Tetris, "run."

Then he was headed downhill to the Secretary of State's room. Her Secret Service agents were at the little oval windows, peering into the tangled maze, pistols in firm two-handed grips. Tetris didn't have the heart to tell them that their weapons were basically BB guns.

"Do we have ranger gear on board? Grapple guns? How many grapple guns?"

"Tetris," said Davis, "did you crash my plane?"

"Do I really have to answer that?"

A Secret Service agent yelped and fell on his rear as the room darkened. Smooth yellow flesh slid across the windows. The plane shuddered. Tetris and Davis watched the scales glide slowly by. Creaks from all sides indicated that the snake had wrapped itself around the fuselage.

"We need to get out of the canopy," said Tetris, "or everyone is going to die."

Shouts and the sound of crumpling metal forced him

back toward the cockpit. The anaconda had its mouth over the nose of the plane, serrated teeth-rows and red throat blocking the windows. Inexorably, the mouth closed. The pilots scrambled free, but one of them was a second too slow, and his lower half was caught in a vise of ruined metal.

Where the fuselage had connected to the roof, canopy air poured through. The smell was fecund, sweet, suggestive of clear water. The snake's cold eye appeared in the gap.

The trapped pilot screamed and screamed.

The eye retreated. Moments later, the snake's nose jammed against the gap, black tongue flickering in. It poked and prodded, trying to get at the source of the tantalizing shrieks, driving the plane deeper and deeper into the canopy.

Tetris had the Secretary of State's arm and was rushing her downhill.

"There was equipment for the mission in the cargo hold," Davis said. "But that's on the underside of the plane."

Li met them in the conference room, along with Dr. Alvarez, Cooper, and a glowering Vincent Chen.

"How do I get the cargo hold open?" asked Tetris.

"There's a switch in the cockpit," said Dr. Alvarez.

"Not anymore."

The plane dropped several feet, groaning. Everyone clutched whatever they could get their hands on. The tip of the anaconda's tail flashed past the window.

"You'd have to use a charge, then," said Cooper. "Blow the lock."

"There's C4 in the back closet," said one of the Secret Service agents. Behind sunglasses, his face was almost as green as Tetris's.

Li followed Tetris down the hall. "I'm coming with you."

Passengers cowered in the rear compartment's seats. They seemed as scared of Tetris as they were of the anaconda.

He opened the closet. Bulletproof vests: useless. M4A1 rifles: slightly less useless. He grabbed one of the rifles, slung the strap over his shoulder, and passed Li two more. The C4 was packaged in blocks; he took a backpack and stuffed it full, then made for the emergency exit.

"The monsters can't see me," said Tetris. "I'm invisible to them. You don't need to come."

"Don't use too much," she said, prodding the pack.

She helped him wrench the exit open. A cavalcade of chirps and shrieks tumbled through, along with a rush of over-oxygenated air. Tetris, wishing for climbing picks, leapt the three foot gap to the nearest branch.

Li slammed the door behind him.

The anaconda was wrapped three times around the upper half of the plane, head out of sight as it probed the underside of the fuselage. The pilot's screams had stopped. Above and beside Tetris, an enormous black widow tiptoed closer on vertiginous legs. The red hourglass on its abdomen was as tall as Tetris. The spider reached out—and out, and out—to touch the fuselage, scraping the aluminum tentatively.

Tetris was always amazed by the complexity of parts around a spider's mouth. Fangs, jaws, mouthparts, little frantically rustling pedipalps, and of course the many unblinking eyes...

A second leg probed out beside the first.

Tetris placed a hand on one of the stationary legs. The exoskeleton was cool and hard, like playground infrastructure. He took a chunk of C4 out of his pack, affixed it to the leg, and inserted a remote detonator.

The spider crossed over to the roof.

Hurry up, said the forest.

He turned and climbed the matted vines to the underside of the plane.

The cargo hold already yawned open. Since the plane was rotated slightly onto its left flank, the door pointed downward, and many of the crates and boxes had already come tumbling out. They littered the branches like an abandoned archaeological dig.

As Tetris approached, a millipede the width of a golden retriever poked its armored head out of the hold. Its tiny eyes examined him dumbly. The remains of a crate were stuck like a wreath around its upper segment.

"Get out of here," said Tetris. The millipede ducked from view.

He sighed and flicked the flashlight attached to his rifle.

The cargo hold was long and dark, with a grooved

metal ceiling. The millipede rustled through boxes near the uphill end. Tetris searched the crates beside the door. The fourth box he checked—with a Vertigo Industries logo stenciled on the side—contained six brand-new grapple guns and accompanying harnesses.

He took a grapple gun and nylon webbing and went outside. Sunlight glared through the interlocking leaves. He aimed upward as the millipede came to watch. Its feelers waved.

"I thought they couldn't see me?" said Tetris as he fired. The grapple gun's hook wrapped around a branch a few stories up.

They can see you, said the forest. *It's just that most of them find you tremendously uninteresting.*

Tetris hooked the webbing around the dangling grapple gun and filled it with gear from the boxes.

When he finally ascended, lugging two full packs, the emergency exit door was open. The carpet beyond gleamed with blood, and the seats in the rear cabin were empty.

Tetris threw the packs down, closed the door, and sprinted up the hall with his rifle at the ready, mind crafting worst-case scenarios beyond his wildest nightmares.

6

A three hundred-pound ant was trying to barge through the door to the conference room, antennae shuddering as it threw its weight against the brittle plastic. Tetris stitched a line of fire down its back, but the bullets merely lodged in the exoskeleton.

The ant backed up. It didn't have room to turn, but it craned its neck to look at him. An electric thrill tickled the back of his neck as the sickle-shaped pincers chewed the air. The ant's eyes were huge, expressionless bulbs.

Li kicked the door open, lunged, and slammed a fire extinguisher through the ant's head. Orange fluid plumed in spouts. She jumped back, leaving the canister embedded in the ruined cranium, as the ant spasmed after her. It bounced off the walls and flipped, every leg moving in its own deranged pattern. Finally, with a whine of escaping air, the carnival of limbs fell still.

"That felt great," said Li, extending a hand to help Tetris clamber over the still-twitching carcass.

The room was packed. Tetris recognized several passengers from the rear cabin.

"Whose blood was that?" he asked.

One of the aides retched. Tetris tried not to look at the brownish dribble that followed. He was beginning to understand why the room smelled so awful.

"Some idiot opened the door," said Li. "Couple of bugs ripped him in half and carted him off." She nodded at the extinguished ant. "That one stuck around. Unlucky for him."

"Her," said Dr. Alvarez. "Workers are female."

"Doc. Not the time for entomological quibbles."

Tetris tossed Li the gun. "Only three?"

"They'll be back," said Dr. Alvarez. "They'll bring the whole colony."

Li checked the magazine. "You find grapple guns?"

"Only six."

Li turned to the crowd. "Tetris, Doc, me—who else knows how to use one?"

"I do," said Secretary of State Toni Davis.

Li looked at her. "Come on."

"No," Davis said, "seriously."

"Where'd you learn that?"

"Does it matter?"

Go go go go go go go, said the forest.

"Who else?" snapped Tetris.

Vincent Chen raised his hand. So did one of the Secret Service agents.

"That's six," said Li. "We'll bring the rest of you down in stages."

But the aides were already clamoring forward, pleading for a spot in the first wave. Along the back wall, the pilots stood silently, arms crossed, with a couple other Secret Service agents and Agent Dale Cooper.

"Everybody shut up," said Davis, and the room fell silent. "Jack Dano. Cooper." She scanned the mob. "Evan. Sasha. Kate. Ben. That's the first six. The rest of you will wait your turn."

"I'll stay," said Cooper quietly. He had a bloody tissue pressed to his nose.

"No," said Dr. Alvarez.

Cooper shook his head. Tetris stared at him.

"Somebody's got to hold down the fort," he said. "You can come back for me."

"Cooper," said Jack Dano, "you are mission-critical personnel."

"Alvarez knows everything that I do," said Cooper.

Why is he doing this, wondered the forest.

Cooper's eyes were an impenetrable blue.

"Let's go," said Li.

Tetris shouldered his pack and vaulted the ant. Right

now the only thing to think about was how to move twenty-four people and a dozen packs from the upper canopy to the relative safety of the lowest branches.

"These are full of harnesses," he said, tossing the packs into the arms of the aides closest behind. "I'll be right back."

He peeked out the porthole and swung the emergency exit open, then leaned out for the bundle of gear. After bringing it inside, he disengaged the grapple gun and tossed it to Li as soon as the silver spearhead finished whizzing back into the barrel. Trusting her to sort through the equipment, he leaned out and fired his own grapple gun, then swung down toward the cargo hold.

The millipede was still there. An antenna wiggled a greeting. Tetris gave it a pat on the head, and was surprised to feel it nudge against his leg like a cat. He grabbed the other packs he'd stuffed with equipment and slung them over his shoulders, then hooked the grapple gun to his harness and ascended. As he rose he saw the first of the ants marching along distant branches. The noose was closing.

Inside, everyone had managed to get their harnesses on. One of the aides was too wide to close all the buckles.

"That's not going to hold," said Li, poking him in the stomach.

"Sure it will," he said.

Li looked at Tetris imploringly. "Can't we bring one of the other ones? Someone with a chance?"

"We have to get everybody out of here eventually," said

Davis.

Tetris could tell that Li didn't expect to make a second trip.

"I'll take you," he said to the bureaucrat. "What's your name?"

"Ben," said the man, face shiny with equal parts terror and gratitude.

"Alright, Ben," said Tetris, "do me a favor and put this on."

"What's in there?"

"A shitload of C4," said Tetris. Then, because he couldn't help himself: "Don't drop it." He tossed the bag, and Ben nearly fell over himself trying to keep it off the ground.

"It won't blow up without a detonator," said Dr. Alvarez, scowling at Tetris.

Cooper stood in the hallway. Tetris went over as the rest of the group geared up.

"Here," he said, pressing the M4A1 into Cooper's arms.

"Better that you have it," said Cooper.

"I found a SCAR," said Tetris. "Don't open the door unless you see my face through the window."

"Understood."

Tetris faked a cough. A day ago, he would have listed this man in his five least-favorite people on the planet. Now he got a painful block in his throat just looking at him.

"Why try to be a hero?"

"That's your job," said Cooper, with an attempt at a

jaunty grin.

"I'll be back for you."

"I appreciate that," said Cooper.

Sixty seconds later, Tetris was strapped to a grapple gun and Ben the State Department staffer, flashing through the leaves while the forest chattered into his brainstem. They landed on a wide branch. Tetris detached from Ben, secured the hook anew, and gave the line a good yank to verify its firmness.

When he turned around, Ben was hunched over, head buried in his arms.

"What?" said Tetris.

"I hate heights," warbled Ben.

"Least of your worries, dude. Get up."

He did have to admit that, pressed against the staffer's sweaty flank, he was not looking forward to the weeks they were preparing to spend together. If Ben couldn't meet the group's pace, he'd be blubbering dead weight, a high-caloric snack to draw hungry creatures from all corners of the forest.

He dropped Ben on one of the lower branches and began planning his ascent. The others were coming down after them. Li had just landed slightly higher up, and was berating her staffer about something. The twiggy man's head bobbed vigorously.

The others were descending slower, taking their time, probably scared out of their little civilian skulls. They were doing alright, though, it seemed like, Vincent Chen maybe the slowest of the bunch. Davis was right beneath him, with a woman from the State Department wrapped around her like an inner tube. Davis was doing great. She was almost past the face in the tree. Soon everyone would be safe. Time to head back up, maybe grab some extra gear if there was . . . face in the tree? Face in the tree *there was a giant cat-eyed face in the tree* next to Davis and before Tetris could shout, the mouth yawned, huge yellow teeth unsheathing, the jaw distending and revealing the skin that covered it to be scaly and fluid, the whole gigantic head perched atop a hideous camouflaged body that, as it moved, seemed to tear a section of tree trunk away—

Tetris fired the grapple gun. Vincent swiveled with his M4A1 held one-handed. The burst he unleashed was short, because he couldn't control his spin and swiftly rotated out of view, but it distracted the monstrosity, and the claw slicing through the air merely severed Davis's grapple line instead of tearing her and the staffer in half.

Davis plummeted. The staffer's arms windmilled. Tetris, feeling the grapple gun's hook latch around a branch, leapt into space. The wind flayed the flesh around his eyes, but he kept his tear-streaked gaze on the fast-dropping target, finessing the switch to adjust his altitude as he swung.

Davis and the aide were slowly tilting heels-over-head as they fell, and when Tetris hit them a knee struck him full in the face. Somehow, biting through his tongue, he managed to keep the starstorm at bay long enough to find a firm hold on Davis's harness, clamping through it and around her torso with both arms. In the limb-flailing shuffle, the switch on his grapple gun was depressed again, and they lurched out of the swing into a breakneck fall, until suddenly there was no more line to give.

The jolt was so violent that it broke the connection between Davis's harness and the staffer's. Tetris watched the red-haired woman tumble the final two hundred feet. It took a long time.

Blood from his truncated tongue swirled in his mouth. He hooked his harness to Davis's and pulled her up.

"No," she said.

The lizard-sphinx leaned off the tree far above them and roared, swiping at Vincent, who dangled just out of reach, grimly continuing his descent. Tetris thumbed the switch and whizzed upward. He'd never seen anything like this, never-not-once had he seen a creature resembling this one in any way, but he had a pretty good idea of how to kill it, actually, now that he thought about it. He left Davis on the branch, snatched Ben's pack, and slung it over his shoulder while the staffer gaped and gargled.

Vincent stood on a limb several stories up, trying to line up another shot, his passenger sticking off his back like some kind of shuddering growth. The lizard-sphinx clambered in slow-motion down the trunk of the tree. Tetris fired his grapple gun at the highest branch he could reach, then zipped into the air.

As he ascended, Tetris unloaded his sidearm left-handed to get the beast's attention. It turned his way, saggy mouth groping the air, and as Tetris passed overhead he tossed a brick of C4 down the wide brown throat.

When he hit the detonator, there were two explosions, the second one echoing down from above. Shit.

The spider, said the forest.

"No shibbt," said Tetris, blood clumping in his mouth. The pain was searing. A big chunk of his tongue hung loose. Hopefully that was another thing the forest could fix.

The canopy crashed and thundered. The black widow exploded through, its remaining legs stabbing hopelessly for purchase. It tumbled into empty air, rolling, the red hourglass flashing by, and somehow caught itself around a branch, landing so heavily that its swollen abdomen crunched. Meanwhile, the lizard-sphinx fled up the tree trunk, emitting horrified noises through a hole the size of an ice cream truck in its leathery neck. It spurted a highway of black blood on the bark as it went.

This has produced considerable noise, observed the forest. *I'd advise abandoning the ones in the plane and fleeing while you can.*

Tetris thought of Cooper and grapple-gunned into the canopy. There was still time.

As he reeled in the hook, trying to discern a path upward, Li popped through the foliage and landed on the branch beside him.

"Turn around," she said.

Every word hurt on the way out of his mouth. "Can't leave the otherth."

"They're not coming," said Li.

"Shtill twelve people on that plane."

"And I'm telling you, nobody else is coming."

Tetris fired through a gap in the leaves and rocketed to a vantage point above the plane. It was covered, tail to nose, by wriggling black ants. They swarmed out of the branches and onto the fuselage, while others flowed the opposite way, producing an industrious rustling buzz.

Tetris sat atop a limb and watched.

"Dead?" he asked the forest.

Almost certainly.

Li, who'd followed him up, put a hand on his shoulder.

"We can't stay here," she said.

Tetris thought he saw a human arm protruding from the mouth of one of the faraway ants.

"I'm sorry, Tetris," said Li.

"Thith ith all my fault," he said.

The hand retreated from his shoulder. "No it's not."

Tetris clenched two tight green fists.

"Pfuck," he said. He spat blood over the edge.

"Look, fuckhead," said Li, "I'm trying real hard not to yell, okay? But there are still living human people down there, and every moment you spend here puts their lives in more danger. So can you nut up and get back to work?"

But before Li could protest, he was swinging out over the plane, dropping rapidly, moisture wicking in flimsy strands from the corners of his eyes.

7

Tetris landed on the tip of the wing and waded into the ants. Antennae prodded his torso through his clothes. He fought to the emergency exit and pried at the edges with a climbing pick.

What are you going to do if you find somebody?

He planted a foot on the fuselage and pushed as hard as he could on the pick's handle. The metal groaned.

An ant stepped on his boot, lancing him through the thick leather. Tetris threw his whole weight against the pick. The door swung open of its own accord, and he stumbled backwards, tossed by a swell of ants. He glimpsed wet human eyes and a gasping mouth, and then everything vanished under a thousand thrashing legs.

The footfalls stabbed him from all sides, and he rolled, covering his face with his arms. Trampled to death by ants. How stupid was that? What had he expected? He tried striking out, but the ants didn't even seem to know he was there.

Then something ignited above him, the heat crackling away all the moisture in the air, leaving a sucking desert emptiness. Drops of molten liquid burned holes in his skin. The view through his closed eyelids was searing orange-red. He rolled away as his lips sizzled, the weight of the ants gone as if swept by a great gust of wind.

Li stood before him, holding aloft the smoking nozzle of a flamethrower.

"How many times do I have to save you before you start listening to me?"

"Where—how -"

She kicked him in the shin. "One of the crates. C'mon."

He stumbled to his feet as Li stowed the nozzle on the fuel-canister backpack.

"We're not jusht leaving," said Tetris, mouth thick with blood.

"Do you have a brain disease?"

Flames licked hungrily from the emergency exit. The interior was an inferno packed with writhing ants.

"There was a person there," said Tetris.

"Emphasis on 'was.'"

Ants streamed out of the flames, roasting in their exoskeletons, tumbling off the wing and vanishing. Tetris gave the plane one last look and secured his grapple line. Li was already descending. He burst through the leaves after her.

The black widow had deflated. Its remaining legs were curled in final agony. Trees like temple columns converged on a mess of roiling vegetation far below. The other survivors were scattered across the branches, enraptured by the flaming ants plummeting out of the canopy like a hailstorm from Hell.

As Tetris and Li rappelled the final fifty feet, a flesh wasp the size of a small helicopter buzzed slow-motion around a trunk. It headed toward Toni Davis and Ben. Tetris drew the SCAR from its sling as the wasp flashed between him and the others, but he didn't dare fire. He thumbed the grapple gun and landed heavily on the nearest branch. As he reeled in the line, the wasp dove for Ben. Through the silver fan of wings, Tetris saw the staffer recoil and pitch over the edge.

The flesh wasp chased the tumbling bureaucrat, caught him out of the air, and carried him off, weaving between trees. The giant stinger pierced flesh, and Tetris stopped watching. He landed beside Davis.

"We're leaving," he said, spitting blood. He wondered if he was supposed to feel guilty for having hoped the wasp would take Ben and not Davis.

Dr. Alvarez swung away to the east. The others followed. Davis, hooked to Tetris's harness, wore one pack and carried another. With so much weight, they bowled through the air like a wrecking ball. Tetris turned his face aside as they smashed into the next tree, but the bark tore his cheek open. He found purchase with a climbing pick and hauled them around to the nearest limb, shoulders screaming from the exertion.

Behind them, the ant-swarmed jetliner came sliding through the leaves. Flames spurted out of the wings and fuselage as the plane fell. When it hit the forest floor, it smashed straight through and into the howling depths.

Tetris and Davis joined the others in flight.

*****

They nursed sore joints and oozing gashes in a ragged circle on the forest floor. Insects buzzed and skirled, eliciting nervous swats. Li sat cross-legged against a tree and examined the flamethrower for damage. There was only enough fluid left for another few spouts. When it ran out she'd take her SCAR back from the twiggy government aide she'd entrusted it with. Speaking of which:

"Brand," she said, "if you don't stop pointing your weapon at people, I'm going to punt you into a ravine."

Evan Brand, a forty-something tetherball-post of a man, sheepishly stowed the SCAR in its sling across his back. He blinked through thick glasses and tried a tentative smile. She didn't smile back.

"We're five hundred miles from the coast," said Tetris. "That's at least four weeks, if we make good time."

Li sighted down the flamethrower nozzle. "We won't."

"Six weeks is a better guess," admitted Tetris.

"Can we survive that long?" asked Davis. Her eyes were icepick-sharp through the grime.

Tetris examined a bloody scrape on his shoulder. "The

forest can help with food and water. But it's not that simple. Our group's too large."

"Then we split up," said Davis.

"Suicide," said Li.

"Tetris could take one group," said Dr. Alvarez. "You and I could take the other."

Li tested her hunting knife's edge on her finger. "You're in no position to be guiding anyone."

"I've been training, studying—"

The knife slammed back into its sheath. "The answer is no, Doc."

Dr. Alvarez yanked her pack straps and turned away.

"The forest has a suggestion," said Tetris, "but you're not going to like it."

Jack Dano, Vincent Chen, and the Secret Service agent wore identical scowls. Their black suits, with slacks stuffed into combat boots, were riddled with gruesome tears. Those clothes would be soon be ribbons, if their owners weren't too.

"There's a neurological center two hundred miles from here," said Tetris. "It's out of the way, but if we make it, the forest could turn you into conduits like me. Then we'd be invisible."

"Absolutely not," said Jack Dano, tugging his tie knot.

Vincent drew his pistol. Li released the flamethrower and rose.

"Drop it," she said, her own pistol gliding out of its holster.

"I knew this was a trap," said Vincent.

"Drop the gun, dipshit," said Li, sighting on his forehead.

Tetris approached until Vincent's pistol was three inches from his eye.

"Think very carefully about what happens after you pull that trigger," he said.

Vincent stared back without flinching.

"Weapons down," said Davis. She spoke quietly, but the force of the command was so great that Li lowered her pistol at once. Vincent followed suit. Jack Dano tore his tie off, balled it up, and threw it into the undergrowth.

Davis glared at each of them in turn.

"No more," she said, the softness of her voice failing to conceal its titanium edge. "No more of this. Do you understand?"

Vincent looked at Tetris.

"Do you understand?" repeated Davis.

"Yes," said Vincent.

"Yes, ma'am," said Li. She holstered her pistol, unable to stymie a grin.

"Tetris," said Davis, "how much time would this detour add?"

Tetris inclined his head, listening. "About a week."

"Li," said Davis, "if we take the direct route, what's your professional opinion of the likelihood that everyone survives?"

"Negligible."

"Come on."

"We left the plane with twelve, and we're already down to ten. What's that tell you?"

"What about the forest's plan? What's that do to our odds?"

"Still two hundred miles to cross," said Li. "I'm sorry, but unless we're extremely lucky, and everybody listens to exactly what Tetris and I say, which I doubt is going to happen, people are going to die."

"Christ Almighty," said Evan Brand, wiping his glasses on his shirt, which served only to smudge them more.

"I do think Tetris's plan is your best chance," said Li.

Tetris seemed to have forgotten they were there. He was tracing lines on his palm, mouthing words they couldn't hear. The faces around the circle were a palette of misery. Li leaned on her right leg, stretching. No point in thinking about anything except the path directly in front of her.

Davis scratched behind her ear. "Who here would become a conduit if the opportunity arose?"

The three staffers raised their hands, along with Dr. Alvarez. After a moment, Davis put her own hand up.

"All that talk," she said to Li, "and you aren't willing to do it yourself?"

"I'm not the one who needs the help," said Li.

"What about you three?"

"No thank you, Madam Secretary," said Jack Dano. Vincent and the agent grunted agreement.

"We'll take the detour," said Davis. "Lead the way."

8

Douglas "Hollywood" Douglas walked along the shore in the evenings, hands in his pockets, gazing only occasionally into the blue-black depths. The Coast Guard had stopped him frequently at first, but now his strolls went largely unmolested. He did technically have clearance to be there, and anyway their job was more to keep things in than out.

He walked outside the floodlights' yellow humps, shrouded, silent, interfacing with the breeze.

A sentient forest was no surprise. He'd felt the truth congeal days after laying eyes on the first obelisk. Even before the dreams. He spat, unsure if he envied Tetris or pitied him.

Most of the dreams had involved his mother. She'd looked avian enough in real life, but in the dreams she'd had feathers sticking off her body at crazy angles, the points jammed bloody under her skin. Completing the nightmare were bulging black eyes and a beakish mouth without teeth. She never formed words, just moved her mouth and screamed, and if he struck out she exploded into polygonal shards, then solidified alternately into a towering bull, a Tyrannosaur, or an aquatic creature of unfathomable bulk. Shadow-black, spouting blood from sewer-drain apertures, howling nonsense words, the visions chased him into consciousness again and again, until one day they simply ceased.

This particular chapter of his altogether dissatisfying past was what Hollywood happened to be mulling over, chewing his lip, at the exact moment when three furtive shapes darted through the floodlights and into the forest ahead.

He pursued on the long, tan, muscular legs that were his proudest possession. People like this were all over the news since Tetris made his announcement. Deluded by pseudo-religious reverence, something like three thousand nutjobs embarked on an ill-fated pilgrimage into the forest every day. (Multitudinous public service announcements, in which Tetris himself had stated bluntly that the forest was not accepting applications, had done nothing to dissuade the legions of faithful.)

The would-be explorers had a considerable head start. Hollywood fought through the brush, following the erratic dance of their flashlight, ducking whenever a thorny branch leapt out to stab him. He was afraid to shout, and the idiots couldn't hear him over their own much clumsier footsteps, so they only noticed his presence when he finally clapped a hand on one man's shoulder.

The man screamed, wriggled out of the grip, and stumbled into a thicket of razorgrass. Then screamed even more, of course, thanks to the lacerations that immediately resulted...

"Shut the fuck up," hissed Hollywood, but it was too late.

As the leader of the group turned, the beam of his upward-swinging floodlight illuminated, ever so briefly, an image soon to be tattooed across Hollywood's brainpan: a wedge-headed titan framed between the trees, legs wider than the trunks, with an acromegalic jaw several stories tall. A fusillade of horns erupted from the beast's smooth skin with a squelch-pop like ten thousand shovels pulled out of the mud at once. The creature's breath bloomed, a green-tinged miasma, forty-five feet above the forest floor.

The sight was cut short when the expedition's leader pointed his light square in Hollywood's eyes. Hollywood only had time to utter the "G" in "Get back" when the creature unleashed a roar so astounding in volume that it literally knocked them all off their feet.

As he scrambled up and began to run, Hollywood cursed the lurid purple splotches left by the flashlight. He felt for obstacles as he went, twice stumbling on the rough ground and only barely managing to right himself.

He could feel someone else behind him, but it wasn't the man with the flashlight. The flashlight was gone, likely crushed alongside its unfortunate owner. The last of the undergrowth whipped by, and then Hollywood was out onto open ground.

The beast followed, submandibular tusks splintering through the outermost trees. Hollywood shouted, waved his arms, and ran, refusing to look back. Then came the massive percussive coughing of the Coast Guard howitzers, the shriek of their shells, and the candent flare of enormous muzzles. He lowered his head, motoring up the steep slope even as his quads begged for relief.

The earth gave its hardest quake yet, and for a moment he thought the beast had somehow leapt and landed close behind him, but when he glanced back its bulk was settling into the ground, gray flesh pockmarked by the great steel guns. Horns retracted and thrust forth and retracted again, a deranged steampunk factory of flesh and bone.

The creature knelt, bellowing, and then a missile streaked in and engulfed the lower portion of its skull in a dodecahedron of flame. The base of the jaw hit the ground a full two seconds before the rest of the head.

What Hollywood found himself thinking about, as the monster's veins proved to course with flammable blood, igniting a conflagration with an aroma not unlike that of a pig on a spit, was not the question of why such an immense creature had been prowling so close to the periphery, nor the fate of the men who had failed to escape, but the shimmering path to pecuniary success that had unfolded before him. He felt the way Rockefeller must have felt, seeing oil for the very first time. His face stretched in what he could hardly have been expected to realize was a predatory leer at the sniveling man who'd escaped alongside him.

"You know," he said, "if you're going to attempt something as ill-advised as an jaunt into the forest, the least you could do is hire a good guide."

He walked off whistling as the carcass popped and crackled behind him, pillars of sparks rising like red gods into the starless sky.

9

From the moment she carried him out of the plane, Evan Brand was in love with Lindsey Li. She reminded him of a girlfriend he'd had back in college. Two decades (had it really been that long?) hadn't dulled memories of that girl, who had been slight and pretty and had covered her mouth when she laughed despite a set of teeth that made Evan's feel yellow and crooked.

Actually, come to think of it, Li was a lot taller than that girl, and nowhere near as slender. Not overweight, just... sturdy. Li's muscles didn't bulge, but when you were pressed against her, as he had a chance to be every time they grapple-gunned in or out of the trees, you couldn't help but notice that her body was made of iron. And her hands... she could catch a cannonball with those hands.

When she laughed, she just plain laughed—no mouth-covering necessary.

So what was it about Li that reminded him of his college girlfriend? Surely it wasn't just that she was Asian. She wasn't even the same kind of Asian. He dimly remembered that his college girlfriend had been either Korean or Japanese, or perhaps (but probably not) Thai, and "Li" was (he was pretty sure) a Chinese name. Li's hair was extremely short, and she scowled a lot, which the college girlfriend had never done, scowling having perhaps been groomed out of her by a strict Korean/Japanese/Thai upbringing, although Evan believed he'd noticed Li scowling a bit less at him, recently, which was as a promising sign.

Evan was not a racist. He worked for an African-American Secretary of State, for Christ's sake! Some of his closest friends were non-white colors, and anyway he'd voted for Obama in both 2008 and 2012. Surely there was some other commonality between Li and his college girlfriend, something subtle, that was causing him to feel this way.

He stood before a wall of vegetation with his zipper down—consumed, as his urine steamed on the leaves, by this same old internal debate—when the vegetation lifted away to reveal a ten-foot-tall, corpulent blue toad, the foot of which Evan had, up until this very moment of prostate-shriveling fear, been piddling upon.

The toad peered down and produced a dissatisfied noise somewhere in the ballpark of "*Glorp.*"

Evan shrieked and turned to flee, yanking frantically

on his zipper, only to run smack into Lindsey Li.

"It won't hurt you," she said, grinning. "Just don't touch it."

"Glorp," the toad agreed.

"Oh my God, no, no no no," said Evan, scampering around her in as dignified a manner as possible.

And that was the exactly the problem, there, and the reason that his pining for Li would never go anywhere: she would never take him seriously. He was aware of his ridiculous appearance—his tattered suit pants tucked into combat boots two sizes too large, his glasses perpetually grimed over now that he no longer had anything dirt-free to clean them with, his shoulders the narrowest in a group that included four women—but even more damaging than that was his incompetence, his audible cowardice, and his overall net-negative impact on their likelihood of survival.

He had to do something to prove himself. But whenever the opportunity arose, his lizard brain took over and sent him running for cover.

The explorers had divided themselves into factions, with Jack Dano, Vincent Chen, and the Secret Service agent unifying around their distrust of Tetris, while Li and Dr. Alvarez set themselves diametrically opposed, and the others wavered somewhere in the middle. Sometimes, when an argument broke out, Evan would try to take Li's side, but for some reason this seemed to piss her off even more. E.g.:

"I'm not eating this shit," said the Secret Service agent, whose name was Clint, as he hefted a pair of the tubers the forest had recommended. "How do I know these aren't full of mind-control chemicals? Let's kill an animal and eat that."

Li took a defiant bite out of her own tuber. "How do you plan to cook an animal, genius? Think even if you can get forest wood to burn, you can roast something without the smell drawing every predator in five miles?"

"I think the roots taste great," lied Evan as he tried to choke a mouthful down. "A complex, buttery flavor with nutty undertones."

Li fixed him in one of her disemboweling glares.

"Joke all you want," she said, "but it's better than going hungry."

"I wasn't—it wasn't supposed to be—"

"You're all ungrateful shitheads," said Li, and went to check on Tetris.

*****

Night falling, the sound of crickets and things much larger than crickets, a gully-rustle of hidden canopy. John Henry wormed deeper into his sleeping bag. The leaves made a sound not unlike rainfall when a breeze went through.

The ferocious female ranger was untying her boots on the branch beside him.

"What's your name?" he asked.

"Lindsey Li. You?"

"John Henry."

"What do you do, John Henry?

"I head the United States Department of State Office of the Legal Adviser."

"You said 'State' twice."

"Yeah, that's a recurring issue. We're all employees of the United States Department of State, so."

"Not all of us."

"Evan Brand, Sasha Montessori over there... that's it, now, I guess."

"What's on your mind?"

He tightened the drawstring, shivering. "I shouldn't be here."

"None of us are particularly happy about this situation."

"No, I mean, the Secretary didn't call my name at first. She called Cooper."

Li scraped mud off her boots with a knife, a pen light held between her teeth.

"I don't know why he passed," said John Henry. "But I suppose I should be grateful."

"Let me ask you something," said Li, stowing her light and affixing the boots to her pack. "Do you think Dale Cooper was a good person?"

He thought about it. "No better than the rest of us, I suppose."

"Then why do you think he gave up his spot?"

Someone stifled a cough in the darkness.

"I imagine I'll spend the rest of my life trying to figure

that one out," he said.

*****

"Can I trust her, Lucia?"

Dr. Alvarez crunched on a tuber. "Madam Secretary—"

"For the last time, Doctor, call me Toni, or I swear to God—"

"Toni, the young rangerette is good-hearted, as much as she tries to disguise it. But she's also the most fiercely loyal person I think I've ever met."

"To her boyfriend."

"He is absolutely not her boyfriend. That I can relay with zero reservations whatsoever."

"But she'd side with him."

"Over anyone."

"Her behavior seems erratic."

"Vincent's behavior is erratic. The forest is erratic. There is nothing—and I mean nothing, Madam Secretary—erratic about Lindsey Li."

*****

It was four in the afternoon, they were stopped before a fungal wall, and the starfish were singing. Thousands of them suspended in the orange murk. Evan Brand ran his tongue over his teeth, the chipped canine with its inadequate cap. He had a rash on both arms and across his chest like a bandolier. Zits were popping out all over his face. He could feel them. There was dirt everywhere, a little less thick where he'd been scratching his rash. His white dress shirt with its neat blue grid pattern was ripped in several places and hanging away from his body. Through the gaps you could see his skin. Insects flew buzzing through the gaps and he swatted them idly, with the air of a practiced and fastidious executioner. Even his eyes itched. His glasses were nebulaic with grease and dirt. He was desperate for a chance to service himself, but of course there was never a free moment, always someone a few feet from him, even at night.

Something evolutionary seemed amiss, there, that he could be distracted from the grave business of survival by a reproductive impulse. His feet in their ill-fitting combat boots were chafed and bleeding in five or six places. His socks were yellow with sweat, brown with dirt, darker brown with dried blood, and stiff as tree bark all over. Some kind of pollen had accumulated in his hair, freezing it like a paintbrush crusted with dried honey.

He was far past dirty, to a plane of existence where his skin could have been replaced by soil and he wouldn't have noticed. The night before, he'd dreamed that mushrooms grew out of his skin, and when he pulled them off, great chunks of flesh came with. Tiny fungi dotted the walls of the weeping wounds.

*****

"You know what needs to be done," said the Secret

Service agent.

Vincent slashed at some ferns with his machete. "Take those sunglasses off. You look like a fucking idiot."

"They're prescription sunglasses, man, I can't—"

"Seriously?"

"Either everything's dark or it's blurry, okay? I pick dark."

"I'm out here with Ray Charles watching my god damn back—"

"It's not just him. Push comes to shove, we have to ice her too."

"Ice, huh? That's your chosen euphemism?"

"Otherwise she'll kill us all, man. You've seen what she can do."

"I know, okay? I know."

*****

Tetris was up in the canopy catching some sunlight when Vincent remarked to Li that the green ranger sure spent a lot of time skulking around behind their backs. Evan Brand ignored the shouting match that ensued, peering at the shifting landscape of speckled leaves. All he wanted was a slice of sky.

When Tetris came zipping out of the canopy, waving his arms, it was Evan who saw him first, which is why he was the only one with a gun out when the monitor lizard hurtled into the clearing. The lizard's blunt gray snout weaved toward Li, tongue flicking, and Evan reacted without thinking, firing wildly as he dove to shove her out of the way.

The lizard flinched under the barrage of bullets, but Evan's magazine emptied far too quickly, and then there was nothing to stop the creature from knocking him on his back. The useless SCAR rebounded from his fingers. He tried to kick as the red-ridged depths yawned before him, but with a sound like all the winds in the world colliding, the teeth closed around him at the waist. With a gentle tug, the lizard separated Evan's lower half from the rest of him. Evan watched the beast toss its head back and swallow his legs.

A jet of fire struck the creature's head. It turned and received a blast of napalm full in the face, and then it was gone, the tip of its tail flashing briefly across Evan's field of view.

He looked at the canopy. The leaves still rustled the same way, whispering over each other, oblivious. Somehow that made him feel like everything was going to be alright.

Li came into view with the flamethrower nozzle in her hand. She was saying something, but he couldn't hear anything over the wind. He looked at her and smiled.

His last thought, as the whiteness swallowed him up and carried him away, was that the reason she reminded him of his college girlfriend was the face she was making right now: the face she made when she was puzzled, squinting with just one eye and biting the corner of her lip.

10

"Don McCarthy has no diplomatic experience, zilcho name recognition, and reptilian mannerisms that would alarm all but my most delusional supporters. What on Earth makes you think he'd be a passable replacement for the most popular Secretary of State in history?"

"Sir, he's the director of the Coast Guard. You've heard what they're saying: 'the President is soft on the forest, the President let the forest murder Toni Davis—'"

"I could go out there and announce that bears shit in the woods and the House would pass a bill claiming the opposite within twenty-four hours."

"Reelection is almost upon us, sir, and the forest is shaping up to be the number one issue."

"That's your rationale? *'It's the forest, stupid?'*"

"Shouldn't you be building a case for why you're the one to deal with it?"

*****

"Douglas."

"Zachary."

"…"

"May I come in?"

"You are aware that it's three o'clock in the morning?"

"So?"

"So I'm going back to bed. Goodbye, good night, good riddance, au revoir."

"Hey!"

"Get your foot out of the door. Just because you've got more legs doesn't mean I can't kick your ass."

"Measure your words, Zip. I'm on a mission of peace."

"Peace? Man, all I've got is peace. My life is unrelenting peace. Move your foot and come back in the morning."

"I've got a job offer for you, dude."

"I don't need a job. I've got a government pension and a dumpsterload of savings."

"Zip, I am not a brilliant man. I'll admit it."

"That's brave of you."

"I am not a smart man. But even I am not dumb enough—Ow, dude, stop it! What's that made of? Adamantium?"

"Rubber tip. The pole's carbon fiber, though. Space-age crutches. I've got a second one for when I really want to move."

"As I was saying: I am not dumb enough to believe for one millisecond that you are the least bit satisfied with the legless life you're living. Nobody goes happily from ranger to invalid unless they've lost a few lobes along the way."

"I'm fucking thrilled, Hollywood. Life is thrilling. You know I've been learning other languages? Spanish, French, Mandarin."

"You know, I'm about to have a lot of time on my hands, too."

"Mhhmm."

"Rangers are going the way of the Australopithecus, thanks to your buds. May they rest in peace."

"I'm not convinced they're dead."

"Their plane crashed in the forest."

"Have you met them?"

"Anyway I'm not here to talk about them, I'm here to talk about us."

"There's no 'us.' You know I've got a ferocious animal, right? Bite through your Achilles if I say the word. Chomper! C'mere."

"I'm starting a company."

"Oh no. No no no."

"Forestourism, Zip. I don't know why nobody's thought of it before."

"I'm not going back out there."

"That's not what I want. I want you to train these morons. Like Rivers did for us."

"Then ask Rivers."

"I did. He told me to fuck off."

"Shocking."

"You can have ten percent, dude."

"Ten?"

"Fifteen."

"Fifty and I'll consider it."

"All due respect, bud, but your job's the easy one."

"Twenty-five."

"Eighteen point seven five. Final offer."

"…"

"And you gotta let me crash at your place tonight."

"…"

"Your fearsome hound appears to have forgotten how to retract his tongue."

"Fine. *Fine.* You can sleep on the couch."

*****

Repelling the monitor lizard used up the last of the flamethrower ammo. Li dumped the empty weapon next to Evan's body. He'd half-closed his eyes at the last moment, and slivers of white peeked between his lids. His head lolled when she lifted him up to get the blood-sodden pack off.

Behind her, John Henry whispered a prayer under his breath, raking his beard with quick strokes of a long-fingered hand.

"I'm next, aren't I?" he said.

"Nobody's next," said Li. "We shouldn't have been

shouting."

Vincent kicked the dirt and refused to look in Evan's direction.

"Get moving," Li barked. "We can't stay here."

Tetris crouched beside the body, muttering and stabbing his finger in the dirt. He was growing. Bulking up, muscles bulging in places she hadn't noticed before, but also growing taller. She could tell by the widening gap between the ends of his sleeves and his hands. She just hoped it was only his body that was changing, and not his mind.

Tetris closed Evan's eyelids with a monstrous green hand.

"Let's go," he said, glancing disinterestedly across her face.

She almost missed the yearning-puppy looks.

*****

"What's Montessori's role?" asked Li, cracking open a tuber. Toni Davis was the only non-ranger who exhibited zero fear of heights. When they were up in the branches, everyone else stayed strapped in, casting nervous glances at the hungry void. Davis didn't seem to care.

"She's the Executive Secretary," said Davis. A gash above her left eye was beginning to scab over. Like the others, she'd sawed her hair short with a combat knife, and rough edges protruded spikily from her skull.

Li took another flavorless bite. "I thought you were the

Secretary."

"She's the director of my Executive Secretariat."

"That clears it up, huh?"

"It's convoluted. I don't blame you for your confusion."

"She's a secretary's secretary."

"And yet she outranks everybody here but me."

"Even Dano?"

"Interdepartmental comparisons get a touch byzantine."

"She never says a word, I've noticed."

"That's because she's mute."

"What?"

"Ha! Got you. No, she's just taciturn."

"Holy shit, Madam Secretary—"

"This 'Madam Secretary' business has got to stop."

Li scratched her neck. "Yes, ma'am."

"Even ma'am is pushing your luck."

"What can I say? I'm an adrenaline junkie."

Li's eyes never stopped moving, flitting across the forest floor, idly checking for the next thing that would try to eat them. It would be dark soon. Elsewhere in the branches, the others talked in voices too quiet to make out, a reassuring tumble of human sound.

"Nah," said Davis.

"Excuse me?"

"You don't have this job because you're an adrenaline junkie. You're something else."

"What's your hypothesis?"

"I don't know you well enough to make one. But I know it's not that."

*****

"I wanted to be a ranger when I was small," said Sasha Montessori, screwing bolts into the branch to secure her sleeping bag.

"What changed?" asked Dr. Alvarez, squinting across the gap at Li and Toni Davis.

"Everybody told me it was a stupid idea."

"Was it?"

"Maybe."

"You made out alright."

"I did."

Dr. Alvarez brushed dirt off her rifle. "Seems unlike you to heed the haters, though."

"It was the last time I ever did."

*****

"When this is over," said Davis, "I want you to come work for me."

Li stopped chewing. "Hwaa?"

"You heard me."

"Sorry, ma'am, but I'm not cut out for Washington."

"You'd be surprised."

"I belong out here."

"You don't seem to be enjoying it much."

"Might have something to do with the company."

"Vincent and Dano get on your nerves. But the rest of

us?"

"I've got a lot of respect for you, Madam . . . ahem, Toni. But right now you're a liability."

A dark shape crashed through the undergrowth far below, pursued by a larger, darker shape with far more legs.

"Anyway," said Li. "You're not in a position to offer me anything. They've probably already given your job away."

"Why did you become a ranger, Li?"

"Same reason you became an astronaut."

Davis shook her head. "I'm never going to escape that book."

"*Fuck Your Opinions, I'm Doing It Anyway*," intoned Li.

"You wouldn't believe how the publisher screamed when I told him I wanted to put the F-word on the cover."

"It's the 21st century. Why do people still care?"

"I guess it makes them uncomfortable, imagining the acts the words describe."

"Tough shit."

"Well. If there's one thing I learned as Secretary of State, it's that common courtesy goes a long way."

"And that's why I couldn't be a politician," said Li.

"You wouldn't have to be a politician to work for me."

Li squinted. The dusk made it hard to discern exactly which emotions were battling it out on Davis's face.

"Why do you even like me?" asked Li. "I've been nothing but rude to you and everyone else. Not that I regret it. I just don't understand how you get from there to here."

"You're blunt. Honest. Smart, and careful. To me it seems like your talents are wasted in your current profession."

"I'm good at my job."

"I know."

A side effect of the grime was an itchiness that rose and fell when you least expected it. Li scratched her legs just above her stiff socks. The skin was raw and papery, but it felt too good to stop.

"There's nothing you need that I could do," she said.

Davis turned her sidearm in her hands and stared down the barrel. Li refrained from snapping about the danger of pointing a gun at yourself. After a while Davis stowed it and released the kind of sigh that, in Li's experience, always preceded a long story.

"When I was young, I did some tremendously stupid things," said Davis. "One of those things resulted in me getting pregnant."

This, Li knew, had not been mentioned in the memoir.

"Becoming a teenage mother would have torpedoed all my plans. No chance of college, or becoming an astronaut. But my parents were religious. They wanted me to keep the baby."

"But you didn't," said Li.

"I went back and forth," said Davis. "What pissed me off was that the father of the child got to go on with his life. For him it was a blip. A speed bump. He could cruise forward and achieve everything he wanted, as long as he made the child support payments. But for me—"

"You had the abortion?"

"I was on my way to the clinic," said Davis, "when I felt something. A kick, except that that was impossible, it was way too early. But a movement. Something. Like it—like she—was saying *stop*. And I decided that I couldn't do it. I told my mom to turn around and drive me home. I'd have the baby. I certainly would never judge another woman for the choice she made. But for me, right then, right there... I just couldn't do it."

Li could barely see Davis's face, now, no matter how she strained.

"You had the baby," she said.

"Two weeks later, I miscarried."

"Oh my God."

"This is the awful part, though: the first thing I felt, when I realized what had happened, wasn't horror. It was pure electric relief. And even though the horror set in afterward, the guilt for that initial moment has never gone away."

"I'm so sorry," said Li.

"Anyway, the reason I bring it up," said Davis, shifting on the branch, "is that she'd be about your age. So I guess you remind me of her. Of what she might have grown up to be."

The leaves whispered over one another, innumerable in perfect darkness.

"How do you know it was a girl?" asked Li.

"Good night, Li," said Davis, unzipping her sleeping bag.

11

The next time Vincent started an argument, Tetris, at this point well over six feet tall, walked up and struck him on the chin. Vincent fell like an unmoored elevator. Tetris crashed down close behind. When the agent pulled his gun, Tetris plucked it from his hand and socked him another one in the jaw.

"I could kill you," observed Tetris.

"Stand down," said Toni Davis.

"Get off him, T," said Li, SCAR pointed at nothing in particular. Her eyes were glued to Jack Dano and the Secret Service agent.

Tetris loomed over Vincent, green fists twitching.

"Please, Tetris," said Dr. Alvarez.

Blood trickled from Vincent's split lip. "Fuck you," he said, and spat.

"I'm trying to save you," said Tetris, oblivious to the blood speckling his face.

"Like you saved Cooper?"

Tetris hit him again. Vincent's head snapped back like a yo-yo. Davis rushed in and shoved Tetris aside. Tried to, at least. Tetris examined her face, then stepped abruptly away. The pistol fell from his fingers. He stalked into the undergrowth, shrugging out of his grapple gun and harness as he went.

"Good riddance," said Jack Dano.

"He'll be back," said Li.

Vincent spat red-black phlegm.

"Your boyfriend is a psychopath," he said. "We'll be better off without him."

"Are you sure he's coming back?" asked Sasha Montessori.

"He'll come back," said Li, gathering up the gear he'd dropped.

They waited all afternoon. When they made camp for the evening, Tetris was nowhere to be found. Li's relief that he'd taken some time to cool off turned to fury as she imagined him sulking in a tree somewhere.

"Do we go on without him?" asked Davis the next morning.

Li hefted the SCAR.

"I'm sure he's just out of sight," said Dr. Alvarez.

Li wanted to shout something into the undergrowth—"Hey shithead, get over yourself"—but making that much noise was irresponsible. She'd never seen him do anything this petulant. Maybe the forest was getting to him.

By lunch there was still no sign of him.

"Let's go," said Li. "He'll catch up."

It was impossible to imagine him abandoning them. And yet... two days passed as they trudged along in the general direction they'd been headed, and Tetris never showed himself.

"It's time to stop going north," said Vincent. "We've got to go east, toward the coast."

"We'll never make it," said Li.

"We'll never find the anomaly without him anyway," said Dr. Alvarez.

A pillbug snuffled in the weeds. Sasha Montessori eyed it with quiet fascination. John Henry stood as far away from the creature as possible.

"East it is," said Li, shouldering her pack.

She figured that straying off the path might lure Tetris out of his pout. Except it didn't. With each passing hour, Li grew angrier at him, and simultaneously more worried. The whole situation was bizarre. There was no explanation for his behavior. Tetris would never have abandoned them like this. Which meant that he was no longer Tetris.

One afternoon, as they passed an oblong meadow packed with brownish-yellow butter mushrooms, a scorpion burst out of the undergrowth and hurtled toward them, pincers raised.

"Go!" shouted Vincent, standing his ground, the SCAR roaring in his hands. Li had already started running, but when she saw him standing back there, something caught in her throat.

The scorpion zig-zagged closer, bullets sparking off its thick black carapace. Before Li could make up her mind, the creature reached Vincent, stinger rising in preparation for a strike. Then it lurched as if struck by a tank shell. Li caught the flash of green and knew at once that the scorpion had stepped on a creeper vine. Legs flailing ridiculously, the fearsome beast crumple-scrunched through a tiny hole in the ground.

"Grapple!" barked Li, grabbing John Henry and hooking him to her harness.

That was it: their lives had been endangered, and Tetris hadn't intervened. He was gone. Li spent the rest of the afternoon repeating it in her head.

"I think we can do this," said Dr. Alvarez when they turned in for the night.

"I think you're right," said Li, and punched her on the shoulder. Dr. Alvarez winced, but then a glow of pride swept over her face.

"Yeah," she said, dreamily.

"Don't get cocky, though," said Li as the scowl returned.

Two slow days later, their path ran up against a ravine. As they made their way along the edge, the undergrowth closed in, dense and tall, until they were forced into single file. Then the undergrowth turned to thornwall, a predatory plant that eviscerated anything unfortunate enough to run through it, and Li began to feel cornered.

She led the way. The ravine leered on her left, and the thornwall leaned in from the right. She felt a wetness on her cheek and sprang away, teetering on the edge. One of the plant's teeth had grazed her cheek as she passed. The skin was sliced open neatly, as if by laser beam, and her fingers came away with a vermillion sheen of blood.

A drop of something hit the ground and sizzled. Li looked up.

Eight huge spiders descended on cables of silk, spooling it dexterously from their rear ends. Another drop of venom emerged from an erect fang; she ducked out of the way as it whipped by to spit and smoke on the leaves.

"Run," she shouted, bolting for the end of the corridor, where the ravine fell away and the forest resumed, but already the calculations were completing in her mind, and she knew that the rearmost members of the group would never make it out in time—

*****

One week earlier

Tetris stalked out of the clearing, fists pulsing, and walked for ten minutes, muttering under his breath. Eventually he came to a steep slope and stopped. He leaned against a fallen branch and shook himself.

"Why am I so mad?" he cried. The anger was a radioactive orange filter over everything. He closed his eyes and rubbed them. Dagger-points of red light exploded and multiplied and faded and exploded again.

Ah, said the forest, *might be a side effect of bulking you up. Hormonal imbalance.*

"Why didn't you tell me?"

I warned you about side effects, said the forest. *But you told me to do it anyway.*

Tetris kept replaying the last blow, Vincent's eyes going unfocused as his head snapped back. Murdering him would have felt even better. Wet carnivorous pleasure. He remembered the taste of raw pillbug, the slimy salty blood. His stomach writhed. He really did want to beat the shit out of someone. The only thing that could relieve the itch in his rib cage would be to bludgeon something into twitching chunks of meat.

He looked around for something to kill, and, finding nothing, felt the bubble of anger dissipate and flow away on the breeze.

"Ah, shit," he said, and sighed. "Guess I should go apologize."

Three inattentive steps later, he stepped on a false patch of moss and plummeted into an inky abyss.

*****

Clear of the corridor, Li shouted and sprayed bullets and generally tried to distract the descending spiders from the half of the group who had yet to make it to safety. The spiders didn't notice her fire, even when it rang against their fat bellies, so focused were they on the meals at hand. Li wished for a rocket launcher, an RPG, a railgun, anything bigger than what she had, but it was no use. The lowest spider was about to reach Dr. Alvarez. Three long, evil legs crossed the void—

Something huge and sleek ripped between the trees and snatched the spider out of the air. A dragon, with leathery wings and clustered black eyes. Gouts of green blood arced as innumerable teeth snapped and popped. Then another dragon exploded out of the branches, and another. The air was thick with them, their wing-beats buffeting Dr. Alvarez and the others as they cleared the ravine and ran. Li saw three more of the spiders struck and then she was running too.

They skirted the edge of the thornwall and slid down a leafy slope, sucking air, ears bombarded by ferocious blasts of sound. The dragons swirled around them, leaping from tree to tree, but by some miracle no one was touched. At the bottom of the slope Li led them right, picking the direction at random, but then a five-story praying mantis burst full-scuttle to block their way. Its segmented razor-blade arms snapped out and descended and were promptly dismembered as three dragons tore the mantis to pieces. The head came bouncing off, a mighty compound eyeball crushed and leaking, as Li and the others cut back the way they'd come.

But the way was blocked, every path was blocked, the dragons had cordoned off all escape and were prowling along the ground, now, awkward the way a grounded eagle is awkward, tip-topping on limbs designed for flight and not stalking.

Li and the others stood in a bubble thirty feet in

diameter, around which dragons nipped and screeched and roared, and then out of the midst came the tall-striding form of Tetris, his clothes ripped, his pack gone, a smile splitting his face like a melon struck with a meat cleaver.

"Boy," said Tetris, wrapping Li in a hug that lifted her well off the ground, "have I got some shit to tell you."

12

"They don't bite," said Tetris as they walked, waving a dismissive hand in the direction of the nearest dragon. A pair of the creatures traipsed and hopped a few yards away, weaving in and out, sometimes dipping to poke a snout into a burrow or crevice, scavenging perpetually for their next meal. The ground trembled.

"If you say so," said Toni Davis. Beside her, John Henry quaked with fright, his Adam's apple bobbing.

"Where were you?" demanded Li.

"I fell down a hole," said Tetris, scratching his nose.

"I thought you had a supercomputer in your brain. How do you just fall down a hole?"

"I wasn't paying attention. Most of the past week was just lying there waiting for my bones to knit back together."

"Uh huh."

"Climbing out wasn't easy, I'll tell you that."

"What's with the dragons?"

"Apparently the forest has been working on a way to control them. Something to do with magnetism."

Tetris stopped walking, listening.

"Umm," he said, "I'm being told that the term is *electromagnetism*. Signals, encrypted and broadcast over low-band frequency—it's saying something about spectrum?"

He rolled his eyes at Li, gesticulating like someone apologizing for a over-long phone call.

"Okay, will you shut up? Nobody cares," he said to the air. "The gist of it is that the forest can send commands to dragons, but only dragons and not any other animals, because the dragons happen to have evolved some special receiver in their brains. So the forest can say, like, 'Don't eat those humans.'"

"But eat everything else."

"Well, they don't need to be told that part."

"Are we still going to the anomaly?" asked Dr. Alvarez.

"I say we put ourselves on the quickest vector out of here," said Jack Dano. It was clear that the miles were taking a toll on him.

Actually, everyone looked bad. Their once-crisp clothes hung in tatters. John Henry still wore his suit jacket under his harness. The fabric was riddled with thorn-holes and rips. All the moisture in his body seemed to leak out of his watery eyes and the pores on his cheeks. He was slick with misery, except for his lips, which were desiccated beyond recognition. But his biggest problem was that the mosquitoes loved him. He was lumpy all over with bites, red and bleeding from agitated scratching.

Later in the afternoon, a dull hum filled the air. Starting out nearly inaudible, it grew and grew until they could no longer ignore it.

"What's that noise?" asked John Henry.

Tetris turned pale, listening.

"Cut south," he said. "We'll try to go around."

"What do you mean, try?" asked Li as they crashed through the undergrowth. "Can't the dragons kill it?"

"Not this," said Tetris grimly. "We've just got to get out of its way."

They hurried on. After a while they trampled across a clearing of rotten pink flowers and came to a steep, rocky slope.

"We have to move faster," said Tetris, leading them down.

The hum had grown into an echoing drone. It was a monolithic wall of sound, and Li didn't want to think about what it meant. Nothing good, judging by the way the dragons snapped and roared.

The storm reached them a few minutes later. A swarm of tiny insects poured between the tree trunks and enveloped them. Clouds of black-bodied creatures drowned everything in a fury of buzzing wings. There were bugs of all kinds, from normal gnats and mosquitoes to beetles the size of baseball mitts. Buffeted by the storm, the dragons snapped and screeched and retired out of earshot, although every once in a while a tail could be seen whipping through the trees.

"How do we get out of this?" shouted Li into Tetris's ear.

"Just have to keep going!" he shouted back. "We're right in the middle!"

They soldiered on, squinting as hard black shells rebounded off their eyelids. Not all the insects stayed aloft. Li couldn't brush them off fast enough, and she'd learned her lesson about smashing them. The smeared blood only drew bigger bugs. A hand-sized dragonfly landed on her neck. She grasped its tumescent abdomen and flung it into the maelstrom.

John Henry screamed. A beetle had his earlobe in its pincers.

"Get it off get it off get it off!"

Vincent yanked the bug away. Most of the ear came with it. An impossible amount of blood poured out of the hole. John's shriek was lost in the roar of insects drawn by the steaming wound. He vanished under a writhing black shroud. The others crowded around, snatching and batting at the insects, but for every one they dislodged, another three zoomed to take their place. Li felt pincers biting into her skin but kept fighting, sweeping bugs away with both arms, and for a moment she managed to uncover John Henry's face—

His eyes were gone.

"Leave him!" she screamed. They plowed ahead, heads lowered, leaving John Henry a convulsing heap on the forest floor.

The next morning, Tetris grapple-gunned up to a branch where Vincent, Jack Dano, and the Secret Service agent were sharing breakfast. There, as instructed by Toni Davis, he attempted to apologize. It did not go well. He was forced to retreat to Dr. Alvarez's branch to avoid a full-blown shouting match.

"Ignore them," said Dr. Alvarez.

"How do I convince them that I'm on their side?"

"It's impossible."

"People change their minds all the time."

"Hardly. Take a look at our political system."

Tetris scratched a scab on his neck. "Anybody will listen to incontrovertible proof."

"There's no such thing as incontrovertible proof," said Dr. Alvarez. She slapped a mosquito.

"Doc," said Tetris, "what's your first name?"

Dr. Alvarez gave him a long look. "Lucia."

"You wanna know mine?"

"I already do."

"Oh."

"It was all over the news."

"Right. It doesn't feel like my real name."

"I like 'Tetris.'"

"When we're back on land," he said, "do you want to get coffee?"

She laughed. "Creative."

"Doesn't have to be that," said Tetris. "Go-karts? Bocce ball? What do normal people do?"

"Coffee sounds great," said Dr. Alvarez.

The days passed uneventfully. Even this deep into the forest, few creatures were bold enough to challenge thirty dragons. At night their reptilian guardians filled the air with rattling snores. Gradually, the survivors grew used to their presence. Even Li's scowl began to fade. The memory of John Henry's demise kept them grounded, but with the forest on their side, it was hard to avoid feeling that survival was well within reach.

One day they came across a spiderweb that reached up to the canopy and as far as they could see in either direction. Contours of web zig-zagged from trunk to trunk.

"Can the dragons rip a hole through this?" asked Tetris.

Maybe, said the forest, *but there are six thousand spiders waiting for it to twitch.*

Tetris kicked leaves on his way back to the group. "Have to go around. Come on."

They stayed as far back as they could without losing sight of the web. The dragons, uncharacteristically wary, retreated out of earshot. It was hard to believe that the immense white wall was biological in origin. It looked like it had been there for centuries. Maybe it had. Tetris scanned the branches as he walked, but all was still.

"How are things back home?" he asked the forest.

Not great. Lots of bluster about how I'm trying to eradicate humanity.

"Wasn't that your original plan?"

Plans change.

The web went on forever. It quivered sometimes in the wind. Tree trunks, lonely columns leading into the gray distance, showed through thinner patches in the silvery wall. Hours of hiking later, there was no sign that they were getting any closer to the end.

Two dragons crashed through the undergrowth, fighting over a spike-toothed worm. The worm telescoped and writhed. When the dragons wrenched it in half, caramel goo pumped out in viscous folds.

"That's disgusting," said Davis. Beside her, Sasha Montessori looked more fascinated than alarmed. Jack Dano leaned against a tree and sighed.

"Keep going," said Tetris. "We can rest when we're on the other side."

They passed a stand of vegetation and suddenly everything fell away to their right. The ground was sandy and smooth, with no shrubs or ferns, and the trees rose like naked stakes out of the emptiness. With nothing to block his view, Tetris could see all the dragons at once, threading through the branches in the distance. They paused occasionally to preen and stretch their wings, but they never touched the ground.

The sand kills on contact, said the forest. *Keep going. It's not much further. You'll know you're close when——*

Something sucked the forest out of his head. Tetris staggered in the silence, ears ringing.

"Hey," he said. "Hello?"

No answer. The closest dragons, the ones who'd been fighting over the worm, paused mid-tussle. Their mouths hung open. Slimy eyelids slid over featureless eyeballs.

Tetris turned to face the group as the dragons lumbered into gear. "Run!"

The first dragon hurtled into their long straggly line and snapped up Sasha Montessori. One instant she was running, slim arms motoring, and the next she'd vanished down the gullet of the tumbling beast.

Li broke away from the spiderweb and led them right, toward the sand.

"Not onto the sand," shouted Tetris, but she didn't seem to hear.

The distant dragons leapt from tree to tree, closing the gap. One of them fell out of the sky, knocked down by its comrades. As soon as it touched the sand, a hundred pink tendrils exploded out, dragging it, flailing and squawking, into the depths. Li skidded and reversed direction.

Tetris heard gunfire and turned to shout at whoever it was, to tell them there was no sense in firing, but it was too late—the second dragon fell upon the Secret Service agent and shook him vigorously from side to side. The legs detached and flew.

More gunfire. Dr. Alvarez stood with her back to the spiderweb, resolutely spraying.

"No!" shouted Tetris. A third dragon swooped in. Dr. Alvarez dove aside, covering ten feet in an instant, as the dragon careened through the space where she'd been and impacted the spiderweb.

The dragon shrieked, but couldn't free itself from the viscid silk. Above, black legs whirred into motion. A host of spiders poured down the web. The dragon's struggle only enmeshed it further, but its efforts opened a hole further down the line, and it was through this hole that Dr. Alvarez led the others. Tetris, scrambling, was the last one through.

They'd just cleared the web when more dragons flung themselves against it, tangling in the sticky strands. Tetris stopped to watch as the first spiders arrived. Fueled by a fury that went beyond hunger, the spiders overran their heaving prey. Jaws snapped and crunched, popping spider abdomens like stomped-upon yogurt canisters, but there were far more arachnids than reptiles, and the scales tipped almost immediately. The dragons vanished under a churning black tide.

Tetris fled. The others had opened a considerable gap, and when he finally caught up, crashing through the undergrowth and into the clearing where they stood, he registered just a glimpse of Jack Dano raising his pistol before hurling himself down. Three bullets ripped through the air where his head had been. He scrambled in the dirt, extending a hand to say stop, but the CIA director tracked him, finger tightening.

Toni Davis pulled her own trigger. Jack Dano, struck in the arm, spun in a tight circle. The pistol pinwheeled from his hand.

"Weapons down," ordered Davis. Tetris threw his SCAR at her feet.

"What the fuck, Tetris?" said Li.

Vincent bent over Jack Dano, ripping the shirt away.

"Is he okay?" asked Tetris.

"Bandages," snapped Vincent. Dr. Alvarez slid down and removed her pack. Jack Dano's good arm lifted, the hand grasping at nothing, then fell. He hadn't made a sound.

Tetris took a quick head count. Li, Dr. Alvarez, Toni Davis, Vincent. Jack Dano, with a bullet in him. Everyone else was dead.

"He's hurt bad," said Li, examining Dano over Dr. Alvarez's shoulder.

Davis squeezed the bridge of her nose. "I'm sorry, Jack."

Dano groaned. His head lolled to the side.

"Something cut my link to the forest," said Tetris. "It must have cut the link to the dragons, too."

"If I'd known that was possible," said Li, "I never would have let them follow us."

"I didn't know either," said Tetris. "I've never lost the link before."

A cold void throbbed in the corner of his head where the forest usually lurked.

"We can stop the bleeding," said Dr. Alvarez, leaning on the wound, hands and the cloth she held both slick with blood, "but I don't know how long he's going to last."

Vincent thumbed his pistol and glared at Tetris. Toni Davis turned away, arms crossed.

"We can save him," said Tetris. "The anomaly's only a

couple days away. The forest can fix him."

"Not a fucking chance," said Vincent. "We put him on a stretcher and head for the coast."

"He won't make it," said Dr. Alvarez.

"Tetris can't even talk to the forest," said Li. "What's the point of going to the anomaly?"

"It'll come back," said Tetris.

"You don't know that."

"It's the forest, Li. It's not going anywhere."

"And yet it's gone."

"It'll come back."

She tugged her fingerless gloves tighter. "Maybe it found another conduit."

"It went away mid-sentence."

He remembered the last time he'd convinced her to go against her instincts. Had it been a mistake, in the end?

"Trust me, Li," he said.

He could tell from her eyes that she no longer did.

13

Tetris carried Jack Dano piggy-back, arms under his skinny legs, their harnesses hooked together. Every once in a while the CIA director stirred and groaned, but otherwise he laid his cheek on Tetris's shoulder and slept.

It had probably been exhaustion as much as anything that made him pull the trigger. Tetris didn't hold it against him. Not after he'd traded his pack for Jack Dano and realized the CIA director was the lighter load. Except for the C4, they'd distributed the contents of Tetris's pack across the group. The C4 was stowed in a pouch on Jack Dano's back.

They trudged silently onward, Li in front, Tetris bringing up the rear. How many weeks had it been? How many more did they have to go?

It was odd to discover that he missed the alien presence in his head.

He kept having to squash a suspicion that Dr. Alvarez would die next. She took the craziest risks. The fact that she was alive right now was an honest-to-God miracle. When he closed his eyes, her insane leap out of the dragon's path played again and again. It was only a matter of time before gambles like that caught up with her.

He'd rather somebody else took the risk next time. He really didn't want her to die. But who would he prefer in her place? Vincent? If he had to choose... Then again, since Jack Dano was already wounded, he was probably the utilitarian choice.

What if it came down to Li and Dr. Alvarez? He wanted to believe that he'd sacrifice himself to let them live.

Okay, but say that wasn't an option. Who would he choose?

Months ago, after the forest fixed him, the path forward had seemed so simple. Talk to the press, talk to the government, convince everyone to work together, save the world. How hard could it be to unite humanity when the planet faced destruction?

Pretty hard, it turned out. He was back at square one. Worse than that: he was further away from the goal than he'd been to begin with. People were dead. His appearance had splintered the world along its preexisting fault lines. For every Toni Davis, there were two or three Vincents, people who would hate and fear and distrust him no matter what he did.

Well. Maybe if he managed to avoid punching people in the face from now on, he'd have an easier time winning them over.

When they turned in for the night, Jack Dano refused his dinner-tuber and went straight to sleep. In the morning he seemed a bit more alert, and with the increased processing power came a visible surge of fear.

By the late afternoon he'd even started to talk again.

"I am going to die," he said into Tetris's ear.

"No you're not," said Tetris.

The spindly arms tightened around Tetris's neck. "Tell my wife I died saving someone. Okay?"

"You're not going to die."

"My daughters too. Lie to them. Understand?"

"Stop saying that."

Sheafs of moss hung from the lower branches, swaying lugubriously in the breeze.

"Sorry I tried to shoot you," said Jack Dano.

"It's all good."

"If this works, and I wind up like you, will you be able to read my mind?"

Tetris scrunched his nose. "I have no idea, actually."

Dano was silent for a long time.

"What's it like?" he asked at last.

"What's what like?"

"Having that thing in your head."

"It's not so bad. I miss it, actually."

"You miss it."

"It's smart. And it seems to have our best interests in mind."

"Hmph."

"Well. I guess it would be more accurate to say that its interests happen to align with ours."

Tetris had come to rely on the forest for amplified sensory data, and as a result his own senses had dulled somewhat. At his rangering prime, he would have heard the quiet rustle of air and known that a creature was diving toward him. As it was, he didn't notice anything until a shadow swept across him, and by then it was far too late.

The blood bat fell out of the sky, thirty-foot wings braking its descent. Tetris had only taken two lunging steps when the claws closed around Jack Dano and hoisted both of them off the ground. The bat launched skyward. Tetris dangled, attached by his harness, as Jack Dano released a bubbling scream. Below, Li held her fire, afraid to hit one of them. The bat shifted its grip, leaving them momentarily unmoored, then closed its claws tighter with a wet and horrible crunch. The screams ceased. Blood poured onto Tetris's neck, back and arms. He lifted his grapple gun, watching the trees whip past as he swung uncontrollably from side to side. At this speed it was almost impossible to line up a shot.

The bat approached the canopy. Tetris figured that being soaked in Jack Dano's blood increased the chances of being deemed a meal once they landed. With one hand on the latch that held the harnesses together, he aimed the grapple gun and waited. There would only be one chance. If he missed, he'd free fall two hundred feet, which would turn him into a green pancake not even the forest could fix.

He took a deep breath, squinted, detached himself, and fired.

For a moment he floated. Then the hook caught a branch. He slammed the button; the line yanked him forward as he began to reel it in. The speed of the swing was uncontrollable. Rising, he careened toward an inconveniently-located tree—

He raised an arm to protect his face and bounced hard off the bark. The skin on his arms and legs tore open, but his bones seemed more or less intact. Rebounding, he ascended to the branch where his line was wrapped.

The blood bat screeched. Tetris peered into the canopy and caught a flash of wing. He'd jumped off just short of its nest. Blood welled from his scrapes. He remembered the C4 on Jack Dano's back and grimaced. It didn't make sense to leave it. He'd sneak into the nest, grab the pack, and find his way back to the others.

It couldn't be more than an hour until dark. He'd have to move quickly. Luckily, the bat hadn't carried him far, and he was pretty sure he knew which direction to go. He'd trust Li and the others to wait for him.

When he crested the edge of the nest, it was already deserted. Jack Dano's husk lay in the corner, the clothes tattered, two red craters in the chest where the fangs had entered. Tetris tried not to look at the face.

As he retrieved the pack, a torrent of psychic energy flooded his skull. He fell against the wall and vomited. His vision whirled. His stomach did backflips. It felt like somebody had shunted six thousand volts directly into his spinal column. He fell to his knees, clutching his head. The nausea and headache and swirling dizziness intensified until, right when he thought he was going to pass out, the assault relented.

Sorry about that, said the forest.

"Where did you go?"

No time. Get the pack and move.

*****

Li walked in tight circles, kicking the weeds.

"He's not coming back," said Vincent.

"He'll come back," said Li.

"We've had this discussion."

"I was right last time."

"He's bat food."

"Dano's bat food. Tetris just happened to be attached."

"How will he locate us?" asked Dr. Alvarez.

"He'll find us," said Toni Davis. "We're staying put."

It always amazed Li that everyone listened to Davis the first time she said something.

"Davis," said Li.

"Yeah?"

"I thought about your offer."

"And?"

The ground swelled, cakes of dirt crumbling to reveal an expanse of orange-brown exoskeleton. A giant crab, awakened from its slumber, shuddered to the surface. Li and the others scattered, firing into spiky corners of shell as the beast rose on segmented legs. Li's bullets sent an eyeball bouncing back on its stalk. The crab skittered left. Toni Davis tried to dive out of the way, but she was too slow, and one of the sharp feet pinned her thigh to the ground.

Davis didn't make a sound, just rolled away when the crab passed, clutching the wound. The crab must have smelled the blood, because after a few steps it wheeled and faced her, weathering the fusillade with one claw clacking greedily. Li fired and shouted and ran closer, but the crab only had eyes for Davis.

Then a blood-drenched Tetris came hurtling out of the trees, free-falling the final fifteen feet as his grappling hook whistled down behind him. He landed on the crab's back like a spider and slapped something against it. The crab bucked and grasped, flinging Tetris away. He slammed against a tree trunk and pressed the detonator.

A yellow-orange globe of flame bloomed on the crab's back. Li ducked as a shell-shard the size of a manhole cover whizzed past. Razor-edged fragments embedded in tree trunks like ninja stars. Then a rain of half-seared crab meat filled the clearing with a salty crustacean reek. Li's ears rang, but she rushed to Davis's side, hefting the Secretary of State up and over her shoulder. Four grapple guns popped, and they zipped into the safety of the branches as the cries of creatures drawn by the explosion began to rend the air.

Li worked to contain the bleeding, her hands crimson and slick. Davis had passed out. Her mouth hung open, and her head tilted lightly as they shifted her. Everything they wrapped around the ruined leg soaked through in moments.

"We're close to the anomaly," said Tetris. "We can get

there before dark."

"That's only forty-five minutes," said Li. Below them, centipedes fought over a crab leg. A maggoty creature slurped its sucker-mouth across gently smoking shell.

"She's not going to last through the night," said Tetris. "She's not going to last two hours, Li. We're really close. We don't have to get all the way there. Just close enough."

"I take it the forest's back?" said Dr. Alvarez.

"Yeah."

"Where'd it go?"

Tetris hefted Toni Davis and hooked her to his harness. Vincent held his head in his hands. Li watched him carefully. With Davis unconscious, he might become a threat, but that was a problem for later.

"North Korea launched a nuke at a nerve center in the Pacific," said Tetris. "Took down the whole global system. Caused a reboot, basically, the way it's being described to me."

They swung away from the chaos and descended when the coast was clear. Tetris sprinted ahead with Toni Davis cradled in his arms. Li and the others pounded after him.

When they reached a ravine, Tetris wasted no time securing his line around a tree trunk.

"Is she going to be alright?" asked Dr. Alvarez.

Davis's slack-mouthed face shone in the dusk.

"It has to do to her what it did to me," said Tetris, "so I really have no idea."

He stepped over the edge and rappelled into darkness.

That night, Li dreamed she was in Toni Davis's White

House office. The Secretary of State was nowhere to be found. Li sat in the leather chair and drank in the aroma of books and ancient furniture. After a while she noticed that she still wore her clothes from the forest and stood with a start. She'd gotten mud all over the room. She planned on sneaking out before someone noticed the mess, but when she flung the door open there was nothing on the other side but the plunging red gullet of a subway snake.

In the morning, as she waited with Dr. Alvarez and Vincent at the edge of the ravine, it occurred to Li that two universes were about to diverge. In one, Toni Davis would survive. She'd emerge, transformed, from the pit. They would make it to shore, find the nearest US Embassy, and from there Li and Tetris would have only a small part to play. Davis would retake her position as Secretary of State. She would win over the world's leaders and unify all of humanity. Then, together with the forest, they would fend off the alien invasion.

In the second universe, Toni Davis would die. But no matter how hard she tried, Li couldn't figure out what happened after that. The second future was a bleak wall of fog. Her mind hit it and glanced off.

So Li focused on the universe she could comprehend. She imagined talking to the press, discussing their journey, making the argument that Davis should be appointed Secretary again despite her green skin. She imagined working for Davis in her office, Davis practicing her speeches, her calls for humanity to confront the threat together.

When Tetris's head poked over the lip of the ravine, Li was still running through plans for the future, weighing the most politically correct response to this or that journalistic inquiry, foiling hypothetical attempts on the Secretary's life, when it dawned on her that Tetris was alone, and his arms were empty, and the universe she'd landed in was, impossibly, the second one, the one too awful to imagine.

14

Someone in the back of Zip's head kept saying in a small and garbled voice that it was time to consider maybe getting out of the shower, where he'd been for an indeterminate but undoubtedly prodigious number of minutes, and put on his clothes to go meet Hollywood in the lobby. Unless he wanted to be late. He didn't particularly want to be late, but then he didn't particularly want to get out of the shower, either. It was extremely warm in here. The hotel room was colder than the polar wastes by comparison.

He stood on his one magnificent leg, the prominent muscles of which flexed and twitched incessantly, thousands of microscopic readjustments together producing the kind of balance that two-legged people assumed without thinking. Every once in a while he touched the wall to correct himself when he tilted too far, but never more than a light brush of his fingers. Never once a lean.

Well. When he needed to turn around, for instance to turn up the heat, he had no choice but to lean. Or hold onto something and hop and twist. He did this now, hopping and twisting, wishing for the steel bar he'd installed in his shower back home, when suddenly the frictionless floor let him go.

His first instinct was to reach with the phantom leg to arrest his descent. Instead all he found was a faceful of shower curtain, followed by more shower curtain (it felt for a moment as though he were thrashing through a bottomless pit of shower curtains), followed by the cold ceramic edge of the toilet bowl.

Rolling on the fake tile, he ripped the curtain away. Water ramping off the fabric and his glistening body created a lake on the bathroom floor. He planted a hand on the toilet seat and levered himself up, then lunged into the tub and turned off the water.

The mirror revealed a bruise on his cheek already beginning to blossom. Zip toweled off and went to get dressed.

"What happened to your face?" asked Hollywood downstairs, with a grin that said he knew the answer.

Zip ignored him and tore into the free continental breakfast.

"I seem to recall you saying you didn't need a handicapped room," said Hollywood.

"Blow me," said Zip around a mouthful of croissant.

Across the room, a woman wearing nothing but yellow—yellow sundress, yellow shoes, a pair of yellow-rimmed sunglasses perched in her shiny black hair—read the newspaper while she pushed oatmeal around in a disposable bowl. The curves of her face converged on a pair of lips held in prim repose. Her chin jutted defiantly. Zip felt a pang of inscrutable sadness.

"In global news," said the television suspended behind Hollywood, "tensions in East Asia remain high following North Korea's launch of a nuclear missile into the Pacific Forest."

The spot where the prosthetic connected to Zip's leg stump was itching again. He undid the straps, letting the leg hang loose, and vigorously scratched the area beneath.

"Japanese leaders are calling for renewed sanctions on North Korea, citing the nuclear missile's path over mainland Japan as a violation of international law, but the effectiveness of any sanctions will depend on China's agreement and participation. As of this morning, Beijing still has yet to comment on the matter. It remains unclear whether the strike was carried out in cooperation with, or against the wishes of, North Korea's largest ally."

"This is exactly the kind of shit that's going to make us rich," said Hollywood, pointing at the TV.

"I fail to see how the first deployment of a nuclear weapon in eighty years could possibly be viewed as a positive."

"Well, it shows you that people are losing their minds. And since our whole business model depends on swindling crazy rich people, I'd say the future looks lucrative."

"Money won't mean anything once the apocalypse hits."

"That's exactly what our customers think. Hell, I think we should triple our rates."

The yellow-clad girl's left arm was sleeved in a complicated tattoo. Zip thought he could make out a spider entwined in the design, its long legs arcing around her bicep.

"We haven't even run our first expedition yet," he said. "What if everybody dies? Who's going to be dumb enough to sign up the second time?"

The grin spread across Hollywood's face like a rash. "Two words: security deposits. I've got expeditions booked out for months. Any time somebody gets cold feet, I—*we*—pocket two hundred grand."

Zip whistled. The girl turned at the sound and stared him down. After a moment he had to look away. When he glanced back she was perusing the newspaper again.

"Our rates are a joke," he said.

"Why do you think I'm always laughing?"

They'd rented a campground outside Seattle for the training. Hollywood drove Zip out in a pickup truck laden with supplies. On the main field, ten minutes before the trainees were scheduled to arrive, Zip jogged a few laps, testing out the prosthetic.

Hollywood slipped a flask into his jacket as Zip lurched to a halt in front of him.

"You mind if I get out of here?" said Hollywood, "I have business things to attend to."

"Business things."

"Interviews," said Hollywood. "We've gotta get multiple expeditions running at once, right? Which means we need more guides."

"As long as my cut doesn't change."

"Jeez, dude, we signed papers, didn't we? In the business world, paper is sacred."

"Uh huh."

"These guys will get a sliver of my share. I've got it all figured out. Don't worry about that. You're looking at a born entrepreneur, here."

"Douglas Douglas, CEO."

"Zachary Chase, Executive Vice President of Customer Ballbreaking."

"Does have a nice ring to it."

"Make these fuckers cry, Zip. It's for their own good."

As Hollywood pulled away, a dilapidated bus carrying the trainees came trundling around the edge of the trees. The distant peak of Mt. Rainier stared down disapprovingly. Zip waited beside the supply crates, savoring the full-bodied aroma of pine trees and earth.

The trainees spilled out of the bus talking and laughing like twelve-year-olds arriving at summer camp. Half of them wore flip-flops. Zip spotted a couple of dresses among the female recruits.

"Your clothes," he moaned.

No one heard him. The bus driver had popped open the luggage areas on the sides of the bus, and the recruits were busy sorting through their gear. One woman let out a laugh so piercing that Zip couldn't help but wince.

"Shut up," he shouted.

Thirty wide eyes swiveled to face him.

"What are you wearing?" he demanded. "How are you going to run in flip-flops?"

Nobody answered, so he focused his glare on one woman in particular.

"Run?" she said. "Today's the first day. I didn't think we'd—"

"Yeah," cut in one of the chubbier men. "Orientation, right? There's never—I mean, it's the first day."

Zip massaged his jaw. Their clothes were spotless and visibly expensive, as were their gear bags and tents. The confidence with which they held their pale millionaire bodies made him want to grab and shake them one by one. Made him want to pummel them until they sniveled and groveled at his feet.

"Drop the bags," said Zip.

"I thought you wanted us to change shoes?"

He stared at her, fighting the red film settling over his vision.

"If it's running you intend us to do," said a man in his fifties, "you might could allow us to don appropriate attire beforehand."

"Fine," said Zip. "You have three minutes to change."

"Where?" cried a woman in a floral dress.

"Three minutes!"

He walked away, counting the seconds under his breath. These people would never respect him the way he'd respected Rivers. They were too entitled, too used to getting exactly what they wanted. He'd make them miserable. Break them down. Tear their egos to shreds and stuff the shreds down their mottled, fleshy throats.

"Six laps," said Zip when the group had reassembled. "The bottom five do a seventh lap while the rest of you rest."

The trainees gaped.

"Well?" he said, pointing at the edge of the field.

"What," said one woman, "you mean, like, now?"

"Yes. Now."

One by one, they began to jog.

"Faster," shouted Zip.

It was like watching a herd of well-fed antelope wobbling toward a watering hole. Zip turned away, stomach wriggling with rage. He wasn't sure why he was so mad. Maybe it was all these perfectly functional legs attached to such pampered, wasted bodies.

"I don't envy you a bit," said the bus driver, and whistled.

Zip kept them moving all afternoon. When they weren't running, they were alternating push-ups and sit-ups, or hiking along the trails that encircled the campground. When the sun began to dip beneath the treeline, the trainees were considerably quieter than they'd been that morning, and had acquired a satisfactory coat of filth. Zip rounded them up near their luggage for a final word as Hollywood's pickup came rumbling around the corner.

"Congratulations," he said, "you're all hopeless."

The general response to this statement was a groan.

"I mean that seriously. None of you are qualified for this. Odds are pretty good that you're going to die. But if you work hard—if you work hard, and you listen to me—I may be able to improve your chances. A little."

The pickup truck rolled to a stop. Moths danced in the headlight beams.

"You're not sleeping here?" warbled one of the trainees, empty tent bag drooping from his hand.

"What a hilarious question," said Zip as he hauled himself into the truck.

"What about bears?" asked another recruit.

Hollywood leaned across Zip and beamed.

"Ladies and gentlemen," he said, "if you're afraid of bears, the forest will make you shit your pants."

Zip slammed the door as they rolled away.

"How'd it go?" asked Hollywood.

"They're hopelessly out of shape and grossly incompetent, I hate them, and I'm pretty sure they hate me too."

"Excellent," said Hollywood. "How much progress do you think you can make in a month?"

"Absolutely none," said Zip.

"Well," said Hollywood as they rattled over a gulch, "as long as they end up thinking they made progress, I suppose that's all that matters."

Zip stared out the window into the shifting green darkness.

Back at the hotel, he went looking for the girl in yellow, but the bar was deserted. He didn't see a single human being on the way to his room. The hotel was quiet as a morgue, although a slight hum filled its halls. A gash of plywood peeked through his door above the card slot. He had to swipe five times before it let him in. Inside he stripped to his boxers, flung everything in a pile, and fell into bed.

Five minutes later, somebody knocked on the door.

"No thank you," said Zip, and rolled over, pulling the blankets tighter.

The knocks came again, twice as forceful as before.

"Go away," shouted Zip. Probably a drunk who'd picked the wrong room.

The knocks kept coming.

Zip yanked the cord to turn on the light and leapt out of bed. He hopped across the room, not bothering with the prosthetic, and tugged the door open. In the hall stood a small man with a ferocious nose.

"Hello," said the man.

"What do you want?"

"My name is George," said the man.

"Thanks for sharing. What do you *want*?"

"I would like to join your next expedition."

Zip scratched the back of his head.

"Talk to my boss," he said.

"I did," said the man. "But he wasn't interested."

Zip snorted. "If you had the money, I don't see why he'd turn you down."

"That's the thing."

"Well, then, buddy, you're out of luck. We're not a charity. We are, in fact, the polar opposite of a charity."

"Please."

"Look, you're actually the lucky one, okay? All these other people—they're fucked. You realize that, right? They're almost certainly going to die. This whole thing is a scam. We just figured we'd try to get some money out of them before they went out there on their own."

"I know it's dangerous."

"Jeez, man, the answer is no. I'm sorry."

The man's eyes watered. He wiped them curtly on his sleeve.

"Did you know my son?" he asked.

Zip leaned his head against the doorframe. "Who?"

"Because you were a ranger, I mean. I think they called him Tetris?"

Zip stared.

"He was the one—you know, the green one. The one in the news."

"Holy shit," said Zip. "You're Tetris's dad?"

"You knew him?"

"Now I definitely can't let you go."

"No!"

"Jesus, man, just because he might be dead doesn't mean you have to follow him down."

There were real tears in the man's eyes. He kept swiping at them, but it only smeared the moisture across his face.

"I just want to say goodbye," he said.

Zip considered that for a moment. "How's going into the forest supposed to help?"

Somewhere down the hall, an ice machine gargled.

"If part of the forest wound up in him," said Tetris's dad, "don't you think it's possible that part of him wound up in it?"

15

"Him again?" said Hollywood when he arrived at the hotel and found Zip and George sharing breakfast.

"Hear me out," said Zip.

The smile rotted and fell away. "Absolutely not."

"It's Tetris's dad."

"I don't care if he's the Pope. No money, no trip. It's that simple."

Zip pushed a hand through his hair. "I knew this would happen."

Hollywood squinted but didn't say anything.

"Take his ticket out of my share," said Zip.

"Ha!"

"I'm serious."

"You want to pay two million dollars to probably get your best friend's grieving father killed? Shit, Zip, if you want him dead that bad, I know people who'll handle it for four hundred bucks."

"Just promise you'll keep him alive."

"I'm going to try to keep them all alive, *Zachary*. That doesn't mean it's going to happen."

"Sit down," Zip said to George. George remained standing.

The scrambled eggs had lost whatever watery flavor they'd had to begin with. The breakfast rolls tasted like ash. Zip pushed his plate back. The girl in the yellow sundress was nowhere to be found. She'd probably checked out. Somehow the fact that he'd never see her again seemed like the real tragedy in all of this.

When they pulled up to the training camp, Zip almost laughed at the tents, which were clumped so close together that the trainees were having trouble extricating themselves.

"Who's he?" demanded someone, pointing an indignant finger at George.

"He showed up late," said Zip.

"Where's his tent?"

George's possessions were limited to a ratty backpack and a green sleeping bag.

"Somebody gets to share," said Zip.

Groans.

"Whoever lets my good friend George sleep in their tent can skip the first two laps," said Zip.

Nobody volunteered, although a few trainees winced, stretching creaking muscles.

"Let's try that again. In five seconds, you're all running laps until somebody volunteers."

A man with thick eyebrows proffered a pudgy hand. Zip clapped once, a gunshot-sound. Several trainees jumped.

"Magnificent. Show him the way."

George tiptoed through the maze of stakes and tent-lines after the bushy-eyebrowed man. The others grumbled. Zip felt a speech coming on.

"Sixty million generations ago," he said, "your ancestors were snot-nosed rats sniveling in tunnels carved from dinosaur shit. Those ancestors relied on fear to survive. Nothing has changed. I can fill your brain with knowledge, but the most important trait to foster is cowardice. In the forest, you are prey. You are a cocktail sausage. A couple of you," he paused, scratching his nose, "are sticks of beef jerky, or hemispheres of ham. But all of you are food. Is that clear?"

He could tell that they wanted to roll their eyes, but were prevented from doing so by the desire to avoid additional laps.

Well. He'd never paid attention to the speeches Rivers gave, either. Although then, at least, he'd had the excuse of being a teenager.

*****

The man who'd agreed to let George sleep in his tent was coincidently also named George, although everyone called him by his last name, which was Matherson. He owned a chain of dealerships that sold tractors, forklifts, cherry-pickers, and other equipment of similar scale. His net worth was around fourteen million dollars; he was spending two million on this expedition.

Sherry would never would have allowed it.

He was alone in a fast-decaying world. People were loud and selfish, and more and more of them were adopting ideas he found repulsive. He quarantined those trends in the corner of his brain labeled "Concerning But Ultimately Not Worth Worrying About." Though it gave him great satisfaction, during election season, to stamp a big red "NO" on all the depravity. Still, at the end of the day, it didn't bother him. It didn't. People were going to do whatever they were going to do. He just wished they would stop shoving his face in it.

The worrying thing was that his side kept losing, and sooner or later he figured he was going to have to choose between presidential candidates who BOTH thought it was okay for men to marry each other, and women to recklessly murder their babies, and when that happened it would probably sicken him so much that he'd retreat from politics entirely, and cancel his cable subscription, and live out the rest of his days on the porch of his ranch house, watching the wind ruffle the trees and nursing an American beer while his Mexican gardener (the legal kind) drove neat loops around the enormous lawn in a high-end mower taken directly from the stock of Matherson Mid-sized Machinery.

At least that had been the plan until the forest business took off. Matherson had seen the Green Ranger on television and known at once that he was staring at the next step in human evolution. Online he found hundreds of forums obsessing over the forest and the Green Ranger himself. "Immortality" was the word being bandied about. Rumormongers said that the forest could mend wounds, cure illnesses, and bestow eternal youth. Some even claimed that the transformation allowed you to read minds. The nuttiest of the nutty went so far as to suggest that the transformation enabled photosynthesis, so that you'd never have to eat again.

He'd tried to squelch the idea. Opened two new dealerships, commissioned television ads, stayed up late crunching numbers... but there was only so much to do. He always had time left over. He took a month-long vacation, sat around Italian cafes trying to look comfortable, and snapped pictures of the idiotic tourists pretending to prop up the Leaning Tower of Pisa. The trip only stressed him out more.

He even gave online dating a try, but every woman who expressed interest was chubby, ugly, or both. This infuriated him. He had money, right? Where were all the gold diggers?

The longer it continued, the more the purposeless thumb-twiddling life began to grate on him, and the larger the Green Ranger loomed in his imagination. He read dozens of books about the forest, binge-watched old ranger programs, and hired a personal trainer. Thirty pounds slipped off him in four months, leaving him a spry two hundred and twenty, practically an Olympic long-jumper, or so he quite humorously remarked to his employees.

Once the idea took root, it was impossible to think about anything else. So when Matherson heard about Hollywood's program—run by real rangers!—all the self-control came crumbling down at once.

*****

"Man, I'd give three branches—bank branches—for a decent rib eye," said Bob Bradley, prodding the Vienna sausages that wallowed in yellow preservative goo on his damp paper plate.

The others ate in silence, watching the campfire kick up sparks. George Aphelion, forty-nine years old, matted clumps of hair protruding from the edges of his sweat-streaked bald spot, shins borderline splinted, nose jutting huge and defiant as ever—father with a grand total of zero extant children, down from a peak of two—sniffed one of his own Vienna sausages, steeled himself, and wolfed it down whole. The processed meat cylinder hit his stomach with gruesome force. He gulped water from a canteen.

"Yes, three branches," said Bob Bradley, examining a sausage's pallid casing. "Three branches. I think I could spare those."

He peered around the somnolent circle and decided to make it absolutely clear:

"I've got seventeen, you know, so I really think I could spare three without much trouble. For a good well-done steak."

Rosalina, she of the withering laugh: "Branches?"

"Bank branches," repeated Bob Bradley, beaming.

"How cute," said Rosalina. "Do you give out credit cards with little panda bears on them?"

The smile curdled. "No."

"Now, my husband," said Rosalina, shoulder-patting her husband, whose name nobody knew—he was "Rosalina's husband" to them, which seemed to suit him fine—"my husband owns a law practice. How many law offices do we have, again, honey?"

Rosalina's husband grunted.

"That was it. Fifteen! So—not quite as many."

"No, not quite as many," said Bob, putting his plate down and crossing his meaty arms.

"Of course, it's not a one-to-one comparison. A good law office... well, I don't have to tell you how much money a good law firm pulls in. You're an economically-inclined individual, Bob, ah ha ha ha!"

George Aphelion cleared his plate. He breathed deeply, trying to calm his wriggling stomach.

"Although I don't think my husband would trade even one of those law offices for something as ephemeral as a steak. He built them from nothing, you understand. Pulled himself up the mountain by his bootstraps. Those offices mean an awful heaping lot to him!"

"I built my business from scratch as well," said Bob in

a not-quite whine. "I wouldn't actually trade—that's ridiculous."

"Banks," said Rosalina. "What a nice business. Fun! You have those little pipes, right? The ones that shoot capsules back and forth?"

"Of course we have those," said Bob, stabbing a sausage so hard that two tines of his plastic fork went careening into the darkness. "Those are an integral element of the modern banking business model. We'd be fools not to leverage such technology."

"How fun," said Rosalina.

Across the campfire, George Matherson, of Matherson Mid-sized Machinery, chewed and swallowed and chewed and swallowed. He'd learned early on that his own fortunes were pitiable compared to those of the more-successful trainees. When the others asked him what he did, he told them curtly that he ran his own business, and left it at that.

"Well," said Rosalina, "We've finally learned what everyone does for a living."

The fire crackled and spat.

"Except you," said Rosalina, pointing a long finger at George Aphelion, who froze with a pilfered sausage (Bob's) halfway to his mouth.

"Um," said George.

"What did you say your name was, again?"

"George," said George.

"What do you do for a living, George?"

He placed his fork down. "I'm a toll booth operator."

Open mouths coruscated in the firelight.

"I don't like it very much," he offered.

"Well," said Rosalina, affixing a smile to her plasticized face, "I suppose you meet a lot of awful interesting people. That must be nice!"

Rosalina's husband made a noise like a constipated hippopotamus.

"Not really," said George. "You don't really get to meet anyone, to be honest. They drive right by."

The corners of Rosalina's eyes scrunched up. "Well, no, I'm sure they just, hmm. But how good of you, though, looking out for the common man? Somebody has to do it, after all. Somebody must. Maintain the integrity of our highways, and so on."

"How are you paying for this?" blurted Bob Bradley.

"Bob!" said Rosalina, hand fluttering before her throat.

"I'm not," said George, and flung a fistful of pine needles into the fire.

"That's not fair," said Matherson. The others sounded their agreement. "I've got half a mind to demand a refund."

"The instructor's paying my share," said George.

The murmurs intensified.

"Playing favorites," said Bob. "I should have known. That slimy, one-legged little-"

"Hey," said George.

Bob shut his mouth.

"Easy, boys," said Rosalina. "I'm sure there was a good reason for Mr. Chase's largesse."

She eyed George, hoping he'd share, but the toll booth operator only stared into the fire.

16

After they completed their training, the would-be-adventurers were allowed two weeks to recuperate. They exchanged handshakes and back slaps in the parking lot before climbing into turbocharged European sports coupes and roaring away. George Aphelion sat on the curb tossing a pebble in the air.

"Go home, George," said Zip.

"Home has been repossessed," said George. The pebble flew, hung at its apex, and plummeted back to his hand.

"Whatever," said Hollywood, and turned to go.

Zip sat on the curb beside George and watched two ants try to drag a dead beetle out of a crack in the asphalt.

"You think we're ready to go in there?" asked George.

Zip said nothing. The ants had the beetle on the edge

of the crevice. They tugged and tugged. One of them lost its grip, and the payload tumbled to its original position. The ants climbed down and resumed their efforts.

"I'll take that as a no," said George.

"Hungry?" asked Zip.

George nodded.

"Come on," said Zip, and levered himself to his feet.

They went to Thai Restaurant and sat on the patio. It was the kind of cloudy day that looked like it should have been colder than it was. George flipped through the menu, frown lines engaged.

"Do they have a hamburger?"

Zip laughed. "Please."

"I don't like ethnic food," said George.

"How Midwestern of you."

George's mouth twitched.

"Look," said Zip, "just get pad Thai. White people love pad Thai."

George found it in the menu. "Not a fan of shrimp."

"Get it with chicken. You'll like it. It's like sweet and spicy pasta."

The waitress filled their glasses with clinking ice water.

"We used to go here all the time," said Zip.

George played with the paper tube from his straw, wrapping it around his index finger.

"Tetris didn't like 'ethnic food' either. I always blamed it on y'all."

George didn't respond.

"I'm just kidding, man, sorry," said Zip.

"I wasn't a very good father," said George.

Zip blew air through pursed lips. "And here we were, having such a normal conversation, too."

A group of sparrows hopped and twittered on an empty table. Every once in a while, a gust of wind sent them fluttering, but they always returned, rearranging their positions, little heads rotating inquisitively.

"Being a parent is hard?" said Zip. "Is that what you want me to say?"

George crushed his straw-paper spiral into a ball.

"I can't shake the feeling that Tetris isn't dead," said Zip.

"Don't taunt me."

"He and Li chased me down a chasm and carried me two weeks out of the forest. A plane crash is nothing."

George examined his chopsticks. Tried to hold them, failed, and set them next to his plate.

"I see a little bit of that in you," said Zip. "The stubbornness, I mean."

"Will stubbornness help me survive?"

"Absolutely not. Have you listened to anything I've said?"

"The louder bits."

"Look," said Zip, "here's the most important lesson. You ready?"

George nodded.

"If you ever have the chance to risk your life to save someone else," said Zip, "let them die."

George twisted his nose histrionically when he tasted

his pad Thai. Then he cleared his plate, scraping up every last bit of noodle and sauce, and chewed mournfully on a toothpick until Zip ordered him a second serving.

*****

Counting George Aphelion, there were sixteen men and women in the first batch of explorers. Eight of them went into the forest with Hollywood; the other eight went with a bearlike ranger named Bo Jr.

Both Georges were in Hollywood's group, along with Bob Bradley, Rosalina Waters, and her husband. There was a young British millionaire named Jeremy Mitchell, who never stopped smiling, and a burly man named Roger Murlock, who communicated largely in grunts, and therefore got along swimmingly with Rosalina's husband. They'd often been seen sharing a cigar during boot camp evenings, sitting a comfortable distance away from one another on a thick log. The final member of the group was a man named Frank, whose laserlike attention to Zip's words during training betrayed a military background. Frank was not fucking around. He was the first trainee to master the grapple gun, and the only one who displayed any proficiency whatsoever with a firearm (everyone had been issued a 10mm handgun as something of a formality).

It was illegal for civilians to enter the forest from the American coastline, so Hollywood drove them across the

Mexican border in a dilapidated bus. Bo Jr. followed in a truck laden with supplies, his windows down, strands of reggae blasting out and sometimes wafting through the rear windows of the bus.

"Why didn't you hire a driver?" asked Bob Bradley, appalled to see his expedition's leader driving a bus like a common laborer.

"I've got my margin to think of," said Hollywood.

This earned begrudging nods from the self-made businessmen among them.

"Can we stop by the outlets in San Ysidro?" asked Rosalina. "My mother used to take me there on weekends."

"Nope," said Hollywood, and thumbed a CD out of a black plastic carrying case. "Everyone sit down and shut up."

The rest of the drive, he bombarded them with Outkast, the Jurassic Five, and A Tribe Called Quest. The only explorer who nodded along, even mouthing a few of the words to "Hey Ya," was Roger Murlock, earning him a wounded glare from Rosalina's husband.

South of Tijuana, Hollywood pulled off onto a dirt road and rumbled toward the coast. The Mexican coastline was dotted with tiny huts, each with a single satellite dish. Hollywood parked beside one of these outposts and jumped out, speaking in rapid but broken Spanish to the Mexican Coast Guard representative who came out to meet him. After everyone had trickled out, the guardsman leapt into the driver's seat and drove the bus away.

"He stole your bus!" said George Matherson.

"It's his bus, Einstein," said Hollywood.

Matherson seemed unconvinced.

As George Aphelion stood before the towering treeline, ancient memories barraged him, childhood trips with his parents into the Blue Ridge Mountains, camping in Shenandoah National Park... streams and waterfalls and trees that had seemed as titanic at the time as the ones in front of him now.

Looking into the forest was like staring down the green-black gullet of infinity. So why wasn't he afraid?

He breathed deeply as they hiked. The ground sloped gently beneath his feet. Thick, earthy air expanded long-withered regions of his lungs. Birds and insects whizzed and sang all around them, and squirrels caroused in the undergrowth. A goofy grin crept across George's face. The forest felt like home.

Nothing happened the first two days. Hollywood led the way, chewing bubble gum, pointing out traps for them to avoid. The first creeper vine appeared halfway through their second day; the first spider trapdoor, just before their second evening.

On the third day, they came across a stand of stunning turquoise flowers.

"Don't touch those," said Hollywood as he passed.

Jeremy Mitchell, the wily British millionaire, winked at the others and bent his head to take a great whiff.

"Simply marvelous," he whispered, knobby fingers brushing the petals.

The next morning, a wild boar the size of a post office came rumbling around a stand of razorgrass.

"Grapple guns!" barked Hollywood, aiming and firing in a single smooth motion.

Blood thu-thunked in George's head. Like the others, he'd fired a grapple gun hundreds of times in training, but the mountain of pigflesh growing in his peripheral vision had erased all confidence. He aimed, bit his tongue, and fired.

The hook crossed the vertical space in slow motion. It paused at its apex and descended, wrapping around the branch.

George slammed the button, bracing himself, and welcomed the tug against his harness as the grapple gun rocketed him skyward. Safe high above, he conducted a quick census. Eight, counting Hollywood and himself. Where was the ninth?

Gunshots popped. Far below, Frank, who'd shown so much promise in training, stood suicidally firm, grapple gun untouched, firing his pistol two-handed, the gun kicking up with each shot. He pumped a full magazine into the charging boar. Then, as he reloaded— stupendously calm, hands moving deftly, no hint of fear— it hit him.

The tusks weren't even necessary. The boar's snout knocked him down and under the hooves as the beast tried and failed to slurp him up on the first pass. By the time it wheeled around, Frank was bloody trampled meat, which the boar promptly tossed down its throat.

"Fucking idiot," said Hollywood.

The boar stared blearily up at them. It snorted. Pawed the ground. Nudged their tree with its snout. Then, after one last baleful glare, it departed, gargantuan hindquarters rolling, brown fur bristling over prodigious slabs of muscle.

"Stupid motherfucker," said Hollywood, wiping his pale-green face. "You stupid, stupid motherfucker."

17

Jeremy Mitchell soon stopped smiling. He staggered along, eyes glazed, until Hollywood asked him what the matter was. The British millionaire prepared to speak, and an army of tiny black beetles came swarming out of his open mouth.

"You touched them!" yelped Hollywood, leaping back as Jeremy convulsed to the ground. "You fucking Neanderthal! I told you not to!"

As Jeremy gurgled and wriggled, his skin erupted from head to toe, innumerable beetles fighting their way free. Hollywood raised his SCAR several times, but didn't pull the trigger, though it clearly pained him. As the others backed away, scratching arms and scalps that suddenly itched furiously, Hollywood knelt a safe distance from Jeremy and bowed his head.

"I tried to warn you," he said.

Roger Murlock stepped up and put a bullet through Jeremy's skull. Two mornings later, when a flesh wasp snatched Murlock, stung him, and dropped him in a gully, a larva wriggling in the depths of his paralyzed gut, Hollywood returned the favor.

On the sixth day, a pack of squawking velociraptors hurtled down a slope to their right, feathers rustling. Sickle claws flashed. Three feet high, the reptiles would have posed relatively little threat if they hadn't come in such astounding numbers. Hollywood sprayed down several as they descended, then drew an enormous hunting knife and launched into the fray. The silver blade flashed from target to target like a bolt of steely lightning. The ferocity of his attack, combined with frenzied pistol fire from the other explorers, quickly routed the raptors, sending them screeching into the jungle, but not before Rosalina's husband had his throat ripped out.

Bob Bradley missed a grapple and was torn in half by a pair of scorpions.

Rosalina tripped on a leaf-scattered slope and tumbled down, landing against a funnel-shaped silvery web. George Aphelion, standing at the top of the hill, battled an urge to follow. Before he could decide, a green-bodied spider came around the edge of the web, and the question of whether to risk his life was rendered wholly moot.

George Matherson dreamed of his dead wife. She stood in a undulating field of tall grass and smiled wider than he'd ever seen her smile. The sun beamed down and set her hair ablaze. He went to her, crying, but just as he reached his arms out to embrace her, he woke to the same dusky forest. Two hours later, he stepped on a creeper vine and vanished forever into the abyss.

Just like that, Hollywood and George Aphelion were alone.

*****

"I really thought I could do it," said Hollywood, legs dangling off the branch.

George Aphelion examined a gigantic bug bite on his arm. "Keep them alive, you mean."

Hollywood spat off the edge.

"You thought you could keep them alive," said George.

"No. God, no."

"Then what?"

"How did they get so rich if they were stupid, huh? Answer me that."

George scraped the bug bite with a couple of fingernails. Dark blood oozed out. He didn't feel anything at all.

"It's like when you make up your mind to dump a girl," said Hollywood, tugging at a loose edge of bark. "You get all the reasons straight in your head. Logically, you know it's correct. You know you're supposed to do it. It's as good as done. And then, the moment you start talking to her, you feel that sickness in your stomach. Like you swallowed a snake."

The forest trilled and buzzed.

"You thought you could keep them alive," said George, "but you couldn't."

"No," said Hollywood. "You're not listening to me."

He took out a piece of gum and bit into it viciously.

"I don't understand," said George.

"It's not my fault," said Hollywood. "Why does it feel like my fault?"

He'd managed to pull a strip of bark free, and was turning it around in his hands.

"Nobody forced them to sign up for this," said Hollywood. "They were going to do it no matter what."

"Hmm," said George.

Hollywood threw the bark away and pressed knuckles against his eyelids.

"I knew they were going to die," he said, so quietly that George barely heard him.

George closed his eyes and tried to hear the blood pulsing through his temples.

"We go back tomorrow," said Hollywood.

"No."

"Excuse me?"

"You haven't taken me to the forest."

"Where do you think you are, genius? The moon?"

"I mean the real forest. The part that can talk to me."

Hollywood laughed sadly. "I don't know where that is."

"Your brochures—"

"Said we could give you a chance of turning green. If the forest 'chose' you. Which, for all we know, is true. But our whole plan was to drag you out here, traipse around for a few days, then drag you back."

"I'm going to keep looking," said George, eyes stinging.

They listened to the forest move.

"Why?" said Hollywood eventually.

George squeezed blood out of the bug bite and stared into the distant canopy, where the leaves blended together into a deep green paste.

"To say goodbye to my son," he said.

Hollywood stayed quiet for a long time. Eventually he shifted, found a more comfortable seat on the branch, and crossed his arms across his chest.

"There might be a way," he said.

George watched him from the corner of his eye.

"On my very first expedition," said Hollywood, "Tetris and I found something out here."

Far below, a three-story praying mantis picked its way through the undergrowth, oblivious to their presence.

"Since then, I feel a little pull. A tug in the back of my head. It's brought me to monoliths, tablets, pyramids... I could take you. Maybe then, if you got real close, you'd be able to talk to it."

George closed his eyes. Frank, Murlock, Matherson, Bradley, Mitchell, Rosalina and her husband: ribbons of meat. Did he want to end up like that? He thought about the future awaiting him on shore. It was impossible to picture. When he tried, his imagination ran up against a concrete wall.

Somewhere above, a birdlike creature unleashed a string of high, clear notes.

"Take me," said George.

*****

It rained for days, mercilessly, relentlessly, a flood that sorted itself through the leaves and fell in pummeling columns to the forest floor. Hollywood and George didn't exchange a word the whole time. Their ponchos were inadequate. The air hung heavy with moisture, sticking to their skin, pearling along spiderwebs, dripping languidly off the leaves of giant forest plants. Mushrooms sprouted everywhere.

While it rained, the forest slept. They passed the carcass of a scorpion, untouched by scavengers, its stinger draped limply against a fallen tree.

George's skin, perpetually damp, began to itch. He dreamed that it started sloughing off, leaving him a red-muscled freak, his bare eyeballs rolling in their sockets. Still the rain fell. The many intermixing sounds—dull patter, restless leaf-rustle, lurking distant roar— burrowed into his ears, so that he couldn't hear them unless he really focused.

One day, as he passed beneath a thin strand of plummeting rainwater, George slipped on a wet leaf and went sliding toward a chasm. As he scrambled for purchase, hurtling down the slope, a fleshy pink creature heaved itself out of the ravine and opened its mouth to receive him. The creature's eyeless head was rimmed with hundreds of undulating flagella. The throat beyond the mouth was ridged and bottomless. George dug his feet in uselessly, watching the demon-slug grow larger, and then Hollywood came sliding headfirst after him.

The ranger slammed against George's back, wrapping an arm through his harness. They spun, accelerating despite George's frenzied kicks, and then something yanked hard against him: Hollywood had somehow landed a grapple. They leapt skyward, George dangling inches above the blind worm's head. One of his feet kicked a wriggling flagellum, and the beast reacted instantly, lunging into the air.

As the hot, reeking breath enveloped him, George hugged his knees to his chest. For a moment they were inside the worm's mouth. The round lips puckered inward. Just before the aperture closed, Hollywood and George slipped through.

Jaws clamped around nothing but air, the creature fell, pink bulk quivering, into the chasm.

George and Hollywood rested on a branch high above and savored the clean, sweet air.

"Well," said George after a while.

They were drenched in rainwater and slug slime. George scratched his nose.

"I have no fucking clue why I did that," said Hollywood.

George stared at his hands, trying to stop them from

shaking. "I'm glad you did, though."

Hollywood spit off the edge.

"Yeah," he said, "me too."

Two hours later, the rain stopped. They found a branch over a wide ravine, beneath a sparse section of canopy, and lay there sunning themselves. Hollywood stripped to his underwear and spread his clothes out to dry. George followed suit. They stayed there all afternoon, listening to nothing, drinking in the sunlight that filtered through the leaves.

"Do you want to hear a joke?" asked Hollywood.

George shrugged.

"A man has three young daughters," said Hollywood. "One afternoon his oldest comes up with a puzzled look on her face.

"'Daddy,' she says, 'why did you name me Rose?'

"'Well,' he says, 'when you were born, a rose petal drifted down and landed on your head.'"

George watched the leaves rustle through one another.

"The little girl is satisfied by this answer. She skips away. A few minutes later, the next-oldest daughter comes up.

"'Daddy,' she says, 'why did you name me Daisy?'

"'Well,' says the man, 'when you were born, a daisy petal floated over and landed on your head.'"

Hollywood's voice was low and smooth, the contours of the story slipping off his tongue with the ease of endless practice.

"This daughter is satisfied too. She skips away, singing,

curls abounce, et cetera. The father smiles and returns to his newspaper. Before he finishes a paragraph, his youngest daughter comes lumbering around the corner.

"'Ehhhyeearrrghh! Eurnhg Grugggn?' she shouts.

"The man looks at her. 'Shut up, Cinderblock,' he says, and turns the page."

A bug flew into George's mouth. He coughed and spit it out.

"That's pretty good," he said.

Hollywood rolled over to lie on his stomach, chasing a beetle along the side of the branch with a dangling finger. "It's alright."

"Your name's Douglas Douglas, right?"

"Nobody calls me that."

"Well."

On the other side of the canyon, a tarantula made its way down a tree trunk, hairy legs feeling the air. George watched it drowsily, wondering if he could count on Hollywood to stay awake if he slipped into a nap.

"It's an awful name," said Hollywood. "My dad had it out for me from the start."

George closed his eyes. A whisper of undergrowth signaled the passage of some huge creature far below.

"He's a lot like the guys we came in here with," said Hollywood. "Rich. Arrogant. Self-assured."

"Still your dad," said George.

"Nah," said Hollywood.

They lay there, listening, cocooned by tropical heat.

"He disowned me," said Hollywood.

George looked at him for the first time in half an hour. There were scars, huge claw marks, across the ranger's back.

"Why?"

"I backed over his poodle. In the Luxury SUV."

"On purpose?"

"Kind of, yeah."

"Ah."

"Last-straw kind of thing. We'd been fighting for years. Stepmom didn't like me either."

"Hmm," said George, who couldn't imagine disowning a child.

"For the record," said Hollywood, "the poodle deserved it."

*****

They came upon the monolith in a clearing ringed by brilliant beetleflowers. Hollywood refused to approach, but he gestured onward. As George approached, everything seemed to fall silent. He ran his hands along the cool gray surface, the immaculately-edged grooves. After a moment he sank down, closed his eyes, and pressed his ear against it.

The stone was cold. He thought he heard a distant ringing, a jet engine cutting the sky. He felt infinitely old. His muscles, stringy but tough from months of exertion, thrummed.

He thought about his wife. Ex-wife. About Todd. About Thomas. About George Matherson, who'd shared his tent, and Bob Bradley, and Rosalina and her husband, and all the other trainees. His hands trembled. Maybe he was alive because he didn't fear death. Maybe that was the secret. He didn't welcome it, exactly, but he didn't think he'd mind, either. He'd given life a good try.

He missed so many people. He missed people he'd only met once or twice, like his uncle Rob, who'd turned him upside down at age seven and spun him around by his heels. Rob, whose first wife had convinced him to get a vasectomy, then left him when the procedure went horribly wrong. Whose second wife had not-so-secretly wanted kids. Rob, who himself had loved kids. Rob, who at forty-five had stuck a shotgun in his mouth and—

Every story George could think of terminated in tragedy. But for some reason, sitting here one hundred miles from the nearest non-Hollywood human being, enveloped in esurient jungle, with insects lighting on his neck to drink his sweat, that didn't seem so sad. It seemed natural. Every story ultimately ended in death. So why worry about it? It was like worrying about the sun coming up.

He listened. The monolith was cold and still and silent.

Thoughts rattled around his head. He was disintegrating. The parts of his mind that defined him were tearing apart, revealing glistening thought-filaments packed with memories and dreams, regrets and hatreds and fears. Fiber-optic neural strands surged with electric-blue energy.

Here he was. The gray fog obscuring his future had begun to clear. Sunbeams pierced the clouds. Deep inside, he felt a kernel of hope. Hope for what, exactly, he couldn't say. Something different. As different as a man his age could expect. Maybe he'd go to school. Study engineering. Start over from scratch.

Or maybe he'd just sit here, ear against the cold stone, and keep his eyes closed, and wait for something to consume him.

Either option was fine.

18

Hollywood waited as long as he could, and then, when he saw that George had dozed off, he took a deep breath, squared his pack on his shoulders, and marched into the clearing. The humming in his head intensified, but he set his eyes straight, step-step-stepped into range, grabbed George under the shoulders, and dragged him away.

Once he was far enough that the cerebral buzzing had subsided to bearable levels, Hollywood slapped George's face, but the older man only groaned and turned his head from side to side. Adrenaline spiking, Hollywood lifted the inert body over his shoulders and jogged, knees creaking. His back hurt. The forest roared and rustled around him. He crossed a hundred yards and grapple-gunned into the branches.

The elevation seemed to help. After a moment or two, George stirred, blinking as if waking for the first time in years.

Hollywood held up a canteen. "Hey. Hey. You alright?"

George, an incandescent grin splitting his face: "He's alive."

"Say again?"

"My son's alive."

Hollywood sighed.

"It showed me," said George.

"It showed me lots of shit," said Hollywood. "None of it came true."

They turned back. One day they were crossing a fallen tree that lay across a ravine when Hollywood, uncharacteristically distracted, slipped and went over the edge. As he fell, he spun, grasping at splinters of bark, and it crystallized that he was about to die in the most embarrassing possible way. Then George caught his arm.

That night Hollywood dreamed that a giant horned moth picked him up and carried him through the canopy and over the forest. A thousand miles of rolling green passed beneath them, the wind a cold sheet wrapped around his face.

Hollywood asked the moth: "Where are you taking

me?"

And the moth replied: "Back to where you started."

But Hollywood could tell from the position of the chalky moon that they were headed west, deeper into the Pacific, not toward the shore. Before he could ask the moth what it meant, a mountain rose out of the forest. The misty green peak blasted all thoughts from his mind.

*****

Zip watched a documentary series on the trains and superhighways spanning the polar wastes. The series was an effort to make the frozen north as intriguing and adventurous as the forest—an attempt, in other words, to replicate the tremendous commercial success of the ranger programs with significantly lower overhead. Unfortunately, the polar wastes were by definition boring, endless stretches of tundra broken only by the occasional malnourished polar bear. Journeys across the expanse, except in the case of mechanical failure, were by-and-large uneventful. Nor were the people who worked the wastes particularly interesting. Rangers tended to have big personalities. Polar waste workers were taciturn misanthropes who'd chosen their profession specifically to get away from other human beings.

He watched the whole series anyway. He couldn't stand the ranger programs, and nothing else was anywhere near as entertaining. He tried and failed to read books. Rock climbing, his original passion, now only infuriated him. Routes that would once have been trivial were now impossible. He spent hours on his apartment balcony, watching people walk by. Lots of them were ugly. Sometimes he'd go all day without seeing a beautiful one.

The sky was always gray. When it wasn't gray it was white. When it wasn't white or gray it was black, and rain fell out of it. But it was never blue.

Hollywood didn't come back when he said he would. Zip stayed in his apartment. When he thought about things to do, they all sounded awful, so he didn't do anything. Doing nothing felt awful too. It was the same with food: nothing sounded appetizing, so he ate whatever was easiest, potato chips and fast food and cans of soup. The days dragged on, and still Hollywood failed to appear.

One day, Zip called his mother and talked to her for a long time. Then he dropped the phone on the floor and lay on his back in the living room, counting dimples in the stucco ceiling.

The best metaphor for how he felt was that he was trapped in a cloud of black flies. When he opened his mouth they flowed inside and he had to spit them out. Their bodies crunched and oozed between his molars. Trying to spit simply let more flies inside, their wings adhering to the roof of his mouth, so at last he had to swallow. It was no use shouting for help, because the buzz drowned out every sound.

When he couldn't stand it anymore, he put on his sneakers and drove to the nearest state park.

It was the middle of the week and the park was

deserted. He picked a trail that led to a cliff and set off at once. It didn't take long to realize that he'd forgotten a water bottle. His sweatshirt and jeans became a sweltering, swampy prison. He tied the sweatshirt around his waist, but sweat still poured hot and fast down his face.

The trail was rough. After half a mile, the dirt path metamorphosed into uneven stone steps. He struggled up, his prosthetic leg stiff, the unwieldy foot with its worn-out sneaker sliding around and twice sending him crashing down. His elbows and knee turned bright red and bled. He stuck a pebble in his mouth to fend off the thirst.

He passed a bush that rustled menacingly, but kept on going, prompting a rattlesnake to burst out and strike his prosthetic leg. Pink-webbed fangs glanced off. Undeterred, the snake struck again, but the prosthetic leg repelled the fangs. Zip stood still, breathing through his nose. The snake coiled and hissed, tail jittering. Zip picked up a big rock. The snake watched him.

"Hissssssssss," it said.

"Fuck off," said Zip.

The rock was a satisfying weight in his hand. Half of his brain said: kill the snake. Look at its mean fucking eyes. The other half said: don't kill it. It's just scared. Look at its beautiful scales. Look at those gold and brown diamonds.

He closed his eyes and tasted the sweet air, rolling the pebble around in his mouth. Then he extended his prosthetic, baiting another strike. When the snake fell for the trick, fangs rebounding uselessly, Zip obliterated its head. It took a couple blows, and when the snake stopped moving Zip felt so nauseous that he had to drop the rock and stagger away. He tried to throw up behind a tree, but he hadn't eaten anything that morning, so the retches brought up nothing at all.

The trees were a tenth the size of forest trees, but they still towered above him. He watched the ground, not the sky, as he fought his way up the mountain. Birds laughed and taunted with their cries. A chunk of stone crumbled away as he stepped on it, and he fell, body weight landing on his prosthetic leg, which snapped at the shin. He tried to take another few steps, licking sour, chapped lips, but the leg kept buckling under him. He found a stick to prop himself up and continued up the slope.

Eventually he came to a stream, which cascaded down a series of steps to his left and crossed the trail before vanishing into the forest. He lapped up water as it trickled down. It tasted clear and pure. He gulped down mouthfuls, blinking as drops clung to his eyelashes.

Something round and smooth touched his tongue and he spat. A tadpole, expelled, writhed on the gravelly trail. Zip tried to brush it back into the stream, but its sensitive belly split open on the rough stones, leaving a trail of guts and blood. The nausea swelled again. Zip distracted himself by looking upstream.

A few stair-steps above, the stream pattered across a broad-leafed plant painted white and black with bird feces.

Zip spat and rubbed his tongue on his sleeve. His

mouth tasted foul. He spat again and swore, hauling himself up. Stupid. His stomach hurt. It had to be his imagination. You couldn't get sick that fast.

He dragged himself up the slope, worthless prosthetic leg buckling, the gnarled walking stick barely keeping him upright. It felt like he'd been walking for hours. He would have checked his phone to see the exact time, but he'd forgotten it in the car. He spat into the undergrowth again and again, but the taste remained.

Zip wasn't sure why it was so important that he reached the top of the trail. He stumped along, leaning on the stick, grunting with every step. The broken prosthetic dug into his stump. He was pretty sure he was bleeding down there, but he refused to stop and take a look. His good leg's muscles screamed.

When Tetris and Li had showed up in D.C., if he'd gone to see them immediately, would they still have gotten on that plane? Would he have gone too? Would he be dead now?

Why hadn't he gone? He'd stayed at home, watching them on the television screen.

Everything had gone to shit since he'd lost the leg.

Although. Now that he really thought about it—he settled onto a mossy rock to give his aching joints a rest— he hadn't really been happy before he lost it, either. Spikes of happiness, sure. There'd been times in the forest, with Tetris and Li, that he'd felt normal. And he was pretty sure he'd always maintained a convincing illusion of happiness. To conceal the buzzing flies. Maybe he'd even managed to delude himself.

His left eye itched, so he rubbed it, but the itching only intensified. He squinted at his fingers. They were dirty. He tried to find a clean scrap of clothing or skin to rub his eye on, but everything was covered in dirt. Finally he turned up his shirt and rubbed a section of sweaty interior against his eye. It stung, but the itching stopped.

What was he planning on doing when he reached the cliff?

Zip closed his eyes and conjured the scene in the forest. He'd stood on a flimsy branch above the spider, brazen, firing his worthless pistol. Why? It could have climbed up after him. He should have grappled away. But he stayed.

Was it possible that the rage he'd felt when he woke in the branches had not been directed at his injuries, or at Tetris and Li for risking their lives, but at his failure to—

Well. He hadn't really wanted to kill the rattlesnake, either, had he?

His gashes sang. Afterward there would be no pain, only silence. Would that be any better?

He removed his prosthetic and examined the place where it had cracked. Imagined sitting on the edge of the cliff, looking over the lumpy treetops, the mountain rising against the gray sky to his left. He imagined the breeze kissing his sweaty cheeks. He imagined slipping as he turned to leave, tumbling over the edge, the seconds of orgasmic flight before swift sharp pain and then nothing.

He sat and listened to the birds for a long time. A ladybug landed on his arm and he left it there. The forest around him was extremely green. The air tasted nice.

Well, there was no rush. He reattached the prosthetic, grabbed his walking stick, and hobbled down the mountain.

When he got back to his apartment, poured a glass of water, and sank into his armchair, Chomper orbiting his leg, Zip noticed a missed call on his phone.

Hollywood.

He'd listen to the voicemail in a second. For now, all he wanted to do was sit, drink his water, and scratch Chomper on the spot beneath his collar where he best liked to be scratched.

19

When Zip opened the door to Hollywood's office, he found the blond ranger sweeping the contents of a mahogany desk into cardboard boxes. The bookshelf along the wall had been gutted, as had the wall with various fake awards printed and framed by Hollywood himself.

"Hey," said Hollywood, wiping sweat from his crooked nose.

"Packing up?"

"Just canceled all the expeditions and the office lease."

Zip kicked a stress relief ball. It flew across the room and molded around a leg of the desk.

"At least we got a nice payout, right?" said Hollywood, and laughed. Zip thought it sounded a bit forced.

"Where's George?"

"He wandered off," said Hollywood. "Before you chew me out: he didn't leave empty-handed. I gave him fifty thousand bucks."

"You let him leave? Also, what? That's nothing."

"What was I supposed to do? Handcuff him? I'd say we left him significantly better off than we found him."

Zip fingered a drawstring on his hoodie. Someone tapped the wall and cleared their throat behind him.

"Excuse me," said a man in the hallway, in a lilting accent Zip didn't recognize, "would this happen to be the office of Forest Adventuring Travels, LLC?"

"Sorry, bud," said Hollywood, trying to figure out how to fit a massive three-hole-punch into a box already brimming with supplies, "we here at FAT just closed our doors. Not accepting new customers."

The man, who barely came up to Zip's shoulder, squeezed his eyes in a vaguely avian approximation of a smile. "Oh, but I am not a customer. I am an attorney. I represent a foreign client who would like to retain your capabilities for a unique, one-time engagement."

He bustled past Zip, extending a business card to Hollywood. Light glinted off gold lettering.

"This is just a phone number," observed Hollywood.

"My client values discretion," said the man.

"Whatever you're buying, I don't sell it," said

Hollywood, and tossed the card in the trash.

The man's eyes followed the card's flight. His mouth remained open for a moment. Then he reached into his pocket and produced another card. This one he held up like a dog treat.

"My client," said the man, waving the card, "will reward you handsomely for your service."

Hollywood snorted. "I just pulled down twenty million dollars," he said. "You can't buy me."

"One expedition. Fifty million dollars, each."

Hollywood froze with a stapler halfway to the box.

"Think about it," said the man, laying the card on the desk. He extended a hand for a shake. Hollywood looked at it like it was a bloody stump. After a moment the hand withdrew.

"Good day," said the man, and departed.

"Absolutely not," said Zip.

"Absolutely FIFTY MILLION DOLLARS," said Hollywood.

"You're already rich. You said it yourself."

"Not rich enough. Fifty million dollars—Zip, with that kind of money—"

"Then do it. Without me."

"Zip. Please. They're not going to take you into the forest. Show up, train another batch of suckers, take your check, and adios. C'mon, man! It's a no-brainer!"

Zip kneaded his forehead.

"Listen to me, Zip. My father is a jackass.

Unfortunately he is also a millionaire. Except for killing his insufferable poodle, I have never been able to give him even the tiniest spoonful of the dastardly comeuppance he so desperately deserves."

"What does fifty million do that twenty million doesn't?"

"I'm getting to that. My father lives next to another jackass millionaire, whose equally preposterous fortune stems from the fact that he invented the moist towelette. Every time you swab your mouth, typically at a restaurant with 'Shack' in its name, this guy gets a cut. If I had fifty million dollars, I would buy the Moist Towelette Tyrant's property. And do you know what I would build there? I would erect, Zip, on the plot of land directly adjacent to my father's, a towering golden phallus the likes of which the world has never seen. A ten-story, tumescent wiener, piercing the very heavens, glistening gold, bulging with veins. Imagine!"

Zip nodded. "I'm imagining."

"No you're—you're not, I can tell by your face. I can tell that you're not."

"I am. I really am. A giant metal penis, is what you're saying. This isn't a fucking M.C. Escher you're trying to—

"Zip! A macro-dong of obscene proportions! The turgid, empyrean majesty! Can't you feel it?"

Zip gave up. "Okay. I feel it."

"Surely there's something you'd do with fifty million dollars."

"I'd give a couple million to each of my parents," said

Zip, "so they'd finally divorce each other."

Hollywood gaped. "You are one depressing guy, huh?"

Zip scratched the beard that had begun accumulating along his jawline. "I'd also get a blimp."

"Cruise liner? Aircraft carrier? Luxury speedliner? What kind of airship are we talking, here, captain?"

"Something modest."

"No. Nooooo. This is not the occasion for modesty. We are talking about fifty million dollars, Zip."

"Jeez, man, you know how much an airship costs? Gotta be five million just for a little one."

"It's free money! Splurge!"

"I'd buy a big fucking airship and paint a pin-up girl on the side. Is that what you want me to say?"

"Her tits hanging out. Yeah. I could see that."

"No, I mean, in a bikini? Because I'm not a weirdo?"

Hollywood tapped his chin. "I see what you're going for. My opinion, though, you'd really want her to be full-on nude. For artistic effect."

Zip, over his growling stomach: "I'll take that under advisement."

"Shit," said Hollywood, checking his oversized watch, "it's two o'clock. Pizza?"

So they went to Pete's Pizza Shack and demolished an extra-large pie with all the toppings. When they were done they wiped their faces with lemon-scented moist towelettes.

On the sidewalk, Hollywood fished out the business card. Zip, teetering on the edge of a food coma, watched sunlight play off the golden script.

"You in?" asked Hollywood.

"I honestly don't know," said Zip.

"Tell you what," said Hollywood, putting the card between his teeth and digging for his wallet. He held out a quarter and motioned.

After a second, Zip took the quarter.

"Heads you go," said Hollywood, "tails you don't."

Zip flipped the coin. It caught the sun on its way up, and he had to look away. When he turned back, the coin was rolling down the sidewalk, bouncing on its edge. It hopped off the curb and vanished through a sewer grate.

"What's that mean?" asked Zip.

"It means you owe me a quarter," said Hollywood, the phone already pressed against his ear.

Three days later they were standing together in the airport security line, Hollywood with gigantic aviators on his face and a chunk of bubble gum popping in his mouth, Zip lugging the same beat-up suitcase he'd brought to boot camp five years earlier.

"They'll take me aside for a pat down," said Zip, "just you watch."

Hollywood peered over his aviators. "Nah, man, you're black, not Muslim. It's the Ay-rabs they're after."

"Look at this beard. Plus the prosthetic. I could have a bomb in there. I bet you a million bucks."

"Whoa. Shake on that?"

They shook.

"That guy's a racist," said Zip, motioning with his head.

"Like, more than usual, I mean. I can tell."

Hollywood looked. A group of TSA officers socialized beside the X-Ray machine. "The fat one?"

"The one with the beady little eyes. The goatee. Look, he's staring. If that fucker doesn't have a Confederate flag on his pick-up truck, I'll eat a bucket of pig slop."

"God bless America," said Hollywood, sizing up a buxom blonde as she bent to remove her shoes. "You seeing her, though?"

"Hmm," said Zip.

"I'd hit that so hard it would orbit the Sun," said Hollywood.

"That doesn't—that doesn't make any sense."

"Halley's Comet that hoe."

"It's amazing you managed to mispronounce that word."

"'Halley?'"

"No. Never mind."

"What—how am I supposed to say it, then?"

"Don't," said Zip, producing his boarding pass. "Just don't."

"See," said Hollywood, "*that's* racism."

The TSA officials couldn't figure out why Zip laughed when they asked him to step aside for a pat down, so they put him in a little room for a few minutes and searched his luggage. When he emerged, Hollywood greeted him with a shrug.

"Easiest one million dollars of my young life," said Zip.

"While you were in there I came up with a great rap

line," said Hollywood.

"No," said Zip. "Please, no."

"Slam that hoe so hard that she orbits the sun—"

"God, no—stop. Please stop."

"—they be call her Hailey's Comet by the time I is done."

"Holy shit, Hollywood."

"Get it? Like, 'Hailey?' Like the name?"

"Did you honestly say 'they be call her?' Is that what you said?"

"It was for flow. Flow, man. Look, I know all about this stuff. I'm a hip hop head."

"Oh my God."

"I listen to Outkast, man! I listen to Kanye!"

"Oh my God."

"I'm practically as black as you are, Zachary."

Zip put a hand on his shoulder.

"Douglas," he said, "you are so white that you not only have the whitest name imaginable, you have it twice."

"There are plenty of black guys named Douglas," said Hollywood.

"On top of that, Douglas, you are nicknamed after a place that is notorious for being full of white people."

"Did you not see that Tarantino movie? The one about the slave?"

"Douglas, you are the whitest person I know. You are whiter than Tetris, which is saying something, because Tetris is an Indiana trailer park boy."

"Well, he's green, actually. Not white."

"You are whiter than Twinkie filling, Douglas."

"Was, I mean," said Hollywood.

"What?"

"Tetris *was* green."

Zip closed his mouth. His suitcase wheels growled against the tile. A lady came over the intercom, loud and unintelligible.

"I forget sometimes," Zip said after a while.

"Yeah," said Hollywood. "I get that."

*****

Zip and Hollywood had seats in first class, but a trip from Seattle to Portugal was still a trip from Seattle to Portugal, and with a four hour layover in Philadelphia it added up to seventeen consecutive hours of travel. Half an hour into the first flight, it was clear that Hollywood's strategy to cope was to get utterly shit-faced on tiny bottles of airplane liquor. Zip, who'd won the rock-paper-scissors match for the window seat, watched the checkered green and brown plains of the Midwest roll by. Eventually he acquiesced to Hollywood's repeated and importunate demands that he partake in the free alcohol, and downed a miniature bottle of whiskey himself. Then another. Things went downhill from there.

When they staggered off the plane in Philadelphia, arms around each other's shoulders, the world looked a whole lot brighter. They stood, swaying, obstructing the entrance to the boarding tunnel, oblivious to the mob of passengers struggling to squeeze by.

"I want a smoothie," announced Zip.

"Me too," said Hollywood.

They bought smoothies. Five minutes passed in silence.

"You know what I want?" said Hollywood. "An iPod."

He tried to drop his half-full smoothie into a trash can and missed. The cup hit the ground and ruptured, strawberry goop splorting out in an alluvial pink fan.

"Whoops," said Zip, and laughed.

Hollywood snorted. "I did not mean to do that."

They wandered the airport, riding the moving walkways, in search of a vending machine with electronics. Eventually they found one. It took Hollywood several minutes to decipher the touchscreen menu, but in the end he purchased an iPod. Several iPods, in fact. They came raining down into the collection slot like square white missiles.

"Man," said Zip, "what are you going to do with eleven iPods?"

"Help me hold them," said Hollywood, taking the boxes out of the slot and passing them over. Zip's arms were quickly filled. Hollywood pulled Zip's roller bag, and Zip carried the teetering pile of iPods. He didn't do a very good job. They were down to six by the time they reached the gate.

"Shit," said Zip, "I must have dropped a bunch."

Hollywood didn't look particularly upset. He turned a box over in his hands, trying to figure out how to open it.

Suddenly his fingers froze.

"Wait," he said, "how am I going to get music onto this?"

Zip shrugged. "I didn't even know they still *made* iPods."

Horror spread across Hollywood's face. "I don't even *want* an iPod."

A TSA agent walked by, arms stacked with the five missing iPod boxes.

"Hey," said Hollywood, lunging to his feet. "Those are mine!"

"Hollywood, no," shouted Zip, staggering after him.

"Give those back," bellowed Hollywood, accelerating to a clumsy sprint.

Startled by the slap of their footsteps, the TSA agent turned. For a moment his eyes went wide. Then Hollywood tackled him, and Zip tackled Hollywood, and the three of them hit the ground, iPods jettisoned in all directions, and Zip began to realize, as a shouting horde of officers came running, that they probably weren't going to make it to Portugal today after all.

*****

"Officer," said Hollywood, "this is all a huge misunderstanding."

"I heard you the first time," said the officer, his feet up on the desk, as he worked his way through the Sports section of the Philadelphia Tribune.

Zip, on the bunk in the back of the cell, sighed and rubbed the spots on his wrists where the cuffs had dug in.

"Honestly, I think it was a blatant case of racial profiling, because of my friend here," said Hollywood, pointing at Zip. "You'd probably know all about that, right?"

The officer slowly turned his head. "Excuse me?"

"I mean, because you're black. You probably get racially profiled all the time."

"Hollywood," said Zip.

"Doesn't it bother you? To see a couple of guys locked up for no reason except racism? Doesn't that hurt, somewhere deep in your black heart?"

The officer put his newspaper down and rose from his chair.

"No, wait, no. No no no," said Hollywood, "that's not what I meant. 'Black heart' as in: black-hearted, you know? Not as in: because you are black. Ha! Whoops. Black-hearted! It's a saying!"

"I told you," rumbled the officer, "to stop talking."

Hollywood snorted. "This is America, man. I know my rights."

"Hollywood," said Zip.

The police officer's nostrils flared. He raised a finger the diameter of a rifle barrel and opened his mouth. Then the station's double doors swung open, revealing the diminutive attorney they'd met in Hollywood's office.

"Alright," said the attorney, "let them out."

Three tight-jawed policemen entered after him.

"What?" said the officer by their cell.

"I already explained this to several dozen of your colleagues. No one is pressing charges. It is your legal imperative to release my clients."

"They assaulted a law enforcement officer," said the towering policeman, stabbing his index finger in Hollywood's direction.

"Allegedly," said the attorney primly. "Now let them out, please."

Outside, Zip hurried to catch the attorney. "How'd you get us off the hook?"

"The individual you attacked," said the attorney, "decided not to press charges."

"Just like that?"

The attorney glanced over. "Upon a thorough investigation, the TSA opted to let the incident slide."

They headed towards a black Lincoln.

"We rebooked your flight," said the attorney as he ducked into the shotgun seat. "I will be accompanying you to forestall any further complications."

He meant it. When they boarded the plane, and Hollywood asked the stewardess for a nightcap, the attorney cleared his throat and stared him down.

"Fine," said Hollywood, and pouted for two hours, until finally he succumbed to exhaustion and fell asleep.

The attorney, who still hadn't mentioned his name, saw them personally to their hotel in Lisbon. It was afternoon in Portugal, the sun dangling above tiers of orange-roofed buildings.

"I will return at seven o'clock tomorrow morning to retrieve you," said the attorney. "Can I trust that you will refrain from further trouble-making in the interim?"

"Man," said Hollywood, "what's your problem?"

The attorney bristled. "If it were up to me, we would never have solicited your participation in the first place. Rest assured that I continue to make frequent and impassioned arguments for your termination. All of which is to say, if you insist on acting like children, sirs, expect to be treated like children."

"Eat a dick," said Zip.

"How eloquent," said the attorney, and climbed back into the car.

In the morning he drove them across the city, whizzing through narrow white-walled alleys, rattling up slopes and flying down hills. For a reserved man, he drove like a maniac, but it was a controlled kind of madness, the aggression moderated by quick reflexes and manic precision. When a truck careened out of an alley in front of them, the attorney whipped their car into the opposite lane, gunned the engine, and swung them back into the original lane just in time for another car to hurtle past in the opposite direction. The whole maneuver happened so quickly that Zip hardly had time to register the near-collision. Nor did the attorney react in any way to the superhuman feat he'd just performed.

They came to a stodgy gray building on the far side of Lisbon. Zip and Hollywood followed the attorney to the front door, echoing each others' yawns.

"Please behave," said the attorney, and led the way.

On the other side of the door stood the buxom blonde from the airport security line.

"Holy shit," said Hollywood.

"Hi," she said, unveiling a six thousand-lumen smile. "It's nice to meet you. My name is Hailey Sumner."

"Holy shit," said Zip.

"I trust Mr. Terpsichorean has been taking care of you?"

It took Zip a minute to realize she was talking about the attorney.

"Uh," he said.

"For God's sake," said Mr. Terpsichorean.

"He's a bundle of laughs," said Hollywood.

"Fantastic," said Sumner, tossing her hair back and shaking Hollywood's hand. "Sorry about the inconveniences in Philadelphia."

They followed her down an unmarked hallway and into a conference room with padded leather chairs.

"What is this place?" asked Zip.

"Take a seat," said Sumner, "and I'll get you up to speed."

Zip settled dubiously into one of the voluminous chairs.

"It may not look like much," said Sumner, "but these are the headquarters of the Omphalos Initiative."

"Never heard of it," said Hollywood.

"That's because it's secret."

"Okay. It's just that, the way you said it, you kind of—

it sounded like you expected me to know what it was."

"Well," said Sumner, smiling patiently, "I didn't."

"Great. Good. Got it."

"Do you want to know—"

"What the Oompa-Loompa Institute does? Sure. But first I have a more important question."

The smile slipped off Sumner's face. She tapped a pen on the table. "Go ahead."

"Want to grab a drink tonight?" asked Hollywood.

The room was very quiet. Mr. Terpsichorean expelled all the air from his lungs in a single explosive burst.

"I do not," said Sumner curtly. All traces of the smile had vanished. "The Omphalos Initiative is an international organization supported by a worldwide network of powerful donors. Our goal is to help humanity reach the next stage of evolution by merging with the World Forest."

"Okay," said Hollywood, "I get that. I get that. I see where you're coming from. Is it because I was too forward? Or do you not find me attractive."

"Mr. Douglas," hissed the attorney.

Sumner tilted her head. "Around here, Mr. Douglas, behavior like that will not be tolerated. Do I make myself clear?"

In her blue-flecked eyes, Zip saw a glint of something he didn't like at all.

Hollywood straightened. "I'm just messing around, ma'am."

"I am not," she said, placing each word deliberately,

"someone with whom you wish to mess around."

"I think I'd like to speak to your boss," said Hollywood.

Faster than a striking viper, Sumner's smile returned.

"Unfortunately for you," she said, "I am the boss."

Hollywood frowned. "Oh."

"Yes. 'Oh.'"

Mr. Terpsichorean looked like he was about to faint.

"I would like to retain your services," said Sumner, "but rest assured, if you prove to be a dissatisfactory partner, I will find an alternative."

"I understand," said Hollywood. Zip felt like laughing and crying at the same time.

"Mr. Douglas," said Sumner, "how long does it typically take one of your expeditions to reach an electromagnetic anomaly?"

Hollywood gaped.

"Mr. Douglas?"

"Uh. Well, it usually—we're usually out there for about two weeks."

"I don't understand. What do you mean, 'usually?' Do the anomalies move?"

"Ah," said Hollywood, "I don't—when you say anomaly, do you mean—"

Sumner raised her immaculate eyebrows. "If you don't even know what an anomaly is, how on Earth do your clients hope to achieve transcendence?"

Zip snorted.

Sumner swiveled. "Mr. Chase?"

"Ma'am," said Zip, "with all due respect, we're just tour

guides. We take wealthy suckers out and walk them around. That's it."

He struggled to meet her blistering stare.

She pressed three fingertips on the table. "It appears that Mr. Terpsichorean was correct. You're a couple of con men."

"We're a couple of rangers," said Hollywood.

"You don't know anything at all."

"Ma'am," said Hollywood, "I know as much about the forest as anyone alive. My physical condition is impeccable. My tactical poise is peerless. If it's a guide you need, I have all the necessary qualifications."

"You have a big fucking mouth, is what you have," said Sumner.

"Look," said Zip, "we thought you needed a trainer and a guide. If that's not what you need, we're happy to get out of your hair. No harm done. Give us a week and we'll forget all about the Ompalooze Imbroglio."

"Omphalos Initiative," snapped Sumner. Zip scratched his nose. All of a sudden Sumner smoothed her face out.

"There's another way," she said.

"Ms. Sumner," said Mr. Terpsichorean sharply, "it's far too risky."

"Maybe not," she said.

"It," said Mr. Terpsichorean, face contorted as if in response to a horrible taste, "is too unpredictable."

"We can regulate that. Have regulated that."

"Hello?" said Hollywood. "Forget we were here?"

Sumner's gaze snapped back to him. She stood. "Come

with me."

"Where?" demanded Hollywood.

But she was already on her way out the door.

As they strode down the hall, Sumner blasted a stream of words over her shoulder.

"Rapid healing. Photosynthesis. Immunity to all disease. Telepathic communication. Functional immortality. These are the gifts of transcendence. By merging with the forest, a human being can reach an entirely new plane of existence."

"And you think you figured out how to do that," said Zip.

"I don't think," said Sumner. "I know."

They rode an elevator several stories down. Sumner led them along yet another unmarked hallway. Here and there they passed other people, subordinates in curious black-and-green uniforms, but no one made eye contact or spoke to Sumner. They practically pressed themselves against the wall when she passed.

"What makes you so sure?" asked Zip.

They came to a section of hallway lined with tall steel doors. Armed guards stood at attention in front of every second or third entryway. Ignoring them, Sumner tapped a code into a keypad, and a door slid open.

"See for yourself," she said.

The room beyond was small and dark. A floor-to-ceiling window, which Zip took to be a one-way mirror, looked out over a concrete cell. Inside the cell, there was a toilet, a cot, and a small steel desk. The desk and the cot were bolted to the floor.

In the center of the cell, staring up at them with molar-grinding hatred, sat Tetris Aphelion, cross-legged, crackling with pent-up fury, a gray collar fitted around his thick green neck.

20

"Holy shit," said Zip, hands behind his head as he paced the hotel room.

"Fuck," said Hollywood from the armchair.

"Fuck," said Zip.

"Holy shit," said Hollywood.

"That was Tetris!"

"Did you see all those guns?"

"We have to get him out of there. What about Li? Is Li in there? What happened to her?"

"We are so fucked," moaned Hollywood.

"Yeah, you made sure of that, huh? Couldn't keep your fucking mouth shut."

"How was I supposed to know she was a supervillain? How was I even supposed to know she was in charge?"

"What, because she's a woman?"

"No, dude," said Hollywood, exasperated, "because she's a *babe*."

Zip parted the blinds and peered out. Tetris was alive. For now.

"How do we get him out of there?"

"Forget Tetris," said Hollywood, "what are *we* going to do?"

"What's wrong with you?"

"The unarmed ranger and his one-legged sidekick stage an elaborate jailbreak. Real fucking likely."

"Man," said Zip, "you know they're torturing him. How else did they get that information? You think he gave it up because they asked nicely?"

"Alright, then, boss," said Hollywood, "what do you suggest? You saw the guards. Those guys are not fucking around. Kevlar! P90s! Night vision goggles! That's part of their protocol, by the way. Cut the lights if there's an intruder. So we need guns, one, and night vision goggles, two... and a way to get through all the locked doors... and a place to hide for the rest of our miserable fucking lives afterward, because they KNOW WHO WE ARE, and KNOW WHERE WE LIVE, and I don't know if you noticed, Zip, but they appear to be PRETTY WELL FUNDED, since they're paying us a hundred million for one lousy trip!"

Zip ran a hand along his jaw.

"Well?" said Hollywood. "Any bright ideas?"

"We have to try," said Zip.

Hollywood snorted. "Be still, my heart."

"We have the element of surprise."

"Right. We'll just run in there with our dicks out, brandishing our element of surprise."

"We play along. Listen to what they have to say. Get them to trust us, and look for an opening."

"What if there is no opening?"

"What do you want me to say? If we leave him, he'll die."

"What makes you think they won't let him go the moment they grow another green person?"

"I don't know, man. Maybe the fact that they were psychotic enough to imprison him in the first place?"

*****

The recruits Zip was expected to train had little in common with his previous batch. Eight white males between the ages of twenty-five and thirty, in peak physical condition, they paid him unflinching attention as he stumbled through an introductory speech. Their stares unnerved him. He fastened his eyes above their heads and told them to run five laps, which they did, effortlessly. He told them to do a hundred push-ups, then gave them five more laps. No one voiced a complaint. He kept them at it all afternoon.

The next day they went to a grapple-gun course. The trainees attacked the challenge with fervor. They'd clearly been practicing ahead of time. Zip began to wonder how he would fill the weeks to come.

He wondered if the trainees knew about the prisoners. Maybe some of them had tortured Tetris themselves.

"Mr. Chase," said one of the recruits, "we've heard conflicting instructions for what to do when confronted by a tarantula. Are you supposed to stand very still, or are you supposed to run away?"

Your only chance is to try a grapple, thought Zip, because the spider will find you by your heartbeat.

He surveyed the hard faces of the trainees. He imagined them standing stock-still as a tarantula approached, pawing the air with its hairy legs. Imagined the horror when the spider folded one of them up. How could he wish that fate on someone? But then he thought of Tetris, alone in his cell, scarred from months of torture.

"Stand still," said Zip. "That goes for a lot of big things. They'll catch you if you try to flee. So stand perfectly still and hope they don't notice."

He dismissed the class early and walked back to the hotel with a smoldering satisfaction in his belly.

*****

One of the trainees was a freckled twenty-something American named James. The others were various persuasions of European, sporting diverse but uniformly heavy accents. James, who it turned out had grown up a few towns down the road from Zip, spoke with an earnest Southern twang. Like the others, he was in peak physical condition, although overall he was a bit smaller than average, around Zip's height. Unlike the others, who treated Zip with the careful deference reserved for authority figures of uncertain temperament, James was warm and conversational.

One evening after training, James stayed late, pestering Zip with questions. A tuft of hair stuck off the back of his head and wiggled whenever he nodded, which happened a lot. Thirty minutes passed. Just as it occurred to Zip that he was actually enjoying the company of an Omphalos Initiate, James slapped a hand against his worry-crinkled forehead.

"What's wrong?" asked Zip.

"It's my mom's birthday," said James. "I was going to meet her for dinner, but it's my night to feed the prisoners."

A thrill coursed down Zip's spine.

"I can handle that for you," he said. His voice sounded like it was being broadcast back to him through a long cardboard tube.

"Could you?"

"I'm not sure where the prisoners are kept, and I'm not sure my card key gets me access, but..."

"Hell, you can borrow my card. Go to the mess—you know where the mess is, right?—and ask the cook. Eduardo, I think. Take the tray down to B3-11. It's the sixth door on the left."

Zip forced himself to stay very still. "B3-11. Got it." His carefully crafted nonchalance disintegrated when James gave a vapid grin and turned to leave without handing over the access card. "Hey. Hey! Forgetting something?"

James slapped his forehead again. "Sorry about that."

Zip's fingers closed around the card. "Have a good night, man."

He waited, watching the sun splat against the horizon, until James's car vanished from sight. Then he sprinted to his SUV, tossed his bag on the passenger-side floor, and cranked the key in the ignition.

It took Franciscan restraint not to drive like a maniac. Finally an opening. It had been weeks without a sighting of Tetris, but now there was a chance.

He jittered through the front door of Omphalos headquarters—it took him five tries to get the card swipe right—and sauntered down the hall to the cafeteria. Well, tried to saunter, anyway. He was newly aware of his prosthetic leg's inflexibility. Was it always this awkward when he walked? Did people notice?

In the cafeteria he found a tray stacked with prepackaged dinners. The label read "B3-11." No sign of Eduardo. Grateful for the chef's absence, Zip grabbed the tray and slipped out.

The elevator moved much slower than usual. As it descended, it released a slight metallic groan. The doors opened with a hiss.

Heart pounding, Zip traversed the hallway, which smelled like industrial cleaners and fresh-polished steel. The guards he passed nodded when they saw him. Somehow he managed to nod back. Didn't they wonder what an unfamiliar face was doing here? He wasn't even in uniform.

At last he came to the cell. Guards on either side sized him up, then returned to drilling ocular holes in the opposite wall.

"Food for the prisoners," Zip said.

The leftmost guard raised an insouciant hand.

Zip waited. A rivulet of sweat trickled down his neck and curled into his armpit. From there he could feel it dripping to his elbow. His missing leg was kicking up phantom pain again. The prosthetic was itchy and tough against his sweaty stump.

At last the door opened. To Zip's absolute gibbering horror, Hailey Sumner walked out. She closed the door behind her, turned, and paused, her face a frosty mask.

"Mr. Chase."

"Sorry," said Zip, "I'm—well, one of the trainees asked me to stand in for him. To bring the prisoners their food."

He struggled to balance the tray in one hand as he rooted in his pocket with the other.

Sumner, eyes flat: "Which trainee." It was a statement, not a question.

"His name is James. He wanted to meet his mother for dinner," said Zip. He showed the pass card. The food almost tipped, and he lunged after it, barely regaining his balance.

"I see," said Sumner.

He lofted the tray. "Should I—"

"Go ahead."

He felt her eyes on his back as he passed. The cell

yawned before him. Inside, under the aquatic fluorescents, were cots, a toilet, and a desk. On one cot sat a woman with piercing eyes and hair tied up behind her head. On the other cot sprawled Lindsey Li.

Zip walked to the exact center of the room and knelt, prosthetic leg creaking, to set the tray on the floor. As he swiveled and rose, his gaze crossed Li's momentarily. She looked half dead in the pallid light, but her eyes were very much alive. Her hair was longer than he'd ever seen it. If she was surprised, she hid it completely.

Then he was out of the room, the door clanging shut behind him.

"Give me the pass card, please," said Sumner. His fingers brushed hers as he placed it in her hand. Her skin was unbelievably soft. She curled perfect unpainted nails around the card and left without a word.

Outside, he sat in the SUV and counted long, deep breaths. The parking lot gradually darkened. Blue lights flickered to life atop tall steel poles. When someone climbed into the car next to him, Zip shook himself and stuck the keys in the ignition.

Back at the hotel, he pounded furiously on Hollywood's door.

"No hablo room service," shouted Hollywood.

"It's me," said Zip, and pounded some more.

There was a commotion of rustling fabric and pattering feet. The door swung open to reveal a glowering Hollywood clad in nothing but clover-patterned boxer shorts.

"What?" he said.

"I found where they're keeping Li," said Zip.

"Congratulations," said Hollywood, thunking his head against the narrow edge of the door. "Let's talk about it in the morning."

A woman edged around the corner behind him, blanket held up to her neck. Naked skin glistened on either side. She said something sharp in Portuguese.

"Babe," said Hollywood, still thunking his head on the door, "you know I don't understand that shit."

His forehead had accrued a red rectangular mark.

"Who is the man?" asked the woman, eyes flashing like bug zappers.

Hollywood sighed.

"Alright," he muttered, "fine."

He pushed himself off the door and turned, revealing a musclebound back covered in scars.

"Git," he said, popping a thumb toward the door. "I'll call you tomorrow. Si?"

More Portuguese, very fast and close together. Hollywood squeezed the bridge of his misshapen nose. "Beat it, baby. Vamos. I'll buy you dinner, okay? Dinner?"

Rolling his eyes at Zip, he closed the door, cutting the torrent of invective in half. Zip observed his shoes until the door opened and she stormed past him, chin high, tugging a halter-top strap over her shoulder. She left a cloud of cloying perfume in her wake.

"I saw Li, Hollywood," said Zip as he lunged into the room. "She's alive."

"Unsurprising," said Hollywood. "She was always tougher than him."

"I know where she is," said Zip. "We can get them both out at once."

"Well," said Hollywood, "I had a productive day too."

Zip surveyed the graveyard of alcohol and street food. A fly circumnavigated a half-eaten döner kebab on the room's obligatory faded green armchair.

"Don't make that face," said Hollywood. "I found a guy who'll sell us guns."

"What kind?"

"Whatever we want. RPGs. Anti-personnel mines. Flamethrowers. He's a Russian dude. Eight feet tall, bald as an Egyptian cat, grizzly bear tattoo, three missing teeth... the works."

"So when are we doing it?"

"Fuck, man."

"Next week. Let's do it next week."

"We need more time."

"Two weeks after that, training will be wrapping up, they'll be trying to send you into the forest."

"We can't just— look, man, we need a *plan*."

Someone knocked insistently on the door.

"For the love of God," shouted Hollywood, stomping over and wrenching it open.

Hailey Sumner stood in the hallway, one eyebrow raised. Behind her loomed two hypervascular guards. Zip's lungs shriveled.

"You again," she said flatly.

"Um," said Zip.

"That's okay," said Sumner, flicking a hand at her craggy bodyguards, who took up positions in the hallway. "This concerns both of you."

"What does?" asked Hollywood.

"We need to move the schedule up," said Sumner. If it bothered her that Hollywood was clad only in boxers, she didn't show it.

"The trainees need more time," said Zip, thinking of James.

"They have the rest of the week," said Sumner, turning to Hollywood. "Sunday. Understood? And there's been a change of plans."

Hollywood ran a hand gingerly up the back of his neck. "Of course."

"The green one," said Sumner. "He's going with you."

Zip's jaw fell open. He snapped it shut.

"He'll still have the shock collar," said Sumner, "and we've figured out how to block his psychic link, so he can't call in reinforcements. But he's going to be your guide to the anomaly. Do you understand?"

"Yes ma'am," said Hollywood.

Sumner's eyes lingered on Zip.

"Wonderful," she said, and beamed. "You gentlemen have a pleasant evening, now."

The next morning, James didn't show up to training. He wasn't there the day after that, either. When Zip asked the others about him, they avoided his eyes. Eventually he stopped asking.

21

As they made their way into the forest, Hollywood studied the eccentricities of his Omphalos companions. The biggest, meanest one, who by virtue of his bigness and meanness seemed to be the leader, had a name like Klaus or Krauss. He carried one of the devices that activated Tetris's shock collar. Klaus or possibly Krauss had demonstrated this capability early on the first day, when Tetris failed to rise from his lunch break with sufficient alacrity. A judicious button press on Klaus/Krauss's transmitter had sent the green ranger convulsing to his knees.

Three of the seven soldiers had mustaches. All seven

had at least one visible tattoo, several of which depicted snakes intertwined. One of the mustached men had scales tattooed on his neck. A heavyset man everybody called Dondo carried a preposterous six-barreled minigun, with ribbons of ammo draped all over him, but he didn't seem to notice the weight. Dondo had, in addition to the bushy hair on his upper lip, a full-bodied red beard tied in little knots. He'd cut off the sleeves of his uniform, revealing enormous biceps, upon the right of which an anatomically precise tattoo of a human heart throbbed as he walked.

One of the more modestly-tattooed individuals was a skittish, swarthy man who could have appeared, smiling confidently, on a package of boxer briefs. His dark hair maintained its pointy front edge no matter the humidity. Hollywood woke one morning to find him hard at work with a comb and travel mirror.

The soldiers took turns leading Tetris by the chain attached to his collar. His hands remained shackled at all times. At night, they affixed the chain to the branch and kept watch in shifts. The close surveillance prevented Hollywood from getting in range, until one afternoon the soldier on duty asked him to hold the chain while he stepped around a tree for a piss.

"Surprise," hissed Hollywood, examining Tetris's shock collar. It was disconcerting to have to look up at him. One of his pinkies was missing, and his arms were criss-crossed with gnarly scars. Across the clearing, Klaus/Krauss eyed them suspiciously.

"I've known for weeks," said Tetris.

The soldier returned before he could explain any further. Hollywood handed the chain over and stepped away, picking at grime on his SCAR-17.

Though he never would have admitted it, Hollywood didn't have a plan. Even if they overpowered the soldiers, there was no way to unlock the collar, which contained a tracker. Leaving the collar intact was hardly an option if they wanted to avoid a warm welcome on shore. The problem seemed unsolvable. He'd think of something, though. He always did.

On a normal expedition, Hollywood and Zip would have argued vehemently against loading up with ponderous firepower, but in this case they hadn't bothered. As a result, the group that ventured into the forest was larger, louder, and better-armed than any Hollywood had ever seen. A man named Andri had an AK-47 and three sidearms strapped to his body—one on each hip, plus an enormous revolver holstered under his left arm. Another man had an antitank rocket launcher, with an ammo case over his shoulder that kept slipping off. Rocket launcher guy, spooked, fired into a hollow log on the second day. Centipedes came wriggling out while Hollywood armed his grapple gun and grimly ascended.

Soldiers trying to operate grapple guns while carrying rocket launchers and miniguns, not to mention ammunition, were a thing of comic beauty. Half the time they couldn't figure out how to clamber onto the branches they'd hooked, so they dangled underneath like lopsided fruit until it was time to descend. Andri fumbled his AK-

47 during one ascent and had to root in the undergrowth afterward. Along the way he brushed a plant that gave him a ferocious rash.

On the third night, Hollywood had a dream. An unshackled Tetris with dead eyes led him around a skyscraper-sized tree, pausing on the other side to point out a stand of orange flowers. Hollywood looked at the flowers. He looked at dream-Tetris, who pointed again at the flowers. Hollywood looked back at the flowers. Then he woke up.

When they stopped for lunch the next day, and Hollywood took a few steps out of the clearing to relieve himself, he found a stand of … orange flowers. Normally he would have left anything that colorful alone, but he was so astounded by the coincidence that he reached out to brush one of the petals.

Just before his fingers made contact, a bee buzzed in and landed on the nest of protuberances in the center. A thread of smoke rose immediately. With a soft hiss, the insect melted, dripping into the depths until only a slight odor of burnt plastic remained.

Hollywood retracted his hand. Gingerly, with a twig, he prodded the flower on all sides. When he pressed the tip against the petals, it released a tiny wisp of chemical smoke. But the flower's green underside was harmless. Hollywood dropped the smoldering twig and wiped his sweaty hands on his pants. The plant's leaves were wide and shiny. He tore one off and touched it to the blossom. Sure enough, the leaf was unharmed. He ripped off several more and carefully wrapped a flower, then folded the package up in yet more leaves and tucked it in the side of his pack.

That night, as he tried to fall asleep, he heard Tetris talking to the soldier on watch.

"Nocturnal predators hunt by heat," said Tetris.

"Shut up," said the soldier.

"There could be a blood bat zeroing in right now. You wouldn't know until it grabbed you."

Hollywood heard the slight buzz and accompanying grunt that indicated a low-grade jolt from the shock collar.

"That wasn't very nice," said Tetris.

"Shut up," said the soldier again, in the slightly muffled way of a person who has his molars clenched together.

Tetris chuckled. It was a deep sound, minatory, and Hollywood swallowed despite himself. Green Tetris reminded him of a caged and brutalized pit bull.

Before they set out the next morning, Klaus/Krauss took hold of Hollywood's jacket.

"It just occurred to me," he growled, "that you were a ranger."

The others stopped to watch. Tetris stared into the green distance, still as a stone idol.

"Just now? It's alright. We can't all be Stephen Hawking-grade intellects," said Hollywood.

"Careful with this mouth of yours."

"I suppose you thought I landed the job with a strongly worded cover letter."

"He was a ranger too."

"So I've heard."

"You wouldn't have happened to run across him, I hope. In your previous life."

"There are lots of rangers. What was your name, again?"

The soldier stuck a finger in his ear and twisted, then examined the accumulation of orange wax. "My name is Felix Krauss."

"Klaus? Like as in 'Santa Claus?'"

"Like as in, there is an 'R,' not an 'L.'"

"Krauss. Thanks for clearing that up."

"Stay away from the prisoner."

"Fine by me. He's got a bit of an aroma. Y'all ever let him shower?"

"You are expendable," said Krauss. "If it becomes necessary, I will expend you."

"Taking some liberties with my native language, there, but I get your drift."

"I will spoon your eyeballs from your skull. With a spoon. Does that make for an understanding?"

"Loud and clear, boss. No spoonerisms necessary."

Three hours later, they came across a Megadodo. The harmless giant came stumbling out of the vegetation and, upon seeing them, produced an extremely loud noise. The nuances of the noise—terror, surprise, and general brainlessness—were lost on the soldiers, whose basic impression of the situation was that a three-story bird intended to eat them.

Dondo unleashed the minigun. Andri emptied his AK-

47. Rocket launcher guy fired his rocket launcher and missed, taking a big chunk out of an innocent tree. The Megadodo ran away, as it had intended to do anyway. Taking advantage of the general disarray, a trapdoor spider burst from its burrow, snatched a soldier, and dragged him kicking and screaming into its tunnel.

The others ran over and poured an otiose flood of lead into the burrow. Grenades were hurled, detonating with great subterranean thunks. Hollywood washed his hands of the situation and grapple-gunned away. Tetris stood grinning at the soldier who held his leash, who trembled like a newborn giraffe, finger hovering over the shock transmitter's big red button.

A few days earlier, the rocket launcher's discharge into a hollow log had gone more or less unnoticed, perhaps because the single loud crash approximated the sound of a falling tree. The amount of firepower discharged at and around the Megadodo, and subsequently into the trapdoor spider's burrow, could not be attributed to natural forces. It was probably the most aurally stimulating occurrence in this part of the forest's recent memory, and it provoked a correspondingly enthusiastic response.

A scorpion skidded out of the vegetation, shrugged off blistering fire, and speared the handsome swarthy soldier with its stinger. A pterodactyl dove past Hollywood on titanic leathery wings, only to be tackled out of the air by a creature with a body like a frog and a huge, circular mouth where its face was supposed to be. The buzzsawmouthed frog-thing had leapt some forty feet into the air to catch its prey, and the two creatures fell in a complex bloody tumble into a copse of thornbushes, while from the opposite direction a six-legged lizard came tail-lashing into the clearing. The soldiers dispersed as the lizard darted between them, flinching under the blunt percussive force of Dondo's minigun.

Standing amid the chaos, Tetris smiled. His teeth shone white as naked bone. He turned to the soldier with his chain, who was enthralled by a tarantula clambering delicately down a nearby tree. When the soldier began to back away, Tetris stuck out a foot and tripped him. The soldier slammed a hand on the transmitter's button as he fell, and Tetris crumpled. The tarantula paused, feeling the air with two enormous legs, a few yards away. The lizard had gotten hold of Andri and stood chewing him contemplatively as the others bellowed and unloaded their worthless weapons.

Convulsing, Tetris crawled toward the man with the transmitter as fire directed at both the lizard and the tarantula whizzed over his head. The clearing crackled with gunfire, shouts, and the screeches of approaching wildlife. The soldier with the transmitter scrabbled and kicked, trying to keep away from Tetris. Not fast enough. Tetris grasped a foot and yanked him closer. The man let go of the device and took up his rifle. Tetris, hands still shackled, pushed the barrel away. Bullets sprayed up in a deadly arc. On a branch high above, Hollywood ducked. When he peered down again, the rifle had been tossed aside. Tetris wrestled the transmitter out of the man's hand and turned it off. He dragged the man to his feet, oblivious to the tracers filling the air, and hurled him at the tarantula. Fangs slipped effortlessly through the man's back and out his front as the horrible legs folded him up and brought him under the mouth to feed.

Tetris didn't bother watching. Hands still cuffed, he stalked toward Krauss, who had the key to the handcuffs in a loop at his waist. The unfolding madness might has well have been a hologram for all the attention he paid it. As the lizard that had just finished Andri turned with interest to a Dondo frantically loading another ribbon into his smoking minigun, Krauss dropped his empty rifle and fled. Tetris sprinted after him. On the far side of a tree, Krauss stopped, transmitter in one hand and a pistol in the other. He hit the button just as Tetris rounded the corner. The hulking ranger fell. Krauss leaned down and pressed the pistol against Tetris's broad green forehead.

Hollywood removed the top of Krauss's skull with a staccato burst from his SCAR-17.

"Stick a spoon in that, bitch," he shouted.

Tetris, drenched in blood and brain matter, shoved the corpse away and grasped the transmitter with spasming fingers. He turned it off, ripped the keys from Krauss's belt, contorted to unlock his cuffs, and, thusly freed, rolled onto his back with arms splayed wide. He closed his eyes. Bullets ripped overhead. A giant rat snuffled past him, took hold of the half-headless corpse, and tugged it through a hole in the ground.

Ten seconds passed. Hollywood didn't dare leave his tree. The action had moved elsewhere, out of sight, though the sound of gunfire had not abated. Finally Tetris climbed to his feet, armed his grapple gun, and joined Hollywood on the branch.

"Get my collar off," said Tetris.

"What?" said Hollywood.

"The flower," said Tetris. "Use it on the collar."

Hollywood rummaged in his pack and retrieved the leaf-wrapped orange blossom. The air convulsed with screeches and screams. Gingerly, holding the base in a shiny leaf, Hollywood pressed the petals against the collar. The air filled with the smell of burning copper. Foul black smoke rose in twisting columns. Hollywood held his breath. His eyes watered and stung. After a few seconds, he took the flower away.

Tetris grasped the collar with both hands. As it continued to smoke, the metal visibly blistering, he tensed his arms and wrenched once, hard. The collar split open. He removed it from his neck, wincing as a tiny streak of corrosive substance ate into his skin, and flung the heavy ring into empty space.

No sooner had Tetris's arm completed the motion of the throw than he buckled and nearly fell off the branch. His eyes rolled up in his head, and his mouth worked soundlessly. A dull roar built from the depths of his throat. The roar increased in volume until it became clear that it wasn't just coming from him. The trees flexed and whipped as if struck by hurricane winds. Hollywood slammed a climbing pick into the branch and held Tetris tight. Out of the canopy poured black-winged dragons. The forest floor shuddered and caved as a legion of subway snakes roiled to the surface. Hollywood pressed his cheek against the bark and held his breath. He wished his hands were free so he could stick fingers in his ears. Far below, a minigunless Dondo attempted to navigate the tremoring ground and fell, windmilling, into the maw of a snake.

Tetris roared anew. Like a reanimated corpse, he jerked around to stare at Hollywood.

His pupils were black pits. Worms wriggled in the whites of his eyes.

Hollywood let him go and grasped the climbing pick with both hands. Tetris grapple-gunned away. A tornado of dragons swirled after him. The air itself leapt and sang. Great heaving snakes tore the ground to shreds as they went, revealing bottomless chasms and skeletons of trees long dead, the whole subterranean hellscape teeming with spiders, while behind it all, Hollywood closed his eyes and prayed to every god he'd ever heard of for the cataclysm to end.

22

Later the video would be replayed one billion times, broken down frame by frame and pixel by pixel. Total clarity was impossible. The camera responsible for the footage, which was mounted on a Portuguese Coast Guard tower, had the resolution of a department store security feed.

The black and white video opened with the forest at night, spotlights lapping at the treeline, the canopy rippling gently in the cool winter breeze. A human figure emerged. His arms were long, with big hands swinging at the ends, and his walk was purposeful. For a few moments the footage went on like that, the man stalking alone across the frame as the forest swayed ever-so-slightly behind him. Then spiders began to pour out of the trees. Thousands of legs flashed, the creatures carrying themselves low to the ground, hurrying as though pained

421

by the stark pools of light. There was no end to them.

Next came enormous snakes. The spiders gave them a wide berth, scuttling to keep the rumbling paths clear. Huge shapes burst from the canopy and cut rapidly across the view. Freeze frames would reveal these creatures to be tremendous reptiles with clustered black eyes and mouths packed with so many slender teeth that they seemed to be perpetually smiling.

The flood continued until a snake bumped against the base of the concrete tower. For a moment the camera caught a view of the ground below, a landscape of tangled arachnids and torrential, scaly flesh, and then, after a few frames of plummet, the feed cut out.

*****

Tetris's army had barely crossed the perimeter when the Portuguese military met them head-on. The horde produced a chittering roar, laced by steel-on-glass screams from the dragons that swirled overhead, but even that couldn't mask the shuddering cry of jet fighters puncturing the troposphere.

When the first air-to-ground missiles struck, all sound ceased, orange plumes leaping up to Tetris's right and left, spider parts flying, a gutted subway snake rising near-vertically out of the flames. The heat seared Tetris's neck—and as suddenly as the sounds had cut out, they came rushing back. The force of the nearest explosion knocked him off his feet as his army burst in all directions.

Ahead, white light erupted from a dozen apertures. There came a whistling sensation and the belated retort of tanks firing, while dirt rose spattering and crescents of shrapnel hummed overhead.

He stumbled onward, surrounded by spiders. A dragon fell out of the sky and wrenched a tank barrel upward just as it fired. The backblast sent tank and dragon up in a candent yellow-white pillar. Other dragons fell upon soldiers huddled behind makeshift barriers. Chuckling gunfire did little to dissuade their fearsome claws and teeth.

Tetris ran. A subway snake bulled down a line, bucking tanks like toy cars. Treads spun worthlessly against smoky dark space. The creature's mouth worked relentlessly, half distended, snapping up soldiers and equipment and earth. Spiders threw themselves into the barriers and fell twitching under withering fire, only to be replaced by more and more and more, an endless wriggling curtain. Another tank detonated as Tetris slid into a crater.

KILLKILLKILLKILLKILLKILL, said the forest.

A soldier rose out of the darkness with a rifle and Tetris ducked. He catapulted underneath screaming orange tracers, slammed against the soldier and rolled, hands working on their own to find the vulnerable skull and twist. Vertebrae popped. The hunger glowed all the stronger. Some part of him reeled, trying to vomit, but that part was not in control.

He didn't look at the dead soldier's face, just picked himself up and kept going. The air smelled of sulfur and blood. Immense wreaths of gunsmoke clouded his night vision. Into the fog he plunged, trusting the windmilling legs all around him, following the cries and clicks of a swarm in which he was just another hungry mouth.

By the time he reached Omphalos headquarters, air raid sirens blared from the center of Lisbon. The forest buzzed in his skull. He aimed his grapple gun at a window and fired, but the silver spearhead bounced right off. He tried the door. Spiders milled in the parking lot. Several clustered around a car, probing it with hooked feet. Tetris approached.

"Back," he shouted, projecting the command with telepathic force. The spiders retreated.

Inside cowered a fat man with enormous fleshy ears, wearing the green and black uniform of the Omphalos Initiative. Tetris knocked on the glass. The man didn't respond. Tetris smashed the window with his elbow. Glass rained everywhere. His boot soles crunched as he reached inside and flicked the lock. He opened the door and dragged the man out.

KILLKILLKILLKILLKILLKILL

"Tell me where the prisoners are," said Tetris.

"B3," said the man. "11 and 14. Oh God, please!"

"Badge," said Tetris.

The man clawed at the green hand constricting his neck.

"*Badge*," said Tetris.

The man rooted in his pocket and produced the access badge. Tetris snatched it, but his other hand refused to release.

KILLKILLKILLKILLKILLKILL

He grit his teeth and fought the forest. Sweat droplets burst across his forehead.

KILLKILLKILLKILLKILLKILL

Spiders closed in, caressing the man with their forelegs, chittering in Tetris's ear. The man screamed high and long. Tetris expelled air, fighting the command, veins bulging along his neck. With a final cry, he tore his hand away. The spiders recoiled. The forest's voice retreated to a distant throb.

"Go," Tetris panted. "Go!"

The man sobbed, climbed into his car, and swerved away.

Tetris staggered to the door, scanned the badge, and stood back as he pulled it open, expecting a flood of lead. Nothing happened. He peered around the edge. It was dark as the far side of Jupiter, though that didn't matter to him anymore. The hallway was empty. He strode inside and the spiders flowed after him, a complex black-carapaced tapestry.

The elevator was locked. Tetris cracked his knuckles and squeezed his fingers into the gap between the doors. Strained. Took a deep breath and pulled, to no avail. The spiders joined him, braced against the opposite wall and each other. They chattered and hissed, pulling. The doors groaned. Slowly, laboriously, they began to slide open. Cold air rushed out of the shaft.

Tetris leaned in and hooked his grapple gun around a

metal outcropping. As he rappelled, the spiders followed, working their way down the wall. The shaft filled with their clicking speech.

Three floors down, Tetris kicked the override switch on the wall, and the doors sprang open.

He rolled into the hall, inches beneath a blistering wall of fire. If the spiders hadn't burst out after him, catching the bullets with their armored exoskeletons, he would have been perforated like a cheese grater. When the last of the spiders had passed, and the gunshots had been replaced by the patter of six thousand chitinous feet, Tetris rose and followed.

He passed a mangled pile of corpses at the T-intersection just as a soldier groggily rolled a green and black-uniformed body aside and raised a tremulous pistol. Tetris snatched the pistol, stuck it in his belt, and lifted the man to his feet.

"Where's B3-11?" he demanded. "Where are the prisoners?"

The soldier mouthed silently. Blood flowed freely from a gash in his neck.

"Flown away," he choked. His eyes rolled up in his head.

Tetris dropped him and pressed onward. He found two empty cells, 11 and 14. He pounded a four-fingered fist into his palm until the stub of his pinky finger screamed. Where?

He sprinted back to the elevator. Outside, the clouds had cleared, revealing a moon like an cross-section of broken femur. Tetris stood in the empty parking lot and allowed his body to quake. The southwest horizon glowed orange-purple, flames scrabbling against the star-flecked sky. Distant cries and roars intermixed with jet engine skirls and thumping artillery fire. Tetris extended his arms and called the chaos to him, vibrating, beaming messages at a forest whose attention was divided among a million skittering fingers.

As the cries of dragons grew louder, an SUV careened around the corner. Tetris drew the pistol from his belt and approached. The passenger-side window rolled down.

"Get in," shouted Zip, leaning over to shove the door open.

Stunned, Tetris climbed inside.

"I figured you'd come here," said Zip.

"Li and Doc," said Tetris.

"Gone?"

Tetris closed his eyes. *Where?*

He tapped the gold strand linking him to the forest. Images flicker-flashed: a subway snake bursting into an artillery encampment and knocking the great gun on its side. A dragon carrying a soldier to the red roof of a building before shredding the gooey meal through meat-grinder teeth.

Flown away.

"The airport," said Tetris.

Zip spun the wheel and floored it. They roared down desolate boulevards as flames glowed and trembled in the rear-view mirror. Spiders poured out of the shadows and galloped after them. Dragons whirled and beat their wings above.

As they neared the airport, Tetris received another image-flash. Three figures in shackles, accompanied by a mob of soldiers, a single tall figure at the front of the pack, all of them walking the long distance to a private jet marooned on the tarmac. The engines were spinning up.

"They're on the runway," said Tetris.

Zip wrenched the SUV off the main road and toward a series of abandoned guard towers. Fences rose like silver webs on either side, tipped with bundled barbed wire. They smashed through the yellow-black arms of a security checkpoint and onto the tarmac.

Tetris beamed his need at the forest. Another blast of images: this time a sunny place, China, defoliants dropped by the ton on the coastal canopy. The screaming psychic pain of innumerable neurons shriveling.

KILLKILLKILLKILLKILLKILL

"Stop the plane," Tetris thought/said.

A dragon fell out of the sky and struck the private jet, knocking it down the runway with big holes in the fuselage. An engine slurped up the tip of the dragon's lashing tail. As the beast screamed and spun and tried to pull away, black blood spitting out the back of the turbine, the whole wing went up in a ball of flame. Then the swarm arrived, with Zip and Tetris at its ravenous head.

When Tetris saw the burn scars on the man at the front of the line, an animal hatred consumed him. As Zip hit the handbrake and swung the vehicle around, Tetris kicked the door open and flung himself out. He tumbled across the pavement, rolled roughly on his shoulder, and righted himself. Canines bared, he lunged for the scar-faced man.

Taking advantage of the commotion, Li struck the nearest guard with two hands. She wrapped her cuffs around his neck, spun, and kicked another guard in the chin. Vincent and Dr. Alvarez struggled with their own assailants. Then the spiders arrived. Gunfire snapped as Tetris pounded a fist into the scarred man's jaw again and again.

Soldiers fled down the runway, spiders in pursuit. As Li and the others un-clicked their handcuffs, Tetris lifted the burn-faced man's hand and bit off two of his fingers.

KILLKILLKILLKILLKILLKILL, said the forest.

The burn-faced man screamed. Tetris tasted salty-sweet blood and spit the fingers away. He dropped the hand, grabbed the man's hair, and slammed his skull down. The man kept screaming. Blood fountained from his finger stumps. Li and Dr. Alvarez froze just shy of intervening while Vincent staggered up behind them, clutching his shoulder.

Tetris cradled the man's head with two enormous green thumbs poised half an inch over the eyeballs.

"Don't do it," said Li.

The man lay frozen and silent, staring at the thumbs occupying his entire field of view.

The forest thrummed and roared in Tetris's skull. He imagined plunging his thumbs into the eyeballs, then through into the brain, the wonderful squelching give. He wanted it so bad. The blood in his mouth hummed and sang. He was a cosmic force, one with the universe.

"It's unnecessary," said Li.

The scarred man stared at the thumbs. Tetris fought, panting. How many times had cigarettes been pressed against his skin? How many fingernails and toenails had been ripped off, only to see them grow back again? How many times had the car battery been wheeled into the room? Tetris closed his eyes and caressed the eyelids. So fragile. So easy. The ease of it called to him. Easy as the scarred man's meat cleaver separating a green pinky from its shivering hand. Press quickly and hard, ignore the thrashing, ignore the blood. Catharsis. He knew he didn't have to. He knew, on some level, that it would be wrong. But he wanted it so bad.

His fingers twitched. Across the tarmac, the flaming jet crackled quietly. A breeze swept across the airfield, heavy with the scent of ash and death.

KILL, said the forest.

Tetris released the torturer's head, struck him hard under the jaw to knock him out, and stood.

"Not today," he mumbled, and tottered toward the SUV.

23

"Where's your finger, T?"

Tetris glanced at his hands on the wheel. No left pinky.

"They wanted to see if it would grow back," he said.

"It did not."

"No, it did not."

The others were asleep in the back seat. Li had her window open and a hand in the shape of a wing swooping up and down in the wind.

"I killed a lot of people," said Tetris.

"Don't think about it."

"I want to think about it, but I can't."

"Good."

"The only thing I can think about, after months of the shit they fed us, is how bad I want a milkshake."

"Do they have those here?"

"They've gotta have fast food chains, right?"

"Presumably."

He turn-signaled into an exit lane.

"Which flavor would you want?" asked Li.

"Chocolate. No. Strawberry."

"A place near me had peach milkshakes during the summer. Simply incredible."

"I snapped a guy's neck, Li."

"Mint chocolate chip. Now that's tried and true."

"Some soldier. I felt his spine snap. Like twisting a plastic tower until the pieces went flying. Blood shot out of his mouth."

"You did what you had to do."

"I had a choice. I think I wanted to kill him."

Li watched scattered buildings flicker by. "What's the plan, here? This is a hamlet. They don't have chain restaurants. They might not even have plumbing."

Tetris kept driving, out the far side of the town and into the empty countryside. Farmland unfurled between meandering hedges. The sound of the wind through Li's open window was a flexing, snapping roar. She put a knife in her hair and sawed.

"I think I enjoyed it, is the thing," said Tetris. "I think I enjoy killing people."

"Tetris, shut the fuck up."

For a long time, nobody said anything. They stopped for gas around six in the morning. Li disembarked to handle it. When Tetris checked on the others, Zip was grinning at him. Dr. Alvarez lay asleep on his shoulder.

"You crazy motherfuckers," said Zip. "You're alive. You're actually alive."

*****

It had been a rough couple of months for the forest. First its only conduit and link to the human world had vanished. Then China began covertly testing defoliants on the canopy off their coast. Through the world's radio transmissions, the forest heard itself endlessly vilified. Extremist politicians everywhere took advantage of forest-fear to win elections against odds that had previously seemed insurmountable. Still reeling from the nuclear strike on one of its neurological centers, the forest began to lose intermittent control of its extremities. Trees along the borders with the polar wastes shriveled and fell. A section of forest off the Western European coast went fuzzy and faded in and out.

With no response to its exhaustive psychic probings, the forest came to the logical conclusion: Tetris had been imprisoned, experimented upon, and dissected by the Portuguese government. After all, it was the police who'd turned him over. Seething over the abduction and murder of its sole ambassador, the forest plotted retribution.

Roots trapped spider queens and subway snakes, holding them close and venting anesthetic clouds so that the forest's pseudopods could conduct the surgeries and genetic engineering necessary to bring their electromagnetic receptors in line. Dragons served for reconnaissance and aerial intimidation, while subway snakes provided raw armored force, and spiders filled the gaps. An army of fangs and claws and mountainous muscle began to coalesce.

A week before Tetris's reappearance, the Chinese went public with plans to defoliate a thirty-mile buffer along their entire coast. The staggering expense didn't dissuade them, although it did enrage a certain world-spanning entity that would much rather have seen those funds invested in planetary defense. Plus the defoliation hurt. Every tree in the forest was essentially a neuron. A certain amount of attrition was to be expected, and the psychic structure of the forest adjusted constantly to compensate, but full-scale deforestation cascaded static across the entire network.

*****

"We go now to the US Embassy in Portugal for an exclusive interview with American private security contractor Jehovah Donahue, a former Army captain who participated in yesterday's frantic eleventh-hour defense. Jehovah: how's it going over there?"

"It's a real clusterfu—a real bad situation, Kathy."

"We've all seen the reports. An unprecedented terrestrial incursion by the forest. Thousands of casualties. What I want to know is, how did it feel on the ground?"

"Well, Kathy, there's no surrendering to a giant snake.

And the flying fu—ahem, *creatures*—I saw one rip a man in half and eat both halves. Grisly stuff. Blood everywhere. Theirs and ours. Whole rivers of blood. The ground just muddy with it. The air like whumping and cracking with wingbeats. I was in the Army for ten years, Kathy. I served in Afghanistan. Nothing prepared me for this."

"In the wake of this disaster, do you think training regimens will have to adapt?"

"Oh, absolutely. I mean, it's a war, right? It's our enemy. So we'll obviously have to learn to fight it better."

"I understand that your defense in Lisbon was successful, though, in the sense that it drove back the invaders?"

"Yes."

"So you won."

"I mean, 'won' kind of fails to capture the on-the-ground reality, if I'm honest, ma'am. More like the other side decided to leave."

"Why Portugal, do you think? Why attack there, of all places?"

"If you ask me, it's a message. The forest wants to scare us. My biggest worry is that our current administration isn't up to the challenge."

"You don't think the President is tough enough on the forest?"

"With all due respect, ma'am, I do not. He's a nice guy. I'd love to grab a beer with him. But when it comes to leading the free world against the greatest threat humanity's ever faced—I don't think he's qualified."

"If our link was blocked, how did you send me those dreams?"

What dreams?

"About the orange flowers that could eat through my collar."

Silence.

"Hello?"

I didn't send any dreams.

"How is that possible?"

But the forest was gone again.

They were holed up in a barn in the Spanish countryside. Dr. Alvarez had negotiated with the owner for a one-week stay. The barn smelled of manure and horse sweat. Hay bales served as beds. Tetris paced, peeking through cloudy windows into the flat black night. Somewhere out there, Hollywood was headed toward them. When he reached the coast he'd give Zip a call on the burner they'd prepared for this purpose.

Everyone was asleep. Tetris couldn't stand the stillness, so he slipped out the door.

Moisture beaded on his skin. He wished for a jacket. A big moon hung just overhead, backed by a spray of white-blue stars. The Milky Way smeared across the sky. Trees that formed the edge of the farmer's property stooped in the breeze. Whenever he closed his eyes, he saw the Portuguese soldier's shadowed face, or the gruesome amphitheater of Krauss's ruptured skull.

Crickets creaked. An animal rooted in the undergrowth. Tetris lay down in the wet grass and rubbed his eyes with the heel of his hand. It was dangerous to be out here. The farmer hadn't seen him yet, and would surely inform the authorities if he did. But the grass felt good.

After a while he climbed a tree.

When the sun finally rose, he slipped back into the barn and prepared breakfast, SPAM and eggs sizzling on a propane stove.

"Chef Tetris on the case," said Zip, who came hopping over, affixing his prosthetic, when he smelled the food.

"Old family recipe," said Tetris.

He held the pancake mix in one hand, trying to decipher the instructions, while he flipped eggs with the other.

"I missed you, buddy," said Zip.

"You too," said Tetris. He put the spatula down and rooted in the cooler for a milk carton.

"I didn't take you for a cook," said Dr. Alvarez. She sat beside Zip on the long oak bench.

"Prepare for pancakes that will blow your mind."

He poured the mixture into a bowl, added milk, and stirred. Li stretched near the door, touching her nose to her knee.

"Your eggs are burning," she called as she switched to the other leg.

He almost dropped the batter bowl. "Shit. Shit!"

"Yeah," said Zip, giving the scraped-up eggs a dubious look, "those ones are yours, big guy."

The pancakes were done by the time Vincent made it over. The agent took a plate without comment and retreated to his corner.

"What's wrong with him?" asked Zip.

Tetris wiped his hands on a rag.

"He's just sulking," said Li. "You'll get used to it."

After breakfast Li and Dr. Alvarez climbed into the loft. Vincent sat in the corner, massaging his shoulder and doodling on a pad of warped yellow paper.

"I didn't know you could draw," said Tetris when he walked by to dump the trash out. A jungle landscape sprawled across Vincent's notepad, populated by spiders and snakes. The lines were confident and strong.

"It's nothing," said Vincent. He tore the page off and wadded it up.

"Man," said Tetris, catching the crumpled ball en route to the trash can, "that's really amazing."

Vincent rubbed his shoulder. Tetris unfolded the drawing.

"You hurt?" he asked, trying to smooth the creases.

"I'm fine," said Vincent.

"You keep touching your shoulder."

"Old injury."

"What happened?"

"Gunshot."

Tetris peered at him. "Gunshot."

"I was a cop," said Vincent.

"I could believe that."

The agent picked at skin around his fingernails.

"You're the kind of guy who only believes in black and white," said Tetris. "Right and wrong."

"No."

"That's why you don't like me. No patience for the chaotic neutral."

"Reason I don't like you is you're an asshole."

"You were an only child, I suspect."

"I had two brothers."

"Well. I bet you got along real well with them, huh?"

Vincent didn't reply. He rotated the pencil stub back and forth.

*****

The days dragged on, each more monotonous than the last. Sometimes the farmer came to visit, forcing Tetris to hide in the loft, wedged beneath the sloped ceiling, until Li gave him the all-clear. He wasn't the only one feeling cooped up. When the food ran out, everyone was so eager to get off the farm that they went to town and left Tetris behind. He prowled and paced and counted knots in the bare plank walls. Somehow he'd expected that escaping the cell would mean an end to inaction. Instead he was back to doing nothing, dribbling time through his fingers like mud, unsure whether he wanted it to flow slower or faster.

If the days were purgatory, the nights were far worse.

Eight hours of uninterrupted silence, without even the forest to keep him company most of the time. He got so bored that he began to pray for something to happen. Anything at all.

One lonesome nocturnal vigil, he spotted a pair of hunched shapes making their way across the night-glassed lawn. The way they moved, furtive and scuttling, you could tell they were up to no good. Burglars? Murderers? Tetris closed his eyes and reached out the way he'd learned to do in the Omphalos cell. The trespassers' auras tasted like melted plastic. Emitting acrid psychic fumes, they drifted towards the farmhouse.

Tetris opened his eyes just in time to see knives come twinkling out of sheaths as the figures stepped onto the farmer's porch. One man's shoulder brushed a wind chime. In the motionless air, the tinkling sounded somehow profane.

Tetris went to the back door of the barn and slid it quietly open.

His night vision didn't make things brighter—it was dark as a walled-off mine shaft—but he could see nonetheless. Every edge of grass stood out in calcified relief. Only a portion of the image was visual. According to the forest, Tetris's custom-built night vision pooled echolocation and electromagnetic spectra on the fringes of visible light, the clamoring sensory potpourri relayed down sparking nerve networks to a newly swollen region of his brain, where overtime neural efforts produced a composite image more reminiscent of an etching in obsidian than a photograph.

Point being that his days of stumbling after rabbits were over. This was Tetris Aphelion v1.3, a far cry from Vanilla T, with more patches undoubtedly on the way. Night vision had come fully online during their march through the Atlantic. When he'd descended into the chasm with Toni Davis in his arms, Tetris had been able to see the tendrils gather her in. The look on her unconscious face, he remembered, had been peaceful, her mouth hanging open as the leg wound suppurated through its wrappings...

He stalked across the open ground, quiet and ominous as an upper-canopy breeze.

The robbers had left the door swinging gently on its hinges. Tetris traced a finger along the wood as he passed. He rode the liquid darkness that rushed ahead to lap against peeling wallpaper and framed family photos. Red-rimmed auras led him up the stairs and down the hall to the master bedroom.

Lights snapped on, casting huge knife-wielding shadows into the hallway. A voice cried out. Tetris stood a few yards back, the balls of his bare feet kissing the hardwood, and took a deep breath through his nose.

The trespasser on the left was thickset and bald, with a purple splotch the shape of France on his shiny skull. On the right slouched a man as hirsute as the first burglar was hairless. Black curls protruded from the collar of his worn blue polo.

On the far side of the room, shielded by a massive four-poster bed, the farmer held a WWII-era rifle, its ancient barrel vacillating from target to target.

The bald trespasser said something in Spanish and gestured with his knife.

The farmer's gun froze. He stared at Tetris, who loomed above and behind the thugs, head just shy of the doorframe.

Spitting, the hirsute trespasser said something that sounded like a curse. He took a step forward. The bald one took a step in the opposite direction, pincering around the bed.

Tetris stepped in, palmed the skull of the bald trespasser, and flung him face-first into the wall. He enjoyed the movement, the simple casual flick, the deep shuddering boom when face met siding. Enjoyed the quick pivot and reach for the second man, whose spinning face broadcast the abject terror of a horror movie jump-scare. For the thug, the darkness had parted to reveal six and a half feet of huge-pupiled boogeyman. Before the would-be robber's brain could begin to parse the impending fight/flight dilemma, Tetris's knee planted itself midway up his chest.

The whole process took no more than two seconds: Tetris appearing, one quick step, first trespasser flung, a pivot so swift that splayed toes squeaked on wood, then one more step and a falcon-like strike with the non-stepping knee. The kneed, hairy thug approached the wall with velocity that suggested, like, two hundred percent, easy. The sound was BOOM-squeak-BOOM, followed by the double-whump of bodies hitting the floor milliseconds apart.

"You're okay," said Tetris, raising a calming hand to the farmer and his wife.

The farmer pointed the antique firearm at Tetris's head and pulled the trigger. Nothing happened.

"Jesus, man," said Tetris, coming up from a duck. "What's wrong with you?"

The thug who'd received the knee lunged along the floor with his serrated knife Achilles-bound. Tetris leapt the strike and landed stumbling on the man's back while the other thug came staggering over, knife wavering, nose not so much broken as forcibly retracted into his face.

On the other side of the bed, the farmer frantically worked at unjamming his weapon, a detail Tetris noted with some trepidation while he tried to figure out how to avoid the two crazily-slashing knives. A blade bit his arm and he roared, right hand dribbling the prone assailant's face against the hardwood while his free hand reached and grabbed what turned out to be the crotch of the upright slashing bloody-faced bald guy. Then, with some kind of off-kilter drunken surge, Tetris rose, applying his shoulder liberally to the chest of the man whose you-know-whats were clutched so unpleasantly in his huge green hand. A flip and a shove and the bald man returned to the wall he'd hit originally, upside down and with considerably more force, actually rupturing the drywall this time, and then a shot rang out, as the farmer at last convinced his weapon to fire.

Despite squirming slabs of muscle occupying sixty to seventy percent of his field of view, the farmer missed everything. The 50s-era heirloom bullet screamed across the hall into the bathroom, where it busted a pipe. As water shrieked through the gap, Tetris hunched and hobbled around the face-down home invader's blind desperate knife swings, finally dropping a fist on the back of the shaggy head. The knife arm went boneless.

Another shot, this one tickling his hair—

Out Tetris went, into the hall, slipping on cascading water and nearly pitching headfirst down the stairs before righting himself against a railing. One two three huge steps and out into the darkness again, bolting across the field, stupid stupid stupid, of course they were going to react like that, they'd had no idea he was in the barn, plus they'd probably heard more than a few things about big murderous green men on the news—

"Holy fuck we have to go we have to go," he shouted, bursting through the double doors—

—to find the whole crew awake and dressed, cramming supplies into flimsy duffel bags—

—while at the other end of the barn Douglas "Hollywood" Douglas worked on molding wide-eyed surprise into trademark sardonic sneer.

*****

The airship station in Porto resembled a giant Soviet playground, with towering concrete spires and grim dingy chasms between loading plinths that stretched for miles. Tethered to the spires, airships drifted near-imperceptibly in the brisk wind, such that if you stared at them too long you began to feel that the ground was moving beneath you. Everything in sight was gray or black or an extremely jaundiced yellow. Zip, Li, Dr. Alvarez, Vincent, Hollywood, and Tetris, who felt naked beneath his thick impasto of body paint, battled through the teeming crowds to loading dock seventeen, where an airship was scheduled to depart within the hour for New York City.

While the body paint succeeded in de-greening Tetris, it did not render him inconspicuous. It was supposed to be Caucasian skin-colored, but in reality it was closer to orange. Tetris looked either aggressively spray-tanned or afflicted with a horrible skin condition. Based on the berth he was being given, the passersby seemed to have decided on the latter.

"I know you missed me," said Hollywood, throwing an arm around Zip as they walked.

"Sure," said Zip, shrugging out of the arm.

"Partners in crime."

Vincent walked beside them, face hidden behind enormous aviators.

Hollywood popped a bright pink wad of gum. "Li, I don't believe your countryman here has said a word since I arrived."

"I didn't miss you a bit, if you're wondering," said Li.

"You realize I helped save you, right?"

"I would have escaped on my own."

Hollywood snorted, dodging an elderly woman with a pushcart who seemed wholly oblivious to their presence. "Yeah, okay. Buried under forty feet of concrete and bosom-deep in armed guards. Stage a regular old El Chapo kind of deal, I'm sure."

"We had a few ideas," said Dr. Alvarez.

"Science," said Hollywood, seizing on the only fact he knew about Dr. Alvarez, "can only get you so far, gorgeous."

Tetris bristled. "Shut up and keep an eye out."

Hollywood bent back dramatically to stare up at him. "Wow! Here I was thinking you were so deep in the brooding-hero shtick that you wouldn't speak up for at least another couple of days."

Tetris hefted his pack.

Hollywood danced around in front of him. "Look, bud, your twelve-inch green boner for the Doctor is nobody's secret whatsoever."

Tetris stopped walking.

"What?" said Hollywood, hopping from foot to foot with a chimpanzee grin. "Why the smoldering look, hmm? You think you're subtle? I've been here five minutes and I figured it out."

Tetris glimpsed Dr. Alvarez stifling a smile behind her hand.

"You know what," he said, "I did actually miss you, man. I'm thankful you helped me escape, and glad you made it out okay."

Hollywood squinted. The grin vanished. "Umm."

Tetris laid a gentle hand on his shoulder. "I respect and appreciate your friendship. Thank you for everything you've done."

"Think you're clever, huh?"

"Thank you, Hollywood. I am in your debt."

The blond ranger walked the rest of the way in sullen, glowering silence.

24

Tetris was sequestered in narrow quarters usually reserved for the airship's housecleaning staff. Zip and Hollywood had bribed a surly officer for access to the room, which with its bed folded out was barely wide enough for a normal adult male, let alone a hulking green one, to turn 180 degrees. Everyone but Tetris had normal quarters elsewhere on the ship. They came down regularly to visit him, bearing food and stories of adventures on the upper decks, but he couldn't help feeling imprisoned. He folded up the bed to get as much space as possible and paced the room. His shoulders brushed the walls whenever the airship swayed.

Dr. Alvarez kept bringing him books to read (there was a bookstore on deck five), and he kept having to come up with lame excuses for why he hadn't gotten around to opening them. He wasn't in the mood. Instead he spent most of his stationary time gazing out the porthole at the

Atlantic Forest. The canopy was a motionless rug from this height. When clouds obscured his view, he closed his eyes and watched visual feeds from the forest.

The latest vision took him somewhere in the South Pacific, where a ten-story blue heron stalked between the trees with fierce orange eyes beneath black-feathered brows. The creature's beak was a twenty-foot spear. The heron strode crisply to a huge pool of scum-rimmed water.

Lakes were a rarity in the forest, because water tended to drain away through the interlocking debris into the onyx depths. This lake, with the heron stepping carefully along its edge, was actually a rainwater-filled hemisphere of some enormous creature's skull, the jagged bone-edges still protruding through the leaves and dirt in certain spots along the rim.

The heron stopped. For a moment it was still, surveying the water. Then its cocked head began to inch downward, the long neck unfurling, the movement slow and controlled.

When it struck, the heron's head moved so fast that it simply vanished from the sky and reappeared exploding out of the water, reeling back with an alligator speared on the tip of its cruel yellow beak. The reptile's crenellated tail flapped. The heron tilted its head back and tossed the meal down, swallowing in multiple tremoring gulps. It shrugged its wings a little, shifted from foot to foot, and settled itself, long neck reassuming its precise s-curve, ready to strike again.

Sitting on the edge of the folded-out bed, leaning his head on the window, Tetris barely registered the opening of the door.

"Thank God," he said, turning. "I was starv—"

Instead of Li or Dr. Alvarez, a dark-skinned man in a crisp button-up, wide eyes framed by curly hair and a thick beard, stared back at him.

"Pardon me, sir," said the man. He tugged the door closed as fast as he could. Not fast enough, as Tetris lunged across the room to drag him inside.

*****

"Stewart," said Hollywood, "you are not pulling your weight, man."

"Your pal's a real asshole," said Stewart to Zip. They were huddled at one end of the basketball court on the airship's top deck. Their opponents leaned against the far wall, scratching matching chinstraps. One of the opponents had the ball and was spinning it idly on his finger.

"Don't I know it," said Zip.

"Focus!" hissed Hollywood. "Focus! I am not losing to these clowns!"

"Hollywood," said Zip, "we're down fifteen points in a first-to-thirty. I'm pretty sure we lost."

"Quitter."

"Yeah, I quit," said Stewart, who'd introduced himself as an accountant from Maine. Sweat poured down the soft folds of his face.

"No—No. No, you do NOT quit," said Hollywood, grabbing his arm. "And you!" He glowered at Zip. "I thought you'd be good at this."

Zip bristled. "And why's that, huh? Because if you say what I think you're going to say—"

"Never mind."

"Dude. I'm playing with a prosthetic."

"I wish Tetris were here. We need somebody who can dunk."

"I don't understand why you care so much," said Stewart, massaging his wrist where Hollywood had grabbed him. "It's just a game, man."

Hollywood's voice jumped two octaves. "Just a game, he says! Look at them! Look at their cocky faces!"

"Hey idiots," called Li, tossing aside the mesh door, "we've got a situation."

"Not now," said Hollywood. "We're in the middle of a game."

"This is an emergency," said Li. "Involving our friend. The, uh, special one."

Zip dragged Hollywood off the court. They power-walked through the maze of corridors and down the corrugated iron stairs near the back of the ship, Hollywood complaining the whole way.

"I just don't understand what was so important that it couldn't wait ten minutes," he whined.

"If I ever have kids, and they turn out like you, I'm going to smother them," said Li, leaping down the stairs.

They rushed down the hall toward Tetris's room. The door, when it opened, slammed into Tetris's back. He grunted and stepped aside. The dark-skinned man stood, chest puffed out bravely, in the far corner.

"Who's that?" asked Hollywood, up on his tiptoes.

"Move," said Li, shoving Tetris out of the way. When everyone was inside, she crammed the door shut. Dr. Alvarez, sitting on the bed next to the prisoner, brought her legs up to give them room.

"My name is Tejas Ramalingam," said the curly-haired man. "I demand that you release me at once."

"Buddy," said Zip, thinking about the Omphalos Initiative, "why are you here?"

"I'm on my way to a conference in New York," said Mr. Ramalingam.

"No, I mean, why are you in this room?"

"I was looking for a restroom when this gorilla abducted me."

"He opened the door and walked right in," said Tetris. "I figured I couldn't let him go."

"I am an executive and a human being," said Mr. Ramalingam. "I have inalienable rights."

"An executive where?" asked Hollywood, peering around Zip and Li.

"If you must know," said Mr. Ramalingam, "I'm an executive director of sales and marketing for a multinational breakfast foods conglomerate."

"Breakfast foods," said Li.

"Quite. I'm in the toaster pastry division. You'd be surprised all the intricacies that go into—"

"Shut up," said Li.

"What do we do?" asked Tetris.

"You can't just keep him prisoner," said Dr. Alvarez. "Someone will notice that he's gone."

"Someone will most certainly notice that I'm gone," agreed Mr. Ramalingam.

"If we let him go, he'll tell them Tetris is here," said Li.

"I would do no such thing," said Mr. Ramalingam.

"Shut up!"

"I object to your rudeness."

Someone knocked insistently on the door.

"Shit," said Li, turning to Tetris. "Hide."

"Where?"

"Under the bed," said Dr. Alvarez. "We'll stand in front of you."

Tetris wedged himself beneath the fold-out cot.

"Don't say a word," said Li, planting a finger in Mr. Ramalingam's chest. He opened his mouth, saw the look in her eyes, and thought better of whatever he'd intended to say.

Hollywood opened the door. On the other side, a pair of uniformed crewmen stood staring, epaulets shiny and blue.

"What can we do for you gentlemen?" asked Zip.

"What on Earth," said the shorter crewman, whose extremely thick glasses made his eyes look two or three times their actual size.

"We're looking for a Mr. Tejas Rangalingo?" said the taller crewman, hand frozen mid-scratch along his jaw. "His wife sent—we saw on the security cameras that he was—"

"It's Ramalingam," said Mr. Ramalingam over Li's shoulder, prompting her to turn and give him a death glare.

"Who gave you permission to occupy this room?" squeaked the shorter crewman. "These are crew quarters. No passengers—"

Hollywood had his wallet out. "Alright, gentlemen, which currency do we prefer—"

"—my name is Mr. Tejas Ramalingam, I am a citizen of the Republic of India and an executive director of sales and marketing for—"

"—Shut your mouth you little—"

"—is that a bribe? Are you attempting to bribe me?"

"—DON'T HURT ME EEEE THERE IS A GIANT GREEN MAN UNDER THE BED PLEASE HELP ME EEEE—"

"—this is very disorderly, very disorderly conduct indeed, I believe I'll have to call—"

"—no no, I understand, that offer was a bit low, how about let's double it, hmmm? Zip, do you by any chance happen to have your wallet on you? I'm thinking these men are—"

"HELP! I'VE BEEN KIDNAPPED! THEY'RE GOING TO FEED ME TO THE GREEN MAN!"

"—under the bed, is that—is there another person in

this room? What's the meaning—"

Soon the two crewmen had joined Mr. Ramalingam beside the window, and things had quieted down substantially.

"Can I come out now?" asked Tetris, his voice muffled. Dr. Alvarez stepped off the bed and flipped it out of the way. Tetris put a hand on his knee and levered himself up.

"The Green Giant," breathed the shorter crewman, eyes filling up his glasses.

"In retrospect, I much preferred 'Green Ranger,'" said Tetris, stretching his cramped neck.

"Who knows you're here?" demanded Li. "How long until they come looking?"

"I'll never tell you anything," said the shorter crewman, raising his chin.

"The captain and the first mate and the quartermaster and the head of security," babbled the tall one, earning ocular daggers from his companion. "Oh God I'm sorry please don't kill me."

"How long do we have?" asked Li.

"Twenty minutes? I don't know! I don't know!"

"Guys," said Dr. Alvarez, "we aren't going to hurt you. We just need to make it to New York without anybody knowing we're on board. Okay? That's all."

"Free us," said Mr. Ramalingam. "We won't breathe a word to anyone."

Hollywood snorted.

"It's not like you have another choice," said Mr. Ramalingam. "You can only fit so many kidnapees in this room."

The room was indeed growing extremely crowded. Tetris yearned for fresh air.

"Here's the plan," said Li. "Tetris, stay here. Doc, retrieve the body paint and get Tetris suited up, just in case. Everybody else: we're going to the bridge."

Just like that, the room emptied out. Tetris, alone again, pushed a hand through his hair and exhaled heavily. Then he popped the bed, sat down, and cracked open one of the books from Dr. Alvarez.

25

"I've been thinking about the plane crash," said Dr. Alvarez as she rubbed body paint on the back of Tetris's neck.

"What about it?"

"'Airplane engines don't just explode' is common knowledge, I feel. Especially on carefully maintained government aircraft."

"That feels," he rumbled, "super good, by the way."

"So obviously the plane was sabotaged."

"Oh, obviously, yeah. Uh huh."

"The question is who sabotaged it."

"Hmm."

Her hands retreated. Tetris sighed.

"Whoever it was," she said, "they had access to the

runway, right? The plane landed, picked us up, soared away. Blew up in midair."

"China," he said. "Russia?"

"That was my first thought. But if news got out—that they tried to kill the Secretary of State—think about the disaster that would be. Why take the risk? If they wanted you dead, why not murder you in your sleep?"

"Me?"

"So I assumed terrorism. But I've been doing some research, and it seems like nobody took credit. Everyone seems to think it was a malfunction. It was made to look like a malfunction. Which only leaves one possibility."

Vincent Chen bulldozed into the room. "What the fuck is going on?"

Tetris rose. "You ever heard of knocking?"

"Everyone is missing," said Vincent. "People are saying the ship's been hijacked. The captain came over the intercom and told us to stay in our rooms." He turned and spat quickly into the hall. "And you're back in body paint."

"Vince," said Dr. Alvarez, "take it easy."

In the expression Vincent directed at Dr. Alvarez, a familiar internal battle unfolded. His lip curled and uncurled like a worm trapped on the sidewalk.

"Walk with us," she said.

They made their way to the bridge, Vincent prowling, Tetris's long arms swinging at his side. When they knocked, the heavy door swung open, and Zip ushered them through.

"Word is out," said Dr. Alvarez. "What happened?"

"Housecleaning caught me unpacking my gun," said Hollywood, leaning on the console beside the captain, whose trim blue-lined hat was sorely askew. "The lady ran before I could add her to our collection."

He gestured toward the corner where six crew members and one Indian breakfast pastry executive sported matching scowls. Under Li's raptor gaze, none of them seemed inclined to budge.

"What's to stop the passengers from notifying the authorities?" asked Dr. Alvarez.

"We disabled the satellite internet," said Li, nodding at a panel that showed signs of repeated bludgeoning. A battle-scarred fire extinguisher lay nearby. "And until we're closer to shore, they can't get signal to use cell phones."

The captain swallowed hard. His Adam's apple jumped up and down.

Hollywood scratched himself under the chin with the barrel of his gun. "We've got our buddy here making regular announcements. 'Apologies for the broken internet,' 'Remain in your rooms until the turbulence subsides,' 'Dinner canceled but we'll send housekeeping around with some extra mints,' et cetera. He's got a great voice. Dude should be calling ball games."

"Please," said the captain, "put the gun away. We're cooperating."

He really did have a deep and sonorous voice. Hollywood shrugged and stuck the pistol in his waistband.

"We would like to avoid hurting anyone," said Li.

One of the prisoners, whose face was sprouting purple lumps in several places, snorted.

Li shrugged. "Anyone else, I mean."

"What happened to him?" asked Tetris.

"Our friend here fancied himself a kickboxer," said Li primly. She examined her knuckles.

"I'm a black belt," said the bruised prisoner defensively.

Li faked toward him, shoulder jutting, and the prisoner flung himself into the arms of his comrades.

Vincent blew air through pursed lips. "Hijacking. I believe I draw the line at hijacking."

"Nobody asked your opinion," said Hollywood.

"You're committing a federal crime," said Vincent. "This is terrorism. There's no going back from here."

"Oh, come on," said Li. "We'll let them go when we arrive."

"Doctor," said Vincent, "you don't have to be a part of this."

Dr. Alvarez gave him a crooked smile. "It's way too late for that, Vince."

"This is wrong," he said.

"If we stop now, we'll fall right into the FBI's arms," said Zip.

"If you're innocent, you have nothing to fear."

"We're not innocent," said Tetris. "But neither are they."

Vincent didn't look at him, just pounded a fist into an open palm, turned, and thrust the heavy steel door out of his way. It slammed shut behind him.

"I am wondering," said Tetris when the silence had curdled, "how we intend to keep this a secret when we get within cell range."

"We'll be long gone by then," said Li.

*****

That night, Tetris and Zip had first shift watching the prisoners.

"There's something I've been meaning to tell you," said Zip.

"Whatever it is, don't worry about it."

"We met your dad, man. Back when everybody thought you were dead."

Tetris didn't know how to respond, so he didn't say anything at all.

After a while Zip shifted, crossing his prosthetic leg beneath the other. "I liked him, actually."

"Hmm."

"Hollywood didn't want to take him. Your dad couldn't pay, obviously. But I paid for him. I don't know if I'm afraid of you being mad about that, or what."

"I'm not mad."

Zip wiped his mouth on the back of his hand. "He cares about you, I think."

"That's what you think?"

"It's none of my business."

One of the prisoners snored like a row of laundromat

dryers. Tetris battled an urge to kick him.

"So are you telling me this," said Tetris, "because you know where he is, and you want me to visit him? Something like that?"

"I just felt like it was a weird thing to keep from you. Like, hey, I met your dad and almost got him killed, and never told you about it."

Tetris cracked his neck once in each direction.

"Everybody on that trip died except him and Hollywood," said Zip.

"Tougher than he looks."

"Runs in the family, huh?"

"Some of us, anyway."

*****

The New York City skyline was a blip on the horizon when Tetris and the others stepped off the airship's emergency exit deck and into empty air. Tumbling, Tetris extended his arms and legs and thrust his face into the wind. The parachute and gear were a reassuring weight on his back. Finally some action!

He rolled to look up at the others as they plummeted after him. Beating his chest, he unleashed a joyous animal roar, but the wind carried it away. He turned his attention back to the fast-approaching canopy.

Welcome home, said the forest.

Tetris grinned so hard that the edges of his wind-seared face began to hurt.

They floated down like dandelion seeds on plump white parachutes. The treetops, which looked so soft from above, proved to be full of grasping branches and whisking leaf edges. Dragons and spiders scampered through the canopy, rooting out any wildlife likely to prove dangerous to the forest's guests. As Tetris unhitched from his parachute and fell sure-footed to a branch immediately below, he closed his eyes and breathed deep. The fecund oxygen-rich air that filled his lungs was nothing like the harsh cigarette smoke of the airship port or the crisp but flavorless air of the Portuguese countryside. This air was alive.

Why the airship had carried an arsenal of ranger gear in a fusty cargo hold was anybody's guess, but Tetris and the others were certainly grateful for the oversight. Once everyone had landed, they rappelled smartly to the forest floor.

"I didn't realize how much I missed this," said Zip, testing his prosthetic against a fallen branch.

Everyone seemed to share the sentiment. They stood for a while and listened. The air swam with pollen and golden motes. A pillbug poked its head out and wiggled antennae at them. Tetris pressed a palm against a mossy trunk, reveling in the tree's smoky aroma and implacable firmness. The buzz of tiny insects came in waves, an ambient lullaby. Somewhere just out of sight, dragons crashed and caroused, occasionally issuing half-hearted shrieks. The spiders had retreated.

Hurry, said the forest.

"Let's go," said Tetris. They were still fugitives. China and Brazil were still dumping defoliants on the canopy. And the invisible cosmic cataclysm was still grinding toward them, inevitable as the sun's eventual implosion. Back in Seattle, his old answering machine was probably still blinking, crammed full of unanswered messages from his father.

"Hey," said Li a few minutes later, jogging up beside him. Her tight-strapped pack bounced on her shoulders. "Slow down. We can't keep up."

Tetris turned and saw them straggling along, Zip limping in the rear.

"Sorry," he said. "I got distracted."

"Let me lead for a while," she said, and reached up to pat him on the shoulder. "Keep Zip company."

Tetris stood aside and let Hollywood and Dr. Alvarez pass.

"You fuckers better not slow down for me," growled Zip.

"No matter what," said Tetris, "this can't be slower than last time."

Zip stuck his arms out to balance as his prosthetic foot twisted on a loose stone. Tetris caught his elbow.

"Don't touch me," said Zip, tugging his arm free.

"Let me know if you want a piggy-back ride," said Tetris brightly.

The reply, a list of unsanitary objects and corresponding orifices Tetris was invited to insert them into, brought a smile to his worn green face.

26

It was four-thirty a.m. and the sun had just begun to suggest a rise out of the green expanse behind them. Several miles north, a flock of dragons distracted the Coast Guard. Tetris, coat of paint flecking, led the way between spotlights and up the sandy slope. They hurried across the no-man's-land and ducked under the black and yellow bar of a Coast Guard checkpoint. The checkpoint's sole occupant snored in a teetering chair.

Atlantic City. Tetris crossed a deserted boardwalk under three-story crimson letters. The streets beyond were empty. The air was cold and still except for occasional gusts with fluoride edges. A truck rumbled by, trailing cartoonish curls of exhaust.

The few pedestrians in view wrote them off in a single sliding glance. A raccoon rustling in a dumpster poked its head out, deemed them no threat, and returned to scavenging. Even the clouds seemed shriveled from the cold. They were looking for a motel when Zip spotted a familiar figure on the far side of the street.

"George!"

Tetris snapped around. Skyscrapers and parking decks folded down like scenery in a pop-up book. His father looked both ways and crossed the street.

"Thomas," said George Aphelion, "you have to leave. They're coming."

Oh yeah, said the forest, *I forgot to tell you about him.*

Tetris, stepping backward, slipped on the curb and stumbled into the street. Something hummed past his ear. The flat crack of the gunshot arrived afterward, and as Tetris regained his footing he saw his father collapsing, spinning to the pavement and clawing at unconcerned air—

Tetris scooped him up and hurtled behind a parked car. The sidewalk kicked up splinters as a second shot missed. Although he felt no pain, Tetris knew he'd bit hard into his tongue.

George was whiter than bone. A darkening blotch

stained his side.

Li skidded around the corner.

"Stay with him," said Tetris.

Li ripped her pack open. Glass sprayed overhead from a third shot. George, eyes closed, remained still. Tetris rooted in his pack.

"The rooftop," said Li as her hands whisked across George, tearing his shirt open, bandages flying off their rolls. She bit off a length of tape.

"That's my dad," said Tetris.

George mouthed something.

"Fuck," said Tetris, trying to convert the tears to something more useful. His muscles hummed. "Fuck. Fuck."

"It's a scratch," said Li, bandaging the gash. "Tetris. He's fine. It only nicked him."

Tetris wrenched the grapple gun out of his pack and lunged around the corner. There—a flash of sun on scope. Gargoyles leered from the edge of the roof. Tetris raised the grapple gun and fired.

He crossed the void to the rooftop in a single breath. The wind tore tears from his eyes. He reached the gargoyle and grasped its curled stone tail. Fingers raw on time-scarred stone, he went over the lip like a spider. The sniper turned, hefting his awkward rifle, the bipod swinging slack beneath the barrel.

Tetris dove. He caught the man's leg and shoved him back as the rifle discharged overhead. The man released his gun, which toppled over the edge, and struck Tetris on the back of the head. Falling hard on one hand, Tetris righted himself, but the man was already circling, knife flitting out of its sheath.

The man dodged Tetris's reaching hand and opened a gash along his arm. Tetris landed a shoulder to the exposed chest, but his assailant only danced back. The knife came flying in again, ready to bury itself in green abdominal flesh. Tetris caught the hand.

He tried to snap the wrist, but the man rolled with the motion somehow and fired off a kick as he went, foot landing hard against Tetris's temple. As blood pumped from the gash on his inner arm, Tetris grabbed for the man's neck. Again he dodged.

The roof was empty except for a concrete structure behind the assassin, its entryway doorstopped by a folded newspaper.

The assassin shoulder-faked and smiled when Tetris flinched. Above the black turtleneck, his skin was pink. His breath hung crystalline in the air.

Tetris snorted a thundercloud and charged.

He swung and swung, the blows firing off fast and unrestrained, but the man refused to be touched, sneaking in a slash here and there as he ducked and slid. Tetris pulled away, panting. Blood flowed from several cuts, stinging in the grime and body paint. One was just above his eye. He wiped the blood away.

Still the man jeered, silent.

He's playing with you, said the forest.

"Real fucking helpful," said Tetris, spitting blood.

Then he thought about it for a second.

Again he closed the gap, winding up for a haymaker. As the assassin shifted, Tetris abandoned the punch and snapped his torso around. His left fist zipped electric-fast to fill the corridor of space the assassin's dodge had taken him to—

Ribs buckled. The assassin bent almost in half and began at once to recover, the knife slashing around, no kidding this time, aimed at the jugular—and Tetris stepped out of the deadly steel arc. Struck a hard flat blow that snapped the assassin's head back.

That was the opening. Tetris grabbed the wrist and broke it for real this time. His knee met the man's hard midriff as the knife skittered away. Blood spattered from Tetris's wounds as he flung the man against the narrow edge of the door. The impact was so great that Tetris momentarily lost his hold. He drove a knee into the man's stomach as he fell, feeling soft innards give way. Rage screamed in his thunking skull.

The man struggled to his knees. Blood poured from his mouth. Tetris reared back and...

The assassin blinked, waiting.

Tetris dropped his fist. "Who are you?"

The assassin didn't respond. Sirens shrieked. Tetris peered over the edge as cop cars raced around the corner. Li and the others were nowhere to be seen.

Down the stairs, urged the forest. *They may not know you're up here yet.*

A flash of movement and Tetris whirled, but the

assassin wasn't headed for him. Like a demented stork, he staggered to the railing and flung himself off. A thin ribbon of blood trailed after him. Tetris watched him hit the pavement.

"Holy shit."

There's no time.

"You brought my dad," said Tetris as he rushed down the stairs. He wiped his hands on his shirt. Body paint came away with the blood, revealing splotches of green skin.

He wanted to help. I linked to him in the Pacific.

"Is he going to die?"

Silence.

Tetris covered flight after flight. On the bottom floor he paused, unsure which route to take. A pair of hands reached out and grabbed his arm.

"This way," hissed Hollywood, and ran.

They weaved down a hallway and blasted through a swinging door. Beyond was a kitchen, all brushed steel and dangling knives, the narrow aisles bustling with workers. Tetris accidentally knocked a pot out of someone's hands. Noodles smashed in steaming heaps on the blue and white tile.

Then they were outside. Hollywood was fast, had always been fast, and Tetris found that he could really unleash, stretch his legs and not worry about leaving the blond ranger behind. They flew down an alley as police sirens careened off the walls.

"Who was that?" asked Hollywood.

"No idea," said Tetris, "but he's dead."

He felt the words leave his mouth, but somehow they still sounded like they originated from some point outside his body. They paused behind a dumpster as a taxi rolled quietly past.

"Hey," shouted Hollywood, running into the street with his arms waving.

"What about the others?" asked Tetris as the cab slowed.

"What about them?"

"We can't just leave them."

"Can, will, and are about to," said Hollywood, ducking into the cab.

A cop car screamed across a distant intersection, lights flashing, heading back the way they'd come.

"Last chance," said Hollywood, reaching for the door. Tetris caught it and tossed his gear inside.

The turbaned cabby proffered a tall-toothed smile. "Where to, sirs?"

"Pottsville, Pennsylvania," said Hollywood.

The driver blinked. His bushy mustache wriggled. "Too far."

"How's two thousand bucks sound?"

Soon they were on the expressway, roaring northwest.

"Where are we going?" asked Tetris.

"I know a guy," said Hollywood. "We can lay low at his place for a while."

Tetris shifted, trying to position his legs so blood could reach his tingling feet. "How long's the drive?"

"Three hours, sirs," said the cab driver. "Music?"

"No," said Tetris.

"Yes, please," said Hollywood.

The driver reached for the knob, paused, looked at Tetris in the rear view, and retracted his hand. Tetris showed his canines.

"Hey," said Hollywood. "I'm the one paying the bill."

So they listened to the radio. Pop music. The driver hummed along. Tetris leaned against the window and watched the highway unfurl.

"Look, shithead, your dad's going to be fine," said Hollywood.

The trees that weren't already bare were changing, an intermittent frenzy of orange and red. It seemed like half the trucks they passed were hauling lumber. Tetris pinched his arm, twisting the green skin until it turned blue-black.

Every hour or so, they faded out of radio range, and the driver had to fiddle with the dial to find something new. They listened to country, R&B, and another pop station before finally the sign for Pottsville appeared overhead.

"Where do I drop you off?" asked the driver as they cruised down Pottsville's narrow streets. It was 9 a.m. and the residents of the town were walking their dogs down rows of identical red-roofed houses.

"I'm starving," said Hollywood. "What's that say? Right there's fine."

The diner was packed with white-haired, suspendered working men. Waitresses sailed through the aisles with sloshing pots of coffee. Tetris and Hollywood tossed their gear into a booth and slid in after it. Everything was bathed in the saturated yellow light of a courthouse snack shop.

"What'll you have, honey?" asked the gum-munching waitress, plucking a pen from behind her ear.

"Coffee, please," said Hollywood. "Four eggs. Bacon. And sausage. Do you guys have blueberry pancakes? I'll have those too, thanks. Extra butter."

The waitress scrawled three quick hieroglyphs and turned to Tetris. "What about you, hon?"

"Bacon and eggs, please," said Tetris. "And a large Coke."

The best that could be said about the food was that it was warm. Still, it beat the forest tubers they'd been eating for the past week, so their plates were cleaned in minutes. Tetris emptied his soda in two gulps and asked for a refill. Stole one of Hollywood's pancakes when he was in the bathroom, then ordered a stack for himself.

"Y'all have a pay phone?" asked Hollywood when the waitress came to collect their dishes.

"Round the corner at the dollar store," said the waitress. Hollywood tipped her a fifty.

It had begun to warm up a bit. The sun shone out of a pallid blue void. Hollywood watched a young mother push a stroller down the opposite sidewalk.

"Oo-wee," he said, blowing into his hands and rubbing them. His nose was pink.

More than anything else, Tetris wanted a shower. He

searched the windows of every house they passed. Even walking through a real-life Norman Rockwell painting, he couldn't shake the feeling that someone was waiting to leap out of the bushes with an Uzi.

"Hey Dicer," said Hollywood after he'd dialed. "Need a favor."

The voice that came crackling through the receiver was rich and expressive, but Tetris couldn't make out a word it said.

"Pottsville," said Hollywood. "Down the street from, uh, Gramma's Family Diner." He paused, listening. "Yeah, no, I didn't try the roast beef, but I saw some other folks— yeah, no, I hear you. Looked like a winner."

"Who is this guy?" asked Tetris when Hollywood hung up.

"You'll like him," said Hollywood.

Thirty minutes later, Dicer roared up in a pickup truck the size of a bulldozer. He leapt down to greet Hollywood with a handshake that promptly turned into a hug.

"Douglas Squared," said Dicer. "Way too long, comrade."

As quick as he'd wrapped Hollywood in a hug, Dicer sprang back, hopping lightly from toe to toe. He was six and a half feet of dark rolling muscle, bald, with a wreath of curly hair along his cheeks and beneath his chin. His eyes were big and jolly, and his nose looked to have been broken at least four or five times. He wore a tired gray muscle shirt with "MILF Hunter" in faded red letters.

"Jim," said Hollywood, "this is my buddy, Tetris."

"You're a big one," said Dicer. "Ever think about MMA?"

"I don't know if they have a weight class for him," said Hollywood. "Let's split."

They bombed along Pottsville's roads, Tetris in the back seat grabbing the handle over the door every time they hit a curve. Something that sounded like a bunch of steel chains clattered in the truck bed.

"What have you got back there?" asked Tetris.

"Bunch of steel chains," said Dicer. "So what is it this time, Douglas? Y'all rob a nursing home?"

"Yeah," said Hollywood, "we're on a string of nursing home robberies. They call us the Denture Desperados. Got a sack full of fake teeth right here. Just waiting for things to cool down before I flip 'em on the prosthodontic black market."

Douglas looked at him gravely.

"Yeah," he said, "I've been there." He brightened, slaloming into the oncoming lane to zoom past a school bus. "Well, no fear. It's a great time to hole up in the country. Hunting's great! Fishing's great! Yesterday I caught a snapper turtle!"

Hollywood unwrapped a cube of pink bubble gum. "They have those up here?"

"Evidently."

They were out of the city now, bumping along a rugged road.

"Where are you from, big guy?"

It took Tetris a minute to realize the question was

directed at him. "Indianapolis."

"No shit. I love Indy."

Tetris curled and uncurled a hand. "Why's that?"

"Cheese steak. Best cheese steaks in the Midwest."

"Cheese steak?"

"That's correct."

"I wasn't aware—"

"No, they have them, you just have to know where to look."

Eventually they took an exit and drove half an hour down a narrow highway lined closely with trees that had discarded most of their leaves. Then they came to an even smaller road, unmarked, that led into the forest. The road wound back and forth, passing isolated residences, narrowing all the time, until finally it turned to gravel. Onward the great truck roared, its mighty tires kicking up stones.

Dicer's house, on the edge of a kidney-shaped lake, had big glass windows and a truly gigantic satellite dish mounted on the roof.

"You have a dog, Dice?" asked Hollywood. "This looks like the kind of property that has three, four dogs, minimum."

"Nope," said Dicer. "I used to have a cat. Woke up one night and he was on my chest, staring into my eyes, three inches from my face. Freaked me out, man. Never had a pet since."

Inside, Dicer beelined for the fridge and pulled out a carton of orange juice, unscrewed the cap, and glugged.

Tetris and Hollywood stood and watched. When he was finished, Dicer crushed the carton and belched.

"Man," he shouted. "That is fresh SQUEEZED!"

"Can I get some of that?" asked Hollywood.

"Sure," said Dicer, tossing him an unopened carton. Hollywood nearly dropped it. Carton number two sailed Tetris's way, and he snagged it out of the air with one huge hand.

"What happened to that finger?" asked Dicer, pointing.

"I lost it," said Tetris.

Dicer squinted at him for a second. Then he laughed and slapped his belly, producing a sound like a trout smacking against a concrete wall.

"You," he whooped. "You crack me up!"

*****

That night, Dicer and Hollywood watched an entire trilogy of sword-and-sorcery movies. Technically, Tetris was there too, although he kept tuning out, and didn't really follow the action. Something about an old guy in a white bathrobe, with a stick that made light, was what he remembered afterward. Dicer had most of the lines memorized, and liked to shout them, especially the grumpy dwarf's. Hollywood was the kind of incessant movie talker Tetris despised, but Dicer seemed to love the snarky commentary. The two friends finished by 2 a.m. and went straight to bed. Tetris slipped out the back door and walked around the lake.

The night was cold. Tetris walked briskly, and when that wasn't enough to keep his body temperature up, broke into a run. He whipped through the trees, reveling in the snapping chill. A deer crossed his path, eyes glowing under the moon. Tetris thought about chasing it, but straying from the lake was likely to get him lost, so he left it alone and continued his run.

When he made it back to the house, he was huffing and gasping, sweat flying off his body. He went inside and took a long shower. Dirt, dried blood, and body paint washed away, swirling around the drain. Long after Tetris was clean, the debris that had crusted his body kept circling. He stayed in the shower, sucking deep breaths of steam with his eyes closed, until the debris was all gone.

Out of the shower, Tetris saw his clean green body in the mirror and cursed. They hadn't told Dicer. But the body paint was in Dr. Alvarez's pack. He'd just have to do his best to explain the verdant complexion when their host awoke.

In the morning Dicer padded out of his bedroom and nodded at Tetris. He pulled out another carton of orange juice—the fridge was packed with them—and chugged half of it.

"Fresh squeezed," he said, gently twisting the cap back onto the carton.

"Good morning," said Tetris.

"You are green," said Dicer. His bulging pecs were barely restrained by a yellow muscle shirt with the silhouette of a rubber duck on the front.

"Yes I am."

Dicer shrugged, belched, and traded the orange juice for an extra-large carton of eggs, which he set on the counter. He retrieved a block of cheese and a sheaf of bacon as well, placing them next to the eggs, and grabbed a gigantic skillet that hung beside a framed image of a four-armed cartoon pocket monster.

"I do not understand even a single thing about you," said Tetris.

"What was that?" asked Dicer in a deep and pleasant voice. He cracked eggs into the skillet one after the other, tossing the shells in the trash, *bam* toss *bam* toss *bam*. "We start training today, or what?"

"Training?"

"Comrade," said Dicer, gaze fierce beneath thick eyebrows, "I can spot a fighter a mile away."

Tetris looked out the floor-to-ceiling windows at the grasping, leafless trees, the birds flitting in the upper branches, and the lake, a still sheet of glass.

Could hardly hurt, said the forest, before fading away again.

Tetris ran a finger along the ridge of scar tissue above his eye. Eggs and bacon popped and sizzled in the pan. The air was full of greasy breakfast smells. He allowed himself a long, deep sigh.

"Okay," he said, "I'm in."

27

The basement was luminous and carpeted with thick blue mats. Tetris thought they were going to start by going over moves, or at least discussing what MMA was, but instead Dicer went straight to beating the everliving shit out of him. The blows were designed to show that Dicer could have hurt him, rather than to cause actual injury, but there were a lot of them. Tetris, for all his lunges and swings, never landed a solid strike.

Dicer downstairs was completely different from Dicer upstairs. In the basement, he never spoke. He was expressionless, his eyes half-lidded and saurian, his legs in constant liquid motion. Sometimes he dodged a blow, caught Tetris's arm, and flung him to the mat. It was like fighting a cyclone of smoke. Hollywood watched from the corner, leaning on a pendulous punching bag, and occasionally laughed or let loose a hearty "Hoo-wee!"

They kept going after lunch. The mats were cool and crisp beneath Tetris's bare feet, but they soon grew slippery with sweat. The basement filled with the hiss-slide of feet on vinyl and the wet thwacking of fists against green flesh.

The morning had been a maelstrom, Tetris throwing out swing after swing and getting punished for every one. By three o'clock, the pace had slowed considerably. Tetris, clothed in bruises, his mouth coated with sweat-salt, felt like curling up at the bottom of a well. He hung back and considered each move. Dicer paced happily. He didn't seem to mind the slower tempo. It certainly didn't prevent him from landing hits.

Hollywood propped his chair back and slept. A wad of gum was wedged in the side of his open mouth. Tetris, jumbled up, rolled his shoulders and raised his fists. He fired off a careful tap, watching Dicer's hands. Dicer took the weak hit and feinted a reprisal, but didn't follow through. Tetris caught sinewy motion in his peripheral vision, weight transferring subtly to the balls of Dicer's feet. He stepped back, raising his hands in front of his face, as Dicer knifed left and rebounded, striking briskly with one fist and then the other. Tetris's arms cushioned the blows. He pressed forward. The swift response took Dicer by surprise, creating an ephemeral opening. Green hands lashed out. One of them caught Dicer's midriff, eliciting a grunt, but by the time the second hand arrived, Dicer was already compensating, swiveling away, and Tetris's knuckles slid harmlessly off knobby muscle.

"Good," said Dicer, voice as orotund as ever despite hours of disuse. His fearsome fists came down. Two loping steps took him to the towel rack. "Good!"

After a moment, Tetris relaxed. His shoulder blades had been clenched so tightly that they screamed white-hot when he released them. He moved unsteadily to the rack and procured a towel. In the most inaccessible crevices of his body, muscles hissed and twinged and sang. Dicer skipped across the room and snapped Hollywood with the tip of his sweat-drenched towel. The blond ranger flailed awake, lost his balance, and toppled out of the teetering chair. Dicer laughed from the belly and spun the damp fabric like a propeller.

"Motherfuc--" choked Hollywood, "I swallowed my gum--"

Dicer chased him, towel snip-snapping, to the stairs. Hollywood yelped and whooped and booked it out of the basement.

"Is that it?" asked Tetris. "Is that supposed to be a lesson?"

Dicer turned around and stuck a contemplative finger in the sodden curls of his beard. "Pardon me?"

Tetris threw his drenched towel in the hamper and tugged a replacement off the rack. "You didn't teach me anything."

Dicer's shrug was an avalanche. "If that's what you think," he said.

That night Tetris took a kayak out to the middle of the lake and sat bobbing in the dendriform wind. The moon overhead was near-full, a pale orb with a neat bite out of it. As his muscle fibers knit back together, he leaned over the edge and stared into the depths. Submerged a hand. It was liquid nitrogen cold, but he held his hand under the surface until the fingers grew brittle and pinpricked with minuscule needles. The water was pure impenetrable black. It was the kind of water that suggested something huge and menacing lurking just beneath the surface.

He spent a while thinking about what that huge thing might be. A creature with slits for eyes and a mouth big enough to swallow the kayak. Behind the teeth like mountain spires, a gullet of bone-white rings. Smooth black skin, firm but pliable, cartilage, fins protruding at extreme angles, and a mighty broad blade of a tail.

He closed his eyes and stowed his hands in his armpits.

Guilt and fear roiled like water snakes in his gut. Thinking about certain things made the sensation worse. So he tried not to think about those things. But there were so many of them, now. The impending invasion. The Omphalos Initiative. The carnage in Portugal. His father. The misplaced terror on the face of the Spanish farmer. The knowledge that most of the world thought he, Tetris Aphelion, was a murderer. The fact that, in a way, he kind of was.

After a while he turned and paddled back to the house. Meanwhile the spilled liquids that made up his bruises, red and black and yellow, sucked back into the network of veins and slimy sacs from which they'd burst, like the water sucking through the teeming pebbles along the shore.

If Dicer had been unfazed by Tetris's verdant skin, he was at least impressed by the speed at which it shed the previous day's beating.

"Your bruises," he said, bustling over to lift Tetris's arm and examine it from all angles. He pulled up Tetris's shirt, too, head darting down to flit eyes across every inch of unblemished torso. "Wow. Wow! *Wow*!"

"Get off," said Tetris, and pulled away.

"Guess I don't have to go easy on you, then," said Dicer, retreating to take an enormous bite out of a bright green apple.

Things went on like that for a week, Dicer wordlessly pummeling Tetris during the day, the forest doing its best to repair the damage overnight. An elbow-jointed pipe in the corner of the basement's ceiling dripped condensation with metronomic regularity. Eventually Dicer decided that the silent thwacking had served its purpose, and began to teach directly, sparse instructions delivered in a hushed, gravelly tone. They began to incorporate grappling: clinching and takedowns, escapes and submissions. Every time Tetris thought he had a handle on the basics, Dicer introduced something new.

As the days went by, the words they spoke grew fewer and farther between. Tetris thought less and less about the world and his mission to save it. There were still six years to go. He wondered where Li and the others had gone. A strange lethargy quelled any desire to seek them out. Where would he even begin to look?

One day, Tetris and Dicer emerged from the basement to find the lakefront vanishing beneath a fluffy blanket of snow.

When the novelty of watching Tetris get bludgeoned wore off, all Hollywood did was sleep. He slept out on the porch in thick winter clothes borrowed from Dicer, obscured except for the puff of his breath. He slept on the couch in front of the grumbling television. He slept wherever a sunbeam came falling through the tall windows when the gray clouds parted. Some days he woke only for meals, or, when the food ran out, to make a run to the grocery store in Dicer's truck.

"You ever hear the parable of the Houston man and the alligator?" asked Dicer as they toweled off one afternoon. He had a fat purple crescent under his eye where an errant strike had caught him.

"No."

"There's an eighteen-foot alligator living under a bridge."

Tetris pressed his toes against the wall and leaned, stretching his calf.

"A Houston man comes up to the bridge with his girlfriend and takes off his shirt. He wants to go for a swim. And an older man walks by at that exact moment, right? And the older man says--"

"Don't jump in there, mayne," interjected Tetris in a laughable approximation of a Southern accent. "There's a big ol' gater under that there bridge."

"But he doesn't listen," said Dicer.

"He most certainly does not."

"'Fuck that alligator,' he says, and jumps in."

Drip, went the pipe in the corner. Drip. Drip.

"I'm guessing it eats him."

"First Texas alligator fatality in two hundred years."

Tetris touched an earlobe gingerly, trying to discern if a blow from Dicer had knocked it loose. "Moral: obey your elders?"

Dicer shrugged and headed up the stairs. "'Don't fuck with alligators,' is what I figured."

That night, around two o'clock a.m., someone knocked on the door.

Tetris went over. His legs were stiff and sore. After a few moments, he twisted the handle and pulled it open.

On the porch stood Vincent Chen, his cold-reddened face wreathed with scraggly hair. A pistol in his right hand dangled toward the earth.

"Hello," said Vincent.

"Hi," said Tetris.

"I found your cab driver," said Vincent.

Snowflakes drifted across the headlights of his parked sedan.

"Then the pay phone you used in Pottsville."

Tetris leaned against the doorframe. He felt like he was ten feet outside his body, viewing the scene through a foggy window.

"Turn yourself in," said Vincent. "No handcuffs necessary. Just come with me."

Tetris shook his shaggy head. The car's headlights

turned themselves off, shrouding Vincent in shadow.

"I called the feds," said Vincent in a hoarse voice. "They'll be here soon."

Tetris thought about closing the door and running out the back, then fleeing into the forest. Just the thought made him tired. He closed his eyes and saw for a moment the dead-eyed face of the assassin on the rooftop.

"Vince," he said.

When he opened his eyes the pistol was pointed at him.

"I'm sorry," said Vincent, sounding like he really meant it, "but I have to do the right thing."

Break his arm, said the forest.

Tetris thought of the soldiers on the Portuguese coast and in the Omphalos base. Blood seeping into cracks and crevices out of which it could never be scrubbed. He left the door open and walked back inside.

"I'm not kidding," said Vincent, and followed.

Dicer stepped out of the bedroom with a shotgun braced against his shoulder. There was a horrific crash. Vincent bounced hard off the edge of the door, pistol flying from his grasp. Tetris crossed the room before it landed.

"Hold your fire!"

Vincent's abdomen was a ragged mess. Feathers from his ruptured jacket fluttered in the air.

"No can do," said Dicer, although he lowered the shotgun.

Vincent's lips pulled back from his teeth. He rolled away, or tried to, when Tetris touched him.

"They're coming," Vincent choked.

"We have to get him to the hospital," said Tetris, struggling out of his shirt. He wadded it up and pressed it to the wound. Wind ripped through the doorway, a fusillade of frozen daggers.

"*Who's* coming?" demanded Dicer.

Hollywood emerged from his own bedroom. He stood, blinking, and threaded his arms into a heavy sweatshirt. "This fucker again?"

Tetris found Vincent's keys. "I'm taking him to the hospital."

Dicer paced, running a hand over his bald dome. "He talking about who I think he's talking about?"

"Dicer, you have to come along. You have to show me where the hospital is."

"Nope," said Dicer. "They shoot guys like me on sight."

Tetris flew to his bag, teeth jumping from the cold, and pulled on layers as fast as he could. "Hollywood?"

The blond ranger sucked his teeth. "We oughta be headed in the opposite direction."

"He's going to die."

Hollywood blinked. "I thought you hated this guy."

"He's going to die, Hollywood."

"He pulled a gun on you."

"He needs our help."

"Route 66," said Dicer from the bedroom, over the sound of drawers being ransacked, "take exit 85, and follow the signs."

He emerged in a pink tank top and shrugged into a

coat, then slung a duffel bag over his shoulder.

"Good luck," he said.

Tetris picked Vincent up and waded into the swirling snow.

The agent's sleek black sedan was parked beside the mailbox. Tetris lowered him into the passenger seat, fastened the belt, and sprinted around, keys jangling.

"C'mon c'mon c'mon," he said, gunning the engine and spinning the wheel hand over hand. They fishtailed out of the driveway, nearly slamming into the trees on the far side. Vincent groaned.

"Oh, God," he said.

"Stay with me, buddy," said Tetris. "Which direction are the FBI guys coming from? Can we meet them halfway?"

The seatbelt kept Vincent from folding over completely, but his arms were wrapped tight around his darkening midsection.

"Okay, that's okay, no big deal," said Tetris, peering at a sign as they whipped by. The tree trunks were red under the headlights. Vincent slumped against his belt.

"Hey," said Tetris, prodding his shoulder. "Hey. Talk to me."

Vincent shuddered and pulled away. "What?"

"Tell me something. Tell me a story."

Vincent pressed his skull against the headrest.

"My brother," he said. "Oh God. My brother."

"What about him?"

Vincent coughed. "I was a cop."

"You mentioned that."

Yellow dashes snapped past beneath a thin veneer of snow.

"I miss him," said Vincent quietly.

Tetris glanced over. "I miss my brother too," he said.

Vincent didn't respond. His eyes were closed.

Suddenly the road was alive with blistering white-yellow lights. Muscular black vans swarmed everywhere. Snowflakes sprang in the high beams as Tetris jammed the brakes. As they shuddered to a halt, he shifted into park. Vans swerved into place behind and in front. Their exhaust pipes belched black smoke.

Tetris lowered his window.

"All right," he shouted. "You got me. I'm coming quietly."

In the driver-side window appeared the sneering face of the scarred torturer from Portugal.

Tetris began a lunge but was stopped by the cold barrel of an enormous revolver against his forehead. Omphalos soldiers in heavy gear dispersed into the trees. Their boots left harsh marks in the snow.

"I don't believe we were ever properly introduced," said a silky voice behind him.

Tetris removed his forehead carefully from the pistol. He knew the voice. It was the voice that had come over the intercom in his cell, again and again, always in that same cool tone, even when he screamed and begged for mercy.

"My name is Hailey Sumner," said the woman, waving a chrome-plated handgun. "You made quite a mess for us

493

back there."

"Please," said Tetris. "He's hurt. We have to get him to a hospital. You can have me, I don't care, but we have to get him--"

"Who?" asked Hailey. "Oh, you mean him?"

She lifted the shiny pistol and shot Vincent in the head.

"Whoops," she said in the ringing silence that followed, as chunks of skull slid down Tetris's gasping cheeks. "Your friend didn't make it. That's too bad."

Before Tetris could form words or wipe the gore off his face or even force his lungs to draw breath, Dicer's macrognathic truck erupted from the darkness. Its huge tires spun as it arced through furious rifle fire. Sparks cascaded and vanished in the whirling snow. The scarred man stepped back from Tetris's window and raised his revolver.

Hollywood leaned out the truck's passenger-side window and fired a shotgun, unleashing a harsh light and a terrible crack that caught the scarred torturer in the chest and flung him to the ground. Dicer's truck smashed into the van blocking Tetris's way, knocking it aside. As Dicer reversed, the truck's exterior still popping and cracking with gunfire, the front bumper sloughed free.

Hailey Sumner had vanished.

"Go!" shouted Hollywood through the din.

Tetris went. He scraped the van on the way by but kept the pedal bottomed out, wrenching the car into the opposite lane. Three of the sedan's windows burst into shimmering ice. Tetris hunkered low behind the wheel as glass flechettes stung his brow and neck.

Just as he cleared the last van, he glimpsed Dicer's truck bouncing into the forest. Then his rearview mirror shattered. A giant hand seized the sedan and dragged it left with a banshee shriek. Popped tire, he thought in some region of his brain that was still functioning. He wrestled back onto the road and accelerated, but the wheel with the popped tire bounced and screeched on the asphalt. He flew around a bend and into the empty night, fighting the sedan as it tugged him left left left. Then he lost his resolve for just a moment and glanced at Vincent's limp form. The side of the agent's head was a horrible red bowl.

When his eyes returned to the spiderwebbed windshield, Tetris found the forest rushing up before him. He twirled the wheel back toward the center of the road, but not fast enough, as the sedan leapt the rumble strips, vaulted the shoulder, and went tumbling down the slope into stumps and saplings and bushes and rocks and gullies and cool, merciful silence.

*****

For the first time since his transformation, Tetris dreamed.

He climbed a tree in the depths of the forest, hand over hand, grasping tiny outcroppings of bark, tangling his fingers in nests of tough moss. The trunk was so wide that its curve was barely noticeable, like the curve of an empty horizon. There were smells, loam and living wood and the distant fecund sweetness of decay, but no sounds. He climbed and climbed, making no progress at all, until suddenly he reached the top.

As he penetrated the final leaf layer, he caught the herbal aroma of fresh thyme, carried across the canopy by a whispering breeze. The moon overhead was close and huge. He inclined his nose, sniffing, to find the source of the wonderful redolence, and came face to face with an enormous white moth.

He staggered and fell back into the canopy. Somehow he arrested his descent, cradled amid the soft leaves. He clambered back up. The moth was still there, its antennae bent pensively. It was furry; its compound eyes were matte black orbs.

"Hmmmmmmmm," hummed the moth.

Tetris sat cross-legged a few feet away.

"I know you," said the moth.

"Of course you do," said Tetris. "What are you trying to tell me?"

The moth fanned its variegated wings, obscuring the sky, before resettling them with a barely audible sigh. "I don't . . . know."

Tetris looked at the stars. Or where the stars were supposed to be, anyway. There was really only one star, to the left of the leering moon, and it was dim and distant. He stared at the lonely star. When he began to feel that it was staring back, he tore his uneasy eyes away.

"If this is a vision, and you're trying to tell me

something, you should just tell me," said Tetris.

"Who do you think I am, again?" asked the moth.

"The forest," said Tetris.

The moth was quiet for a long time.

"I don't think so," it said.

"Then who?"

"I'm not sure," said the moth, looking past him at the rolling canopy, the treetops blue hills in the meager light. Everything else was dark, but the moth shone with captured moonlight. "Still. I know you."

Tetris's tree began to sink into the depths, but he couldn't find the will to uncross his legs and climb to another one.

"Wait," he shouted, as the moth dwindled above him. "Wait!"

Then darkness swallowed him, and the dreamscape descended into inchoate madness, screeches and black shapes and bristling slender teeth.

*****

The world was light. Hot, candent, electrified light. Tetris opened his eyes a sliver and closed them again. His body felt like a single enormous, lumpy bruise. Thoughts pinged against the walls of his skull, shuddered in the grogginess and thumping pain, and deliquesced.

"Where," he said, and tried opening his eyes again.

His pupils, normally elastic, were slow to contract. Gradually an image emerged: white walls, white-curtained window blazing with light, white rails on the bed atop which he lay. White sheets and a shining white-labeled IV bag swaying as he moved.

In the corner, above and to the left: a square television, the boxy old vacuum-tube kind, volume set to "insistent murmur," displaying a news program, plastic smiles above a glass and steel desk.

Tetris tried to move his legs and found them restrained by leather straps. His arms leapt against similar restraints. The IV pinched his arm.

"He lives," said the man beside the bed, folding his newspaper and handing it to a tall man beside him. A curled black cord led from the tall man's cauliflower ear down the back of his bridge-cable neck.

Tetris screwed his eyes shut again and reached out to the forest. He found nothing except the musk of distant, amorphous fear.

"My name is Don McCarthy," said the man, waving a hand over Tetris's closed eyes. Inside Tetris's lids, the hand was a dark shadow flitting across a webbed green plain. "Hello? Anybody in there? I'm the Secretary of State."

"Toni Davis," said Tetris.

"Is deceased, I'm afraid," said McCarthy, sitting in a metal chair turned backwards, his legs sprawled wide. His eyes were small and sharp as polished onyx. His hair was close-cropped and gray. "I've got her job now."

"Who are you?"

McCarthy waved at the bodyguard. "Leave us alone,

please."

The man left after a glance through his impenetrable sunglasses.

"I used to be in charge of the Coast Guard," said McCarthy. "Lousy job. Nobody appreciates what you do. One monster slips by and gobbles a grandmother out walking her poodle, and they're after your head. Doesn't matter that you stopped another fifty earlier that week. Zero tolerance for error. Sensationalist media." He sighed. "It goes without saying, but I like being Secretary of State a whole lot better."

"Vincent," said Tetris.

"He's dead," said McCarthy, raising a finger. "Also Dale Cooper. Jack Dano." He ticked them off. "Davis. Bunch of government aides. Scientists. Plus a couple thousand innocents in Portugal, and our man in Atlantic City." His hands fluttered amusedly. "It's a funny thing, Mr. Aphelion, the way everyone around you seems to expire."

Tetris drove his head against the white metal bars at the head of the cot. An animal grunt escaped his clamped teeth.

"Well," said McCarthy, leaning in conspiratorially, "I suppose I can't pin all of those on you. A few of them are my fault."

Tetris stopped moving.

"I took your plane down, pal."

The Secretary's breath was foul. Tetris tried not to inhale.

"With national security at stake," said McCarthy, "we

really had no other option."

"You killed them," said Tetris. His side hurt.

McCarthy stood. "I knew what you were the moment I heard about you," he said. "The moment you walked out of the forest, I knew. Knew you were the greatest threat mankind had ever seen."

Tetris spasmed against the bonds.

"I pity you, Aphelion. I really do."

Tetris strained and strained, but the shackles remained firm.

"You let this thing into your mind," said McCarthy, circling the bed. "You believed its lies. Aliens. Invasions. You should have died like a man in the forest. Instead you gave in, came here, and spread your disease. You worked for the enemy. You deceived the Secretary of State. Do you have any idea the work it's taken to undo the damage from those lies?"

"What lies?"

"There are no aliens," said McCarthy. "There's no invasion."

Tetris fell back, heart banging away. "No."

"We looked. There isn't anything out there."

"It's too far," said Tetris. "It's six years away."

McCarthy spat a bitter laugh. "Six years! Time. That's all it wanted. Time to figure out how to kill us without us killing it first. You never questioned it, did you? Not even once."

"Are you listening to this?" Tetris asked the ceiling. "Hello?"

"It's listening," said McCarthy, "even if it pretends it's not."

"You're wrong," said Tetris. "If there wasn't an invasion coming, the forest would already have killed us."

"How?"

"Toxins. Pods of toxins, all over the world. It showed me, in a vision."

"Toxins delivered on what? The air?" McCarthy laughed. "You know how long it would take a cloud of gas to drift on wind currents across an entire continent? Do you—I mean, have you heard of gas masks? Hazmat suits? We would fire our missiles before it did more than tickle New York."

Tetris arced against his bonds, ignoring the blinding pain in his side.

"You idiot," said McCarthy, "it knows we can kill it, and it's playing for more time. All of this, it's a trick. You fell for it. And so did Davis, and Dano, and everyone else on that plane. You all fell for it. But not me."

"You're wrong," said Tetris, although suddenly he wasn't sure.

"Can you believe you got all your friends killed?" He shook his head sadly. "I can't believe it, personally. Some of them were my friends too."

Tetris saw spiders and snakes tearing into masses of soldiers, saw his own hands fling a man into the mouth of a tarantula. McCarthy's phone buzzed, and buzzed, and buzzed again.

"Why won't you answer me?" Tetris shouted at the

ceiling. "Where are you?"

Then the forest was there, filling its corner of his vibrating skull.

Look at the television, it said.

Tetris looked. "Please tell me that's one of yours."

That, said the forest, *has nothing to do with me*.

McCarthy looked too. The phone fell from his hand.

Ten minutes later, when Li and Dr. Alvarez came swinging through the window in a storm of rainbow shards, they found the room deserted, the bed wheeled away, chairs askew, an IV bag leaking a broadening puddle.

Li stowed her gun and ransacked the room for clues. She peered into the hall, checked the corners, and was getting down to explore the space beneath the dresser when Dr. Alvarez laid a hand on her shoulder.

Together they stood, in a room reeking of ammonia, as on the boxy black television something obscenely huge, hundreds of feet tall, raised its head out of billowing meteorite smoke. The head was followed by immeasurable chthonic bulk, size the camera could not capture, swing wildly though it did; and after the head and the bulk, when the too-numerous arms emerged, it became clear, to Li and Dr. Alvarez and all the others watching the grainy vision creeping across their screens, that this section of cratered Kansas farmland had become something terrible, a place of sulfurous fumes and apocalypse, a wasteland that could bear no possible name but Hell.

About the Author

Justin Groot lives in Southern California, where he spends most of his free time reading, writing, playing videogames, and rock climbing.

Twitter: @JustinGroot3